MOTHER OF MARLIN

THE MARLIN CHRONICLES: BOOK 1

Alyson Mountjoy

ALYSON MOUNTJOY

ISBN-10: 1521113572
ISBN-13: 978-1521113578

DEDICATION

To Anna, my daughter, editor and friend - for your continued encouragement, for your kindness, your music, your strength and your indomitable spirit.

To Kev, my husband - for your support and love, for looking after me, for showing me what a soul-mate truly is, for always being by my side, and for the beautiful moth photograph used on the cover of this book.

To Logan, my son - for your humour which has kept me going through the darkest of days, for your strength of character and creativity, for your advice and for always inspiring me to be a better writer.

To Kelly, my daughter-in-law - for your gentleness, your sensitivity, your talent and all that you have brought to our family just by being you.

This book is also dedicated to my friends, few but true, and to my family and everyone else who has been part of my journey so far. You have all in some way made me who I am, and I am grateful. To each of my readers, wherever you may be on your journey, always be happy with who you are.

"In order for the light to shine so brightly, the darkness must be present."

Francis Bacon

CONTENTS

ALYSON MOUNTJOY

PART ONE: THIS OLD MAN

⊚IT WAS MID-AFTERNOON on the 17th June 2015. Stephanie Meares stood on the doorstep of her new home, basking in a shaft of sunlight that had pierced the cotton wool clouds as if to welcome her. As it bathed her upturned face and closed eyelids, she savoured its warmth and smiled to herself. She had finally arrived.

There were several re-usable shopping bags at her feet, the air was heavy with the scent of honeysuckle from the nearby hedgerow, and alive with the sound of birdsong. Blue butterflies darted busily from flower to flower as she waved goodbye to the removal men. She watched as the van backed carefully out of her drive, narrowly missing her car. Hoping that more care had been taken with her possessions, she retrieved the cat carrier from the front seat and surveyed the boxes piled up in the hall.

"Home at last!" she thought to herself.

It was a wonderful thought, one which drew another smile to her lips. Nothing was likely to dampen her spirits on such a special day.

Stephanie's new home was a detached, double-fronted, stone cottage, built in the 1800s from local stone as a home for one of the local estate workers. Known as The Lodge, it was set at the end of a quiet country lane, half-way up a hill. To the front there was only a walled drive, and to the rear of the property was a small garden with a tiny patio and a lawn planted with wild flowers and herbs. The best feature was that the gate at the far end opened onto steps which led directly to the beach below.

The coastline curved around the back and to the left of her property, affording her designated living room a majestic view of the bay. Her mid-blue sofa and matching armchairs with yellow brocade cushions mirrored the view from the wide French windows, bringing the beach indoors with its colours of the sand and the sea. It was to be a sunny, relaxing haven; her sanctuary.

The similarly sized room to the right of the hall was to be her office. Book shelves lined the walls; an antique oak desk housing her laptop and a well-used, leather computer chair afforded her a comfortable workstation. It took pride of place in front of the window, overlooking fields and woods. The reason that she chose this room as her office was because she knew that she would find a sea view too distracting, which was not an ideal scenario when she had work to do.

At the end of the hall lay a small but well-appointed cottage kitchen. It was full of light and sufficient storage space for her needs and it also had a sea view. Upstairs had a similar layout to downstairs, with two bedrooms either side of the landing and a bathroom equidistant between them, at the back above the kitchen.

The sound of scratching prompted Stephanie to open the cat carrier, and her sleek, cream tabby cat bolted passionately for freedom, only to stop and lick her paws on the hall carpet as if nothing untoward had happened. But she soon realised that she was in a strange place, and ran to hide among the boxes, as cats do.

Stephanie took her shopping along the hall to the kitchen. She eventually located a kettle, a mug and a spoon, and enjoyed a quick cup of tea before she unpacked her groceries. As she drank it, she stepped out into the garden to revel in the sunshine, sitting on a step to take in the glorious view over the bay. She decided that she would never tire of waking up to this every day, making a mental note to invest in some patio furniture.

Maisy, the cat, eventually became brave and crept out. She began to sniff every box, piece of furniture and corner of the property, and she was none too sure that she liked it. Like most cats, Maisy hated change. She found her beloved owner in the kitchen, wound her tail around her legs and mewed ingratiatingly for food. Food was always comforting. Stephanie duly fed her, glad that she had called in at the village shop on the way and that they had sold Maisy's favourite brand; it was actually the only food that her feline companion chose to accept. The small supermarket (with its over-inflated tourist prices) would have to suffice as a temporary source of necessities until she could place a regular order with an online supplier.

Suitably refreshed by the tea, Stephanie left Maisy to wander, snooze, or whatever else it was that cats did, and set to work. She had wisely labelled each box with the room that was destined to house its contents. Thanks to the removal men, who had apparently been efficient after all, most of the boxes were already in their allotted rooms, waiting for her attention. The hall collection was the exception, containing boxes of random possessions which she had not yet labelled; the ones without a destination. They were the items that might well end up in the attic, being mostly souvenirs and other objects inherited from her mother. She could imagine her Mum, Grace Meares, describing them as "neither use nor ornament" and they were certainly that. But she couldn't bring herself to throw them away because of the memories which they evoked by their very existence. Their sentimental value was priceless, and even if they had no resting place in her cottage yet, they already held a place in her heart.

***

Stephanie was 29 years old and of medium height and build, an attractive woman with bright, blue eyes and mousy shoulder-length hair. Her hair was naturally wavy; she hated it and straightened it every day, despairing that it became curly and unruly whenever it rained. There was nothing mousy, however, about this woman's character. Yet she was a woman of simple pleasures: she liked tea and cats, walks on the beach and an occasional glass of wine. She was a writer, a recent career development, yet already it felt like writing could easily bring her contentment for the rest of her life.

This quiet little cottage on the north-west coast of Cornwall was her dream house. After yearning to own a cottage like this for years, she came to notice an advertisement in a newspaper at just the right time. She had been both delighted and surprised at how closely it resembled the property in her dreams. She didn't care if it was divine intervention, synchronicity, fate or just sheer luck, it was meant to be her home, she just knew it. It felt as if it had been calling to her for a long time, and now she had claimed it. Or maybe the cottage had claimed her. Either way she was here, and that was all that mattered.

Finding a house so similar to one that she dreamed about might have struck some people as a rather spooky coincidence, but Stephanie was used to such things. They happened to her on a regular basis. Some events were unnerving, but this was one of the good ones, and she didn't believe in coincidence

The cottage would be the ideal location from which to write. Quiet and fairly secluded, it felt as if it was in the middle of nowhere, when it was only a twenty-minute walk to the village of Marlin at the foot of the hill. Less at a good pace. She hoped that she would be left uninterrupted in this perfect location to get on with her work. London had been so busy and noisy (not at all conducive to creativity) and writing the first book had been a little tedious because of that.

After putting away her shopping, Stephanie decided to begin organising her bedroom. Nothing strenuous, just making up her bed and unpacking some clothes and toiletries. She was too tired to do much more after the drive down to Cornwall. She set off up the stairs. Like the office, the spare room faced towards the woods, so she had chosen the bedroom with a sea view as her own. As she opened the bedroom door, the glistening blue water blinded her through large, bare windows.

"Curtains! My first job," she told herself as she squinted and struggled to look for them with spots before her eyes.

Maisy had followed her, thinking there was safety in numbers, and she settled on the bed. She merely lifted one eyelid in acknowledgement of her owner's presence then promptly fell asleep. Just then, a gentle breeze skimmed Stephanie's cheek, drawn past her from the open windows. She felt a chill, even though the room and the breeze were both warm, and it made her shiver. Just for an instant, the room smelled faintly of roses, then the bedroom door slammed shut behind her. She jumped and turned around in surprise. Maisy bolted under the bed as if she had been shot.

Behind the door to the left of the room was a white rocking chair, old and well-loved, a familiar relic from her childhood. Her battered old guitar stood next to it, another heirloom which had once belonged to her mother. But what surprised her more than the door slamming was what was on the chair. It was a doll, but not an ordinary child's doll. It was the figure of an old man, at least on first examination it appeared to be an old man, but it was so worn and crinkled that it was hard to tell.

It was about eight inches in height and dressed in what might once have been a smart, brown tweed suit (now faded), complete with a faintly stained cotton shirt and a brown and cream, striped tie. It looked like it might be an antique. The face was made of faded cloth and painted crudely, yet its piercing, beady eyes gave it an odd expression. There were wisps of what appeared to be dark, human hair bordering its nearly bald little head like a crown. It resembled a misshapen ventriloquist's dummy, or a puppet with no movable parts - and she had never seen it before in her life.

"This is creepy," she thought.

She assumed that it had belonged to the last owner of the property. She was apparently herself a single woman too, but that was all Stephanie knew about her. The removal men must have thought the doll was hers and had placed it carefully on the chair behind the door out of harm's way. But it wasn't hers. Truth be told she found it a bit scary, although to some it might have a sad, scruffy charm.

"Maybe part of a collection?" she thought.

Stephanie looked at the doll from a distance. It fascinated her that people would collect such objects. It wasn't to her taste at all, yet she couldn't bring herself to throw it away, just in case the owner had accidentally forgotten what might be something of great sentimental value. That was a predicament that she could relate to, with all her boxes of memories.

"I certainly don't want it!" she found herself saying out loud as if to confirm the sentiment.

It was Saturday so little could be done today, so she decided to try to return the doll to its rightful owner via the estate agent the following week. She left the little old man where he sat for now, propped up on the chair at a quizzical angle. Maisy thought she has been talking to her when she spoke and started purring, but she wasn't yet brave enough to venture out from under the bed in this new strange place. Stephanie bent down and stroked her reassuringly, then she began putting up curtains and making the room ready for her first night in her new home.

As Stephanie moved around, the bare white painted floorboards creaked underfoot, a comforting sound that spoke to the age and homeliness of her new cottage. Making a mental reminder to buy rugs, she surveyed her handiwork with a smile at a job well done. Then she went downstairs to make herself a snack before taking a shower and having a welcome early night. It had been a tiring day.

Maisy stayed where she was, safe under the bed, eyeing the doll from the safety of her sanctuary. She growled quietly while Stephanie slept. The light of the moon streamed through a chink in the curtains and glinted off the little old man's black, glassy eyes. Had Stephanie been awake, she might have noticed how they seemed to glare at her from across the room.

***

It was Monday, two days later, and her first weekend in Marlin had passed in blissful solitude. Everything was pretty much set out as she wanted it, with all the boxes either emptied or stored intact in the attic or spare room. The curtains and blinds were in place, ornaments had been dusted, books shelved and mirrors polished. With all her belongings arranged around her, it really felt like home. In her bright and airy kitchen, where new pale lemon curtains fluttered in the sea breeze, Stephanie enjoyed a light breakfast of hot tea and buttered toast with orange marmalade, then she set off on her morning walk to the beach. Maisy watched her leave through half-closed eyes until sleep claimed her again.

It was a new ritual, a wonderful start to her working day. She felt grateful; privileged to have achieved what she had longed for. She locked the back door and made her way down the garden path, reaching a gate and a short yet steep set of steps at the end. She resisted looking at the view and cast her eyes downward for safety's sake till she stepped onto the beach.

A familiar serenity washed over her as soon as her feet touched the sand. It felt almost like her own private beach, even though there were already other people walking there. When she looked up, the sight before her made her smile, just as it did every day. An elderly couple walked their dog, and some children played in rock pools while little boats bobbed like toys in the distance to complete the picture- perfect scene. The sand felt cool on her bare feet, being too early in the day to have absorbed enough heat from the sunlight to warm it. As she walked, she felt the tiny golden grains shifting between her toes. The tide was almost fully in, but the water didn't reach the sea wall even at high tide so there was always plenty of room to take a stroll. A light spray moistened her face as she tiptoed into the cool waves. She licked her lips and tasted salt.

She meandered along the shoreline for a while, then stopped and sat on a large, flat rock and faced the sea. She closed her eyes, letting her mind wander and open up to ideas and memories, as fact and fantasy intermingled in her brain and it began weaving the plan for her new book. After a while, she skimmed some pebbles across the incoming waves and scanned the beach for shells, finally putting a particularly pretty, mottled pink one in the pocket of her shorts.

When she felt suitably relaxed and ready to write, she got up and, after one last look at the sea, she turned back towards the steps. She slipped her sandals on again and ventured upwards, using the convenient metal rail to her right to steady herself. Up the winding path to the small weather-beaten wooden garden gate she went. She stepped through the gate and closed it behind her, then turned and glanced up at the cottage. She stopped. There, framed by her bedroom window, was the figure of the little old man. He was standing upright on the windowsill looking down at her, his small palms resting on the glass. A cloud moved and sunlight glinted off the window, momentarily blinding her. Flinching automatically to protect her eyes, she closed them. When she looked back, he was gone.

She was shaken. She ran as fast as she could to the back door, her heart thumping, instinctively fearing that someone had broken in and moved him. Her logical brain did not even have time to wonder why anyone would do that. Maybe the light was playing tricks, or so she hoped. The door was still locked. She unlocked it with the key from her pocket and ran down the hall to check the front door, also locked. Turning, she rushed up the stairs. Flinging her bedroom door wide open, she found the little old man seated, as usual, on the rocking chair under the window. The room was just as she had left it.

"It must have been the light," she thought, catching her breath and closing the door firmly behind her as went downstairs again.

Her heart was still racing. Could she have imagined, it or did she really see him standing there? It seemed impossible. She went into the kitchen to make a strong cup of tea. While she was drinking her tea, she rang the estate agent. No-one answered, so she planned to try again after lunch.

A few moments later the chair on which the doll sat began to rock, slowly; deliberately. Stephanie, busy by now in her office, didn't hear a thing. She took the pretty pink shell from her pocket and placed it on her desk, safe until it could be added to the growing collection on her kitchen windowsill.

***

After a couple of days of concerted effort, the plan for her book was coming along nicely. It was a sequel to her first novel. The story was planned, new characters had been outlined, and she had sent a draft of the first two chapters to her publisher. Stephanie had been writing for years as a hobby while working in the administrative side of local government, but with no real success. She used to stick to a strict plan; the results were fairly good yet sometimes contrived, but her submissions had been rejected time after time. But with the last book she had just created a rough outline to start with, and the characters simply sprang to life, choosing their own direction. The story developed unaided and almost wrote itself, like it took on a life of its own in her mind and she was just the conduit to the laptop. At least that was how it had felt.

The novel had been a runaway success, with the advance on the next two books in the trilogy earning her almost enough money for a deposit on the cottage. The sale of her flat, located in a desirable area of London, had made up the rest of the deposit, with money left over to tide her over between the royalty cheques. The formula had proved successful, so she was determined to write in the same way again. With a minimal outline finished, it was up to the characters to work their magic. She would let it simmer in her imagination and add flesh to the bones later on.

She had decided to take a day away from writing, allowing time for inspiration to appear. One thing she had learned was that this sort of thing could not be forced or rushed, and with a beautiful new home and the nearby coastline to enjoy, she was in no hurry. She had just escaped from a bad long-term relationship, which ended at about the same time as her writing career took off. She knew that running away wasn't the answer and that you take your troubles with you. But Paul was firmly in the past and this cottage, this new life, was her future; her lifeline.

After doing some online research she had lunch and went off to relax while the story fermented unaided. She hummed a familiar tune as she went upstairs to take a long, hot, relaxing bath. She had been waking a lot lately with the same tune going around in her head, but hard as she tried, she couldn't remember what it was.

***

A short while later, Maisy nuzzled her leg as she sat straightening her hair at her dressing table. Stephanie stroked her head gently and the purring cat flopped on the floor beside her, then she caught a glimpse of the doll's reflection in the mirror as she put on her earrings. Something was sticking out of the top pocket of his diminutive jacket. Her smile faded.

"It couldn't be, could it?" she thought.

She stood up and walked over to the doll. Reaching her hand gently down into the breast pocket of its jacket she took put a small object. She stared at it in disbelief; it was the small, pink shell that she had found on the beach two days before. In her efforts to meet her editor's deadline for the book synopsis, she had forgotten all about it, (as she had about ringing the estate agent). Yet there it was, impossible as it seemed. In her bedroom, in the pocket of a dusty old doll.

"How did it get here? Is it the same one?" she thought.

"Only one way to find out!" she pronounced to an empty room and ran down the stairs to her office, still holding the shell.

Maisy was startled. She fled the room and ran after her. In the office, Stephanie found the desk empty apart from her laptop. She looked on the floor under the desk in case her elbow had swept it off. She found nothing but a stray pen and her drinks mat with a cat motif. Then she inspected the kitchen windowsill in case she had absentmindedly placed it there, but the one in her hand was the only pink shell. After staring at it in silent disbelief, she placed it on the windowsill with the other shells. An uneasy feeling crept over her. She thought about seeing the old man at the window, another strange occurrence. Were these things really happening or was she starting to lose her mind? She had been under a lot of stress before the move. She shook off the idea and put the kettle on.

Twenty minutes later, sitting by the window in the kitchen with a mug of hot tea, she tried the estate agent's number again, wishing that she hadn't been so caught up in her book that she had forgotten about the creepy doll. All of a sudden, Stephanie heard a creaking sound followed by a tap. It was coming from the room above her, in a regular, rhythmic pattern. Creak. Tap. Creak. Tap. She jumped up and rushed up to her room.

She stopped in the doorway, unable to believe her eyes. The rocking chair was swaying back and forth, tapping the windowsill as it rocked backwards, the old, bare floorboards creaking with its motion. The little old man was sitting there; the expression on his face was changed from a blank stare to the shadow of a self-satisfied smile.

Maisy appeared in the doorway and started hissing, her back arched and her fur spiked up in all directions. Stephanie's stomach lurched in fear. She began shaking. It was like she was in the middle of a surreal dream. She stepped nervously into the room and the rocking chair stopped dead. Maisy turned and fled, her tail still twice its size, like that of a squirrel. The old man's face was once more expressionless. It was as if she had somehow broken some sort of spell and the room was again silent, normal. All she could hear was the muted crashing of the waves on the beach below and the curtains gently flapping in the breeze. It was a warm day, yet the room felt unnaturally cold.

This time she knew she hadn't imagined it. The paintwork on the chair and the windowsill behind the chair both bore fresh scratches. She jumped up and down on the floorboards to test them, trying to re-create the sound she had heard, but the chair didn't move. She waved the bedroom door to make more of a breeze, mimicking a random gust of wind, but still the rocking chair remained still.

Something else had made the chair rock. Something (or someone) that she didn't even want to think about. She walked to the chair, picked up the doll and took it up the ladder to the attic above, where she threw it into one of her many empty boxes and firmly taped down the lid. She was taking no chances.

Incredible as it seemed even to her, Stephanie had the nagging feeling that this old man was somehow very much alive, aware and watching her every move, and she didn't like the thought one bit. He had to go.

***

The rest of the day passed uneventfully. She tried the number again, and again. Then remembering that it was Wednesday (which meant that they closed at lunchtime) she gave up, ranting to herself about how "it was a wonder they ever did any business when they never answered the phone" and "surely businesses can ill afford to take an afternoon off midweek." She didn't want to admit it, but the doll had made her extremely nervous and irritable. If the estate agent had answered, they would surely have borne the brunt of her mood.

After coaxing Maisy out from under the sofa in the living room, she made dinner and took another short walk on the beach. This made her feel much more settled. She had developed a headache; it felt like there was a band wound tightly around her skull, and it wouldn't go away. So, she had no choice but to go to bed early. The chair remained motionless and Stephanie slept well, safe in the knowledge that the little old man was taped in its box in the attic. Maisy lay next to her feet, eyeing the old chair suspiciously. Soon, sleep overcame her too.

***

The next day dawned bright and sunny, with brilliant rays of light pouring in through the windows. Stephanie felt positive and decisive. She was determined to find out who the old man was and where he came from and send him back to his owner.

After breakfast, she once more rang the estate agent who had sold her the property, fully prepared to drive to Wadebridge with the doll (in its box) if there was no reply this time. As soon as she picked up the phone, Maisy jumped on her lap. Upset that the stupid object held her attention she attempted to nuzzle it from her hand. She received a stroke for her trouble, so she settled down to sleep on her owner's lap. Finally, someone answered. Stephanie asked to speak to the manager and questioned her about contact details for the previous owner.

"Ah, well, that might be a bit difficult Ms Meares," said an annoying voice on the other end of the phone. "As much as Taylor and Hopcroft would like to help, the lady vanished, so to speak!"

"Vanished? What do you mean, vanished?" barked Stephanie, her voice rising in a mixture of annoyance and disbelief. "People don't just disappear like that! Where did my money go?"

Maisy took offence at the noise and jumped down, heading for the kitchen in that huffy way that only cats can muster. Stephanie struggled to keep her temper.

"No need to shout, dear. The sale money was paid to Lord Trevelyan who owns the estate, the land that The Lodge stands on."

Mrs Taylor continued unruffled and with relish, being the type of woman who enjoyed the spreading of rumour and gossip but would never admit to it.

"Ms Trevelyan was a wealthy woman from a good family. When she was, shall we say, spirited away, her parents were devastated. They employed private detectives to comb the house and surrounding area. No expense was spared, but neither hide nor hair of her was found. Poor dear!"

She barely stopped to catch her breath, then continued.

"Missing presumed DEAD, was the consensus at the time," she whispered with all the theatrical skill she could muster. "The tides on this stretch of coastline are treacherous, after all."

Stephanie was shocked. She paused momentarily to gather her thoughts before asking for the address of the family home. Her heart dropped when she was told (in suitably hushed tones) that the parents had left everything and moved to France to get over their loss and start again, instructing her to sell the cottage. They were unreachable.

"Would you at least be able to tell me whether an old doll left behind belonged to Ms Trevelyan? It was in the master bedroom." Stephanie added, hopefully.

"Oh, that old thing? I assume so, the family didn't want any of her possessions. I put them all in storage as instructed, but I left the doll there. They thought it should remain in the house, under the circumstances."

"What circumstances?" Stephanie asked, becoming alarmed.

"Something isn't right here," she thought.

Maisy had returned. Her trip to the kitchen had been in vain: her food bowl was empty. She settled on Stephanie's lap again, gently kneading her knee.

"Because of the legend, of course. The curse! Sorry dear, I have a call waiting. Must rush! I would ask at the antique shop in the village. The owner might be able to help you. Bye!"

She was gone, and the line buzzed with her absence.

Stephanie sat, dazed, her mind racing. She blew the wisps of her errant fringe from her eyes and just sat there. A missing woman? A legend? Her idyllic country retreat might be the site of a murder and the doll in the attic was cursed. Just what she needed.

A sudden clap of thunder shook her from her thoughts and she dropped the phone, sending Maisy scurrying under the sofa as huge drops of rain pelted the windows, soaking the flimsy curtains as they flailed in the wind.

Stephanie hurriedly went around the house, closing all the windows. The flashes and rumbles continued to light up the darkened sky and black clouds drew in before expelling their payload of pelting rain, she abandoned all hope of making it into the village to visit the antique shop. That would have to wait till the morning. She closed the French windows to stop them swinging in the breeze and sat in her living room for a while, watching the drama of nature unfold in the sky above the impressive, raging sea. The lightning flashes rending the sombre clouds with purple shards of radiance were exhilarating. Her garden would benefit from the downpour too. She thought it was magnificent, but Maisy did not agree. She was still hiding under the sofa, and not even a tasty morsel could tempt her out.

Having wasted her day so far and choosing not to venture out in the heavy rain, Stephanie gave in and went into the office. She settled in for the rest of the afternoon, throwing herself into bills and research, catching up with unread email and social media, and passing the time with videos of cats. Hours passed, interspersed with visits to the kitchen for snacks and soft drinks. So absorbed was she in her tasks that she didn't hear the door squeak open on its old hinges as something pushed it open and looked inside. Something ancient, something evil. Maisy hissed and growled softly, ears back, head to the ground, but Stephanie took no notice. She thought she was just objecting to the storm.

The watcher was back. Unseen by his quarry, he waited.

***

The next morning, after a fitful night plagued by nightmares of little old men chasing her (and waking at 3.14 am for no apparent reason), Stephanie rose early, showered quickly and dressed. She skipped breakfast and started off to the village after a quick cup of tea. No time for a leisurely breakfast, or a stroll on the beach today.

She was lost in thought. Her pace was hurried; she ignored the beauty of the morning and failed to see the cheeky robin perched on the gate opposite leading to the fields. She ignored the butterflies that played around the flowers, the tranquil pond and the grass verges dotted with summer flowers. The sounds and sights of her environment passed her by; she was a woman on a mission.

The country lane widened eventually into a small road with a slight downhill incline, and she strode on purposefully, smiling absentmindedly at the people that she met. Some looked like villagers; others were obviously tourists bedecked with cameras and souvenirs. Many of them smiled back, which lifted her spirits. She had made good time, and within fifteen minutes she had reached the village of Marlin.

After passing a butcher's, a greengrocer's and a small post office, she found what she was looking for. She peered in at the front window of the antique shop, annoyed to find that it was not open till ten o'clock. It nestled between a small supermarket and an even smaller pharmacy. Shops lined only one side of the road, and on the other was a river with a narrow footpath. Life was so much more casual in the country, and she had yet to get used to the pace. With forty minutes to wait, she went in search of a distraction.

Walking on from the antique shop, she came to a small bridge on her left which traversed the river. On her side of the road she was pleased to find that the village had a small, pretty café with adjoining bakery. Her lack of breakfast was soon replaced by a coffee and a slice of fruit cake, made to a traditional local recipe (so she was informed by the enthusiastic young woman who served her, tall and thin with piercing, vulture-like eyes).

"Not from round here?" chirped the waitress, stirring her from her thoughts.

"Just moved in," replied Stephanie casually, hoping that the girl would go and interrogate someone else. But sadly, she was the only customer.

"Ooh, where from?" asked the waitress, with a prying glint in her eyes and her head to one side as she surveyed her mark. Strangers were always fodder for discussion.

"London," said Stephanie sharply, in the vain hope of deterring her.

But she had settled in, hand on hip to begin her inquisition.

Then the ancient café doorbell clanged (the type that all such establishments seemed to have in rural villages) and a group of three young men walked in, chatting in French.

"Sorry, customers!" she said, as her eyes lit up and she went in search of more exotic prey, giving the tourists her full attention.

Stephanie sighed inwardly with relief. She enjoyed the rest of her coffee and fruit cake in peace, watching the village come to life through the window, almost forgetting why she was even there. She revisited the occurrences of the past few days in her head again and again. The clock on the wall told her that she still had time to spare before the shop opened, so she paid her bill, and set off to see the rest of the village, what little there was of it.

After leaving the café, she realised that she had already seen nearly all that the village had to offer. In the space of ten minutes she came across the rest; the library, which stood the other side of the bridge next to the primary school and The Marlin Arms, a small, ancient pub just down the lane from that, frequented mostly by locals in the winter. She imagined that it would be very appealing to tourists in the summer because it offered home-cooked food, a beer garden and a safe play area.

Across the road there were three parallel rows of cottages which lined the hill in stages. They stood above the pub, overlooking the village on the other side of the river. Like her own house, they were made from local stone, and many of them offered bed and breakfast. Stephanie suspected that their location gave their guests stunning, undisturbed views across the bay and out to sea towards Ireland beyond.

She mused that tourists might drive to nearby towns if they wanted night-time entertainment. Marlin was more of a sleepy coastal village for those seeking a quiet retreat. It was a place to restore the soul from city stress by sun, sea, sand; by walking and silent reflection. But it seemed to be popular with young families because of the safe, clean beach, although it was likely with so little to see and do that most visitors used the village more as a base for touring the sights of Cornwall, rather than somewhere to spend a whole week. In her view, anyway. Personally, she loved it for its sleepy solitude. It was charming, and she felt like she had stepped back in time. She hadn't had time to visit the village when viewing the cottage, a practice which some would view as a mistake. Yet she needn't have worried; she was warming to the place already. But sightseeing wasn't what had brought her here today. She had a purpose of a different kind.

***

Looking at her watch she saw that it was five past ten. She walked the short distance back to the antique shop, to be greeted by an older man who was engaged in briskly sweeping the pavement outside.

"Tourists!" he said "Dropping crumbs from their pasties and goodness knows what else."

She nodded in agreement and he parked his broom inside the door as he led her into the shop. He closed the door behind him; the obligatory doorbell jangled, making her jump. He was, she suspected, the upper end of middle-aged, balding and wearing a charcoal pinstripe suit, complete with waistcoat and pocket watch. She smiled to herself as she realised he reminded her a little of the creepy doll. Then she shuddered. He passed his hand over the few grey hairs left on the top of his head, straightened his bright red bow tie, and spoke.

"My apologies, no offence intended, he said," referring to his comments about tourists.

"None taken!" Stephanie replied.

"Well, young woman, what can I do for you today?" he enquired.

Stephanie was wandering about the shop, casually glancing at random antiques with no obvious interest in any of them while trying to come up with a way of broaching the subject at hand. An expression fleetingly crossed his face when she turned to face him, as if he recognised her.

"It's, um, quite a delicate matter," she started, looking into his kind eyes.

She decided it would be best to just blurt it out.

"Well, it's like this. It's about the figure of an old man, a doll, or puppet. I'm not sure what to call it. It's in my house, well cottage, and the owner is missing, and…"

She was aware the she was rambling, so she stopped.

"Take a breath my dear!" the owner said.

He was smiling, but he had a worried look in his eyes. "Have a seat."

He pointed to a padded winged chair to her right. "Tea?" he asked.

"Oh no, but thank you," she answered breathlessly, accepting a seat.

"I'm sorry, I'm not making myself very clear," she said, flushing with embarrassment. He pulled up a chair opposite her.

"It's OK, I know exactly what you mean," he replied. "You must be the new owner of The Lodge."

"Yes!" she was surprised. "How did you...?"

"The only person to have gone missing in this area in many years was Sarah Trevelyan from The Lodge. I remember she brought the doll to me some months ago, for some advice. I believe she found it in an old chest the attic. I did warn her," he said with a concerned look.

He began mopping his gleaming brow with a bright red handkerchief with white dots that he retrieved from his trouser pocket, looking nervously downwards like a guilty child, as if he was worried that he was about to be blamed for something.

"Warned her about what?" Stephanie asked.

"The legend!" He paused, looking around to make sure no-one was listening (although nobody else had entered the shop).

"It started nearly a hundred years ago, in the early 1900s. The Trevelyan estate was owned by a cruel man, William Trevelyan. His family had made a fortune from the local tin mines and they lived up at The Manor. The house where you now live belonged to the estate manager. It's on Trevelyan land, you see, as is the rest of the village. It used to be called Trevelyan Lodge." He paused for breath.

"At the time, John Hall and his wife Mary lived on the hill leading down to the village. You passed their house on the way here. The Smithy. He was a blacksmith, you see, but he died in the First World War. After that, Mary made a living by cleaning up at The Manor. They had two sons, Tom and Mark. Tom fell in love with Trevelyan's teenage daughter, Isabel. She was a real beauty. This area was renowned for smuggling in years gone by and the caves were ideal hiding places for contraband. There were rumours that Tom was a thief, started by Trevelyan, the local Justice of the Peace, all lies, of course. "

The man started to become agitated as he continued, his face growing redder.

"In fact, it was his own son Peter Trevelyan who was responsible, storing his stolen goods in those caves. It was the depression and certain goods were hard to come by, so he imported items illegally by boat and sold them at a profit. But the lies proved enough to stop him marrying his daughter, and worse."

Michael took another well-earned breath. By now, Stephanie was sitting on the edge of her chair.

"What happened next?" she asked.

"Tom Hall, the son, was charged with theft and effectively dealing in stolen goods. With the help of forged statements, bribed witnesses and planted evidence provided by Peter, William Trevelyan of course found him guilty. Tom was sentenced to be jailed for three years for profiteering. He was lucky it wasn't more. Isabel was so distraught that she would stand on the cliff top, day and night, waiting for him at their favourite spot until he came home. She lost track of time, barely slept or ate enough to keep body and soul together."

He took another pause. Stephanie felt queasy; this tale was taking a sinister turn. He continued.

"Her family sent her away to relatives that summer to try to make her forget him, but six months later she came home. Finally, one cold blustery autumn night, she fell to her death on the rocks below Fern Leap. It's a popular suicide spot round here. Some say it was deliberate, through grief, some say she was simply weak from hunger."

He paused, mopping his brow again. Suddenly, Stephanie felt very sad.

"Tom endured hell on earth in jail from beatings and isolation. Trevelyan saw to that. But through it all, the thought of coming home to his beloved Isabel kept him going. After three years, he came back, only to find her dead and buried. Tom went off to confront Trevelyan at The Manor, but the poor lad never stood a chance. Trevelyan took his shotgun and shot him, telling people he came upon him in the dark and mistook him for an armed intruder. He was, of course, unarmed and took a single bullet to the lung. Peter stood by and did nothing. Tom's brother Mark, fearing for his safety, had followed him there and found him bleeding profusely, gasping for breath. But he was too late. Nothing could be done."

Michael stopped, obviously becoming emotional, wiping his face with his handkerchief and mopping his brow. It was not an easy story to tell.

"What happened next?" Stephanie coaxed.

"Mark carried Tom home, but when he got there, he… he died in his mother's arms. Mary Hall, their mother, was thought of as a witch in these parts. As well as making herbal remedies, she also cast spells. She cursed Trevelyan and his family. She wished him dead, and swore that all his descendants would die young, like her son. Everyone knew that there was no justice to be had for Tom, what with Trevelyan's position and Tom being a convicted criminal. No justice for the family. But Mary found it in her own way. Trevelyan died soon after. He fell from his horse and broke his neck just weeks later. Trevelyan's wife Julia and their son Peter also perished in a suspicious fire following a party to celebrate his 21ˢᵗ birthday, leaving The Manor in ruins. No-one ever lived there again. They say Peter's evil spirit still haunts his house in the village to this day."

This was disturbing news, not at all what Stephanie had expected.

"Curse? Hauntings?" she thought. It was getting worse by the minute.

Michael carried on.

"When Mary died soon after, some say of a broken heart, Mark found the doll buried near the foundations of their house, its shirt cut from the fabric of her own son's bloody shirt on the day that he died and his suit made from the jacket that her son had worn. It rested in a wooden box with unusual symbols carved on it. It was an effigy of Trevelyan. She even managed to get some of his own hair which she stole from a brush at The Manor while she was cleaning his room. The doll carries the dark magic that binds the curse to the family, you see. After Mary died, Mark hid the doll away, no-one knows where, to keep it from harming anyone else, but it somehow got out of its box. Other descendants have also perished. Somehow the doll made its way back to The Lodge. Sarah Trevelyan found it, she was drawn to its magic and made the mistake of keeping it. She was the last in the line, you see. Her father Andrew was a descendant of distant cousins of William's, from Devon. He and his wife Judy moved to the area when she was a child and built a big house on the coast road. Sarah was such a lovely girl."

At this point he became even more upset.

"I warned her not to keep it, I told her it would activate the curse. You must believe me! But she laughed at me, laughed at the curse. Now she's gone too, poor child."

The man had tears in his eyes. Stephanie didn't know what to do, so she just put a hand on his shoulder. She was stunned by his words. After a few moments, he stopped sobbing. He looked at her with fear in his eyes.

"Get out of that house!" he exclaimed. "Leave The Lodge, get far away like Sarah's parents, before it's too late for you too!"

"I can't," she muttered miserably. "It's all I have."

She looked into his eyes once more. "But I'm not a Trevelyan, surely the curse can't hurt me?"

"The fact that you have come to me today means that there's trouble at The Lodge. The doll has a link to you somehow, and the evil is too strong. It has grown over the years; the beast within it is sick with anger and all it wants is revenge. Maybe the curse will take anyone who owns the house because it's where Tom lived and died? I don't know. I thought that when Sarah went missing that would be the end of it, being the last of the Trevelyan line. But if it is awake again, soon it will be out of control. You must understand, that thing is the living embodiment of hatred and death!"

"But there must be a way of breaking the curse," Stephanie said, desperately. "What can I do?"

"There is one way. It is said that if you find the box, put the doll in it and burn it, the curse will die with it," he said. "But nobody knows where to find it, and even then, it won't be easy. The doll is very devious and powerful. Be careful!"

She got up to leave, shaken beyond belief but determined not to leave her home. As she stood, he grabbed hold of her hand.

"I'm so sorry," he said, "so very sorry!" He pointed to the doorway. "My family... it's all our fault."

Stephanie rose and went to the doorway, opened the door and looked up. Above the door, the shop sign said *'HALL ANTIQUES'*. She understood.

"So, that means...?" She looked back as he nodded. The poor man looked truly miserable.

"Yes, I am Michael Hall. My father was Mark Hall and Mary was my grandmother. I've lived in The Smithy all my life, and my family live there still, but the box isn't there any more. We searched every inch of it. You must find it, my dear, and soon!"

***

After leaving Michael's shop, Stephanie was visibly shaken. She paid a visit to the library and searched the archives, assisted by the dusty librarian, Miss Broom. She picked up a few groceries in the village. With all the books she had found, she couldn't carry much more. She noticed The Smithy as she walked up the lane to her cottage and she rushed nervously past it, only too aware now of its awful past.

She arrived home, hot and bothered, at about two o'clock. Maisy was stretched out decadently in the hall waiting for her; Stephanie had forgotten to feed her in her rush to leave earlier. Maisy jumped up as she came in and was naturally very vocal in her disgust. As any cat owner knows, forgetting a cat's meal time is a cardinal sin. Stephanie fed her, apologising profusely. She made herself a quick sandwich and a mug of tea and settled down in the office to read the books from the library on local history and legends. Maisy was still pouting (this time in comfort, on the sofa in the living room). A soft summer shower trickled down the windows as she slept.

Stephanie had hoped for some hints as to the whereabouts of the box, but after three hours, she gave in; she was none the wiser and had a stiff neck. After that, she scoured the internet and finally came across an old map of Lapwing Cove which encompassed the beach that lay below her cottage. She remembered something that Michael had told her about hiding contraband in caves. She looked closely at the map and found that there was a cave just under the headland, along the beach from the cottage. She hadn't ventured that far yet.

She got up, planning to head out to investigate. The coastal weather had other plans however, as the light shower had turned to heavy rain which thrummed at the windows, accompanied by a rising gale. It would have to wait till the morning. She made dinner and watched a little television. The weather forecaster indicated that more thunderstorms were due later in the week, but tomorrow would be dry and sunny.

"Tomorrow it is then!" she announced to Maisy, who had finally forgiven her after her next meal arrived on time, and was curled up in a ball on her lap, fast asleep: paw on nose, tail on head. The nap was short-lived however, as not long after Maisy was settled, Stephanie wriggled herself free to go upstairs, suddenly struck with a spurt of musical inspiration. Maisy jumped into the newly vacated warm space on the sofa and purred.

"Would you jump on my grave as quickly?" called Stephanie from the hallway, then shuddered at her own words.

Maisy glared after her and fell asleep again.

Music had always been a huge part of Stephanie's life. She would sing as often as she could, having inherited both her mother's passion for singing and her perfect pitch. She sat now, singing and playing her guitar for some time; drawing comfort from the favourite songs from her childhood and teenage years. Songs that her mother sang to her as a child. She played until her fingers started to become sore (recent events had not left her much time to practice) then she went to take a shower. She returned to her bedroom and sat at her dressing table mirror to dry her hair. She looked up and caught a glimpse of a familiar figure in the rocking chair. It was the old man. He had somehow freed himself from the attic.

Dropping the hair dryer in shock, she walked over and picked him up, filled with a mixture of anger, fear and dread. She examined him closely as she carried him out of the room, pausing on the landing. His face was blank, it was just a doll, but just for a split second she saw something else, a demonic glint in his eyes. She took him hastily back to the attic and secured him in a box, this time placing it inside a suitcase which she then locked, and she bolted the trap door to the attic this time too. She doubted it would stop him. She went to bed, but it was not to be a restful night.

***

Sleep did not come easily with her mind racing. After she finally dropped off, her dreams were again nightmares of being pursued by some invisible enemy. An unfamiliar female figure in white floated around her, exuding a bright light. It appeared as if she was trying to speak, but Stephanie could make out neither her words not her features. Then she began to sing, a quiet lilting melody that sounded familiar, timeless yet without lyrics. Her voice was sweet and mystical. Hypnotic. All about her head and hair, like streaks of silver, flew dozens of little ghostly white moths. Stephanie thrashed about, sending Maisy flying in a huff, resigning her to sleep under the bed. At 3.14 am she woke. This was becoming a habit. Maisy was growling gutturally, her hackles up. She was just visible in the bedroom doorway as she stalked something - or someone - on the landing. Stephanie put on the lamp and jumped out of bed; Maisy ran to hide.

As she stepped out of the bedroom, she could see nothing. No-one. As she turned to go back to bed, she felt a strong breeze on her neck and the bedroom door flew shut in her face. Turning around, she caught a glimpse of something white shimmering at the end of the hall.

She walked towards it, her curiosity getting the better of her, not thinking of the consequences. In her haste, she didn't think to put on the light, but the shape shone so brightly that she didn't need it. As she approached, it turned the corner. She followed. She was not prepared for what she saw on the stairs: it was a figure, not of an old man but of a woman. The figure from her dreams. She just stood there, shining like a million stars with the aura of light engulfing her and a single, tiny white moth fluttering around her head.

The woman smiled and beckoned to Stephanie who was rigid with terror although her appearance was not threatening in the least. Then she vanished as quickly as she had appeared, her exit accompanied by that same cool rush of air but this time with a faint scent of roses. Stephanie couldn't believe her eyes. It was like the breeze that had slammed her door that first night in the bedroom. She just stood there in disbelief, gripping the banister so that she wouldn't fall; her legs felt like they were giving way, unable to hold her weight.

After a few minutes of sitting on the stairs, she went down to the kitchen to get a drink of warm milk. But she knew that sleep was out of the question, what with the worries of the day racing round her head and now this.

"She looks like me!" she thought. *"Who is she?"*

She jumped as Maisy landed in her lap, needing attention and reassurance. She stroked her beloved tabby cat and began to cry, warm salty tears soaking the cat's head. The strain was becoming too much for her. Her book was at a stand-still, her dream home had turned into a house of horror. She was hunted by a demonic doll and haunted by a spooky woman that resembled her. She had only one thought.

"Jan!"

She didn't know why she hadn't thought of her before. Jan had been her best friend since childhood, and as well as being a private investigator, some aspects of her job were based among what might be termed the supernatural fringes of society.

Jan was a medium, a 'house-clearer' by trade, and her business proved lucrative. Basically, she could see, hear and speak to the dead, and they spoke to her. She had a team who helped her, and they would visit people's homes and rid them of unwanted spirit visitors and help spirits find peace, find lost items for clients and basically dealing with anything of the supernatural persuasion. They also undertook more mundane investigative cases which Jan found to be decidedly less interesting, but they paid the bills so she wasn't complaining.

Stephanie had always fervently refused invitations to accompany Jan on any of her cases, especially the more unusual ones. Jan also knew all about Stephanie's strange dreams, which more often than not turned out to be premonitions. She had tried encouraging her, telling her that she also had a gift; that she was blocking it and wasting her talent. Stephanie used to just laugh it off, but it looked like Jan had been right. There was definitely something weird going on. It would be worth an "I told you so!" to sort this mess out. She was sure that Jan would know what to do.

She looked at the clock: 3.14 am again. It was far too early to ring yet, so she would have to be patient and wait until a more respectable hour.

Disturbing a sleeping friend in the early hours wasn't the best way to ask for a favour.

With a firm plan in mind, Stephanie headed for bed again, complete with her very purry cat in tow, happy to follow her mistress even if she had made her a little soggy.

After much restlessness, she fell asleep from sheer exhaustion as dawn approached. Silence fell on the cottage once more, save for the sound of the waves softly rolling in with the morning tide and the call of an owl in the distance. Little did Stephanie know it, but a fight between good and evil had begun, and she was caught in the middle. Would she be forfeited for the greater good or live to see victory?

***

A voice was calling from far away. Stepping out of bed she walked effortlessly down the stairs. Then she was at the back door. It was open. A woman's voice was calling her name. Then the figure in white appeared on the path behind the gate. The lady that shone, surrounded by her spirit entourage, a cloud of minute, glimmering moths. Silently she motioned to Stephanie to follow her down the steps and onto the beach. She did as she was asked.

Moonlight bathed the beach with an eerie glow; stars glimmered above as ink-black waves crashed furiously on the shore to her right. A soft mist rolled in and swirled around her feet. On she went, past the headland to a split in the rock, a recess just wide enough to accommodate a slender human form. The lady slid in and she followed. It opened into a dark chamber, the glow from the figure somehow illuminating it well enough for her to see. A cave. She pointed to a jagged corner of rock that stuck out about halfway in and five feet off the sandy floor. Stephanie touched it and it crumbled before her eyes as a shaft of light blinded her.

***

She woke up to find a beam of bright sunlight creeping over her windowsill from behind the clouds. Her curtains had shifted in a gentle breeze and the light stabbed at her eyes. It was noon, and she had overslept. There was no doubt she needed the rest, but she had to call Jan. She jumped out of bed and ran to splash her face with water. Her eyes felt gritty. She didn't notice that she left a trail of sandy footprints which vanished almost as soon as her foot left the floor, or the tiny white moth that flew out of the window. The ever-present Maisy saw it and simply yawned, too tired to give chase: her owner had kept her up half the night.

Stephanie picked up her mobile phone and went straight downstairs to make tea and ring Jan, her number still on speed dial. Maisy followed. Daylight meant breakfast.

"Jan, I need your help…" Stephanie began

Before she could explain anything, Jan said that it would take her a few hours to drive from London and she had some work to finish up first.

"I'll be there tonight," Jan assured her. "Give me the address and chill the wine!"

Stephanie smiled and thanked her. Jan was particular about her wine, favouring a crisp dry white but also partial to a rich, fruity red. It had been a long time since they last spoke, yet it was as if no time had passed. No explanation was necessary when a friend needed help, and no distance was too great. She knew that if Jan ever needed her, she would do the same. Jan hung up, but her last words still rang loudly in Stephanie's heard.

"Don't worry Steph!"

But she was worried; how could she not be? Yet just speaking to Jan had made her feel better already, and hopeful that there was a way out of this nightmare.

She knew that she had isolated herself the past few months since her break-up with Paul. Even the thought of him made her shudder. Paul Richards. What had she been thinking? He had broken her heart and stolen her credit cards then disappeared into the night like the thief that he was. Luckily the police had caught up with him and he had been put away where he belonged (though not for long enough in her opinion).

Her reaction to his betrayal had been to hide from everyone because she felt gullible, weak and stupid. Although it was the time that she needed her friend most, she didn't want to be pitied. She should have known that Jan wouldn't have done that; she was her best friend. Stephanie felt guilty; she had pushed her away for far too long, and she had missed her terribly.

Stephanie had loved London, but it was tainted for her now. So, she had decided to move away, from everyone and everything that reminded her of Paul. Even the mention of his name made her sick. She ran away, sold her flat, abandoned her friends and bought this cottage. She had put everything she had into the place, staking her entire future on the move. She hadn't contacted anyone she knew in months or returned her friends' attempts at contacting her. Her pride was one thing, but this was something that she couldn't handle alone, and she would be stupid to try.

But even if she had been a poor friend in not answering Jan's calls or emails, she knew that she was the one person who understood her best; the one who would always be there for her. However long the absence. Scatter-brained and distracted as she always seemed, she was really quite the opposite. Jan was organised, reliable and loyal; the best person to count on in a crisis. And this was a crisis of monumental proportions, a battle that she might not win by herself, and in trying to do she had already put herself at risk. But with Jan's help, she might have a chance of making it out alive.

So, she pulled herself together, showered, dressed and attempted to do some writing. But she soon abandoned it. Her attention was wandering; she was unable to concentrate. She took some chops out of the freezer for dinner and prepared a salad to go with it. She didn't even fancy a walk on the beach, not with the cave at the other end of it, and she was too scared to venture there alone. Instead she decided to make another visit to the village, leaving Maisy well fed and asleep in the office. She wanted to speak to the one person who might have answers. Michael.

It was another hot day with the promise of thunder later. As she set off, she felt relaxed and happy in the knowledge that Jan would be there soon. But a sense of creeping dread filled her heart, and every sense was heightened as if her brain was on high alert. Today she noticed everything. All the sights, sounds and smells of the world around her were somehow magnified, more intense. The flowers were brighter, their scent was stronger; she had never seen as many brightly coloured butterflies, or heard such noisy birds. Their songs were deafening.

She watched as dragonflies danced above the pond by the derelict mill, seizing the day. She realised that this might be her last day on earth. She jumped at shadows and the sound of grasshoppers. Everyone she met looked like they were watching her. She hated herself for being so jittery; it was exhausting. She had never felt so alive, or so desperate.

***

She stopped halfway for a rest on a strategically placed bench. The heat was relentless. She wished that her mother was still alive; she would have known what to do. She had always been warm and practical, calm and sensible, and she always had all the answers. But she had died in a dreadful car accident when Stephanie was fourteen. Stephanie's father James Meares, a solicitor, had become distant, lost in grief. His sister, her spinster aunt Eleanor, had been enlisted to raise her. She moved in with them and tried her best, but she was ignorant to the needs of a bereft young girl. Although she was well looked after following her mother's death, Stephanie felt unwanted: a burden. She had left home as soon as she was able and moved to London in search of work.

She hadn't spoken to her father for six years. She had never dreamed of contacting him when things went wrong in London. To do so would have brought her little comfort. It was more likely that she would only receive words of recrimination and reproach for trusting so foolishly. Yet deep down she knew that he would only behave like that because he was looking out for her. She missed him too, very much, and had done since her mother died.

She had put up a wall against the world, a barrier of protection against everyone. But in doing so, she found herself alone, and that wasn't really what she wanted, or needed. As tears threatened again, she put aside her memories, stood up and carried on walking. She needed all her emotional strength to face the present, if she was to have a future.

On entering the village, she went straight to the antique shop. It was after ten o'clock   therefore the shop was open for business. Michael Hall became flustered when she walked in, stammering at a customer who nevertheless left happy with his purchase of a carved mantel clock.

"Hello Michael," she said, with an attempt at a smile. She had never felt less like smiling.

Her presence had obviously unnerved him, but he smiled warmly and replied courteously.

"Yes, my dear. What can I do for you today?" he asked.

That is when she dispensed with the pleasantries and regaled him with the tale of her night-time visitor and the moth. His face visibly paled at her words.

"You mean you saw HER?" He looked shaken to the core.

"Yes!" she answered, pleased that he seemed to know who she was talking about. "Who is she Michael? Please tell me."

"Isabel!" he said, wide eyed. "You saw Isabel Trevelyan! But I don't understand..." He cupped his head in his hands and sat down, somewhat urgently, in the winged chair that she had occupied on her last visit.

"Neither do I," she said, starting to lose patience.

"She only appears to family, HER family!" he insisted.

"As I told you before," Stephanie assured him firmly, "I'm not a Trevelyan. My mother was from Bristol and my father was born in Bath. They met at Bristol University and, as far as I know, they never set foot in Cornwall."

"There is no mistake, my dear." He shook his head vehemently.

"So, Isabel, what is she? A ghost? I've been seeing a ghost?" she repeated in disbelief.

"Rumour has it that she's a revenant, a vengeful spirit that has unfinished business on earth. She is also portent of doom, death and disaster. She only appears when one of her family is in grave danger, which is why Sarah saw her, before she…"

"Disappeared. Or died." Stephanie said it flatly, without emotion.

"I'm sorry…" His words caught in his throat.

Stephanie turned away and left him alone with his sorrow. She felt numb. The bell sang as she left and the door slid shut behind her with a grating sound, jarring her nerves even further. Nothing made sense. She wished that Jan was there. She felt so cold, even standing out beneath the summer sun. So lost.

She went to the café, realising that she felt nauseous. She needed something sweet 'for the shock', as her mother used to say. Tea and fruit cake were duly ordered and quickly received. Glaring defiantly at the waitress ensured a lack of unwanted conversation. The place was empty, and she was glad of the chance to gather her thoughts. An hour later, the cake was only half-eaten and all but a few sips of her well-sweetened tea sat there, stone cold. She had been lost inside her head, mulling over the events of a hundred years ago.

She got up and paid her bill. Every step forward was an effort and seemed to take her backwards; her feet and heart felt heavy. Her world had fallen silent, and all colour seemed to have drained from her surroundings. If she passed anyone on the way, their presence didn't register. It took all her strength to walk slowly home. But somewhere along the way Stephanie Meares made up her mind.

"One way or another, this ends tonight!"

***

It was almost four when she opened her front door and was greeted by the figure of the little old man who sat on the bottom step of the stairs, a triumphant look on his face. The air was cold, and she was terrified. She instinctively stepped back into the warmth of the sunlight. She knew she had to secure him somehow until she could find the box. With every fibre of her being screaming for her to leave the cottage forever and just run, she walked forwards and bent down to pick him up. As she did, a spine-chilling laugh filled the air, not a human laugh, something otherworldly and evil. She almost dropped him in shock.

She ran to the kitchen and with one hand holding him round the leg in case he somehow got free (and she had no idea what he was capable of), she clumsily placed him in a black bin bag, knotted the top twice and put him outside in the old steel dustbin. It was ludicrous to think that an inanimate object could inspire such fear. But this was no ordinary doll. Slamming the lid firmly down, she went back inside and locked the front door and kitchen door, then she ran around the house shutting all the windows. She prayed it would hold him long enough.

As she stood in the kitchen, she heard what sounded like singing, as if it was far away yet floating inside her ear; the same song that had mesmerised her the night before as she slept. The song that the woman in white sang in her dream. A few bars wafted on the air, and it was gone, but it was enough for her to recognise it now as a lullaby that her grandmother, Nana Jean, used to sing to her at bedtime. She had died suddenly aged just 49 when Stephanie was only eight and she still missed her. But the voice wasn't hers. Amid all this madness, in some small way it brought her comfort, whoever was singing, and maybe that was its purpose.

Only then did she notice the damage. As she looked around the kitchen she was reminded of the destruction left by a hurricane, except in this case the roof was still on and the cottage was structurally sound. She walked through the house with one hand over her mouth, uttering only small gasps at what she saw, before returning to the kitchen where she had started.

Every piece of crockery, glassware, book, ornament, cushion and any other item which was not stored safely in a cupboard had been swept to the floor. Even the antique teapot belonging to Nana Jean. She remembered the singing, and the tears stung the corners of her eyes as she began to pick up the pieces of the delicate rose-patterned china, refusing to give in, refusing to let him defeat her. Anger rose in her chest, her cheeks flushed.

She could almost hear her mother's voice in her head, talking to her.

"You're a fighter Steffi Meares, never forget it!"

She stood up defiantly, swallowing the lump in her throat, that dry pain you get when you don't want to cry.

"It must have been the doll," she thought. *"But how? This is madness!"*

"Damn you to hell!" she yelled, her throat aching with the effort.

She wished her mother was there to hug her, to ruffle her hair and tell her it would all be OK, enfolding her in strong arms and surrounding her with love. Making her feel safe from the world like she did when she was a child. She had never felt so helpless.

She was shaken from her misery by someone banging on the front door. She wiped away another stray tear and made her way to the door, slowly, nervously at first, then running as she recognised a face through the glass panel at the top. It was Jan. She opened the door and hugged her, dissolving into tears as Jan gasped for breath and hugged her back.

"Good lord, I would have come earlier if I'd known I'd have this much of a welcome!" she gasped. "Put me down, Steph, I can't breathe!"

Stephanie released her grip, sniffed and pulled away to take a good look at her friend.

"I'm sorry Jan. I've been such a terrible friend!" she said with tears burning her eyes. "I can't believe you're really here, and you look fabulous!"

Jan brushed back her bubbly curls and flashed her friend a ready smile, one that even reached her deep blue eyes. Tall, blonde, well-dressed, fully made up and oozing confidence, Jan provided a stark contrast to

Stephanie's current appearance and demeanour. About the same height as her friend, she was just as attractive.

Jan looked her friend up and down. She was shocked by what she saw.

"No apology necessary. I finished work earlier than expected. I always look fabulous. And you, well, words fail me!" Jan shook her head. "You look like death."

"BAD choice of words, Jan," she replied with a wry smile.

Stephanie caught sight of herself in the hall mirror which was askew but unbroken, much like herself. She doubted at this point that she would even survive long enough to endure seven years of bad luck, and she looked truly dreadful. Her hair was a mess; her face deathly pale and streaked with yesterday's make-up and fresh tears, eyes blackened underneath by mascara and bags the size of saucers. She looked like a wild woman. Or a weeping panda.

Jan surveyed the devastation to the cottage, and the damage that had been done to her friend since she last saw her. Despite her best efforts to make contact, that had been over a year ago. Stephanie looked anxious and thinner than she remembered. She didn't know if her present state of mind was due to what had happened with Paul, or to the current situation in Marlin. Or maybe a combination of the two. All she knew was that her friend was a shadow of her formal self and she was worried for her. She decided that the best way to help Stephanie now was to focus on the matter in hand.

"What the hell happened here?" she started, then stopped when Stephanie just stared at her. "On second thoughts, let's get this mess cleaned up first and have something to eat, you look like you haven't eaten in months.

A few hours later, the house was tidy and they had finished the meal of pork chops and salad. They sat in the living room with glasses of Muscadet, Stephanie's favourite wine and well-chilled as directed. Thankfully the glasses had been saved from destruction by their location in the kitchen cupboard.

The wind was rising, making an eerie whistling sound as it whooshed around the garden, adding to Stephanie's state of heightened agitation. It began to blow the curtains around the open French windows. Stephanie thought she had closed them earlier, but that didn't matter now. Much of what had happened in that cottage defied explanation. The flapping sound was grating on her already tattered nerves., and although it was a little stuffy indoors, she couldn't stand the sound any longer so she closed the windows.

Outside it was dusk, with storm clouds hastening the gloom, so she lit the matching pair of yellow-shaded wall lights on either side of the fireplace. She was keen to talk about the reason for her phone call, but Jan had other ideas. Jan had been trying to distract her, telling her about her life, passing on gossip about mutual friends, simply to try to calm Stephanie down. It wasn't helping. The atmosphere was strained. Jan sensed that this was a problem that only she could solve and decided that it was time to address it. She filled her glass and took a healthy sip.

"OK, time for business. Tell me everything!" demanded Jan.

"It's this house..." Stephanie began, but Jan stopped her.

"I know, I can feel it. Actually, say nothing and I'll work it out for myself," she said authoritatively. Stephanie nodded.

Jan picked up her purple Radley handbag and took out a pack of Tarot cards. She shuffled them and placed the pile on the coffee table; Stephanie just stared at them.

"Shuffle the deck!" said Jan, nodding at them.

"You know how I feel about those things; it's a load of rubbish!" Stephanie said.

"Humour me. To be honest, I don't think you're in a position to be picky. Come on, shuffle them!"

Jan looked at Stephanie. Reluctantly she picked up the deck, shuffled them well and placed them back on the coffee table with a sigh.

"Now choose three cards, one for your past, one for the present and one for the future," Jan ordered, and Stephanie did as she was told.

The first card she drew was The High Priestess. Then there was The Hanged Man and finally, Death. Jan took a deep breath, looked into her eyes, and spoke

"OK. This is worse than I thought. There are two entities around you Steph. I can feel them. One is good, a strong, powerful woman in spirit who is protecting you. She's represented by The High Priestess. The other is evil. It isn't even a person, it never has been. It's just a manifestation of hate. They are both powerful. It's some sort of ancient family feud, and you're caught in the middle somehow."

"It's because I bought this house," Stephanie said in panic.

"Yes and no, it's because of who you ARE!" Jan insisted. "You're connected to it all somehow. I think you were drawn to buy the house, to lure you here."

Stephanie remembered how much the cottage had been like the house she had dreamed about, and she felt cold all over. Her new, perfect life was falling apart.

"Michael said that, but I don't understand. Jan, you've known me all nearly my life. They aren't my family, they can't be!" Stephanie was confused beyond belief.

"Who is Michael? Tell me everything, now!" Jan said, frowning, full of concern.

Stephanie explained. When she had finished, Jan closed her eyes.

"Now I understand. It all makes sense. That's why she's here," she said. "I told you to trust your instincts more. It's Isabel, Steph. She's been reaching out to you.

"ISABEL? Really, Isabel Trevelyan?"

Stephanie shuddered, her hands were shaking as she picked upon her glass.

"Is she the woman who has been appearing to me? But she looks like me! Jan, why does she look like me?"

"Calm down Steph!" said Jan, taking her hand and looking her straight in the eye. "She wants to help you. She has many things to tell you, you just need to listen."

"How can you see her? Surely we can't both be related to her?" Stephanie asked.

"I can't physically SEE her; she's sort of in my head, if you know what I mean. Her thoughts are my thoughts. Spirits appear to me like that sometimes," Jan said reassuringly. "I can sense that she's been here trying to speak to you. She isn't actually here right now."

"OK," Stephanie said, settling back on the sofa, ready to listen.

Jan continued reading the cards. Stephanie was starting to relax. If Jan could see Isabel too, no matter how she was doing it, then at least she knew that she wasn't losing her mind. Jan went on.

"She has been fighting for you since you got here, Steph. The next card represents the struggle that's going on now, between good, which is Isabel, and evil, presumably this doll. She is keeping it at bay for now, as indicated by the balance of The Hanged Man card, but it's getting stronger."

Stephanie realised that it did all fit in with what Michael had told her.

"So, what about the third card, Death. Does that mean he's going to kill me?" Stephanie asked, not really wanting to hear the reply.

"Not necessarily. Death represents a change, a shift of some sort. It indicates the end of something, but also the start of something else."

"What does that mean?" Stephanie asked.

"Probably the end if your old life and the start if your new one? Pick another card to amplify the energy and clarify the situation. Place it on the Death card," Jan said.

Stephanie chose another card and placed it as instructed. It was The Tower.

"OK!" Jan said. "Not the best card, but it makes sense. The Tower represents chaos, destruction and despair. But it can also indicate hope. A way out of oppression, by self-sacrifice and transformation." Jan looked thoughtful.

"I don't understand!" said Stephanie close to tears again. Jan put her arm round her shoulder.

"It's OK, Steph," she said gently. "The cards are only a possible future, they offer you a way forward and the rest all depends on you. We'll work it out together. You need to get some sleep, then you'll be able to think more clearly. But first there's something I need to do. Show me the doll!"

***

With Stephanie standing behind her in the kitchen doorway, Jan opened the lid of the bin. She undid the knots in the bin bag, took out the doll, held it by one arm and started chanting in a strange, melodic language. The doll twitched as little as she spoke, then it became still, just hanging there. She put it back in the bin bag, knotted it carefully and returned the bag to the bin with a satisfying clang of the lid.

"He's an ugly little bugger, isn't he?" she said with a smile. "Come on, let's get some sleep. That should keep him quiet for a while!"

Stephanie couldn't believe what she had just witnessed.

"What did you do?" Stephanie asked as she locked the back door and stared at Jan. "Was that, I mean, can you do… mag..?"

"Magic? Yes, you learn all sorts in my job! Just a low-grade binding spell. It won't keep him there for long, I'm not that good yet. But it might help slow him down at least." she said, smiling. "Let's have some more wine, try to relax and watch a film or something, then get some sleep. You look like you need it!"

Stephanie was amazed. Jan never failed to surprise her, even after all these years. They spent a couple of hours catching up on news and gossip. Jan filled her in on her newest cases, recent fleeting but failed attempts at romance, interesting cases and hopes for the future.

Stephanie finally told Jan the full story about Paul. Jan was incensed. At nine o'clock, with two wine bottles and a tub of ice-cream lying empty in the kitchen, they decided to call it a night.

Stephanie helped Jan to make up the bed in the spare room and said goodnight. She lay in bed thinking. She felt a lot better about things now that Jan was there; she certainly seemed to know what she was doing which was exactly as Stephanie had hoped. But there were still so many unanswered questions. Maisy jumped onto the bed and lay in her favourite spot. With the comforting sound of her purring, Stephanie was soon asleep.

***

Stephanie was dreaming. She was walking along the beach, towards the cliffs to the left of her cottage. She saw a figure in white gliding across the sand towards her. It was Isabel, with the little moth fluttering around her head. As they met, Isabel took her hand and Stephanie was transported back in time. She relived the moments with her, saw them through her eyes and felt as she had felt. Isabel was ushered away from Marlin in secrecy. She was pregnant, scared and far from home; she felt so alone. The vision skipped to when Isabel first held her baby in her arms, and Stephanie could feel all the joy and love that Isabel felt for her child as she sang her to sleep with a familiar lullaby. Then she watched, horrified, as the shadowy figure of a man took the child away. Somehow, Stephanie knew he was William Trevelyan. Isabel was in obvious distress and Stephanie felt it all. The rest blended into a montage of misery depicting the aftermath of her father's actions. All she could make out from the disjointed images was the depth of Isabel's despair.

Stephanie woke with hot tears rolling down her cheeks and looked at the clock. It was 3.14 am. Isabel had shared her story with her, a story that had been hidden for far too long. She could see it all now; why she had come and the reason that she was protecting her.

She ran to wake Jan and sat on her bed to tell her what she had seen. The night was warm, but she was shaking.

"Jan, she had a baby in secret. Tom's child! She was taken away to a convent in Bath and her child was born, a girl who was adopted. Her child was my grandmother, Jan, I'm Isabel's great granddaughter! That's the connection! My grandmother, Nana Jean, never knew she was adopted so she and my mother knew nothing about any of this! I AM a Trevelyan after all!"

They thought about it all, logically and it did somehow make sense. Her grandmother, Nana Jean was from Bath and moved to Bristol just before her mother was born. Her family had always said how much Stephanie looked like her grandmother when she was young, and photographs had shown they were right.

"If I look like Nana Jean, then it makes sense that I might look like Isabel. Maybe I look like Sarah too, and that's why Michael appeared to see a resemblance when we first met. No wonder he seemed nervous!" said Stephanie.

Then a distant memory flashed into her head.

"Nana Jean died suddenly too Jan, in a hit and run accident. Oh, my God! Do you think…?"

Jan nodded solemnly.

"Yes, that's probably why she died so young."

It was all falling into place. Stephanie's distress was obvious, and Jan wished so much that she could take it all away.

"The end of the dream was very jumbled and vague," she said. "So, Isabel must have more to tell me," she whispered, her throat dry all of a sudden.

"OK why don't we ask her?" Jan said, determined to try the one thing that she knew she could do; try to contact Isabel again.

Anything that might even remotely help was better than watching Stephanie slowly unravel before her eyes. Jan had never seen her like this, not even when her mother died, and it was heartbreaking to witness.

They went down to the living room and Stephanie shakily made hot chocolate as Jan called on Isabel to come to them. Stephanie was beside herself. This was all so new to her; so terrible. She didn't even want to consider it, but she knew it was a truth she had to face. If the legend was real, she could be next.

***

It was a heavy night with a full moon. Neither of them was going to get back to sleep now. Stars twinkled in the sky above the bay and they sat in silence looking out at them for some time. The wind had subsided. Maisy came downstairs looking for food, then finding none, she fell asleep on Stephanie's lap. They waited. Nothing happened. Jan tried calling out to Isabel again. Just as they were about to give up and go back to bed, the air around them abruptly turned icy and the lights flickered. Stephanie sensed a ringing in her ears. Maisy ran into the office. Then Isabel appeared, clear as day, standing in front of the French windows; gazing wistfully out to sea. She turned to face them, smiled and vanished.

Instantly images flooded into Jan's mind of what Isabel had been trying to say. Terrible images that Jan struggled to understand, let alone find the words to convey. She knew that Stephanie would be devastated, but she had to tell her.

"That night, the night she died, Isabel had a terrible row with her father. The pain of losing her child became too much. She wanted to tell everyone, to force her father into getting her baby back. He refused. She became enraged and fled to the cliff path. He followed her as she ran towards this very cottage to tell the Halls what had happened: that their grandchild was being raised by strangers." Jan paused.

"William, a man of his standing in the community, couldn't risk the truth coming out so he - oh God, Steph - he pushed her over the cliff, he killed his own daughter! I'm so sorry, Steph. William killed Isabel." She hugged Stephanie.

The tears rolled down Stephanie's cheeks as the two women clung to each other. The realisation of the awful truth had come as a great shock. As a member of the Trevelyan family she was indeed a marked woman. Sarah was gone, Sarah the distant cousin whom she had never met, blighted from birth just like the others. Just like she had been. Stephanie had no doubt now that she was being hunted and for the first time in her life, she was truly afraid.

Just then she felt something brush against her ear. She looked up and there was small white moth. Unlike a normal moth, it gave off an unusual glow, like the tail of a firefly, but the whole of its body and wings shone. Close up, with its sparkling feathery wings and red eyes, Stephanie thought that it looked like a tiny, shining angel. Jan pointed at the moth.

"Isabel sent it, Steph," Jan said, "she wants us to follow it. She says you are in great danger."

"You can see the moth?" she asked. "How?"

"I don't know, Isabel is controlling all this, not me! I see what she wants me to see! Now is the time to put things right, but only you can do it."

Stephanie remembered the host of moths in her dream and told Jan.

"But how can we stop this?" she asked, again, drying her eyes with her sleeve.

Jan took Stephanie's hands.

"No idea Steph, I just know that we must do as she says. It's the only way to save you. She couldn't help Sarah because she couldn't reach her. Sarah didn't have your gift or someone like me to help her, so she couldn't make sense of the dreams. I'm so sorry, Sarah is dead, Steph. But I'm sure that Isabel can help you end this, and I'll do everything I can to help."

Jan squeezed her friend's hand and Stephanie was so glad she was there.

The moth flew around the room, waiting for them. They both rushed upstairs and dressed quickly in jeans, hoodies and flat shoes. Stephanie was surprised that Jan had any shoes without stiletto heels, but somehow found comfort in the fact that her friend had come prepared for anything. The moth followed, darting around Stephanie's head as if to hurry her along. When they arrived back downstairs, it flew to the back door.

"Come on, we have to get to the cave, the one from your dream!"

Jan grabbed her friend by the arm. In the kitchen, Stephanie picked up a torch from the drawer of a pine dresser by the back door. Jan unlocked it, the moth flew out into the garden and they followed. Stephanie locked the back door behind them. They rushed past the dustbin, but in their haste neither of them noticed that the lid was missing and the black bag inside was empty.

***

They reached the garden gate where the moth was waiting for them.

Stephanie stopped in her tracks.

"Jan, this means that Michael…" she began.

"Yes, Steph, he's your great uncle! Now, hurry up!" said Jan firmly.

She opened the gate. They descended the path then the steps as quickly as was practical and made their way along the beach under cover of the night sky. Waves crashed heavily on the shore and the mist swirled about their feet, just like in Stephanie's dreamscape. The bright, round moon and glittering stars lit their way. Then clouds drifted over and obscured it, and then the thunder started rumbling and roaring in the distance like a savage beast fighting to be free. The moth sped up, the two women running to catch up with it. Then it stopped, hovering around the entrance to the gap in the rock leading into the cave that Stephanie had seen in her dream.

"Come on!" said Stephanie, but Jan shook her head.

When she had caught her breath, she spoke.

"No, I can't fit in there and this is something you must do alone. It's OK, you'll be safe. I'll wait here for you. But be quick, the tide is coming in!"

Stephanie lit up the torch and squeezed through the gap in the rock. Once inside, the cave smelled musty and dank. She began looking for the jutting out corner of rock that she had seen in her dream, but as if it knew what she was looking for, the moth flew right to it. Stephanie reached out and touched the rock, but instead of crumbling in her hand like it did in her dream, it moved downwards like a lever and a section of the cave wall slid back to reveal an opening. Before she had a chance to call out to Jan to tell her what was going on, the moth flew into the chamber beyond. She had no choice but to follow.

As she stepped in she dropped the torch. It turned itself off as it hit the ground and in the dark, she couldn't find it. She took a deep breath to quell her panic. She could see the moth as it hovered in a circle over the same spot in the centre of the chamber. Her gaze was drawn momentarily upwards to the roof of the chamber as it came alive with light and the gentle flutter of little wings. There were hundreds of the tiny moths, all glowing together. Their bodies and wings were ablaze with light and their eyes shone red.

Stephanie looked back at the floor. She bent down to examine what the guide moth was trying to show her in the centre of the chamber floor. She felt like she was still dreaming; it was all so surreal.

She scraped away the damp sand and felt something buried there. It was a large flat rock, protecting what lay below. She slid her hands under one edge and flipped it over then dug her hands into the sand below. She pulled out a metal box with a closed lid but no lock. She opened it. Inside was a book, wrapped in what appeared to be some sort of waterproof material like oil-cloth and tied with a leather strap. In that light, she couldn't make out any writing. As she took it out, she saw that there was something else at the bottom of the metal box. She reached in and took out a smaller wooden box. In the limited light cast by the moths, she could see that it was carved with mystical shapes and symbols.

"This must be the box Michel told me about!" she thought.

She felt underneath where the metal box had lain and there was nothing else but sand. Suddenly, the moths began dropping from the cave roof and leaving the chamber.

"Time to go," she thought.

She spotted her torch on the ground by the entrance, the lens reflecting the last of their fading luminescence. The guide moth remained to the last. As she turned back into the chamber for one last look, he flew in a circle around her head and flew off, leaving her alone in the dark.

She put the book in her jeans pocket and carried the wooden box in her hand. With the other she picked up the torch and turned it on, making her way out of the cave to the beach where Jan was sitting on a nearby rock, keeping an eye on the incoming tide. When she saw Stephanie, she jumped up.

"What did you find?" asked Jan.

Stephanie showed her the book and the wooden box.

"Let's go Steph," she said, "We have work to do, the tide is almost in and there's a storm coming."

She put a comforting arm round her friend and Stephanie almost started crying again. But she knew this was the time to be strong. Her life depended on it.

They rushed back to the cottage as fast as they could, with thunder rumbling in the distance. The first heavy raindrops landed on their heads as they reached the back door. It was open.

"I thought you closed it?" said Jan.

"I did," Stephanie answered, "and I locked it!"

Then she looked at the dustbin. "He's gone, Jan!"

"I knew that spell wouldn't hold him for long," Jan muttered. "We don't have time to look for him, but I'm sure he'll find us soon enough! Let's see what you have there."

She grabbed Stephanie's hand and led her into the living room. They sat on the sofa and she opened a bottle of wine; red this time. The familiar lullaby rang round and round in Stephanie's head until she felt dizzy. She placed the box on her lap as she unwrapped the book.

"Let me see it!" Jan demanded and Stephanie handed it over.

Maisy felt neglected and lay curled up on the armchair. When a surprisingly loud clap of thunder crashed, momentarily rattling the windows, it sent her scampering off to hide under the desk in the office, her dainty paws sliding in an ungainly manner on the polished wooden floor. Stephanie jumped and reached for her wine.

"What is it Jan?" she asked her friend.

"Isabel's diary," she said, flicking through neatly penned pages.

Then she looked up, her eyes filled with both surprise and sadness.

"I think you should read this," she said kindly, and handed it to her friend.

Stephanie skimmed through the pages and came to a passage that listed clearly the visit to Bath, exactly as in her dream, followed later by Isabel's feelings of indescribable loss and her love for her stolen child. Isabel had written that she barely had any time with her baby. She had been singing to her when William arrived and callously ripped her from her mother's arms. Stephanie gasped, knowing that she had heard that lullaby so many times and not realised its significance. Somehow her grandmother had remembered it. It had been her only memory of Isabel. She held the diary tightly, hugging it close to her.

"This proves what I saw in my dream!" she said. She started reading again.

When she read how Isabel wept for Tom who she might never see again and who would never know his daughter, and the grief that Isabel felt from never being able to hold her baby again, a sob rose in her throat and she wept. Isabel also wrote that she was prepared to wait for Tom forever; how she intended to tell his family everything that night and how much she hoped and prayed that they would help her to find her child. She left the house at three in the morning; even though it was the middle of the night, she felt she had no time to lose. It was her last entry.

"She never made it to the cottage, Jan. No-one here ever knew about the baby," Stephanie said.

Stephanie felt like she had been punched in the stomach when she realised that this was her own family she was reading about. Isabel's unimaginable torment. Her grandmother, her Nana Jean, was the child who had been denied her true family from birth and had never known her mother's love. At this moment, she missed her own mother more than ever. But she also felt grateful that she had at least been given the chance to know her, for however brief a time.

Stephanie felt every ounce of Isabel's pain as if it were her own. Her ancestor had suffered so cruelly, but she could not rest even in death. Or at least, she chose not to. She had been unable to help her child. But now she had come back to help her great granddaughter when she needed her most, just as she had tried to help Sarah, and Stephanie was so grateful for that.

"Did you say she wrote that she left at three o'clock?" Jan asked.

Stephanie nodded. "You told me you've been waking at 3.14. That must be the time she died!" Stephanie felt empty.

Suddenly the room became cold. It was as if all the warmth had been sucked out of it at once and she could see her breath in front of her face.

"Looks like he found us!" Jan said.

The lights went out. Thunder crashed around them. Rain lashed at the windows. Inside it was pitch black apart from the glare of sheet lightning over the sea. Stephanie dropped the diary and grabbed Jan's hand, holding the box tightly in the other hand as Jan reached out for the torch on the table by her glass. She knocked a glass over and it shattered, spilling wine on the table, splashing some onto the floor where it sat like a pool of ruby-red blood. She finally found the torch without cutting herself and, as the lighting flashed again, she saw Stephanie. She was on her feet, clutching the box and pointing at the doorway to the hall.

The room went dark again, and the air grew much colder. Maisy was growling and spitting from where she hid in the office. Stephanie turned to face the door as the room lit up again and saw a glimpse of the little old man standing there, back-lit by the light from the office window, with a demonic grin on his face. He was holding a knife. Time stood still. Jan and Stephanie knew that they had to catch him and put him in the box. But how were they to do that in the dark?

Another flash of lightning lit the room and he was gone. Where was he? Jan shone the torch around as Stephanie screamed and dropped the box. She crawled on her hands and knees trying to reach it as the little old man leaped onto her back, raising up the knife to stab her. Without thinking, Jan threw the torch at him. He gave a cry of pain like a wounded animal. Stephanie stood up and shouted that she was alright. She felt around the floor for the box and Jan tried to mend the torch, but there were pieces everywhere.

The next few flashes showed the old man in various places as if he was bouncing round the walls like a toy ball. It was sickeningly comical but at the same time, horrifying. Without warning, he flew at Stephanie again and was illuminated as his face was inches from hers, the face of pure evil, the knife poised to strike. She did the only thing she could do. She grabbed him.

The doll emitted an unearthly wail, like the screech of a banshee. It was deafening. He wanted revenge, demanding it in the only way he could. Resisting the urge to put her hands over her ears, Stephanie held on tight to the effigy as it wriggled and slashed at her hands and arms with its deadly blade.

She knew its only purpose: its reason for existing now was to kill her. She struggled with the hateful doll until she was finally able to take the knife off him and throw it away from her. Still she held him firmly by the waist.

She felt the material of his shirt under her fingers, the very shirt that had been stained with Tom's blood when Isabel's father murdered him, as he had done his own daughter. Now her own blood stained it too. All at once she understood the pain that her family had experienced at that man's hands and the hatred that had led to the doll's creation. Knowing that Tom's own mother had created the doll meant that the other side of her family had also been responsible. It was born from hatred felt on both sides of her family, and it had to be stopped. Jan had been right, only she could stop this, once and for all. She was the final link between the families.

Just then the lightning flashed brighter than ever in the dark room, the French windows burst open with a crash and there, like the glow of a thousand fireflies in the blackness, stood Isabel. Hair wild, eyes glowing with rage and as red as her moth companions. She flew across the room and glided a few inches above the ground. Jan ran to Stephanie's side.

"My God!" said Jan. "She's awesome!"

"You can see her?" Stephanie asked. "How?"

"Because she wants me to. I keep telling you! She knows I'm here to help you, but I can feel she's getting weaker and time is running out. It takes a phenomenal amount of energy for her to materialise like this and he is drawing it away from her!"

Suddenly Jan began to speak in a voice not her own. Stephanie knew the voice was Isabel's. All of Isabel's energy was being used to appear before them and help Stephanie, so she needed Jan's help to communicate. Jan's arms were outstretched, and in her hands was the open carved box.

"Release him child, I will take him now!" said Isabel.

Jan firmly, but gently, took the wailing creature from Stephanie's grasp, and as she placed it in the box it began hissing, growling, spitting. Its eyes became pinpricks of glowing green, like venomous bile. Jan closed the lid, but the doll could still be heard inside it, screaming and snarling inhumanly, as if they had lowered it into a bath of acid. Once the lid was shut, the lights came back on.

"He cannot get out. Now burn him, send him to hell!" said Jan in Isabel's sweet voice which carried love combined at the same time with such hatred that it was chilling. They watched as Isabel flew out through the open French windows and vanished into the night. Jan began coughing and tried to compose herself. Possession was not pleasant.

"I hate it when spirits do that!" she said and smiled wryly. "Come on!"

Stephanie took the box and followed Jan to the kitchen. The ceaseless keening continued from within the box as they made their way outside. Jan found matches and newspaper and took fire-lighters from the barbecue. She placed the dustbin on the patio and Stephanie put the wooden box inside, stuffing the paper and fire-lighters all around it before dropping in a flaming match. They watched as it burned, covering their ears to the tormented shrieks that came from inside it. They stood and watched until there was silence and the box and its contents were smouldering ash. Jan placed the lid on the dustbin and with one arm around her friend's quivering shoulders, she led her inside.

They heard a faint fluttering and turned to face the windows. The now-familiar shape of Isabel appeared, surrounded once again by her radiant entourage of tiny moths. She glided silently around Stephanie, surveying her, and stopped by the fireplace. Her face was a picture of serenity and love once again.

She spoke to Stephanie, this time directly, energised now that the evil entity had gone.

"You have been brave, my little one. Be happy, we will meet again should you ever need me!"

With that she rushed at Stephanie as if to hug her but instead she passed straight through her before vanishing again through the open window. Stephanie gasped. She felt like she had when her mother had hugged her as a child, like someone just wrapped her in a cloud of pink and orange mist. She felt safe, warm, like she was being cocooned in love. It was as if Isabel's soul had passed through her, leaving an incredible parting gift that said so much more than words. An imprint of the afterlife in a wave of spiritual energy which few are ever lucky enough to experience.

Isabel was gone. The lullaby that she had sung to her baby echoed in her wake, accompanied again by the faintest scent of roses. The room fell silent, the air suddenly felt lighter and moonlight streamed in through the window as the storm passed and the sea became calm. It was over.

Stephanie fell into the nearest chair and wept. For herself, for Isabel and Tom and for her grandmother. But mostly she wept from sheer relief. Jan stood up to go in search of a first aid kit, a new bottle of wine and a fresh glass to replace the broken one. She dressed her friend's wounds which were thankfully quite superficial, thanks to her

hoody. Then she cleaned up the glass, tidied the room and sat silently waiting for Stephanie to compose herself while passing her the occasional tissue.

Maisy appeared from the office and jumped onto Stephanie's lap. She didn't seem to mind as tears fell on her, soaking her head yet again. She was used to it. When Stephanie finally stopped crying, she cuddled the damp cat, smiled at Jan and took the glass from the table.

"So, when is the house-warming party?" Jan asked, with a wink.

Stephanie threw a cushion at her.

"There's only one thing bothering me," she said. "Where is Sarah?"

"Time will tell," said Jan. "Thank God that's over. Steph, pass the wine!"

***

The next morning, apart from a niggling hangover, Stephanie woke to find that the world looked lighter, brighter and a lot more welcoming. After plenty of water and strong coffee, she took Jan to meet Michael and together they told him about what had happened the night before. Jan explained to them that the creature, and all the death and destruction that followed in its wake, could not have been set in motion just by a curse.

"A curse is a spoken utterance wishing someone harm. It usually covers a single event like falling downstairs or breaking a leg. Often, it's born out of rage, in the heat of the moment. What we have here is a classic hex, premeditated to do as much harm as possible and set firmly in place by a dark magic ritual, deliberately intended for prolonged and sustained damage to that person and anyone associated with them. The effects of the hex would remain long after the death of the witch who cast it unless the doll was destroyed. Mary truly was evil, and a very experienced witch. I wouldn't have liked to come across her on a dark night!" she added.

Michael shuddered at the thought. He hugged Stephanie and welcomed her to the family. He also had some sad news for her. A man walking his dog on the beach near the cave had found the body of a young woman washed up. The currents were indeed treacherous; it was lucky that her body had come ashore at all. The flash floods after the storm had apparently helped; but Jan suspected that maybe Isabel had a hand in bringing her home.

He told her that the police had been called in from Wadebridge, the largest town in the area. Unfortunately, local police stations were a thing of the past, and small villages and towns now had a satellite police service only.

"Not much use in an emergency!" she said, and Michael had to agree, adding that the crime rate was mercifully low in Marlin.

The consensus was that Sarah had fallen from the cliffs while out walking. The body had been identified from a small tattoo on her left shoulder: that of a very distinctive white moth.

"Sarah loved those moths, she told me she had been seeing them everywhere." Michael said, "She had even been dreaming about them. But one day they stopped coming. So, she got a tattoo to remind her of them. Poor child."

Stephanie felt as though someone had thrown cold water over her. The moths had stopped coming because Isabel couldn't get through to Sarah to warn her. They were all relieved that the last piece of the puzzle had been found. They all knew that although it looked like suicide or a tragic accident, that could not have been further from the truth. Sarah had been the last victim of the hex.

"There's something I have to do," Stephanie said. Jan nodded.

***

Together they went back to her cottage then down through the garden and walked across the beach together. An area of the beach had been fenced off by police and they bypassed it with sadness. It was the spot where Sarah was found. They bypassed it and continued until they reached the jagged rocks below Fern Leap.

Stephanie stood looking up at the cliff, the warm sea breeze blowing her hair everywhere. Then, as a wave rolled in and the tide lapped the rocks, she threw two pink roses into the sea, taken with permission from Michael's garden on the way there. One for Isabel and one for Sarah. They stood there in silence as the roses were taken out by the tide, and when they were out of sight, they walked back across the beach to The Lodge.

When they got back to the cottage, they had lunch and spent the afternoon enjoying each other's company, talking about everything and nothing as only good friends can. Jan was glad to see again the Stephanie that she knew and loved; the protective shell that she had built around herself was starting to crumble.

Jan took a call from one of her employees at about five o'clock, asking her to join them at a séance in Exeter that evening. Although Stephanie was her priority, Jan sensed that she would be alright now and judged that it was safe to leave her. So, she packed the few things she had brought with her and said goodbye to Maisy. As she opened the front door to go, Stephanie hugged her.

"I wouldn't be here now if it wasn't for you!" she said. "Thank you!"

"Ring me," Jan answered, "and not just when you need my help!" she added with a wink.

Stephanie assured her that she would keep in touch this time. Jan smiled and turned to go. Then she turned back.

"You're a fighter Steffi Meares, never forget it!" she said, as she ruffled her hair and walked off.

As Stephanie stood there in stunned silence, watching the car drive away, she could hear Jan muttering through the car window:

"I really hate it when they do that!"

Stephanie smiled.

"Mum?" she said. "Is that you?"

"YES!" came a voice.

That was the final straw. After everything that she had been through in the last couple of days, Stephanie sat on the stairs and wept like a baby while a pair of invisible arms held her tight and the scent of sandalwood filled the air. Grace had always loved sandalwood.

***

As Stephanie stood in her kitchen washing dishes later that evening, her thoughts drifted back over the events of the past few weeks. Her arrival in Marlin had started her on a path of discovery that she had never anticipated. It had been quite an experience, and she felt fragile; her nerves were frayed, and she needed sleep. Lots of sleep. But did she regret it? Not for one second. For the first time in her life she felt that she truly knew who she was, and that she was exactly where she was meant to be.

She looked through the window, watching the waves lapping the shore and listening to the sea birds. It was so beautiful. Then a chill ran through her.

"Is it over? Do I really have my life back, or does Marlin have more to throw at me?" she wondered.

Her logical brain told her that she should leave Marlin while she still could, to put it all behind her and just get on with her life somewhere else. But she was done with hiding. Her instincts told her that she had been drawn to this little village, to this cottage, for reasons which she was sure were still hidden from her. Here in her cottage, in the village that had called to her over time and space, via a seed sown in her genetic memory or maybe planted there by Isabel. It was as if something had been set in motion that she was powerless to escape, even if she wanted to. Never before had she felt like she belonged anywhere, but now she did.

Something was stirring within her; she could feel it. Her dreams and waking visions were becoming more accurate, her instincts were sharper. Marlin had triggered an awakening. If sensing her mother's presence and hearing her voice was anything to go by, the gift that she had long since buried was growing, demanding to be free, and she couldn't fight it any more. Whatever happened next, whatever horrors this village wanted to throw at her, she would deal with them. Stephanie Meares was here to stay.

PART TWO: INHERITANCE

STEPHANIE WAS ALONE AGAIN. She sat on a rock on the beach below her idyllic Cornish cottage, gazing at the waves and relishing her solitude. A cool breeze stirred the sand into flurries as pale, grey clouds huddled overhead. Gulls screeched and a bouncy Labrador puppy sniffed its way along the rocks and ran gleefully into the water. But she was oblivious; lost in thought.

The past few weeks had been manic since Sarah Trevelyan's body had washed up on the beach. Sarah was supposedly the last of her line until Isabel Trevelyan's diary was found and proved that Stephanie was Isabel's great, great granddaughter, and the rightful heiress to the Trevelyan fortune.

As expected, Sarah's grieving parents Andrew and Judy, the only other remaining Trevelyans, had vehemently contested the validity of the diary. Although Stephanie had laid no formal claim to the estate, they had been alerted by the investigation of her best friend Jan. They were sceptical, to say the least. But when the hand-writing was authenticated as Isabel's by experts enlisted by their own legal team, the Trevelyans had no choice but to accept the shocking facts. Isabel had been murdered by her own father after he forced her to have her newborn baby adopted against her will. In the depths of the Trevelyan family vaults, the adoption papers were duly found, providing further damning evidence. Stephanie was the last Trevelyan.

Illegitimate or not, her Nana Jean was a direct descendant of the Trevelyan line, and poor Sarah's parents, as merely distant cousins by marriage, were not. They stood to lose everything; the land, the title and their wealth; legally, the entire estate belonged to Stephanie. But she didn't want any of it, and chose not to contest it, being only too aware that they had been through enough in losing their only child. Even though no amount of money would ever make up for her loss, she couldn't bear to take their comfortable lifestyle and title from them too. They had never known any other life, and to lose it all would bring social disgrace and financial hardship to people that were now her family.

In Stephanie's opinion, the Trevelyan name had brought nothing but misery, and she wasn't ready yet to be associated with it. So, Sarah's parents had heaved a joint sigh of relief, and kept everything. Stephanie knew that with no other living heir it would pass to her anyway when they died, and she could decide then what to do with it. For now, she just wanted to get back to her life, to anonymity, and to finishing her book.

But then the news had broken. Finding a lost local heiress with a dramatic story steeped in legend had stirred up a media maelstrom. Her Uncle Michael had reluctantly agreed to be interviewed. He had wisely omitted the magical element of the family history; nobody would believe it anyway. The story had what was known in the trade as "mileage" and it had to run its course, gaining attention from some national newspapers, and even a television network or two along the way. Stephanie had declined all offers of publicity, talk shows or articles telling "her side of the story" yet she was still hounded for weeks. Eventually interest waned; but for Stephanie it had been an unpleasant and unwanted intrusion from which she was only now starting to recover.

She had always shied away from the limelight, even after she published her first successful book. She was seriously hoping that this would be an end to it and that she would be left in peace to get on with writing its sequel. But the villagers had read the story and heard the rumours; it was a small village after all, and gossip spread like wildfire. Some of the locals eyed her nervously now that they all knew the Trevelyan legend and the Hall family history of witchcraft. A few even feared her. But mostly she was welcomed with love as a prodigal child who had found her way home. Most of the villagers took her to their hearts and treated her as if she belonged there, and she had finally begun to believe it.

In the meantime, as much as a distraction as anything else, Stephanie had been to visit her new-found uncle Michael and his family who lived at The Smithy. He was, of course, the greatest gossip in the village, and kept her abreast of the rumours. It had been strange meeting relatives that until recently, she had never known existed. It was even stranger still to be sitting in a house once owned by Mary Hall, the woman who had created the freakish doll that tried to kill her. But it was a warm place now, a lovely home.

Michael still blamed himself for his grandmother's actions. But Stephanie explained that he was no more responsible for what Mary Hall did than she had been for the murderous William Trevelyan. They agreed to put it all behind them and look to the future.

Michael had a lovely wife, Lisa, and three sons, John and David who were twins, and Matthew who was born much later. Only Matthew was married, to a lively young woman named Jessie also from the village, and they had a daughter called Lucy who was almost 11. They had all been happy to welcome Stephanie into the family. She called in to see them quite often, now that the press had stopped sitting in a van outside her cottage, and stumbling about on the beach below her house pretending to be tourists and dog-walkers. She had ever had much in the way of family until now, with no siblings or cousins, and she was already quite fond of them all.

***

Stephanie's time in Marlin had so far been quite an experience. Being thrust into a world where spirits roamed freely seeking vengeance and plotting murder, and finding out that magic was real, in truth those things were not what she had expected. In fact, it had been a culture shock of the highest order. Knowing that she was a descendant of a witch on one side and a murderer on the other was even more mind-blowing. But being related to Isabel was something that she considered a privilege; her courage and dignity had impressed her final descendant greatly.

What amazed Stephanie more than anything was the fact that she seemed to have inherited something remarkable from her mother's family: the paranormal abilities that she had been blocking all her life. It made sense now why her dreams had drawn her to Marlin. It was her destiny to unlock her past, finally embrace her gift and build her future there with people who understood her.

After the night that Isabel saved her from the doll and ended the hex, Stephanie had come to realise more and more that Jan had been right about her. Her own sixth sense was awakened and the gift she had been ignoring since childhood now demanded to be free. This was an inheritance of a different kind altogether, one she could not refuse even if she tried. There had been occasional nightmares too since that night, but they had soon passed.

She didn't know if it was the arrival of the spirit of Isabel, or Marlin itself, or the mere fact that she was ready to embrace it at last. But it was forcing its way out and growing daily. The realisation terrified and excited her at the same time. She had a feeling that Marlin had more secrets to reveal, and so far she had only just scratched the surface. Something told her that she hadn't seen the end of death or danger either. What she had been through, as awful as it had been, was only the beginning.

Following the discovery of Sarah's body, Stephanie had been experiencing strange dreams and waking flashbacks from her childhood, disturbing memories which she had suppressed. For some reason, they no longer wanted to stay hidden and assaulted her senses whenever they felt like it. One such memory popped into her head now as she sat alone on the beach.

She was six. Her mother was in hospital for an operation; she didn't know what was wrong because it was not felt appropriate to discuss such matters with small children. Her father had been called away to London for a few days to prepare for a particularly important court case, leaving her in the care of his sister in Bristol. At the time her aunt Eleanor, not at all maternal, owned a house not far from where they lived. She was an accountant who worked from home, so the arrangement suited her better than going to stay at Stephanie's house. Although Stephanie remembered missing her parents, it was to be her first time away from home without them, and she viewed it as an adventure.

It was her first night at her aunt's house. She was alone. Her aunt wasn't the sort who believed in night lights so the main bedroom light was off.

The glow from the landing spilled in through the bedroom door, left slightly ajar as a compromise, and it cast shadows around the room. She remembered feeling a little uneasy once the bedroom light went off. But she lay down as instructed in the double bed, with her trusty teddy bear, and tried to sleep.

She was drifting off to sleep when she became aware of something, a presence in the room. It was suddenly cold, so cold that she pulled up the blankets to her neck and sat up, dragging them with her. She wasn't usually a nervous child, but she was overcome with a feeling of panic. Dread. Her instincts were screaming that there was something very wrong in that room, something that shouldn't be there. It stood by the wardrobe near the window. She couldn't see it, but she felt its presence. Its sadness. The feeling kept growing worse till it developed into panic, and she couldn't stand it any more.

She screamed and ran out of the room and just stood there, a small child shivering on the landing. Her aunt rushed upstairs, and on hearing her account, reassured her that she was just feeling strange, homesick. She knew it was more than that, but didn't have the words to convey the terror that had overcome her or what she had sensed. She was too young.

Her aunt told her that she was over-reacting. She and tried everything she could think of to persuade her to go back to bed, but Stephanie was adamant that she was not going back into that room. In the end her aunt had to take her home and stay there with her till her parents came back a few days later. Her aunt never spoke of it again. Stephanie was glad when Eleanor later moved in with them and sold the old place; Stephanie didn't feel at ease there after that and she had refused point-blank to stay there overnight again.

Stephanie came back to the present. She had totally forgotten that night had even happened. Many years later, she had found out that room, in that bed, was where her paternal grandfather had died only a year earlier. Eleanor had looked after her father during a long illness, right to the end, and consequently never married. That early frightening experience had remained with Stephanie, hidden away all this time. It had caused her to block the episode from her mind, along with the others that were now gnawing their way to the surface.

A recent conversation with Jan also came to mind now.

"Spirits often reach out to the living when they're just dozing off, or just waking. The time when we're half awake and half asleep. It's the time when the veil between this world and the next is at its thinnest. The conscious mind isn't in charge then, to dismiss the feelings that the sensitive among us can detect," Jan had told her.

She was sure that was exactly what had happened that night.

Jan had added that children had the ability to sense spirits until adults told them not to, or persuaded them that it was just their imagination. Or ridiculed them, often out of fear. Stephanie knew that she had chosen to block them out like most children would. But Jan, like others, had accepted and developed her talents from a young age. Jan had stressed that if the aptitude was strong, it would make its presence felt, as it was now doing with Stephanie. Flashbacks, dreams and fragments of memory were bubbling to the surface, but now she welcomed them.

Stephanie never told her parents about any of her early psychic experiences, only sharing them with Jan. She wondered it maybe her mother might have had them too, knowing now who her ancestors were. Maybe she might have understood and many years of anguish would have been avoided. But Stephanie had been too scared to even raise the subject with anyone but Jan. There was no getting away from the fact that the premonitions and ability to sense spirit presence had always been there, despite her denial. But now, instead of fearing it, she was ready to understand it.

It started to rain, and she was ripped from her thoughts by the cold water droplets on her face. She shook off her childhood memory and ran to the shelter of her cottage. She looked back. The sea was grey and a sense of emptiness and loss swept over her. Not for the first time recently, she realised that solitude was just another word for isolation, and running away only meant that you take your problems with you. Or you create new ones. She was glad that she had stopped running.

Back at the cottage, Maisy her faithful cream tabby followed her from room to room, as she had done every day lately, as if she knew that she needed comfort. Cats also have a sixth sense and she was right, Stephanie was still on edge. She picked up her cat and held her until Maisy protested and wriggled free.

***

It was October 2015 and summer was another memory. Days were cooler, nights were longer and leaves were turning from green to orange, yellow and red. The tides came in and went out and everyone adopted an extra layer of clothing and carried an umbrella, but it was not yet cold enough to put on the central heating. Life went on as normal, or the version of normal that it had become. Not much writing had taken place over the past few months and Jan had been a frequent visitor. Wine had flowed, music and laughter filled the cottage and it felt like being on holiday. But Stephanie was painfully aware that she had a deadline to meet and bills to pay. The holiday was well and truly over.

It was early on a Monday afternoon and Stephanie was at home after her usual morning walk on the beach. It had been cold, windy and a sudden squall had blown in with the tide, so she had made it a brief walk followed by a hot shower. Now she was dry and warm, sitting at her desk in her office. Poised over her laptop, she made slow but steady progress on Chapter 8 of her book. Maisy was at her feet, in fact lying on her slippers; colder weather usually meant warm feet to snuggle up to. The book was a romance of the "cosy mystery" genre. She still found it amusing that she was the best-selling author of a book about a whirlwind romance, when her own past relationships had been a disaster, and her love life was now non-existent.

An hour later, half a mug of cold tea and the remnants of a sandwich sat on the desk beside her, evidence of a working lunch. Her characters were developing nicely, a plot was unfurling at her fingertips. Words flowed, ideas burst forth without too much effort. The book was taking shape, but it had been a long time coming. With all that had happened, the new book was still way behind deadline and her editor had already rung in a panic twice in the last week.

"GIVE IT TIME!" said a voice.

She looked up from her laptop.

The hearing of voices was a recent development. Maisy hadn't stirred. She turned around and wasn't surprised to find that she was alone. She sighed, then spoke, as Jan had instructed when she visited last.

"Is anyone there?" she called, braver than she felt. "Mum is that you?"

She had been hearing her late mother's voice and sensing her presence a lot lately. Jan had advised her to call out in case it was someone else. On receiving silence in return, she began feeling around the room for cold spots and found none. Jan had told her that a drop in temperature might indicate a spirit presence. Apparently, they often sucked out the heat from any area they visited because they needed to draw as much energy as they could to be able to enter the earthly plane.

She opened a document on her laptop with the ominous title "Events" and added this latest aberration to the ever-growing list of spooky events. There was a long list devoted just to the "Evil Doll Incident." She thought that recording such occurrences might be a good idea either to show to Jan, or as material for a book of a different kind. Maybe she might write a supernatural autobiography of some sort when she tired of writing in her current genre; if she ever finished the book she was working on.

Stephanie sighed. She was sad that her great grandmother Isabel hadn't visited her again, yet she was happy at the same time. Jan had told her told her it meant that Isabel had moved on, secure in the knowledge that her job was done. This was all so new, and despite being fascinated and surprisingly accepting of her developing abilities, the incidents were random and frustrating. Yet as time went on, she felt no fear, the sign of a true medium, according to Jan. But she still felt a bit lost; she really didn't know what she was doing.

What she did know, however, was that the disembodied voice had made her lose her train of thought, despite their good intentions in encouraging her. So, she wriggled her feet out from under a sleeping Maisy and went to make a fresh mug of tea. Maisy woke up and followed her.

Leaves flitted past the kitchen window like rust-coloured butterflies on the breeze, chasing raindrops which were coming thick and fast now, racing each other down the kitchen window. The tiny specks of water glinting in the sunshine reminded her of Isabel's moths, and the memory made her smile.

As she stared at the leaves swirling and swooping outside the window, intermittently interspersed with heavy rain, there was a loud knock at the front door. She jumped. Tripping over Maisy as she turned around, she banged her leg on the table and swore. Maisy thought that if her human was in the kitchen, she was there for the sole purpose of providing her with food, so she lay patiently in wait under the table, ignoring the random expletive hurled at her. Stephanie made her way quickly down the hall to the front door, rubbing her left shin on the way.

She opened the door to find a man she had never met, holding a bundle of wet, black fluff.

"Hi there, sorry to bother you, but is this yours?" he asked.

The man was tall with thick, dark, wavy hair and eyes of the deepest blue. He gave her a decidedly disarming smile, and she was momentarily mesmerised. After what seemed like a long time, she took a deep breath and spoke.

"I don't know, what is it?" she replied.

"Oh, dear God, I sound like an idiot," she thought.

"A kitten, of course!" he replied.

As he turned it round she could see two large, pale green eyes, surrounded by a small, black, fuzzy head. The head was attached to a scrawny, little body with four paws and a tiny, wiggly tail. It was indeed a kitten. Her heart melted at the sight of the small, bedraggled creature.

"I was walking to the village and found it crying under a hedge," the man added by way of explanation.

"Oh! Oh no, it's not mine," she stammered, still drowning in the deep azure pools of the stranger's eyes.

"Get a grip," she told herself. It didn't seem to work.

"Er, do you mind if we come in?" he asked as the wind and increasingly heavy rain howled around him, sweeping wet leaves onto the hall carpet. He held up the kitten to show that by "we" he meant himself and the cat.

"Oh, yes, I'm so sorry! Please do," she said. "Poor thing."

He stood there dripping in the hallway as she closed the door, her cheeks pink with embarrassment.

"It was dry when I came out," he said, looking down at his soaked wearing a sweatshirt and jeans; he had no coat. The kitten was shivering

"I meant the kitten. But let me get you a towel," she said, with a smile. "Come into the kitchen."

He followed her down the hall, she handed him a towel and took the kitten off him to dry it with another one. He looked a little embarrassed now. The kitten started to purr as soon as she touched it. Maisy, still sitting expectantly by her food bowl, eyed the fur ball suspiciously, and the man even more so.

"Aaw, she's adorable!" she said, wrapping it in a dry towel and placing it in the crook of her arm. The kitten stayed there, happy to be warm.

"She?" said the man. "It looks too small to tell…"

"An educated guess," she said with a grin.

He smiled back and his face lit up. Stephanie felt the colour rising in her cheeks again. Who was this man and why had he brought her a kitten? And why was he having this effect on her?

"YOU KNOW WHY!" said a voice next to her left ear. She jumped.

"Not now!" she thought.

"Shush!" muttered Stephanie. The man looked shocked, yet a little amused.

"I never said anything," he said, looking as surprised as she obviously felt.

"Not you!" said Stephanie. Her cheeks were now scarlet.

"Who then, the kitten?" He smirked.

"He thinks I'm mad!" Stephanie thought.

"Sorry," she mumbled, "I thought I heard the phone. It's always ringing when you least expect it. So, why did you bring this kitten to me?" she asked, deftly changing the subject. She wasn't some crazy cat-lady. That involved having more than one cat, by all accounts.

"Well, I found it on the lane, under the hedge, like I said. It was near the gate opposite your house. I asked around and the villagers said you had a cat. So, I thought, maybe, er, she had... kittens?" his voice drifted off. He took a deep breath and wiped the rain off his brow.

"No, my Maisy is spayed. Here, you'd better take it!" she said as she gave him back the kitten, complete with towel.

"What am I supposed to do with it?" he said, with panic in his voice.

"Take it home and look after it?" she suggested, amused by his reaction.

"I don't live here, I mean I'm just renting for a few months. Willow Cottage just up the hill. I really don't know anything about cats. Could you?" he stumbled over his words. "Please?" he added, batting his huge black eyelashes.

Stephanie felt her face heating up.

"I don't think Maisy would be too impressed," she replied with a smile.

Maisy came out from under the kitchen table right on cue, hissed in the direction of the kitten and strolled into the office with her tail held high.

"I can't just put it back out alone in the rain, can I?" he grinned and raised his eyebrows, beseechingly.

Her cheeks burned, and her heart started beating just a little faster.

"Alright, I'll take her for now. I'll try to find her a home in the village."

"Thanks!" he sighed with obvious relief. "I hope to see you again. I suppose we're neighbours, for now at least. Maybe next time I'll be able to, you know, er, not sound like a tongue-tied teenager!"

"Yes, why is that?" she asked, ushering him to the front door.

"I suppose you make me nervous," he admitted, but his eyes were smiling.

She found herself smiling too. They held each other's glance for a second or two longer than was necessary. Then they both glanced away, focusing instead on the kitten who was now dry, warm, purring and extremely cute. Then their eyes met again.

He held out his hand. "I should introduce myself. Nice to meet you, er…?"

"Stephanie," she said, "Stephanie Meares."

She shook his hand and a jolt of static electricity passed between them, with a hearty crackling noise. The kitten hissed in her arms. She stroked its head, and it calmed down.

"Ouch!" he said. "Jeff Dawson," he said grinning again. "Call me Jeff!"

"Well that was weird," she thought. *"Maybe I should offer him tea?"*

"Pleased to meet you, Jeff. Would you like some tea?" she suggested. The kitten had settled again and was purring in her arms.

"The rain has stopped, so I'd better get going in case it starts again," said Jeff, flashing another amazing smile. "Maybe next time. Bye, then!"

"Next time?" she thought. *"How many kittens does he have?"*

"OK, bye!" said Stephanie, smiling at the thought of him marching along followed by a trail of kittens, like the Pied Piper.

As she closed the door, the kitten looked up at her and began to purr again. Nestled in her arms, it promptly fell asleep.

"That was interesting," she murmured, with a hint of a smile, stroking the kitten's head absent-mindedly as she went to the kitchen.

"YOU LIKE HIM, STEFFI!" said a voice.

Suddenly there was the unmistakable scent of sandalwood, her mother's favourite. This time Stephanie knew without doubt that the voice she was hearing was her mother's spirit, because of that and the fact that nobody else had ever called her Steffi.

"Mum?" she called. But no-one replied. Grace never stayed long enough to hold a conversation.

"Do I like him?" she wondered. She immediately put the idea out of her mind.

"Life is complicated enough without that!"

***

The next few hours were tense. Maisy acknowledged their guest with spits and hisses and spent the evening under the chair in the office, watching the doorway intently as if to ward off the interloper. She did grudgingly accept a plate of food at about 6 o'clock, eaten with her back to her human and accompanied by occasional glances over her shoulder. There was also intermittent growling to which the kitten appeared oblivious.

Stephanie had fed the kitten earlier, grateful to find that it was old enough for solid food. It was ravenous. She tried not to make a fuss of it for fear of upsetting Maisy, but it was hard not to; it was a kitten after all. On close examination, to her surprise it turned out to be a boy, about 12 weeks old according to Stephanie's estimation (and by comparison to her memories of Maisy at around that age).

His fur looked black, having just a tiny white tuft on his belly and a few pale hairs on his chest. But when the light shone on him, she could see some wide chocolate-brown patches on his back. He was, in fact, a very dark tortoiseshell kitten. His eyes were green as she had thought, but on closer inspection she saw deep golden rings round the outside.

"Unusual!" she thought.

He was litter-trained, he had no fleas and was very loving, so someone had obviously taken care of him. But where had he come from? Could a kitten that small simply have escaped from a house nearby? The nearest house was in fact Willow Cottage where Jeff was staying.

"Jeff… No, don't go there!" she told herself sternly, with a sigh.

Her other neighbours were either at least a mile up the hill beyond that, or a farmhouse about two miles away across the fields opposite her house, which belonged to the Trevelyan estate. The Smithy where Michael and his family lived was at the end of a row of cottages a stone's throw from the village, about twenty minutes away. Surely all of them were too far from The Lodge for a tiny kitten to walk? She hoped that the morning might bring some answers.

She put him in a deep cardboard box with an old towel for a blanket and fashioned a makeshift litter box from half a cereal packet.

"Well, I suppose I can't keep calling you Kitten. I'll have to give you a name, even if it is temporary," she said, as he kneaded his new blanket in delight with his little tail standing straight up in the air.

A name popped conveniently into her head.

"Shadow!" she said triumphantly, taking his continued purring as approval.

Maisy stuck her nose in the air and stomped away to the office in a huff, showing her disapproval with a narrowing of her eyes and by wagging her tail, with that obvious level of disdain that only cats can muster. The kitten was affectionate and wanted attention. But there was no way she could keep him (Maisy would never forgive her if that happened). Stephanie thought it best not to get too attached to him. So, she left him alone to sleep, which he did with his tail curled round his chin and one front paw resting on his tiny nose.

***

After a hasty dinner, Stephanie opted for an early night; the day's events had exhausted her. She seemed to need a lot more sleep lately. She had too much on her mind to focus on work, reading or watching television. Shadow was asleep in his new box under the window in her room. He had made no attempt to climb out, seemingly worn out by his ordeal. But he had stayed awake long enough to eat another small dish of Maisy's favourite food which Stephanie had mashed up for him. Maisy sat on the rocking chair behind the door with one eye open, avoiding Stephanie's attempts to coax her to lie in her usual spot on the bed near her owner's stomach.

Maisy never went outside. Her upstairs litter tray was kept in the bathroom as well as one in the porch off the kitchen and she had the run of the house. Nevertheless, she eyed the kitten's new quarters complete with kitten 'en suite' with jealousy, and eyed the kitten itself with sheer rage. Maisy was pouting; visitors having preferential treatment did not go down well.

Outside the sea was calm, a gentle autumn breeze tugged playfully at the curtains and soft waves lapped the shore. Soon Stephanie was asleep. She had recently started to relax again. The house felt like it belonged to her once more and she loved being there. Also, despite vivid dreams her sleep had been more restful after the doll episode was resolved. But tonight was different. Although she had fallen asleep easily, she slept fitfully and was restless. In her dream, she was wandering round her cottage, but the rooms were all wrong. The office was a living-room and what she had as the living-room was set up like a dining room. All the walls of the cottage were covered in variations of old-fashioned wallpaper with tiny flowers. There were heavy curtains, and the kitchen had no units or appliances. There was just a plain white Belfast sink with a drainer, an oak table and four sturdy chairs, an oak dresser with pretty china plates on it and a black cast-iron range where her cooker should be.

The stairs were not carpeted; in fact, the whole house had no carpet, only various round cream rugs dotted here and there on polished wood floors. Each room had a rug with a different coloured stripe around the outer edge.

Upstairs there were three bedrooms, with the bathroom being used as a smaller bedroom with a toilet provided in a shed outside by the back door. Next to it was another shed storing wood, presumably for the kitchen stove. In her dream, the cottage had been transported back in time.

At first the rooms were devoid of people. Then she found herself downstairs in the hall and heard voices coming from her office, but it was being used as a living room. A pretty, fair-haired woman sat on a plump sofa, sewing by the dim light of an oil lamp. She wore a 1930s-style knee-length brown skirt and a white blouse with a lace collar; her hair was pinned up in a tight bun but a wisp of hair escaped each side, trailing down beside her ears. She also wore a wedding ring and a large, oval, silver locket, engraved with a single rosebud.

She was chatting eagerly to a handsome, dark-haired man. He had an impressive, thick moustache and was reading a newspaper. He was sitting in an armchair under the window backing onto the fields; he wore dark trousers and braces and sat in his shirt sleeves. He wore a tie, and his hair was slicked back. His shoes shone, even in the pale lamplight.

The man was watching a small boy with white blond hair, wearing shorts and a blue, short-sleeved, buttoned shirt. The child was wheeling a small, wooden car with red wheels around the blue striped edge of one of the cream rugs, as if it was a race track. An image played in her mind of the man painting its wheels and the little boy opening a parcel on Christmas Day and finding it inside. As the boy played, he hummed a nursery rhyme and his father watched him with pride at the joy his gift had brought. She had the sense that the father had carved the toy himself. There was a large black cat beside the boy on the rug, near an open fire.

Suddenly, the scene changed. The woman was still there, on the sofa near the fireplace, but this time she was dressed in black. She was crying. She looked older, and she was alone in the room. Then she was aware of a soft droning noise…

Stephanie woke up. Then she realised that Shadow had somehow scrambled out of his box and was lying across her chest, purring. That must have been what woke her. Maisy was still asleep on the chair.

"What an odd dream, if it even was a dream," she thought.

She made a mental note to add it to her log of strange incidents, and to examine her office. She had suspected there was a fireplace in there behind her bookcase and if so, she thought to open it up. She envisaged working to the sound of crackling wood from an open fire on snowy evenings.

 She went into the bathroom for a drink of water, putting Shadow back in his box on the way, then lay down and went straight back to sleep. It was only four o'clock. This time she slept till her alarm shook her from a dreamless sleep at nine in the morning.

***

The morning was sunny and dry, slightly chilly, but perfect for a walk to the village to locate Shadow's owner, or to find him one. She also needed to speak to Michael about her dream. It felt too real to be a dream, seeming more like what she had come to know as a psychic vision. She was certain of it; her visions were always more vivid and detailed than dreams, like the replay of a memory belonging to someone else. But who had sent it to her?

She was also sure that Michael would be able to help. When he wasn't running his antique shop, he was also an avid local historian. If anyone knew anything, it would be him; or he would know where to look.

***

Shadow was livelier today; he had already attempted to climb the bedroom curtains and was hanging from them by his claws when she woke. Maisy was unimpressed. He escaped and ran into the bathroom, only to be chased out by Maisy. Shadow stopped at the edge of the stairs, peering over the precipice He was about to launch himself into the unknown when Stephanie picked him up.

"I should have called you Trouble!" she said, smiling.

She didn't remember Maisy being this much bother. Maisy had been a model kitten as memory served. Maisy remembered too and licked a front paw in her superior way.

Rather than carry Shadow to the village with her, Stephanie took a photo of him with her phone and put it in her pocket. She left the poor little scrap asleep in his box in the kitchen, exhausted by the earlier spurt of exercise. She had replaced his litter tray and put down a small dish of food for later, and she made sure to close the kitchen door.

Maisy had been fed and had carefully taken up a position in the hallway with a good view of the kitchen and the kitten. She was displeased that her view of the kitten had been obscured by the closed door, wanting to keep a close eye on him at all times. Stephanie finished her tea in the living room by the French windows, overlooking Lapwing Cove below her cottage, and the open sea beyond. Leaving the mug on the coffee table, she picked up a jacket and her keys from the hall stand and set off for the village. Maisy permitted her to stroke her as she went past, but her eyes followed her to the door with a glare, as if to say "Traitor!"

On the way to the village Stephanie had a lot to think about. The kitten. Jeff. The dream. Jeff. Mum. Jeff. Why was it all happening now when she had just regained some semblance of normality? She began to think her life would never be normal again, or was this a new type of life that she would have to become accustomed to? And what about the book; would she ever get to finish it?

By this time, she had reached Michael's house, so deep in thought that she nearly passed it. She had been oblivious to the bright, blue sky with fluffy clouds speeding along, and to the glorious, brightly coloured adornment of the trees and the abundance of acorns. She usually loved admiring the quaint stone cottages with their picture-perfect gardens. It was like the village that time forgot, and she was beginning to feel part of it all. But today, as usual when her mind was preoccupied, she was blind to them all.

Michael didn't open his antique shop till ten o'clock, but it was ten to ten and she feared he might have already left. She knocked the front door of The Smithy. Michael's wife Lisa answered and happily welcomed her in. Luckily Michael was still there, finishing his breakfast and sipping tea from a fine china cup.

"Morning, Stephanie!" he said, smiling broadly.

He was very fond of her already, as was Lisa who smiled and offered her a cup of tea, which she declined.

"Hi Lisa! Morning, Michael! I was hoping you could help me with something," she replied. First of all, she told them the tale of Jeff and the kitten,

"A handsome young man, so I've heard," Lisa said with a knowing wink. "A writer like yourself. He's rented Willow Cottage till after Christmas to work on a historical piece of some sort. Single, I hear! No idea about the cat though."

Lisa was also a reliable source of local information.

"Yes, and he looks familiar somehow, although he keeps very much to himself." Michael added wistfully.

"*Interesting,*" thought Stephanie, trying not to look interested at all, but turning pink.

"Well I don't know anyone who's missing a kitten, but I can ask around the village for you," offered Michael, kindly changing the subject to cover her obvious embarrassment.

"I know who might want one, if you're not keeping it," said Lisa. "Our Lucy would love a kitten, I'm sure. I'll mention it to Jessie, if you like."

"Thank you both, and yes please to all your suggestions," said Stephanie gratefully.

"Got to rush, time to open up," said Michael. "I'm running a little late today. Will you walk with me, or are you going straight home?"

"Yes, I'll come with you, I need to pick up more cat food," she said.

The arrival of Shadow had threatened to deplete her feline provisions considerably before her next delivery was due. Growing kittens needed a lot of food. She also had other things to discuss with Michael. He was in no great rush today; trade was usually quieter in autumn when tourists were less common although business still ticked over nicely.

Stephanie was determined to get to the bottom of the strange dream, so she began.

"Do you know who lived in The Lodge before Sarah?" she asked Michael, explaining the dream as they walked.

Of course, he already knew all about Isabel and her help in getting rid of the doll. Having a witch as an ancestor, it hadn't been much of a stretch for him to accept that Stephanie had "the gift" as he called it: the family trait of mediumship and psychic ability such as prophetic dreams and other skills. Apparently, it was only present in the females of the Hall line, which she, of course, now knew was her lineage too. Michael was an only child. He didn't have it and obviously neither did his sons. But as for Lucy, time would tell.

Michael agreed that her dream sounded important. Someone was trying to give her a message.

"Now then, let me think," he said.

He stopped and dabbed his near-bald head with his spotted handkerchief then they walked on. The day was warm for the time of year.

"Sarah moved in about Christmas-time in 2014 and lived there till she disappeared late this spring. Before that it was the Blackwells, a nice couple. They lived there from late 1975 to 2013. Mr Blackwell was the Trevelyan estate manager, and The Lodge came rent-free with the job. They had no children, so it can't be them. After they retired and moved away, it remained empty while Sarah was in University. Her parents kept it for her and she moved in when she came home, you see. The place is managed remotely these days, online or whatever you call it, with a manager visiting every few months. That's why it wasn't needed for the estate any more and why young Sarah went to live there," he said. Then he added, "She fell in love with it, just like you did," and he gave a sad smile.

"Now we know why," thought Stephanie and nodded.

"I think the Blackwells would be the wrong era," she said. "Judging by the clothes and décor it looked much older, although I'm no expert. Who lived there before them?"

"Well the manager before them was Bill Judd, but everyone just called him Judd. He lived there alone from just after the end of the war in 1945 to early 1975."

"No family and still too late. I think it was more like 1920s or thirties."

"Oh, in that case it must be the Jones family. Emma, Robert and young Jason. They would have been living there when Isabel…" his voice faltered at the mention of her name. He stopped.

"It's OK." Stephanie placed a hand in his arm. He mopped his brow again, gave her a smile, and they carried on walking.

"Yes, it sounds like it could be them. Are there any photos of them anywhere?" she asked eagerly.

"You might find one of him in the archives. Robert was manager when Trevelyan died and when The Manor burnt down. Saved the estate from ruin after the fire, by all accounts, while they searched for someone to take it on."

"I thought Sarah's family inherited the estate then?" Stephanie asked in surprise.

"Yes, they did. It took them a while to trace him. Andrew Trevelyan's father who inherited it then, from Henry Trevelyan in Devon. He was William's cousin. But he didn't want it for some time, fearing the legend. He died tragically soon after as I remember. It was put in trust for his son Andrew until he came of age. Later Andrew married and he and his wife moved to Marlin. If they hadn't..."

Stephanie knew what he was thinking. If they hadn't, both they and Sarah would still be alive. It crossed her mind that Andrew's father might have been a victim of the curse too, even though he lived in Devon.

"Anyway, Emma Jones, was a strong woman," Michael went on. "She managed the estate after Robert joined up in 1941 and carried on after he came home. He was injured at El Alamein in November 1942. His father had been a soldier too as I recall. He came home, honourably discharged, but sadly died of his injuries three months later, in January 1943."

Stephanie suddenly remembered the man's shiny shoes; she should have known that he was from a military family. She remembered how Nana Jean's husband, her Grampa George, had shoes that always gleamed. He was a retired soldier and old habits died hard. He would always set the shoe polish alight to melt it before cleaning them, and it had fascinated her to watch him. She told Michael about it and he smiled at her account of the memory.

Stephanie realised then that Michael reminded her a little of her grandfather. George had died when she was five. Although Michael looked nothing like him, she remembered how he always made her feel special, and Michel had the same effect. He brought her back to the present as he carried on with his tale. This was certainly a day full of memories, like someone had opened the floodgates.

"So, Emma continued to manage the estate until the war ended. Women had to take over, you see while most of the men were away fighting. They did more than just keep the home fires burning, you know. In 1945 when our soldiers returned home, the owner at the time decided it was more fitting for a man to take on the role again. Men returning form the war needed jobs, and women were expected to go back to being housewives and mothers for the most part. Sexist I know, but that was how things were back then. That was why they took Judd on. He was a year older than Jason. He walked with a limp from a war wound, shrapnel I think."

"Poor Emma. She was homeless?" said Stephanie.

Michael smiled. "Yes. Well, it was a different time back then," he added.

"What happened to Emma and Jason after that?" she asked.

"Well, you see, that's where it gets strange. Emma vanished in the autumn of 1945. She was meant to go and stay with her sister, down the coast. But she never got there. You should speak to Bob Bishop, he lives just up the hill from you, at Curlew House. He was Jason's best friend."

"How old is he?" asked Stephanie in obvious surprise.

"He's 93, and he still has all his marbles. Sharp as a tack is old Bob! But I'd start with the archives if I were you, while you're in the village."

***

By this time, they had reached the antique shop, so Michael said goodbye and left her outside while he went to open up. Stephanie was left reeling by the tale of the former inhabitants of her cottage. She had so much more to think about now. She decided to call in for a quick coffee at the small café. She needed to organise her thoughts before she went in search of the archives. She had no time for cake today and was soon on her way.

Some locals nodded and smiled as she passed them, and one old man even took off his cap to her.

"I didn't know people really did that any more!" she thought, in amusement.

It was a kind gesture. One woman however, grabbed her small son's hand and dragged him to the other side of the street as she approached. She sighed and looked away; some people could be so hurtful.

Once at the library, she located the archives with the help of the librarian. It was only a small library as expected in a small village. But it had an impressive archive, due in no small part to the efforts of her uncle, so she was told by the efficient Miss Broom.

As founder and chair of the local history society, Michael had taken it upon himself to see that the collection of all things relevant to the village of Marlin and the Trevelyan estate was properly maintained. A basement room at the library was a testament to his success, dedicated to the exhibition of many documents and other treasured items. Stephanie found them proudly displayed for the world to see. She could understand his sentiment. He had no personal connection to anything related to the Trevelyans, and she knew that he felt bitterness towards the family (and no little shame at what Mary Hall had done to them). But he obviously understood that local history should be respectfully recorded and preserved, no matter whose family it belonged to, and she admired him for it. Maybe it was also his way of making up for the actions of his ancestor.

Miss Broom was eager to help Stephanie with her search, especially considering her recently acquired fame and status. After only ten minutes she produced a copy of a newspaper article about a local war hero, Robert Jones, who had been awarded a posthumous medal for bravery at the second Battle of Alamein. In November 1942, he was injured helping his comrades to escape enemy fire. He received a medical discharge with full honours and later died at home from his injuries. The newspaper was dated 4th November 1943, almost a year after his death. There was a photograph of him, and Stephanie gasped when she saw that the man staring back at her from the photograph was the same man she had seen in her dream, complete with moustache and slicked back hair. The librarian also drew her attention to his medal which was displayed in a cabinet on the far wall.

Now it made sense. The first scene she had witnessed in her dream was that of a happy family, a husband and wife at home with their young son. It was years before the war started and they had been oblivious to what was to come. Later she had seen the woman alone, now a grieving widow. If her son was fighting in the war too she would have worried that he might also be lost. He would have been about the right age and might even have joined up at the same time as his father. She wondered if he had survived, aware that she forgot to press Michael about what happened to him. After hearing about Emma, she had been her only concern. But she was sure that Bob Bishop would know.

She noticed that on one wall of the archive was an old map of the area. Stephanie smiled when she saw Lapwing Cove and her beloved cottage, The Lodge, which nestled on the cliff above the bay. It showed Fern Leap where Isabel died (which made her shudder) and the rest of the Trevelyan estate surrounding the village. The ancient tin mine, three farms and a quarry occupied an area further along the coast to the left.

The woods behind her cottage also belonged to the estate as did the land and all the buildings in the village, including the pub and the three rows of workers' cottages on the hill above. It seemed that there were areas of the village she hadn't visited yet, further on from the village itself where she thought it was just open countryside.

On the other side of the village, near the crossroads at the top of the hill just past her home, lay two other cottages which she knew had also been sold off. The one nearest to The Lodge was Willow Cottage where Jeff was staying, and the other was Curlew Cottage where Bob Bishop lived.

All the land in the area belonged to the estate, which gave her some perspective on the magnitude of her future inheritance. She was surprised to see that The Manor was on there too. It took up a fair space on the map, obviously an imposingly large building in its time, complete with its own small chapel and a graveyard for the people of the estate and later, the villagers. That was apparently a common provision by the lord of the manor, according to the documents she found.

"The map must have been drawn before The Manor was destroyed," she

thought. *"I wonder if the chapel is still standing?"*

Suddenly she was struck with the realisation that it was her ancestral family home and half of her bloodline lay buried in that graveyard. It was sobering to see that, as the true heiress, she really was the rightful owner of nearly everything on the whole map. One day it would be *her* estate.

The fact that she was the descendant of a murderer also kept playing on her mind. She simply had to visit the ruins of her ancestral home, to search the graveyard and pay her respects to Isabel. But that would have to wait. She had more pressing concerns, like finding out what happened to the people in her vision. As with Isabel, she felt that it had been sent to her for a reason; to right some long-forgotten wrong. If only she knew what it was.

She looked at her phone and it was already noon; time to go. Further research would have to wait. She thanked the librarian on her way out and went to the supermarket. Then she walked home. She still had to feed the cats and herself, have a chat with Bob Bishop, and maybe do some writing before dinner.

***

It had been a fascinating morning, and she felt like she was making progress. Her thoughts raced as she carried a loaf of bread, a dozen tins of kitten food and a small catnip toy in the shape of a puppy (Maisy didn't like to share her toys). Despite the sunshine, the breeze was cold, and she was glad of her jacket as she walked up the hill. She kicked the autumn leaves with childish enthusiasm as she went. Autumn was her favourite season. In a few weeks, the weather would most likely worsen and she would be forced to drive to the village, or risk being drenched or blown away. She loved being able to walk everywhere, to breathe fresh, clean air and enjoy nature in all its glory.

London and its stuffy tubes and buses, fumes and crowds, seemed a lifetime away, yet she had only lived here for a few short months. Although brought up in Bristol, she was used to the bustle of city life. But she had always felt it to be restrictive; claustrophobic even. She felt she could breathe here, with open spaces and fresh, clean air. She decided there and then that this was the place where she would spend the rest of her life, maybe get married and have children and…

"Hi, can I help you with those bags?"

A voice behind her broke her reverie and made her jump. She turned to see Jeff.

"Oh God, did he see me kicking the leaves?" she thought, her face turning the usual shade of pink that appeared whenever he was around.

"Oh, no, that's OK. I'm balanced like this." she mumbled.

"Sorry?" He looked confused.

"The bags, one in each hand, the weight is balanced, it's a phrase my mother used to use."

"Why does he keep appearing, making me feel self-conscious?" she asked herself.

"Ah, OK. How's the kitten? Did you find her owner?" he asked.

"It's a boy, I was wrong," she admitted with a sheepish grin. "It happens occasionally. His name is Shadow."

"I assume you're keeping her, I mean him, now you've you named him?" he asked, also grinning.

"Oh, no, I just thought he deserved a name better than Kitten," she said.

"Fair point," he said. "Everyone deserves a decent name, and it suits him. No luck with finding his owner yet then?" he added

"Not yet, my uncle is asking around the village and I have a home lined up if all else fails," she said cheerily, but her legs were shaking.

"I hope he doesn't notice," she thought.

"That's good," he replied. She stopped walking.

"Home again!" she mumbled, nervously, arriving at The Lodge.

"I could take you up on that offer of tea now, if you have time," he said with a blinding smile.

"Oh, yes OK!" she answered.

"Does he have to keep smiling like that?" she thought. She realised she was scowling.

"Only if it's convenient," he said, seeing her expression and totally misreading it.

"Not at all, please come in. Just don't mind the mess. I haven't tidied up today."

Stephanie unlocked the front door and was met by chaos.

"I see what you mean," muttered Jeff.

"No, I didn't mean… this. NOOO!" she yelled, dropping her shopping on the floor, narrowly missing his feet.

The mess bore all the hallmarks of a cat. Cushions littered the hall with their stuffing oozing out. There were rips in the living room curtains. Pictures were askew. A toilet roll had been unravelled and was draped all the way down the stairs, shredded mercilessly along the way. Tiny pieces of tissue decorated the stairs like a light snowfall. The office was littered with unused printer paper in various stages of demise. Luckily her book was stored digitally on her laptop and backed up on a flash drive which was locked away in a drawer.

Maisy was nowhere to be seen. The door from the hall to the kitchen was open, but Shadow was fast asleep in his box where she had left him. He opened one eye and started to purr. Jeff picked up the shopping bags and closed the front door.

"Wow!" he said.

Stephanie was unable to speak. She couldn't believe that Maisy would have done all this. She had never done anything like this before, not even as a kitten. But if it wasn't her, then how did the kitten manage it? She remembered shutting the kitchen door, so who opened it? She stormed into the kitchen and looked behind the door. She found claw marks on the door and the table. Shadow.

"If Shadow jumped from the table and launched himself at the door handle, then maybe… but surely not!" she thought.

She examined the hall side of the door. Not a mark in sight. That had to be the only explanation. Shadow must have let himself out and caused all this mess.

"Shall I put the kettle on?" Jeff offered, placing the bags on the kitchen table. She had forgotten he was there. She sank into a chair by the table.

"Please," was all she could manage.

Jeff could see her distress and took charge.

"It's OK, we can easily sort this out." he said. "I can start in the living room if you like. Where are your bin bags?"

Stephanie suddenly saw red.

"Bin bags! BIN BAGS?" she yelled. "If you hadn't brought that damned cat here in the first place none of this would have happened!"

"How is it my fault? How do you know it wasn't your cat that did it?" he replied.

He feigned annoyance, but he was smiling.

"Claw marks on the back of the kitchen door, for one thing. And my Maisy would never..." she replied, outraged at the very idea.

Just then Maisy, on hearing her name, appeared as if by magic from under the desk in the office, strolled into the kitchen and sat down by Stephanie, nuzzling her leg. She had bits of tissue and white cushion stuffing caught on each of her front claws.

"Maisy! No!" Stephanie was speechless.

Jeff picked up the kitten from its box and he had the same damning evidence on his claws.

"It looks like a joint effort to me," he said, smiling.

Stephanie glared at him and muttered one word. "Sorry."

"Apology accepted," said Jeff. "Now, where *are* the bin bags?"

***

Soon the house had regained some semblance of order and the cats were fed. Stephanie had made Jeff a sandwich by way of an apology and they were drinking their tea on a bench in the back garden, overlooking the beach. She had relented and given the toy puppy to Shadow and he was currently in his box in the office, throwing it into the air and catching it in his teeth. Maisy was asleep on a chair in the living-room.

"He has GOT to go!" Stephanie said.

"Oh definitely," Jeff answered, stifling a smile.

"I'm sorry for earlier. It wasn't your fault, and you were only trying to help, and…" she began, her voice fading into nothing.

"I told you before, don't worry about it. If that's the worst thing that happens to me today, then…"

Jeff stopped talking and took her hand. Just then an image flashed before her eyes, like a thought that was not her own.

It was night. Jeff was lying on the ground with a head wound, bleeding and unconscious.

She pulled her hand away.

"Sorry, I didn't mean... well, I did, but..." he babbled. "That was presumptuous of me." Now it was his turn to look embarrassed.

"No, it isn't that… well it is, but…"

She couldn't find a way to tell him. How do you warn someone they're going to be attacked? Jan had told her about this sort of thing, but she had never experienced it before. A full-blown waking premonition.

"TELL HIM!" came the now familiar voice of her mother next to her left ear.

"I can't!" she shouted, but she knew she had to. Jeff, of course, misunderstood.

"It's OK. I don't want to seem pushy, I know we only just met, but I felt a connection, and I thought you did too, and… I'll go," said Jeff, standing up and walking into the hallway. "I should go."

"No wait, you don't understand!" she called after him.

He stopped. She hated the confusion in his eyes, the pain she thought she had caused him by pulling her hand away.

"Let me explain," she said.

"What is it? You look like you saw a ghost," he said, obviously concerned.

In as few words as she could, without mentioning Isabel or Jan, the doll or the Trevelyans, Stephanie told him that sometimes she had "visions." She mumbled something about having "good instincts" and "trusting her intuition" and then told him what she had "seen."

"Are you a witch?" he asked.

"No, of course not!" she said.

He seemed relieved to know that. "So, who is going to attack me? When? Why?" he asked.

She said she felt strongly that it would be that night. That was all she knew.

"I think I'd better go home and lock the doors then," he said, smiling.

"You're not taking this seriously," she said.

"Would you, if a virtual stranger came out with that?" he retorted.

"Maybe," she said, then paused. "No. I suppose not."

He had a point.

"OK, well I do have to go now and get some work done," he said, looking at his watch. "Thanks for the lunch."

"Thanks for your help," she said "and please, be careful!"

"I will," he said, his eyes twinkling in the afternoon light.

She walked with him through the cottage and let him out through the front door, with a knot in her stomach as he walked away. She felt sick. But he was right; there was already an unmistakable bond forming between them. An indefinable something. She hoped that her vision had been wrong. If not, whatever was blossoming between them would be over before it even started. As much as she wished it not to be true, unless she did something to stop it Jeff would be injured that night; or worse.

***

After a hot relaxing bath, she sat snuggled in her warm dressing-gown and slippers and tried her best to write. But nothing came to mind; instead, she just felt sleepy. After a short nap, she tried to call Jan, but the number was engaged so she just left her a brief message. She made herself a stir-fry and changed into clothes more suitable for an evening walk. She put Shadow in the safety of the spare room with his blanket, catnip puppy, litter tray and a dish of food. The room contained just a bed, a rug and some storage boxes; not a lot to damage there. But she locked the door just in case he tried to get out and put the key in her pocket. Maisy was relegated to the bathroom with a litter tray and the door was pulled shut, much to her obvious disgust.

"Divide and conquer!" Stephanie thought.

That kitten was a bad influence, and she hoped a home would be found for him soon, one way or another. She put her torch in her jacket pocket, stepped out and locked her front door.

It was early evening, and she was finally on her way to visit Bob Bishop. She knew she had to leave by the time it got dark, to check if there was anyone lurking in the vicinity of Willow Cottage.

She passed it on her way up the hill and she glanced over. One downstairs light was on but she couldn't see him from the road. She felt like a stalker. But if anything happened to Jeff, she would feel terrible because she hadn't been able to make him take her warning seriously. She would have to talk to Jan about this whole vision thing.

"Is there such a thing as an effective technique for giving precognitive warnings?" she wondered.

She found Curlew House easily enough. It was a solid, double-fronted, stone-built, detached property which stood at the top of the hill. Like Willow Cottage it looked similar in design to The Lodge and about the same age. It enjoyed majestic views over the village and the cove. Its windows looked like eyes, wide and watchful, gleaming in the late afternoon light. Somehow, she felt sad; she knew that she was imposing on its solitude, and that of its owner. Did she have the right to disturb a frail old man in the sanctity of his own home and dredge up bad memories?

"Probably not," she thought.

But she knew that she had to do it anyway; she needed answers.

She knocked the door using the large brass knocker in the shape of a bird. Not knowing much about birds and given the house name, she assumed it was meant to represent a curlew. She waited; no-one answered the door, but there was a light on downstairs. She tried again. After the second knock, a voice could be heard behind the door.

"Hold your horses, I'm not as young as I was!" came a voice.

A small man with a walking stick opened the door. He had deep blue eyes and a shock of white hair. His gaze was unnerving. He was dressed smartly in a knitted cardigan with leather buttons, worn over a shirt with small checks, a pair of brown corduroy trousers, thick socks and cosy slippers. He looked sprightly enough, yet his collarbone was visible, poking through his short due to an apparent lack of body fat. He looked light enough to blow away in a half-decent breeze and his complexion was a little pasty, as if he didn't go out much.

"I'm not buying anything!" he declared, as he looked her straight in the eyes.

"I'm not selling anything," she replied with a smile. "I'm sorry to bother you, Mr Bishop. Please could I have a few moments of your time? My uncle, Michael Hall, thinks you might be able to help me with something, if you don't mind?" She took a breath. "My name is Stephanie," she said. "Stephanie Meares."

"Oh, it's you! Yes, I know who you are my dear. Nothing goes on around her that I don't know about." He smiled. "Come in, come in! Leave your jacket on the hall stand, or you won't feel the benefit when you go out."

***

"Just made a pot of tea. Want a cup?" asked Bob lowering himself into a plush yet well-worn armchair next to a roaring fire in his living-room. He propped up his stick between the chair and the hearth. "Take a seat," he urged.

He pointed to a tray on the coffee table with one hand and offered her the equally plump chair next to him by waving the other.

"Yes, please, milk no sugar," she answered. She looked around the charming room with its ageing furniture and homely décor. She sensed that it had once been graced by a woman's touch, but not for some time.

"Sweet enough, I see," he smiled. "Good man, your uncle. Knew his parents, and grandparents," said Bob. "And Isabel, of course. But then you've met her too, haven't you?" he added.

She smiled back nervously. *"How does he know that?"* she thought.

Bob Bishop seemed to know a lot about her. But Isabel was a topic for another day. She had more pressing matters to discuss. He passed her a delicate rose-patterned cup and saucer, without a hint of a tremor in his wrinkled hands, and she thanked him.

"Now what is it you came to ask me?" he asked.

She sipped her tea and began, approving of his directness.

"It's about The Lodge. I'm trying to trace the history of the people who lived there, and I was wondering if you remember anything about..."

He held up his right hand and cut her off.

"Jason and his mother. You want to know what happened, don't you?" he asked with a frown.

"Yes, please," she answered.

"Well, it was a very long time ago, but I remember as if it was yesterday. It was like this..."

Bob Bishop proceeded to tell her that he and Jason Jones had been friends from the time that they were old enough to kick a ball, or climb a tree. Robert Jones had been a good man, respected by all who worked on the estate. His wife, Emma, was a warm woman, devoted to her husband and son. They had welcomed him into her home and treated him as if he was their own child. Bob's mother had died when he was little so he spent more time at their home than his own. Stephanie could relate to that. Jan had practically lived at her house when they were growing up.

"After he was taken, Robert I mean, a part of her died with him. She became withdrawn," he said. "Jason was in the army too, as was I. Joined up together, we did, but we were lucky enough to make it home. So many of us didn't."

He wiped a tear from his eye with a bright, white handkerchief and blew his nose.

"I'm sorry," was all she could think of to say.

He looked at her in silent appreciation, then stared into the flames of the open log fire for a moment or two, lost in the past. Stephanie drank her tea and waited.

"Long time ago, no point dwelling on it," he replied at last, with a faraway smile, then he continued.

"After Robert died and Jason came home, they had to leave The Lodge because it was tied to the job, as I'm sure Michael will have told you. That was when Emma decided to pack up and leave the village. The new estate manager, Judd, offered her a job in his office, typing and so on, but she turned him down flat. Too many memories there, she said." Stephanie nodded and Bob continued.

"She arranged to go and stay with her sister for a while, along the coast at Hewley Point, and then she planned to make a fresh start elsewhere. They set a date and everything was packed, just clothes and personal bits, mind you. The furniture belonged to the estate. Bill Judd himself offered to drive her there himself. He knew her husband see, served with him and was with him when he died. He was one of the men Robert saved. When he arrived that morning, her luggage was ready in the hall. But when Jason went upstairs to fetch her, she was nowhere to be found."

"Oh, so Jason wasn't going with her?" Stephanie was surprised. It sounded strange that a loving mother would leave her son so soon after his father died.

"No indeed! He called the police in, all the way from Wadebridge. People searched high and low. Not a trace was found, apart from this," said Bob.

He stood up with difficulty and opened a small wooden box on the mantelpiece. He took something out and lowered himself back into his chair.

"This was found up in the woods over there," he said, waving his hand in the direction of the woods that backed onto the fields at the rear of The Lodge. "Jason found it himself a couple of weeks later."

Stephanie looked down in shock at what he held in his hands. It was the large, oval, silver locket from her dream, engraved with a single rosebud. He opened it and showed her that it contained two photographs. One was a of handsome young man with blond hair, which had to be Jason, and the other was the face she now recognised as his father, Robert. There was no doubt that the woman she had seen was Emma.

"The police were stumped of course, with no sign of a struggle in the house or any evidence that anything untoward had happened to her. To be honest, I don't think they took it seriously. By the time Jason found the locket they had abandoned the search. It was just after the war and I suppose they had better things to worry about. But if you look carefully at the rose on the front, you can still see the blood."

He passed her the locket. As she tentatively took it from him, she held it in her hand and the room fell away. Stephanie was somewhere else. She found herself in a wooded area. It smelled musty and damp. There was a woman running for her life. The path was steep, muddy. The grass was like ice, heavy with the early morning dew. The woman was Emma. She scrambled up a slight slope and slipped, cutting her hand on a pile of sharp stones to her right as she tried to steady herself. She wore a crisp, white blouse, black jacket and skirt and lace-up shoes, like in the second part of the dream. A woman in mourning.

Her locket was flapping and twisting as she ran as if it had a life of its own. She grabbed it to steady it, then tucked it inside her crisp, white blouse to keep it safe and as she did so she smeared it with blood. A small red stain spread across her blouse from her hand as she touched it.

"He's coming!" Stephanie whispered almost imperceptibly.

"Are you alright?" came a voice. It was Bob.

Stephanie opened her eyes. Bob looked concerned, but not surprised.

"Here, have some more tea," he said.

She realised that she had dropped the locket on the floor. Bob bent down carefully to pick it up, resting heavily on the arm of the chair.

"You saw her, didn't you?" he asked with a slight smile as he eased himself into the chair again.

"How did you…?" she began.

"Your family isn't the only one with the gift, you know!" he said with a wry smile. Stephanie was amazed. What sort of village was this? Stephanie felt like someone had taken all the air from her lungs. This was all so new to her, and more than a little unsettling.

"So, someone was chasing her?" she asked, when she could think clearly.

"That's what you saw is it? I never get beyond the running part. Your gift is strong, my dear!"

It struck her that the story she was trying to piece together was like a mystery to be solved. A puzzle. To her they were strangers who had lived in her house, but this man knew them. He had lived when they lived and was around when her grandmother was born, and when Isabel died. To him it was all so real; so personal.

"So, tell me. Where did the blood come from?" Bob asked eagerly.

He brought her back to the present.

"Her hand, she cut it on a stone. But how did I see that?"

She was shaken and confused and suddenly her head ached and she was very thirsty.

"It's called psychometry, my dear. People with that talent can hold a piece of jewellery or other belongings and feel the energy of the owner, maybe many years afterwards. See what they saw, feel what they felt," he explained gently. "You seem to be very good at it. I knew you would be. I've been waiting for you for a very long time."

"Jan never mentioned THIS!" she thought, taking a large gulp of what turned out to be very sugary tea. She grimaced at the sweetness, but drank again, draining her cup.

"I saw her running through the woods then she cut her hand. But how did she lose the locket?" Stephanie asked. She needed to make sense of it all.

"No-one knows." he said with a smile. "No-one ever got as far as you did."

"What happened to Jason, then?" she asked.

"He left the village soon after, when the police stopped looking and it was obvious his mother wouldn't be found. It was all too much for him." His face clouded over. "Boarded a ship to Australia and never came back. Left me the locket as a keepsake and just started again. Couldn't bear to look at it." He stared into the fire again. "Never heard from him again My best friend, gone just like that."

He stared once more into the fire. A log crackled as it dropped a little in the hearth, sending sparks up the old chimney. As if suddenly drawn back to the present by the sound, Bob stood up gingerly, grasping his walking stick.

"Look how dark it's gone. Time to put the light on, I think." he said.

He walked across and switched on a table lamp hear the door. Stephanie suddenly remembered Jeff.

"I've taken up enough of your time, Mr Bishop," she said, getting up from her chair. "Thank you for the information, and the tea."

"You're welcome, my dear, and please call me Bob," he said. "Will you come again? I don't get many visitors these days."

"Yes of course," she answered, realising she still had more questions to ask him. "Would tomorrow be OK? I think we have a lot more to discuss."

"Fine by me," he replied with a warm smile. "Now let's find your jacket. It'll be cold out tonight."

Then as they reached the front door, he spoke again.

"Take this with you, you might get something more from it," he said, putting the locket into her jacket pocket. "And be careful with that cat, won't you? He's a familiar, but he isn't meant for you."

"How do you know about the cat, and what on earth is a familiar?" she asked, nervously.

"I'll tell you tomorrow!" said Bob, with a wink.

***

Stephanie stepped out into the cold October evening. As predicted by Bob, an unexpected frost was already settling on the ground. She was already chilled to the core by what had just happened and the cold air seeping into her bones made it worse.

"That's why I saw the family at my house," she thought. *"Emma wants me to find her so her spirit can find peace."*

Ethereal wisps of light fog played around the street lights, and swirled around her head like tiny fingers, rising up the hill behind her from the sea. She felt like she had stepped into a dream landscape as she made her way down the hill towards Willow Cottage. She felt for her torch, which was still safe in her jacket pocket. As she reached into her pocket, her hand brushed against the locket. She withdrew her hand sharply, not wanting any more visions, not here and definitely not now. Her life was becoming more complicated by the day; much more interesting than the novel she was writing. Or not writing would be more accurate.

Soon she was standing at the gate. There was a light on in the porch now too. She opened the gate without making a sound, afraid to close it in case it alerted anyone to her presence. She stepped closer and could see to her horror that Jeff was not alone. Someone else was in the room, slightly shorter than Jeff. But their back was towards her so she couldn't see who it was and they were obviously arguing.

"I made it in time," she thought to herself.

"DON'T BE HASTY, STEFFI!" came a familiar voice from somewhere close to her left ear.

"OK, Mother," she replied in a whisper.

It surprised Stephanie how readily she accepted her visions and hearing the random mutterings of the departed now. It was becoming a regular occurrence, and at least she found it comforting to know that her mother was one of them. But that psychometry business would take a lot of getting used to.

Her attention was drawn back to the window as the argument became heated. The voices were very muffled so she couldn't make out what was being said, but arms were waving and Jeff's voice was raised. It looked like they might come to blows. She had to act.

The only thing she could think of was to rap at the window with her knuckles. It hurt; they were already stinging from the cold. Her breath was as moist and misty as the fog which by now had descended like a cloak, shrouding the area. The temperature was indeed dropping as Bob predicted. Sea fog came in suddenly, she knew that. She shuddered and moved across to the front door. Jeff and his visitor had stopped arguing. She could make out the sounds of someone opening the living room door and walking on what sounded like a hard wood floor to the front door. Her nerves were jangling.

***

"Oh, hi!" said Jeff, looking worried. "It's you! Anything wrong? Come in, it's freezing."

Stephanie stepped into his hallway and he closed the door. Walking straight past him she stepped into a comfortable front room and saw someone standing next to the fire warming their hands. Female hands. The person turned around and she saw that his guest was a tall, attractive, dark-haired, athletic-looking woman.

"Hello," said Stephanie curtly.

She felt an odd feeling forming in the pit of her stomach. Was she jealous?

"Hi," said the woman, looking a little tense.

Jeff had come into the room and was standing behind her. "This is

Dana," he said. "She's my... editor."

"Oh, OK." said Stephanie, suddenly lost for words.

Her instincts told her that the woman wasn't anyone's editor. Her demeanour screamed that she was anything of the sort. Stephanie wanted the floor to open up and swallow her whole. How could she get out of this? Jeff looked perfectly well, with no blood or visible signs of injury. She felt like a fool, her cheeks were hot and her palms were sweaty despite the fact that her fingers were still numb.

"I'd better go," said Dana, looking uneasy.

She nodded at Stephanie in the doorway, squeezed past and headed for the front door, whispering a parting comment.

"I'm serious, Jeff," she muttered.

Jeff showed her to the door as Stephanie peered after them.

"Understood," he called as she slammed the front door behind her.

He sighed and turned back to find Stephanie, red-faced behind him.

"Sorry," he said. "I missed another deadline."

Stephanie stammered something about understanding and he offered her tea which she accepted.

"Then you can tell me why you're here," he said, with one of his heart-melting smiles.

"Oh no," she thought. *"How do I explain this?"* She wanted to run.

As she waited, she noticed a pile of documents on the table. There was a brown paper folder on the top. Maybe it was his work. She was eager to see what his writing style was like (from a professional point of view of course). She could just take a quick look before he came back and he would be none the wiser. She hastily flicked the cover open and gasped at what she saw. The folder was full of newspaper clippings. A knot appeared in the pit of her stomach.

"LOCAL AUTHOR HEIRESS!" and "DEAD BODY WASHED UP!" were two of the headlines. Her mind was flooded with questions. Why did he have these? Had he been checking up on her? Was he really researching the Trevelyans? Could he be a reporter? Had he brought her the kitten as a way to get to know her so that he could write an inside story?

She felt appalled, angry. Betrayed. Hot tears burned at the corners of her eyes, stabbing like needles. Her throat was tight.

"Well my taste in men certainly hasn't improved, has it?" she thought.

She was suddenly terribly disappointed with herself, and with him. All at once she felt woefully embarrassed and angry. Very angry. She heard whistling and footsteps on the wooden hall floor.

"What does he have to be cheerful about?" she thought as she turned to face him.

Jeff pushed open the door with a metal tray containing two steaming mugs of tea and a plate of biscuits. Then he saw her dark expression and the folder open on the table. His face crumpled.

"I'm sorry," he said. "But it isn't as bad as it looks. Really!"

"I don't want to hear it," she mumbled, fighting back the tears.

"Stephanie, please, let me explain!" he said.

But she just barged past him, sending the tray flying. Mugs and biscuits dropped to the floor as the tray was forced up into his face, hitting him square on the forehead. It left a nasty cut which began to bleed.

"Ow! Wait!" Jeff called.

He put his left hand on the cut and turned to run after her. But instead he slipped on the hot spilled tea and his feet slid from under him. He was propelled backwards against the fireplace, banging the back of his head on the mantelpiece as he fell. He slumped to the floor like a sack of potatoes as if he had been punched. Stephanie looked back to see him half-lying in the hearth. Luckily it just contained a gas fire which was turned off. Jeff just sat there, motionless. He was conscious, but dazed.

Stephanie felt awful. She rushed over to him.

"Jeff! Are you OK?" she almost shrieked, with a pang of guilt.

"*I didn't want this, even if he does deserve it,*" she thought.

"Oh, I'm good. Great!" he mumbled. "Thanks a lot. Your premonition came true after all."

Somehow, she wasn't at all pleased about it.

He looked a little groggy, but even now he didn't seem angry with her. He held his head, eyes closed as he tried to stand up and failed, slipping again on the tea. She just had to laugh. Suddenly he smiled and opened his eyes.

"Well I'm glad you find it funny!" he said, but a smile crept onto his face too. The situation was ridiculous.

"Stay there, don't move while I get something to clear up this mess," she called.

At the end of the hall she found the kitchen. She hastily grabbed towel, a dust pan and brush and a first aid kit (a standard item at all rental properties). Soon she had cleaned up the tea, the broken mug and sloppy biscuit debris. Jeff was sitting safely in a chair by the table and she sat next to him, dressing the wound. He winced as she applied antiseptic.

She was First Aid trained and had established that he wasn't exhibiting any symptoms of concussion and hadn't appeared to have been knocked out. In any case, he refused point blank to go to hospital. She advised him against alcohol and told him to ring her if he felt nauseous or his headache worsened. She said that she would be happy to drive him to the nearest casualty department, wherever that was. Then she made fresh tea and tried to explain.

"I didn't mean for you to get hurt. Really. I only came to make sure you were OK," she mumbled. "I wish I hadn't bothered now," she said, pointing at the newspaper clippings.

"Strangely enough, I was fine till you arrived!" he said.

"You didn't look fine. What were you and Dana arguing about? I know she isn't your editor!" she said.

"If you would have let me explain," he said. "I was going to tell you I work for Jan!"

She felt like someone had thrown cold water in her face.

"What? Ridiculous!" she snapped. "I would know, she's my best friend."

"She knew you didn't want the inheritance," he continued. "But she also knows that there are certain people out there who want to make sure you never live to claim it. In our business, we deal with all sorts and he knows how to make life very difficult for you."

"Who is HE? What are you rambling on about?" she asked.

She tried to appear unconcerned, but something in his voice, his measured honest tone, made her feel nervous.

"Paul," he said. "It's Paul. Your ex!"

"WHAT? No."

The room started swimming. "But he's in prison. Isn't he?" she added, hopeful that he hadn't been let out.

"Yes, don't worry, he's still locked up. But he has some very shady acquaintances. As well as the inheritance, there's a story, you see. A tale about some sort of priceless contraband hidden somewhere on the estate, and they think you know where to find it."

"But I don't know anything!" Stephanie insisted. This was becoming worse by the second.

"I know. That's what I've been researching. We thought if I could just get to it first and give it to the Trevelyan's solicitor, then they wouldn't bother you any more. They will stop at nothing to get what they want.

Stephanie, please believe me, you aren't safe. Jan really did send me here to protect you."

"Well if you ask me, judging by tonight's performance, you aren't really up to the job, are you!" she declared, feeling suddenly quite scared.

"I suppose not," he grinned, and she couldn't help smiling back. "I'm a former police officer too. It's shaming to be floored by a woman with a tea tray!"

She laughed, despite herself.

"So, anyway, who was that woman earlier?" she demanded.

She sipped her tea, and he did the same.

"Dana is one of my colleagues," he said. "She works for Jan and she's working on this case too. She was annoyed with me because she thinks I'm getting too, well, close to you. She threatened to tell Jan. I wasn't supposed to make contact, you see. I'm so sorry, Stephanie. I hated lying to you and I meant it when I said I felt we had a connection. And that… well, that wasn't part of the plan. Not at all. I'm sorry if I've behaved unprofessionally."

He looked straight at her, his eyes pleading with her to believe him.

Stephanie's hands shook as she held her mug of tea. She knew that Jan had people working for her and that sometimes they had to take on dangerous cases. But she never imagined that she would be one of them.

Her brain was a mixture of emotion and adrenalin and her heart was thumping. She felt anger towards Jan for not telling her and Jeff for lying to her, but also gratitude that they had stepped in to help her, if he was telling her the truth. Otherwise, what he said was too cruel. Her feelings towards him were so mixed. The very mention of Paul's name had dredged up bad memories from when she was with him: his deceit, treachery and greed. There had been other women too, as she had found out in court. She had to sit there and be publicly humiliated by the fact that he had also been unfaithful; that he had never loved her. It had been one of the worst days of her life.

She felt the old churning inside when she thought of how gullible she had been, how innocently she had fallen prey to all his machinations. Would her relationship with Paul ever stop coming back to haunt her? Would it continue to stand in the way of any future relationship she might have? She felt anxious at the possibility of him having anything to do with her, even from a distance. It was nauseating.

She was relieved that Jeff at least wasn't a reporter and that he seemed to be on her side. Even though he had lied to her, it seemed that it was for the right reasons. As for Jan, best friend or not Jan would be getting an earful when she got home. She had to check whether what Jeff had told her was even true. What did she really know about him? Only what he had told her. She felt so confused. Yet again, with more information came more questions. She suddenly felt very tired.

"Are you OK?" said Jeff, pulling her attention back to the room.

She had been so lost in thought that she had forgotten he was there. He put his hand over hers where it rested on the table. The same spark shot between them as before, but this time he didn't pull his hand away, and neither did she. She looked him straight in the eyes and gave him a tired smile.

"I've got to go." she said, and he nodded in understanding. He could see that his news had taken it out of her.

"Are you sure you'll be OK?" he asked. "You look worn out."

"I should be asking you that. Yes, I am very tired," she said. "We can talk about all this tomorrow."

"Let me walk you home, it's the least I can do…" he began.

"No, you need to rest. But thanks," she replied. "I'm sorry again about, you know…"

"Lamping me with a tray? It's OK, I'm alright, really," he said with a smile as he put his other hand on the lump at the back of his head and winced.

"You need witch hazel for that, to bring the bruise out. I'll bring you some in the morning," she said.

"And about the kitten, I did really find it outside your house. I wasn't supposed to speak to you, Jan made it very clear that you weren't to know about me. She's going to kill me," he said, pathetically.

"Not if I get to her first!" Stephanie said. "Don't worry, if what you say is true, she will have a lot to answer for too." She retrieved her hand gently, from where it was still resting beneath his.

"It is true. I swear," he said.

She got up to go then suddenly had a thought and turned back.

"So, if you work with Jan then you know about all the… spooky stuff? Isabel and so on?"

"Oh yes!" he said. "Jan told me everything," he said, smiling.

"But you pretended to not know what I was on about earlier when I told you about my... my vision." She felt foolish.

"I know. Sorry about that too," he replied, with a sheepish grin. "I was trying hard to maintain my cover story, pretending that I knew nothing about you."

Strangely she didn't feel upset about him knowing about her quirks. In fact, she felt relieved.

She simply smiled and said "Stay there, I'll see myself out. Goodnight, Jeff!"

Then he called after her as she left.

"Oh, and by the way, your mother said to tell you 'Hi, Steffi!'"

She slammed the door without looking back and hurried out into the fog, which was thicker now.

"He's like me!" she thought, with a grin.

She knew Jan employed other psychics, and he was obviously one of them. For some reason that felt comforting, important. Essential even. She was amused at the thought that her mother had encouraged her to tell him what she had foreseen. However, it surprised her that Grace had been speaking to Jeff too.

"So, the spirit of my dead mother is trying to set me up with Jeff." she thought. *"Wait till Jan hears about this!"*

She took her torch out of her pocket and made her way down the hill through the fog. Soon she was back at The Lodge. She found Maisy asleep in the bathroom and Shadow curled up on the bed in the spare room, and that was where she hoped they would stay until morning. She wasn't in the mood for dealing with any more cat antics. She was too tired even to call Jan to give her a piece of her mind, or eat dinner. Instead, she just sat with a cup of hot chocolate in her living room, overlooking the bay.

Knowing her friend had done all that to protect her, and that Jeff had come riding into the village like a white knight, made her feel somehow safe. If his story was to be believed. She had never felt more confused. Her life was like a tangled spider's web, with all the strands leading back to her. She sat in the middle, but far from being the spider in control of the situation and knowing what each strand was leading to, she was a prisoner. The prey. A victim of her own inheritance, in more ways than one.

Her life was bouncing further and further out of control as each strand was plucked and twisted by unknown people, unseen forces. She realised that far from being over when the doll had been destroyed, the mysteries of Marlin had only just started. Her gut feeling had been right. She looked out over the fog as it wafted relentlessly inward with the dark tide and shivered. Not from the cold, but from a growing sense of panic.

It was late by this time so she decided that her chat with Jan could wait till the morning. So, she checked her doors and windows twice and went to bed. Just when she had started to feel safe in her own home, something else had to come along to spoil it.

***

Stephanie woke when the alarm went off, having slept undisturbed and without dreaming; she was grateful for the welcome respite of refreshing rest. She had set the alarm for eight o'clock because she knew she had a busy day ahead.

She was surprised to find that Shadow was lying on the bed at her feet, all curled up, a tiny mass of warm, purring fur. Or maybe deep down she wasn't surprised at all. She picked him up; he made a chirpy noise when she touched him and purred loudly as she carried him to the spare room. The door was open. She put him back in the box. She knew that not only had she closed the door, but she had also locked it again before bed. He stared up at her, a picture of innocence with his large gleaming eyes, like tiny green grapes edged with honey.

"Don't play the innocent with me!" she said, stroking him for a while and listening to his comforting purr.

The tiny catnip puppy that she had given him was sitting in his food bowl; somehow it always ended up in there after every meal. She smiled, took it out and threw it to him then, retrieved the dish. Shadow pounced on his tiny toy and rolled with it, bopping it about the box, gleefully.

"Breakfast won't be long," she said.

He replied with a meow and went back to playing with his toy. After locking him in again, she made her way to the bathroom. Maisy shot out as she opened the door and ran down the stairs. Her cat was far from happy. Stephanie sighed.

Bob's comment rang in her head: that Shadow was a familiar, whatever that was. She needed to speak to Bob again. There was something decidedly odd about this kitten, in spite of his cuteness.

***

After a quick shower, Stephanie dressed, leaving her hair to dry naturally. She knew it would dry in waves, just like her mother's used to, but she didn't care. She didn't have time to dry it or straighten it. She fed the cats then started on the first task on a long list she had to get through that day. She had to speak to Jan.

Jan's number was engaged, as was often the case, so she left a stern, brief message, indicating that she knew about Jeff and wasn't happy. Then she rang her editor to explain that she had some personal matters to deal with and that she wouldn't be able to send her the next three chapters by Monday as promised. Her editor was experienced and understood that a writer worked better when their mind was on the job; without distractions. She also knew that quality work, which Stephanie's first book had been, was worth the wait. They agreed on a two-week extension, but she knew she couldn't delay the deadline forever.

She found her bottle of witch hazel in the bathroom and this time decided to give Maisy free roam of the house again. Shadow was locked in the spare room and she hoped he would stay there, but she had no time to worry about it. Hopefully he would soon have a new owner.

A little before nine she was knocking on Jeff's door. He stood there, grinning, looking better than anyone had a right to look first thing in the morning, especially after being injured. He handed her a mug of tea as she stepped in through the door.

"Right on time!" he said.

"How did you...?" she started.

"You're not the only person who has the gift in this village."

"Someone else said that to me yesterday," she replied.

"Yes, I know, I hear you've already met my great uncle Bob."

"Great uncle Bob?" she was somehow not that surprised. She could see a family resemblance now in his piercing blue eyes.

"Yes, my grandmother was a Bishop, Bob's sister. He rang me this morning to tell me about your visit yesterday. He seems pretty taken with you."

"I suppose you know all about this?" She put her hand in her jacket and pulled out the locket.

As she did so, the room began to spin. She was aware of being transported somewhere, back to the woods. Emma was there. She was hiding; terrified. A man approached but Stephanie couldn't see his face.

"I'm sorry, I don't know anything," said Emma. "If Robert knew about it he never told me. Please!"

Then she was aware of someone holding her, a voice calling her name.

"Stephanie! Are you OK?"

She became aware of her surroundings. She was lying in the hallway, Jeff had his arms around her. She was crying.

Effortlessly he picked her up, carried her to the living-room and laid her on the sofa. He covered her with a blanket and left the room for a moment, then returned with a glass of water.

"Here, drink this," he said, passing her the glass. "Spirit work can make you dehydrated."

She did feel very thirsty and drank the whole glass of water. She remembered her thirst at Bob' the night before too. She could sense his eyes scanning her face and looked up.

"You were shouting and crying," he said. "Did you see Emma again? What happened?"

He looked so worried that it made her feel protected, suddenly safer.

"It's OK, I'm fine now. Yes, it was Emma, the man chasing her was looking for something. She didn't know where it was. She said Robert never told her then he… my God I think that was when he killed her! Jeff, do you think they were looking for the same thing as Paul? Is that going to happen to me?"

She started shaking. He put his arms round her and spoke gently.

"No-one will ever hurt you again," he said. "Not Paul, not anyone."

And she believed him.

She looked up at him, their eyes met and the world melted away. But then she pushed him away, threw off the blanket and stood up.

"Come on, she said, we have to speak to Bob!"

***

Stephanie had made sure to dab some witch hazel on Jeff's head before setting off. Soon they were sitting in Bob's front room drinking tea. On the way, Jeff had told her that he spoke to Jan that morning. Jan had told him not to leave her side and that she would ring Stephanie that night if she couldn't do so before. She had said that she had a particularly nasty "house clearance" to deal with. Stephanie understood what that meant; a difficult case of spirit infestation. Still she was keen to speak to Jan, for confirmation that Jeff was who he claimed to be. To put her mind at rest. The mere mention of Paul had sent her lingering paranoia into overdrive.

Jeff was certainly attentive, watching her carefully, anxiously, making sure she was alright after what happened earlier. The fire was blazing and Bob noticed the stolen glances between them, the spark of a new relationship, and he was silently pleased. Outwardly he was still chortling to himself about the plaster on Jeff's head.

"She got you good there, son!" he said.

"Yes, I know, very funny Uncle Bob," said Jeff, smiling too.

Stephanie was bursting to tell him what just happened, and he picked up on that.

"So, what did you want to tell me?" asked Bob.

"I don't know for sure," she said "but I think the man chasing Emma was Judd!"

"Judd? You mean Bill Judd? How do you know that?" asked Jeff, amazed.

143

"He had a limp," she said, wide-eyed now. "The man chasing Emma had a limp. I noticed it as he followed her. Michael said Judd was injured in the war, so it's possible it was him."

Bob nodded.

"The man caught her while she stopped for breath hiding behind a tree. If she had just kept going, maybe…" she added, with tears in her eyes.

"It's in the past," said Bob, reassuringly. "Don't upset yourself, my dear. All we can do now is find out the truth and find where she is. That's why Jason gave me the locket; he knew about the gift and that someday, someone would be able to use it to find her and lay her to rest, properly. He was my friend, and he trusted me to do it, and with your help and Jeff's I will. I promised him, you see."

Tears glinted in his eyes too and he turned away to face the fire. Momentarily, he was lost again in the past.

"She had no idea what he was looking for," Stephanie repeated. "She said Robert never told her anything, so that means her husband must have known about it, or at least Judd thought he did."

"I think you're right," said Jeff. "They were old army comrades, weren't they Uncle Bob?"

"Yes, they were," said Bob, pulling himself together. "And I know just the man you need to speak to. Old Bill Judd himself!"

"You mean contact his spirit?" asked Stephanie in surprise.

"No, I meant to just go and visit him," said Bob with a smile.

"He's still alive?" asked Stephanie in amazement.

"Why shouldn't he be?" asked Bob, pretending to be offended, then grinning. "He lives in the sheltered accommodation complex the other side of the village, just past the old Manor."

"Let's pay him a visit then," said Jeff.

Bob was visibly cheered by the thought that they might finally be able to get answers and find Emma.

"Ring me afterwards." he told Jeff. "And don't forget about that familiar," he said to Stephanie.

"Oh yes," she said. "You were going to explain to me about that."

Bob took a deep breath. "A familiar is a protective spirit in the form of an animal, usually a cat. Cats are magical creatures and they have a habit of finding their way to just where they're meant to be, to the person they rightfully belong to. And that kitten belongs to Lucy Hall!"

"Lucy? Why?" she asked in surprise.

"Because she's a witch, like Mary Hall, and every witch needs a familiar. They belong together. And don't think about finding out where it came from, it simply appeared and took that form. Don't worry, it won't harm you. It came to you so that you can take it to Lucy. It knows you have the gift, you see."

"This gift that just keeps giving!" she thought.

Jeff didn't look surprised, he just nodded occasionally. Nothing much surprised him about what Bob had to say; or anything concerning

Stephanie, come to that.

"Lucy's a witch!" she thought. She wondered if Michael suspected.

Just then her phone rang. It was Lisa saying that she had spoken to Jessie about the kitten. They would love to give it to Lucy for her birthday on Friday, so could she keep it for her till then. Strangely though, she added, she had asked around and nobody in the village had lost a kitten. Stephanie smiled and told Lisa that she would be happy to keep the kitten for Lucy. She would bring it down to them at The Smithy, early on Friday morning. It was only two days away.

There was no need to explain to either Bob or Jeff what the phone call had been about, they had gathered the gist from her comments alone. Bob smiled smugly.

"Told you!" he said.

She smiled and shrugged her shoulders in a resigned way. It had been a long few days and so much had happened already. She feared that this was turning into another week from hell. She wanted an end to this mystery; she owed it to Emma. But she knew that there was worse to come when it dawned on her that sooner or later they might really find Emma's body. Spirits she could just about handle, but corpses?

"Be careful what you wish for!" she thought, with a shudder.

PART THREE: BETRAYAL

STEPHANIE AND JEFF made their way through the village to see Bill Judd. Bob had given them directions to Marlin House where he now lived in sheltered accommodation. As they walked, people paid Stephanie a lot of attention, which Jeff found quite amusing.

"The villagers seem to like you!" he said, grinning.

Stephanie raised her eyebrows then glared as a young boy shouted "Witch!" as he sped past on his bicycle.

"Not all of them," she said. Her thoughts turned to Emma.

"Bill Judd offered Emma that job as his secretary to keep her here, didn't he?" she said.

"I expect so," Jeff replied. "If he thought she knew where the treasure was, whatever it is, then he wouldn't want her leaving without finding out what she knew."

"That's why he promised to drive them that day," she said, realising what a devious, dangerous man they were about to meet, and she shivered. Jeff noticed.

"Are you cold? Here, take my scarf," he said. She shook her head.

"No, it's not that, it's this whole situation that's making me shiver. Anyone that would do that is evil," she said.

"I agree," said Jeff. "My mother told me not to fear spirits because the living are far more dangerous."

"Your mother never met the doll," she said.

"Yes, but that was a hexed object, not strictly a spirit," he explained. "But Jan and I have seen a few that would make your hair curl. Oh, it already does! By the way it suits you like that," he said with a grin.

"Oh, er thanks!" she said, with pink cheeks yet again. "Didn't have time to straighten it," she mumbled.

She thought back to what Bob had said, about Justin leaving Marlin after his mother's disappearance. Something didn't quite ring true.

"Why didn't Justin stay and find out what happened to Emma?" she asked.

"I wondered about that too," Jeff replied. "If it was someone I loved..."

He stopped speaking and his face clouded over, like he was going to say something and thought better of it. Suddenly he was lost in thought. Something was bothering him, and it wasn't Emma, but Stephanie didn't feel it was appropriate to ask him about it. Maybe Jan would know; if she ever, answered her phone.

They strolled on in silence for a while. The sun was shining down from a clear sky and the air was pleasantly warm. Stephanie stole a couple of glances at Jeff, then focused on her surroundings and saw that she had never been to this part of the village before. They had walked all the way to the end of the village and beyond without her noticing.

"You seem to know the way. Did you grow up in Marlin?" she asked.

"I'm originally from Wadebridge, but I spent all my summers here in Willow Cottage as a boy. My mother still owns it and rents it out, so I wasn't lying about that. Although she won't take money from me, of course. I used to live in London, but these days I move around a lot, wherever P.I. takes me."

"I'm surprised Jan never mentioned you," Stephanie whispered, old doubts creeping in.

He stopped and turned to face her. He looked deeply hurt.

"You still don't trust me, do you?" he asked, frowning.

"It's not that... I just..." she muttered. Did she trust him? "Yes, I do!" she said, this time with conviction. But did she truly believe it, or did she just need to believe that she had found a man she could trust? She wished Jan would call her back.

Just then a voice next to her ear said "STEFFI, RUN!"

Without saying a word, she grabbed Jeff's hand and started running down the road; luckily, he took the hint and ran too. She didn't know where or why, just that her life depended on it. Despite her gnawing doubts, she felt that with him she would be safe anywhere.

"Did you...?" she asked, breathing heavily.

"Yes, I heard her too," he answered. "Grace!"

She was convinced that his gift was genuine, at the very least. It was definitely her mother's voice.

She ran on instinct through streets she had never seen before, as if some invisible beacon was guiding her. She pulled him into a narrow, cobbled pedestrian alleyway she had never even know was there, through an arch into a courtyard. They stopped, catching their breath, surrounded by old, empty houses.

A silent row of three terraced cottages formed each of the other three sides to the courtyard; all were empty and their windows were boarded up. The atmosphere was menacing, one of deep despair and emptiness. It was a place where sadness lived. Stephanie felt it oozing from every building.

Jeff peered back around the corner to the alley as a black car drove past, speeding away from them. It had been following them since they entered the village. Jeff had spotted it earlier, but hadn't wanted to frighten her. Heeding her mother's warning, her instincts had led them to safety in an area where cars couldn't follow, out of sight of their pursuers.

"That was close," he said, panting, as he joined her by in the centre of the courtyard.

"You knew they were following us?" she asked. He nodded.

"Where are we?" she asked.

"Quarry Lane. It's where some of the tin miners and quarry workers used to live. It's been abandoned for many years, since well before I was born. Nobody wants to live here now."

She could understand why.

"Pardon my ignorance, but why was there a quarry when the tin was mined underground?" she asked. Jeff smiled.

"The quarry provided granite for local buildings," he said simply.

"I see," she answered, feeling even more stupid.

They looked around them. One house in particular drew her attention: the epicentre of the darkness. It was dark and gloomy, and it felt horrible.

"This house, it feels familiar," she said. "But I don't know why." Stephanie stood and stared at the house facing her. She began to suspect that she had been drawn to this place for another reason, one which had nothing to do with her safety.

The house had an aged, engraved, brass plaque outside which said "Quarry House". The property took up one whole side of the courtyard. It was, at first glance, three floors high, with three windows at each floor. But there was also evidence of a basement; she could see brick arches just above ground level that outlined ancient windows, with metal grating on the ground nearby to let the light into the rooms below.

"Servants' quarters," she thought.

"It was Peter Trevelyan's house," said Jeff.

"Isabel's brother," she said, and he nodded.

"He was quarry manager before his untimely death. It's been empty since he died, just like the rest of the courtyard. Nobody can cope with his presence, if you know what I mean! It's like his negative presence contaminates the whole area. One by one they all moved out. It all belongs to the estate. Such a waste."

"He's still there? Why hasn't anyone moved him on?" she asked in surprise.

"Many have tried, believe me, including myself and Uncle Bob. Peter simply won't go."

"He's waiting for me!" she said and marched across the cobbles.

Somehow, she knew. She just felt it. The soles of her shoes made no sound. It was as though the courtyard was sucking even sound away, like it had with the very life of the place itself. She felt unafraid and strode with purpose to the door.

"It's locked, and anyway it's trespassing!" Jeff called after her.

"If it belongs to the estate, it belongs to me!" she said.

Jeff couldn't argue with that, although she hadn't applied to take ownership of the estate yet.

"A technicality!" he thought, and followed her. One look at her face told him that she would not be dissuaded.

There were three planks of wood nailed across the doorway forming a barrier. As she approached it, the nails from the middle plank slowly worked themselves loose and dropped, one by one, with a soft clink onto the cobbles. The door swung slowly inward as if pulled from inside. She was expected.

There was room for a person to climb through, by bending their head a little and stepping over the lower plank. Not at all perturbed by the strange occurrence, she went in.

"Wait!" he called. "Jan said we should stay together!"

"Come on then!" she said, her voice muffled by the dark hallway. Jeff sighed and followed her into the house.

***

She was grateful that her torch was still in her pocket from the night before. She avoided touching the locket and peered down the hallway. There was a grand central staircase and there were rooms on either side. She felt drawn to the second one on the right. As she entered, she felt a strong, ice-cold breeze ruffle her hair, and she sneezed as it disturbed years of dust. The room was empty of furniture, and held only a few wooden crates and a large, rectangular, gilt-edged mirror which hung above an ornate wooden fireplace.

The room had bare, wooden floorboards; thick black curtains shrouded the windows, so that the only light came from her torch. Specks of dust flickered in its beams like hundreds of fairies dancing. But this was not a place where fairies would dwell, this was a house ruled by evil. A malevolent spirit rested here, that of a man who had assisted with the false imprisonment of her great grandfather, Tom Hall, framed for Peter's own crimes. This was a man whose actions had helped lead to the adoption of his baby niece and the murder of his own sister, and he also did nothing to prevent Tom's murder. All actions which had resulted in his own untimely death by the curse of Mary Hall. This was not a soul at peace. This spirit wanted revenge on her as the last true descendant of his sister's child, and he had waited a long time.

The dust in the room started to swirl around her, rising and spinning as if moved by some unseen vortex; a tornado of unnatural origin. Suddenly a crate hurled itself across the room narrowly missing her head. Her torch went out.

"Come out of there, it isn't safe!" said Jeff from the doorway.

The house was freezing, and shadows danced in every corner in the dim light from the broken doorway. He knew that meant a strong spirit presence. He shone his torch into the room, but that too was soon drained of energy, another sign. The room was pitch black.

"Show yourself, coward!" Stephanie called out.

Jeff knew she wasn't talking to him yet he couldn't see anyone in the room, or anything. She pulled open the tattered curtains, and they crumbled at her touch. A few more rays of light flickered in, forcing their way between the slats of wood that veiled the outside of the grimy windows. Her eyes acclimatised, and she watched as the shadowy figure of a man appeared out of thin air.

He stood by the fireplace. He was wearing a 1930s-style evening suit, he had a thin weasel-like face, curly hair as black as coal and his eyes burned in a venomous stare

"You came!" he said in a silky sweet voice full of bile and hate.

The mirror flew off the wall above his head, across the room, straight towards Stephanie and missed her as she waved her hand. An invisible force emitted from her palm had gently batted it away. It crashed to the floor at her feet, yet surprisingly the glass remained intact.

"What the hell!" said Jeff in surprise.

"How did she do that?" he thought.

"You can't hurt me! This is my house now and you have no place here!" she said, in a voice that made the hairs on Jeff's arms stand up.

"You won't hurt anyone, every again! GET OUT!"

As she said it, light sprang from her eyes, her hands glowed and the room lit up as if someone had flipped a switch. It was a beautiful room, full of expensive Art Deco furniture. There were paintings and fresh flowers, and the room looked as it had in the 1930s. It was flooded with radiance. Peter hid his eyes from the light, howling like an injured beast. Jeff didn't hide; he knew what it was and he had no reason to fear it. It was the light of pure goodness, the type of light that can't be extinguished by evil. This woman was truly gifted.

"You have been in the dark too long, Peter Trevelyan! There's no saving you now! Go where you belong!" she called, in a voice that echoed round the room, filling every corner like the glow that pulsed from her hands.

His spirit started to dissolve before them till it was no more than a smoky shape that disintegrated into nothingness. As it did so, it emitted a gurgling noise that made Jeff's blood run cold. With a popping sound, like the top coming off a beer bottle, the last remnant of the spirit of Peter Trevelyan was sucked into the floor, and beyond. Down to a place where he could never harm anyone again.

His darkness disappeared, then all the boards on the windows shattered, the vestiges of curtains shrivelled and turned to ash as daylight burst into the room. Within the space of a second, every room in the house exploded with sunlight and the last trace of him was gone. The room was empty once more, just a shell. Stephanie collapsed onto the floor, her torch falling from her hand. Jeff ran to her. She opened her eyes and looked up at him.

"What happened? Did I do OK?" she asked.

The past few moments had passed as if she was in a dream.

"Spectacular!" he said. "Jan would be proud!"

***

Minutes later she woke up. She looked up to see Jeff's worried face, he had been cradling her in his arms the whole time. He helped her to her feet and retrieved her torch.

"Are you alright?" he asked. She nodded.

"Let's go!" she said.

As they stepped from the cold, damp house into the courtyard, the sun was warm in contrast. They saw that the boards also had vanished from the windows of all the houses around the courtyard and every hint of darkness was chased away. The place felt warm again, alive, a place where people would be happy to make a home. Like Peter, the pervading cloud of negativity that had shrouded the courtyard for so many years had been banished.

They just stood and stared. Jeff was amazed. He knew from talking to Uncle Bob that she was capable of great things, but he had never expected that. Neither he nor Jan could have done *that*; not even come close. It was beyond remarkable.

When Jeff told her what she had done, Stephanie was stunned. She had acted purely on instinct, as if she had always known what to do, without thought, without hesitation. This was her true inheritance. She felt an invisible hand ruffle her hair. A voice whispered one word in her

MOTHER OF MARLIN

ear, a word that reduced her to tears.

"PROUD!"

It was what her mother always used to say to her. It comforted her to know that Grace was with her. But at the same time, it made her heart ache, reminding her of the emptiness inside because she missed her so much.

She wiped away the tears. Another strand was broken of the web that encompassed her. She patted the outside of her jacket pocket, making sure the locket was still there. It was, but she was afraid to touch it again so soon. The process was exhausting.

Next, they had to talk to Bill Judd, and she was not looking forward to that. They set off again, and this time Jeff led the way. She had no idea where to go without instinct to lead her, and her energy was weak: depleted by her recent confrontation.

"You OK?" asked Jeff, taking hold of her hand as they walked. It felt right, and his obvious concern was also very touching.

"Yes, good, thanks!" she answered. "How much further?"

The effort of sending Peter Trevelyan on his way was taking its toll.

"We're here!" he said as they rounded a bend. It was the last row of houses in the village. It had been fenced in and there was a gate. The grounds were full of bushes and trees, almost bare of leaves now. The house on the left of the row had a sign outside that said "MANAGER."

They went in through the gate and knocked on the door. They asked where Mr Judd lived and if it was OK to call on him. The manager told

157

them it was fine, but they weren't likely to get much by way of conversation from him. She led them to his maisonette and Jeff rang the doorbell. After a short while, a frail old man in a wheelchair opened the door.

"Yes!" he snarled

"Bill, these young people have come to visit you!" she said. "Invite them in!"

"Don't want visitors!" he mumbled.

"Now that isn't polite, is it! They took the trouble to come to see you, please let them in!" said the manager gently.

"Please?" asked Stephanie gently. "We won't keep you long."

Something about her made his glare soften.

"I suppose you'd best come in!" he said.

He led the way, Jeff followed, and the manager waved goodbye as Stephanie shut the door.

They both settled on a rather hard sofa in a small, immaculate but sparsely furnished living area. It made Stephanie feel sad. It was functional, but it lacked personality. It was the home of a lonely old man who had never been married. She took the locket quickly out of her pocket and laid it on the coffee table in front of her.

"Do you recognise this?" she asked.

Bill Judd looked like he had been shot. Terror spread across his face.

"Where is she Mr Judd?" asked Jeff. "Where is Emma?"

"It wasn't me!" he said. "I didn't mean to frighten her. I would never have hurt Emma. I loved her, you see. I know she was older, but, well the heart wants what the heart wants, doesn't it? She was beautiful and so kind."

Jeff and Stephanie looked at each other. This wasn't what they were expecting at all. The old man continued with tears in his eyes. He had been waiting a long time to tell his story.

"Yes, I admit I chased her, and she ran from me. I didn't mean her any harm. I tried to get her to tell me what she knew, to get her to safety. But she wouldn't hear of it. She laughed at me. I overheard them, you see. They found out about the treasure and they said she knew too much. I knew what that meant. After that day in the woods, I never saw her again and I suppose I just suspected the worst."

Stephanie looked at Jeff. His story was plausible. and he was obviously distressed.

"Who are they Mr Judd? Who was after Emma?" she asked.

"Why those boys of course, Bob Bishop and her son young Jason Jones!" he said, as if it was obvious.

Jeff's face wore an expression of both anger and incredulity. Stephanie just stared.

"Now wait a minute, you can't just put the blame on Bob!" he stood up, pointing a finger at the old man.

"Hear him out Jeff, please," Stephanie said quietly, raising a hand to touch his arm. Jeff sat down.

"Carry on, Mr Judd," she said, in a voice much calmer than she felt.

"They wanted the treasure, you see, the treasure that Robert told Jason about after the war. When he died, I thought it was the end of it. At least, I prayed it was, until it looked like he was going to confront his mother. He thought she knew something. I would have done anything for Emma. I offered her a job, I wanted us to make a life together after her husband died. To keep her safe from Jason and his friend. But she wouldn't have me. God help me, I couldn't make her believe me!"

The old man started to cry. Stephanie felt bad for him, reliving such pain.

"When she ran from me that day in the woods, seeing her so frightened of me, I couldn't bear it. Then when she... when she disappeared, it broke my heart."

He collapsed into sobs and Stephanie put a hand on his shoulder. Jeff's face was white.

"I'll make some tea," she said.

She was very thirsty again after what had happened at Quarry House, and she wanted and excuse to leave them alone to talk.

"Now it made sense why Emma was leaving alone; she was scared of her son!" she thought.

She soon found all she needed in the basic kitchen and brought through a pot of tea for them all.

After a while Jeff spoke. "I don't understand," he said. "Bob Bishop, my great uncle Bob, he would never do such a thing!"

"You must be Jeff then," said Bill, wiping his eyes with a clean, white handkerchief from his trouser pocket. "I'm sorry, son. He plays the part well, does old Bob. Hides behind that mask of respectability he's built up over the years. Good old Bob, kind old Bob. But he's evil! Him and that cold-blooded killer of a mate of his! Wicked through and through!" Bill's face wore a sneer.

"Stop it!" said Jeff. "I don't believe he could have fooled me like that. Stephanie, you don't believe this, don't you?" His eyes were pleading.

"I don't know what to think," said Stephanie as she poured the tea. "Hang on, did I hear you say that Jason was the... the killer?"

"Yes. But Bob would have helped him cover it up. Your great uncle was just after the treasure, whatever that was," said Judd, sipping his tea and starting to look a little better.

"Well that's a relief anyway," she said. "At least Bob didn't kill her!"

She looked at Jeff and felt a pang of sadness at the sight of his defeated expression. Bob obviously meant the world to him.

"I still can't believe he had anything to do with it," Jeff said with determination. "Did Jason know you knew about Emma? If so, why did he let you live? And why didn't you tell anyone?"

There were still so many unanswered questions.

"I told them they could kill me if they wanted. Jason tried to get me to leave, even offered me money, but there was no way I would ever leave

Marlin till Emma was found. But nobody ever found her. Before long Jason left for Australia. After he left, I told the police my suspicions, but Bob gave him an alibi. But without a body they couldn't arrest him. But Bob didn't dare touch me after that!" he said defiantly, then stared wistfully into his teacup, lost in thought.

As she finished her tea and poured another, Stephanie could see that the old man looked totally grief-stricken, and it didn't appear to be an act.

"Jason disappeared too shortly afterwards. Possibly he had fled overseas to avoid detection or arrest?" she thought.

"Maybe you're too close to this Jeff. He is your family after all. I think we need a fresh set of eyes, someone who won't be taken in. Someone like…"

"Jan!" Jeff and Stephanie said it together.

Stephanie put their mugs in the kitchen, then they hastily said their goodbyes to Mr Judd and left, heading for Stephanie's cottage.

"Be careful, won't you?" he called after them through the doorway. "He's still out there, somewhere! And please, find Emma if you can!"

"We'll do our best!" Stephanie called back.

But she had no idea how to go about it. They left Judd to his memories and made their way back through the village.

"About the men following us earlier," she said, just after they left Bill Judd's meagre home, "how did they know where we'd be? Did you text or call anyone to say we were going to see Mr Judd?"

"No!" he said. "The only other person that knew, was... Bob!"

Jeff looked like he had been slapped in the face; he seemed genuinely horrified. Maybe there was some truth in what Bill Judd had said after all. Could Bob have been playing them all this time, putting their lives in danger just for money? Or was Jeff still lying to her, deceiving her like Paul had? Was he working with Bob and the people that were following her? Dana too? Maybe she couldn't reach Jan because he had sent Dana to hurt her, or worse.

Stephanie was scared and becoming more suspicious by the minute. Her mind was all over the place. She rang Jan, but she still wasn't answering her phone. To either of them, it seemed. She thought about what might have happened to Jan and felt tears forming. She blinked them away. If she was on her own now, she would need to be stronger than this.

***

On the way, back to The Lodge, Stephanie felt dizzy again, so she sat down on a bench outside the library. Jeff walked out of earshot to make some private calls, but he was still close enough to keep an eye on her. Five minutes later, he came over to her and said he had rung the office, leaving an urgent message saying he needed Jan to drive down and meet them at The Lodge as soon as she could. Also, he said he'd rung Dana, to get someone to investigate his uncle and to see if she could locate any police records from when Emma disappeared.

"At least that was what you said you did!" Stephanie thought.

She scanned his face for any indication that he was lying. She was starting to doubt him again, and she hated herself for it. Worrying thoughts wormed their way into her mind.

"If Jeff and Bob are in it with the others, then they need me to tell them where the treasure is. But if they believe that Emma died without telling anyone, and I can't give them any more information from the locket, what use am I to them now? I'm expendable!"

She still only had Jeff's word that he even knew Jan, that Jan had sent him to help her, or that Jan had told him to stay with her. Would her oldest and dearest friend do all that without even telling her, and why wasn't Jan answering her phone?

Stephanie realised that there was so much that she didn't know. Had she really been taken in by Bob? By Jeff? Grace obviously trusted this man, this stranger; if indeed it was her mother speaking to her from beyond the grave. Was she losing her mind? She remembered reading once that the insane never doubted their sanity. Well she was doubting hers. She might be sane, but stupid. Her instincts were failing her. She felt vulnerable and alone.

***

They walked the rest of the way to The Lodge in silence; Jeff was lost in thought too.

"Is he genuinely upset about Bob? Or about what I might think of him? Or is he planning something?"

Stephanie was on her guard. She had no idea if she was only apprehensive again because Judd had put questions in her mind about Bob, leading her to suspect Jeff by association. If Judd was right, she had fallen for Bob's lies too. But then again, she realised that she had only known Jeff just over two days. She was usually a good judge of character, but he had already lied to her at least once that she knew about.

By the time they reached The Lodge, it was mid-afternoon. She concocted an excuse to get rid of him. She needed time to think.

"I have a terrible migraine, Jeff. Would you mind if we talked about this tomorrow?"

"But Jan wanted me to stay with you. I..." Jeff tried his best to talk her round.

"I don't care what Jan wants, I need to sleep. Please, just go home!" she yelled.

His eyes were full of concern and pain.

"OK, I'll be here first thing in the morning, here's my number. If you need anything…"

Their eyes met.

"How can I doubt him," she thought, *"he looks so upset, so caring!"*

"Thank you!" she said, taking the business card he offered.

As he turned to walk up the hill, she stood on her doorstep and watched him go. She felt sad, empty, and very guilty. She wanted to run after him, but decided against it. She wanted to believe him. He already meant more to her than she was even ready to admit. But could she trust her feelings? After all, they had let her down before. Her logical mind said to wait for proof, either way.

The migraine was partly genuine. She had a niggling pain behind her eyes; lack of sleep or food always started it off. Maybe a few hours of peace, a proper rest and a good meal were what she needed after all. She took her key out of her picket and put it in the door.

Then she glanced down at the card in her hand. It was embossed with Jan's company name, "P.I. Ltd." with her unique silver logo on the front, and it identified Jeff Dawson as one of her senior investigators.

To most people the letters "P.I." meant Private Investigator, but she knew it also stood for Paranormal Investigator, a service catering for certain clients that had a more supernatural kind of problem. Jan was fiercely protective of her business and the identity of her staff. Stephanie already knew that, so it wasn't that unusual that Jan had never mentioned Jeff. Some people liked to keep their psychic gifts to themselves and protecting his identity as a private investigator was also a safety consideration. But then again, anyone can have business cards printed.

Stephanie was so conflicted. She needed to know once and for all. Just then her phone rang.

"Steph, it's me are you OK? Jeff called and left a message to say you needed me. I'll be there in a couple of hours!"

Stephanie slumped onto on her doorstep, unable to stop the tears streaming down her face.

"Steph what is it, talk to me!" Jan ordered.

She explained her doubts about Jeff, ending with the all-important question.

"Jan, do you trust him?" she asked.

"With my life," her friend replied. "And more importantly, with yours! He's saved my arse more times than I can count. He's good people, Steph. Now, I have to go, but I will see you later! You OK now?"

"Yes, I'll be fine. See you soon!" she mumbled through her tears.

She said goodbye to her friend and stood up, taking her door key from the pocket of her jeans.

"He is who he says he is!" she thought.

She was elated. Jeff was who she thought he was; a man she could trust. A man she could… She stopped in the hallway. She was brought back to the present with a crash. Her house was a mess. No, that was an understatement. It was a disaster, worse than any damage caused by cats, more than even Shadow could manage.

Furniture was overturned, drawers had been emptied, her sofa and chair cushions were slashed open, and even the stair carpet had been ripped up. This was definitely human in origin. Someone had broken into her home while she had been out, and they had obviously been searching for something.

Instinct took over. They could still be in the house! She turned, slamming the front door behind her and ran up the hill, texting Jeff's number as she did so.

"HELP!" was the message she sent.

He somehow knew something was wrong and had already turned back to her house. They met just a little way up the lane. She ran to him and flung her arms round his neck. Clinging to him, both out of sheer relief for him being there, and for being the man that she'd hoped he was.

"I'm so sorry!" she sobbed, leaving her tears all over his shoulder. "Sorry for… for not believing you!"

He pulled away, and looked into her eyes.

"I understand," he said warmly. "Jan already told me all about Paul. Scum like that can put you off men for life and he deserves to rot in hell!"

She dried her eyes. "Jan just rang me and she will be here this evening."

"I know, she just called to tell me to come to your house! She said you sounded upset, then you texted. What happened?"

Then she remembered. Her house.

"The Lodge, it's been ransacked! Oh no, the cats, I forgot about the cats!"

They both ran back down the hill. Jeff took charge, which seemed to be a habit of his, but although usually fiercely independent, she found that with him she didn't mind. It felt good to be looked after for a change. He took her keys and let himself in, telling her to stay outside. But, of course, she didn't listen. He searched methodically, room by room. She followed behind him through the house, greeted by a scene of devastation in every room.

But the cats were safe, and that was her main concern. They had both been locked in the spare room by the intruders. Shadow was on the bed fast asleep and Maisy sat on the windowsill with one eye open, watching him. Stephanie hoped she'd given them a few scratches for their trouble; she disliked being picked up by anyone apart from her chosen human and showed her displeasure with her claws. Especially to men. She had hated Paul with a passion, but Stephanie had put that down to good taste in the end. Her cat had been wiser than she was. Her hackles were up when Jeff opened the door, her tail like a squirrel's, bushy and twice its size. She spat at him, not seeing Stephanie, then quickly jumped down, ran past them and down the stairs, hissing loudly. Maisy was frightened.

"Thank God!" said Stephanie, picking up Shadow and snuggling his warm kitten fur to her cheek. He gave a deep, throaty purr and bopped her on the nose. He seemed unfazed.

"Meeoo!" said Shadow.

His toy puppy sat once more in the food bowl; it made her smile, bringing back a little hint of normality. Jeff was on the landing ringing the police on his mobile phone. He came into the spare room.

"Don't touch anything," he said, becoming very professional. "They will need to dust for fingerprints. Has anything been stolen?"

Stephanie wandered round the cottage. After the cats, her second priority was her laptop containing her book draft. Next came her family photographs, which were still intact although the frames were smashed; they were her most valued possessions apart from her memories. She went in search of Jeff and found him in the kitchen.

"Hard to tell with all this mess, but, no, I don't think so," she said, feeling quite faint and sitting down, hard, on the nearest chair. She patted her jacket pocket, the locket was still there. They couldn't have been after that because Bob knew she had it with her. Her face was ashen, her skin clammy. Her beautiful home had been ruined; again. Her sanctuary had been trashed and it was all too much.

"I'll get you some water," Jeff said. "You've had a shock."

He sat with his arm around her shoulders until twenty minutes later when an unmarked police car arrived. Neither of them spoke, he just held her. She was barely aware of his presence at first. But when she realised, it felt right. In his arms, she felt safe.

Jeff opened the door to two detectives. He knew the officers and introduced them as Detective Sergeant Philip Dennis and Detective Constable Mike Adams. They had been liaising with Jan's company on this case and others and knew Jeff well. He chatted to them quietly on the drive for a while, then he gave a statement, and by then Stephanie had recovered enough to do the same. They put on latex gloves and paper shoes and wandered round the house for a while. Soon after, a "Scenes of Crime" team arrived from Wadebridge, and three men in white overalls scoured the cottage. They took her fingerprints; Jeff's were already on record as a former police officer, apparently a Detective Sergeant. Then they searched for any other evidence which might identify the people who had trashed her home. They found nothing.

"They were obviously looking for something, Phil," Jeff said. He had already explained about the legendary treasure.

"Well they didn't bloody find it!" said Stephanie.

Her shock had turned to anger and righteous indignation. How dare they do this to her home, whoever they were. Jeff gave the detectives a car registration number, taken from the car which had been following them that afternoon. He had taken a photo on his phone as it sped past the courtyard while Stephanie had been looking around the courtyard. She was impressed.

"They want something which I don't have. I don't even know what it is!" she said. "Unless they thought Judd had given us something?"

"You'd better make sure the old man is safe," Jeff said.

Mike said that he would and warned them to be careful. They had reason to believe that the men were career criminals with a history of violence, even murder. Phil said he would be in touch. Jeff nodded, and they left, with the Scenes of Crime van following close behind. The implication was obvious; they knew where she lived and she wasn't safe, and Jan had been right to be concerned. They thought she had what they were seeking and now Stephanie might as well have had a target painted on her back.

***

Stephanie was still visibly shaken. Jeff had promised to help her get the house in order, but first he insisted on making her sweet tea and a sandwich. Maisy had appeared in search of food, apparently recovered from her fright, so Jeff fed her. She sat purring on his lap as they sat in the kitchen. He was her new best friend, it seemed, because since the kitten arrived, her owner was out of favour. But Stephanie simply viewed the fact that she had taken to him so willingly as a testament to his good character. The doorbell rang and Stephanie jumped. Jeff lowered Maisy gently to the floor went to answer it. It was Jan.

"Steph!" she yelled, dropping her case on the hall mat, and running down the hall. She was dressed immaculately, as usual, in a grey

171

business suit and pale lemon silk blouse. Her soft, blonde curls bobbed as she ran to Stephanie at the kitchen table and hugged her tightly.

Jeff had never seen Jan like this before. She was his employer, but also his friend, and although she could be a little eccentric at times, as most psychics usually are, normally she was all business. A true professional, even when off duty. This side of her made him smile. The bond between the women was obviously very strong; they seemed more like sisters. At that moment, she was just what Stephanie needed.

"Hi Jeff!" she said a few seconds later, as she kicked off her unfeasibly high heels. "I'll get an update from you shortly, but for now will you PLEASE get me a glass of wine, it was a hell of a journey down here. The traffic was horrendous."

She took off her jacket and hung it on the coat rack. "This place is a mess!" she added, looking around.

Stephanie and Jeff both started laughing. Stephanie at her old friend and her familiar ways, and Jeff and this new side of Jan that it would take a while to get used to. He looked at Stephanie; the glow was back in her cheeks and her eyes shone. He smiled to himself and as Stephanie caught his eye and smiled at him, he felt as if his heart skipped a beat. Jan, of course had noticed. *"YES!"* she thought.

"How long are you staying, Boss?" asked Jeff.

"As long as I'm needed, and I've told you before, don't call me Boss!" she said with a smile to Jeff. Then with a wink to Stephanie she added, "Or until the wine runs out!"

***

As they all sipped chilled, white wine, they were thankful that the intruders had at least left a couple of her glasses and the contents of her fridge intact, although Jeff had to drink his wine from a mug. He updated Jan on recent events. He had informed the police about Bob despite his loyalty to him, omitting of course any mention of the locket and Stephanie's psychometry. If it proved relevant to her death, they could declare it later. Her despatching of Peter Trevelyan to the next life was also left out. It was a feat which had greatly impressed Jan.

"Knew you had it in you, Steph!" she said with a broad smile.

"She was amazing!" said Jeff, beaming. "Better than the time we sent that woman on her way at the theatre in Blackpool! Remember? Miles better!"

"The actress? That good?" Jeff nodded. Wow Steph!" she gushed. "If you ever need a job..."

Then Jeff explained about the light that Stephanie had produced. At that Jan was speechless and became very quiet. She topped up her glass; Jeff and Stephanie had only just started theirs. Jeff was amused. He had never seen Jan drink anything stronger than coffee before this.

"Well if I don't get a chance to finish this book soon. I might just have to take you up on that!" There was an awkward pause and Jeff took her hand in sympathy. Jan smiled.

"So... Bob!" said Jan, referring at last to the elephant in the room. "I had a call from Dana just before I left London. She said that she found out Paul had been ringing two numbers from prison. One of them was, in fact, Bob."

Jeff sighed.

"How much does Bob know? What's the damage Jeff?" Jan asked.

"As far as he knows, and everyone else in the village, I'm just a former police officer who took up writing after leaving the force. I told him I'm investigating the history of the farm and our family tree, and how that links in to the history of the estate. It's what I am doing on the side actually, it's pretty interesting stuff!"

With that, he winked at Stephanie. "Don't worry, he has no idea I'm here on a case. Nobody does. He thinks I have designs on Stephanie and has probably used that to his advantage," he said with an embarrassed smile.

"*Which you do!*" Stephanie thought. Jan grinned to herself.

"The other one was a man we know of as Jason Jones. As we thought, he moved to Australia soon after his mother went missing. But what we didn't know is that he returned two years later and changed his name, then bullied his way into the London criminal underworld and established himself as the head of one of the leading UK crime syndicates. His name is Jason Richards. I'm sorry Steph, he's Paul's father."

"WHAT? No. This isn't happening." She looked at him as if he had just grown another head.

Not for the first time, Stephanie's world started to crumble around her. Jeff put his arm around her protectively. He had no idea what was going on either, but he could see she couldn't take much more.

"With the news of her lineage all over the papers, that confirmed their suspicions. So, Jason used his contacts to set the wheels in motion to recover whatever it is they're looking for. It must be pretty valuable to go to all this trouble!" said Jan.

Jeff squeezed her hand. "I was wrong. He's worse than scum!" he said.

She squeezed his hand in return.

Then Stephanie became very calm. She glanced over at Jan and she looked into Jeff's eyes. She seemed to draw strength from what she saw.

"You know what, I don't care about him any more!" she said. "He is safe where he should be. Locked away from the world. We must figure out what this thing is and find it, before anyone else gets hurt, and before Jason gets his filthy hands on it! He is the dangerous one. Not Paul, or Bob, and certainly not Bill Judd!"

"Agreed!" said Jeff. "But just how do you suppose we go about it?"

"I know!" said Jan. "A séance!"

"What?" said Jeff. "That wouldn't work because Emma doesn't know anything."

"I know that!" she said. "But her husband Richard Jones does..."

"First, we have to tidy this place up, and we need food," said Stephanie. "I'm starving! Who wants Chinese?"

***

Stephanie had already discovered that the next village along the coast had probably the finest Chinese restaurant on the Cornish coast. Jeff was allowed to take Jan's car to collect their order while she and Jan put the cottage back in order.

"She must trust him because she doesn't let anyone touch her car, not even me!" thought Stephanie as she made up the bed for Jan in the spare room.

"Would you like to explain to me why you felt the need to attack my best investigator with a tea tray?" Jan asked, standing in the doorway. "The poor man comes all the way here to protect you and..."

"Would you stop! You know that's not what happened!" she said, laughing.

"Yea, I know, but I couldn't resist." "He's already the talk of the office over that! So, you like him then!" Jan poked her in the ribs as Steph plumped a pillow.

"Ouch! Stop it! You sent him here on purpose didn't you! What have I told you about matchmaking?"

Jan giggled.

"You do like him, don't you? Even your mother likes him!"

Stephanie blushed.

"I realise you've been ganging up on me with my dead mother! I meant to ask you about that. How does it work? How come he can hear what she's saying, but only sometimes?"

"He can hear her when she wants him to," she said. "Come on Steph give the man a chance! It's about time you had some fun, and you deserve a good man like him, someone to look after you. You moved down here from London without a word, got attacked by a possessed doll and inherited a crazy family. It's too much to deal with by yourself Steph! And he needs someone too after…"

She stopped, biting her lip.

"After what? Come on Jan, you can't leave me hanging like that!" Stephanie put down the pillow and faced her.

"After… his wife. She was murdered Steph. It was three years ago, and he's hardly looked at another woman since. All he does is work. But a few days with you, seeing you together, well Steph you've brought him back to life! If ever a couple were made for each other…"

The front door slammed. "I'm back!" called Jeff. "Where are the plates kept?"

"Later! I want a full history!" said Stephanie in a whisper. She remembered the conversation she had with Jeff earlier, and his face when speaking about what he would do if something happened to someone he loved. It made sense now.

"Got it!" whispered Jan. "But please don't tell him I mentioned it."

Stephanie shouted "On my way!" and ran downstairs.

"*Wife?*" she thought.

***

After a wonderful meal and a bottle of wine, they had coffee to clear their heads.

"You should never perform a séance whilst under the influence of alcohol," Jan said. "But as this is an emergency, I'll risk it!"

Jeff explained that you need to be in full control in case something nasty tried to come through the veil, the barrier between this life and the next. But he reassured her that Jan was an expert and would put plenty of spiritual protection in place, both around the room and around them.

"OK, let's do this!" said Stephanie, with more than a little trepidation.

Maisy was put in the bathroom with Shadow to avoid distractions, much to her disgust, then they all sat around the kitchen table by candlelight. They joined hands around Jan's crystal ball in the centre of the table, one of the items retrieved from her kit in the car. Jan had burning bundles of white sage propped up in glasses, both to cleanse the room and purify the energy. She said a prayer of protection, then she rang a small, ornate, antique, silver bell three times to summon the spirits and to further purge the room of any negativity.

Jan told them not to let go of each other's hands, whatever happened. This was obviously not Jeff's first séance, judging by his stoic air of calmness, but Stephanie was a novice and even with her recent experiences, she was becoming increasingly nervous. Jeff was sitting on her right and he smiled at her, sensing her anxiety, then Jan gave her a wink and she began.

Jan called in her guides and theirs to protect them and asked, in love and light, if anyone in spirit was there who wished to speak to them. If so, would they knock the table once. Nothing happened. If her guides were there, Stephanie was oblivious to the fact; to her knowledge she had never met them. She wondered if Grace was there. They waited for several minutes as Jan tried again and again to make contact.

Just as they were about to call it a night, a blast of cold air whooshed around the room and it became full of the sound of voices, surrounding them and all talking at once. But no recognisable words could be plucked from the din. The temperature in the room dropped like a stone and the candles flickered. Stephanie began to feel queasy; their energy was so strong. Then Jan called directly on the spirit of Robert Jones and said that no-one else was needed at this time. Silence reigned, so Stephanie assumed that they had all left. Then a stream of icy air blew out one of the candles.

"Knock the table once if you are Robert Jones!" commanded Jan.

RAP came the sound of knuckles on the kitchen table where none could be seen.

"Hello are you Robert Jones? Please knock once for yes and twice for no."

RAP again.

"Welcome Robert! Do you know what Bob and Jason are looking for? One knock for yes, two for no."

RAP

A big smile spread across Jan's face. Stephanie held Jeff's hand even tighter.

"OK, thank you. Did you hide it?"

RAP

"Yes!" Jan said, in delight.

"Now we're getting somewhere!" said Jan. "Is it in the village?"

RAP RAP

"Thank you, Robert." said Jan. "Not in the village then! Is it hidden somewhere in the woods?"

RAP RAP came the reply.

"OK, not in the woods. Robert, is it somewhere here, in The Lodge?"

RAP

This time the table shook with the force of the rapping and started to wobble. Stephanie jumped.

"Don't break the circle!" Jan warned. "Thank you, Robert! How do we find it? Jason's men searched the place today. Or maybe they already found it? Robert, tell me, did they find it?"

RAP RAP

"Good!" said Jan. "Robert, what did you hide?"

Stephanie spoke. "I can see him Jan. He's showing me a memory. He's standing in the office, when it was his living-room. He's holding something, a metal tin with a rosebud painted on it, just like the carving on the locket he gave to Emma. He's hiding it."

"Where?" asked Jan.

"It faded, he's gone," Stephanie said sadly.

Jan swore; Stephanie smelled sandalwood and her mother's voice spoke loudly in her left ear.

"HE HAD TO GO, HE SAID TO TELL YOU IT'S IN THE HEAR…."

"Did you hear that?" she asked Jan. "That was Grace."

Jan shook her head.

"I heard her," said Jeff. "I think she said it's in the heart?"

"What heart?" said Jan.

"No not heart, it was HEARTH!" said Stephanie. "She sent me an image, in the office, where the desk is, behind the plaster board is a fireplace. I saw it in my dream the other night. He hid it up the chimney!"

"What sort of treasure could withstand the heat of a fire in a metal box?" asked Jan. "Surely paper would singe or burn and gold would melt."

"Only one way to find out," said Jeff.

"Thank you, Robert and Grace," said Jan. "Go in peace!" she said, and blew out all the candles. She said a short prayer.

"Now we can break the circle" she said, and they all stood up to leave the kitchen.

It was already night outside. The room was momentarily in darkness, then it became   flooded with moonlight as the clouds shifted.

"Wait!" said Jeff. "We still have to find out where Emma is."

"I already know," said Stephanie. "Before she left, Mum gave me a message from Emma. She showed me a place in the woods near an old oak tree that looked like it had been sheared in half by lightning, close to a stone bridge. Does that sound familiar, Jeff!"

"Yes, I know exactly where that is," said Jeff.

"That can wait till tomorrow," said Jan. "Tonight we need to find whatever it is that is hidden in this house. It must be important if they are willing to kill for it, and none of us will be safe till it's found."

***

Jeff drove Jan's car to his house to collect tools while Stephanie and Jan cleared her bookcase in the office and moved it away from the wall.

Minutes later, Jeff returned with a red metal toolbox and a sledgehammer. To his surprise, Stephanie marched over and took the sledgehammer off him and knocked through the plasterboard covering the fireplace. It felt liberating to release all the tension of the past few days. Stephanie reached into the chimney on the left, and as shown by her mother, she found a ledge. At about a hand's length in, on the ledge she found a tin box. It was covered in soot. Rain had at one time found its way down the chimney and rusted it shut, so with the help of some pliers, Jeff prised it open. Inside lay a dull looking crystal about the size of his palm, pale pink in colour.

"It looks like Rose Quartz," said Jan, having a fine collection of crystals at her flat.

"Maybe it does," Stephanie said. "But that, as I was reliably informed by Robert, is the Rose of Alexandria! It's a rare, pink, uncut diamond that went missing at the end of the Second World War. It was mined in South Africa and stolen from a jeweller in Alexandria, its namesake, not too far along the coast from where the battle of El Alamein took place. How it came into his possession is unclear, but Robert brought it home with him, meaning to retrieve it and sell it some years later when it was no longer fresh in people's memory. But he died of his war wounds before he had a chance. Someone must have known he had it and wanted it for themselves, and poor Emma died because of it. I can't even bear to look at it."

Jan took out her phone and researched it on the internet.

"I found it! It's worth in excess of fifty million pounds in its uncut form!" she said. "It's one of the rarest diamonds in the world!"

"No wonder people were willing to kill for it," said Jeff soberly.

Jan touched the crystal and instantly drew her hand away.

"It feels horrible," she said. "It has very negative energy and no wonder, given its history," said Jan. "Crystals can carry the energy of past events, owners or rough treatment and what we have here is a blood diamond. Diamonds are often sold to fund wars, hence the name, and it would have been blasted out of the ground by unscrupulous miners. People have died since because of it too, as we know only too well. I'm not surprised it feels like that, especially with all the other events that surround it. I'll have to cleanse it."

She went to the kitchen and came back with the white sage, still burning, and wafted the smoke over and around the diamond three times. Then she placed it back in the tin and cleansed that too, setting it down on the desk.

"I'll stay here tonight, on your sofa, if that's OK," Jeff said to Stephanie. "I don't want to leave you both unguarded in case they come back."

"Fine by me!" Stephanie said.

"First thing in the morning I'll take the diamond up to London, to the Trevelyan family solicitor. It doesn't belong to them of course, but at least they can put it in their safe while we work out the details with the police!"

"Surely if it was found in my house it belongs to me?" said Stephanie with a smile, opening the tin and looking at it.

"Sorry, it's stolen property!" said Jeff with a shrug of his shoulders.

"Well you can have it if you want to find a way to deal with the curse." said Jan, looking at her phone again. "It says here…"

"Take it!" said Steph slamming the lid of the tin and handing it to Jan. "I've had enough of curses to last me a lifetime!"

"I've told you, that was a hex!" said Jan.

"Same difference!" said Stephanie, yawning.

"What do you want to do about the fireplace?" asked Jeff.

"Leave it open, I like it," she said smiling.

"What about the cats?" he asked. "They would love climbing up there."

"Ah, I hadn't thought of that! We'll close the door for now and work it out in the morning!" she said, stifling another yawn. They all went into the living-room

"Let me get you a pillow and a blanket," she said to Jeff. "I think we all need some sleep, and tomorrow we can go and find Emma."

"Er, it's OK, I picked up a sleeping bag from home earlier," he said. "And this."

He reached behind the kitchen door where he had been hiding a shotgun. He saw her look of panic.

"It's OK, I have a licence!" he said. "It belongs to Willow Cottage. My father used to farm the land opposite, and he needed it to stop stray dogs and foxes from worrying the sheep. Anyway, I'd feel more comfortable knowing I was armed, because I'm certain the people who came here earlier would be!"

"Not helping," she asked, her face pale

"Listen, Steph, the people that followed you and broke in today have probably killed before. Best to be cautious," warned Jan.

"What about you?" she asked Jan, not knowing what to expect. "Are you armed?"

"Don't be ridiculous. I might break a nail!" Jan said, with a flick of her hair.

Stephanie and Jeff both laughed. This had been a very strange week, and it wasn't over yet. Half an hour later, the cats had been fed and everyone was asleep.

***

They were all awake early: no-one had slept well. It was a beautiful sunny day, unseasonably warm again, but with clouds that threatened showers. Stephanie knew by now that these could easily blow over by lunchtime, or they could bring rain, hail, sleet or snow. Living by the sea meant changeable weather, which sometimes made it difficult to know what to wear, but it was certainly never boring. At about eight o'clock, as they were having breakfast in the kitchen, Jan's phone rang. Her face became serious. Stephanie instantly had an image in her head of herself standing in her living room, dressed all in black. She looked at Jeff.

"Death," she said. "Someone has died."

Jeff stared at her with concern. She explained what she had seen. He put an arm around her shoulders. Amid all this mess, she was happy because she knew he understood her. As soon as Jan finished her call, he spoke.

"Was that Dana? Tell me," Jeff said. "What happened?"

"Yes, it was Dana. Turn on the local radio," Jan answered gravely.

Stephanie obliged. There was a news bulletin stating that a local couple had been involved in a shooting while staying at their villa in the south of France. Their names were Andrew and Judy Trevelyan. Local detectives were liaising with the French authorities and the motive was as yet unknown. They all looked at each other in silence. The hex had been broken, but they had died anyway. How was that possible?

Then almost immediately, Jeff's phone rang. He hardly spoke except to confirm that he understood what they had told him.

"That was Phil, one of the detectives who came here yesterday. He warned us to be on the lookout. It looks like Jason Richards is getting desperate and has been seen in Wadebridge. They think he's on his way here!"

"I need to get rid of the diamond. We'll proceed as planned," said Jan. "But please be very careful. Steph, you will be safe with Jeff."

She drained her mug of coffee, in a hurry to set off.

"I know!" Stephanie said, looking at him. He was more determined and self-assured than she had ever seen him.

"What should we do about Bob?" he asked.

"Let the police take care of him," Jan replied. "They're picking up anyone even remotely connected to Jason." she said.

Jan grabbed her bag, making sure the tin containing the diamond was in there, then she picked up her jacket and headed for the front door.

"Don't worry, she'll be safe with me!" he said with a wink to Stephanie.

"I know you'll look after her," Jan said. Then she hugged them both and made a hasty exit.

After she left, Stephanie turned and looked at Jeff.

"I trust you to look after me," she said with a smile.

"Finally," he said, and grinned. "Let's feed the cats and go. We have work to do."

Jeff wanted to speak to Bob, to clear the air, to try to understand why he had betrayed them. But that would have to wait. They had a body to find.

***

They took Stephanie's car to save time. The woods were beyond the fields between The Lodge and Willow Cottage, fields which Jeff's family had once farmed. Although they could walk there, it was safer and less conspicuous to go by car, and quicker. By driving to the top of the hill and turning left then driving down a bit, they came out at the back entrance to the woods. Although she wanted to find Emma and free her spirit, which they suspected was still bound to the spot where she died, Stephanie was not relishing the idea of spending the morning searching for her remains. Jeff had brought a shovel and other tools, transferred from the boot of Jan's car before breakfast, as well as the shotgun.

"She will be OK, won't she?" Stephanie said.

"Jan? Yes, of course! Dana is meeting her in Wadebridge and they will drive back to London together. Dana will look after her. She's ex-army and extremely good at her job."

"She looked it!" thought Stephanie, suddenly feeling a little better.

Soon they reached the entrance to the woods. Not for the first time in recent days she was glad that she had her torch in her pocket. Jeff gave her the shovel and took the torch from her, carrying it in his teeth so his hands were free to hold the shotgun. He walked in front. Stephanie had no idea where she was going, never having been there before, and she stumbled along behind him as he led the way to the bridge that she had described.

The woods smelled musty and the air was damp as in her vision. Leafless brambles tore at their clothes and low branches waved ominously at them. Occasional shafts of light burst through the treetops and a river bisected the woods, no doubt draining into the sea at Tern Cove. They followed it downwards on a slight slope until they came to a clearing. There was the old stone bridge, exactly as she had foreseen.

"Look," said Stephanie, "there's the oak tree!"

Jeff laid the gun against a tree while he turned off the torch and put it safely in the pocket of his hoody; he had extra shotgun cartridges zipped up in the other. Then he picked up the gun again.

"Now where do we look?" Jeff asked.

"I don't know!" Stephanie said, sitting on a rock.

The area had an odd feeling to it, timeless and eerie, largely due to the strange tree, which looked like it might have been split in two by some sort of otherworldly flaming axe, but she suspected that it was probably lightning. She listened to the river burbling over stones on its way to the sea. There were no birds anywhere. No creatures.

"They call this Dead Tree Dell," said Jeff. "I found it mentioned in one of the books I was reading. No-one ever comes here."

"I don't blame them!" said Stephanie.

As she turned to look back into the woods, a shadowy mist appeared which grew and changed until it took the shape of a woman, walking purposefully towards her from the woods. As she approached, she could see that it was Emma.

"It's reputedly haunted," said Jeff.

"I can see why!" she said, looking round nervously and gripping the shovel as if her life depended on it.

Nothing stirred, not even the leaves. There was silence; even the rushing noise of the nearby river seemed to have faded away. The place was still and somehow held an air of reverence. Stephanie felt as if she was in a vacuum, then her ears popped.

"She's here, Emma is here! Look, over there." She pointed.

"I can't see her," Jeff said, disappointed.

Emma's face was deathly white and now and then she vanished and unnervingly re-appeared a step or two nearer, walking with a jerky, twitching sort of gait. As she came close, it was obvious why. Her neck had obviously been broken prior to her death, and her head was lolling about from side to side in a disturbing way.

"Believe me, you're lucky you can't see her!" said Stephanie.

Emma smiled at her in a creepy sort of way, and, without a word, pointed to the rock that Stephanie was sitting on. Stephanie shivered, like icy water was trickling down her spine, and jumped off the rock as if it was electrified, dropping the shovel she was holding.

"Here?" she said, in surprise. Emma nodded.

"Hear what?" said Jeff. "I can't hear anything!"

"No, she's buried *here*! Emma's pointing to the ground at my feet. I think that's where her body is!"

"Oh, I see! Move over there so I can dig," he said pointing to the oak tree, as if it was the most natural thing in the world to dig up a corpse in the middle of the woods.

"And take this," he added as she moved away from the rock.

He gave her the shotgun and picked up the shovel from where it lay on the ground.

"What am I supposed to do with *this?*" she asked, holding it gingerly.

"Just keep a look out while I dig," he said. She held the weapon nervously, looking around, breathing deeply as she watched Jeff digging.

"Grip it properly!" he said. "If you drop it, one of us could be injured."

"Oh, OK!" she said, holding it firmly, keeping her fingers well away from the trigger.

He grinned, reassuringly. Nothing about this scenario felt normal; it was like a terrible dream.

For about 30 minutes Jeff dug with Stephanie keeping watch. Emma stood there the whole time, with her head leaning on her right shoulder and her wide eyes staring at Jeff, who couldn't see her. For some reason, Stephanie found the whole scenario decidedly amusing.

"*It's hysteria,*" she thought. "*I'm obviously getting hysterical!*"

Then Jeff called out. "I think I found something!"

Jeff unearthed what looked like an old rug. Stephanie couldn't take her eyes off the rug; she recognised it. It was round. What had had once been cream was darkened and dirty, a little threadbare and caked in mud. But she could still make out a blue stripe around the edge. She was sure it was the one from her vision of The Lodge all those years ago, the one that Jason had played on as child in front of the living-room fire. Emma reappeared and stood there, looking down into her grave, humming a lullaby, the same one that her son had been humming in her vision of them as a happy family.

"It's you!" Stephanie said.

Emma nodded, then she vanished, and Stephanie explained the significance of the rug to Jeff.

"It looks like Jason did kill her then, if the rug came from The Lodge," he said, obviously sad at the implication of Bob's involvement.

Jeff dug around the outside of the rug till he had room to stand in the hole without standing on it. Then, putting on surgical gloves which he took from his pocket, he opened it up. There, on the rug beneath the burnt old tree next to the stone bridge lay the decayed remains of Emma Jones.

The rug had opened out in such a way that it looked like wings, encompassing a shrivelled body devoid of much other than bone and a few wisps of dark brown hair. She lay there like a withered, macabre angel. She wore the same clothes that Stephanie had seen in her vision: her ragged black suit and a white blouse which was now filthy. Her skeletal hands had seemingly been deliberately placed respectfully across her chest; on one she wore a wedding ring and in the other she clasped a small wooden car with red wheels. There was no doubt in her mind: it was Emma.

"Jason loved her!" said Stephanie, realising what happened, her eyes filling with tears. "See the care he took to lay her to rest? He even gave her his favourite toy car, the one that Robert made, just so she wouldn't be lonely. Emma wants us to know that. That's why she sent me the visions and why she brought us here!"

Stephanie turned and through the tears which were now flowing freely down her face, she saw that Emma had appeared again. She was different, radiant as if back-lit by sunlight although the clearing was still virtually shrouded in darkness. She was dressed as she was in life, and she looked happy. Her head stood proudly on her shoulders, upright as it should be, and she nodded to Stephanie. Then a scenario played out in Stephanie's mind and she related it to Jeff as he sat, exhausted on the rock.

"Judd was chasing Emma. They came the other way through the woods, as Judd said, through the fields behind The Lodge. She crossed the bridge, he caught up with her and tried to grab her arm, trying to explain the danger she was in, but not from him. He tried to persuade her to tell him what she knew, but she knew nothing. He heard voices behind him and ran away the way we came here today, just as Jason and Bob ran over the bridge. They didn't see him. Then Jason found Emma and confronted her about the treasure. He tried to get her to go back with him. They argued and she pulled away from him, losing her balance on the wet grass. She fell sideways, struck her head on the rock and snapped her neck. He ran to her, but it was too late. She was gone. She died instantly, and Jason was heartbroken."

Stephanie paused to wipe her eyes.

"My God, Jeff, Jason didn't kill her. It was an accident!" she said. "Bill Judd didn't see what happened, so he just assumed Jason was responsible."

"What was Bob's part in all this?" Jeff asked quietly.

Stephanie continued to convey, as best she could, the images that Emma was showing her. It was as if a video was replaying in her head of Emma's last moments and what happened next.

"It was Jason's idea to hide her body. He thought that no-one would believe the truth. He'd already been in trouble with the police before, so Bob agreed to help him. Jason went to fetch a shovel and a rug from the house to wrap her in. Bob dug the hole and Jason laid her there. He said goodbye and gave her the toy car which his father had made him as a boy, collected from the house when he went back for the shovel. He wanted something of his to be buried with her. She wasn't wearing her locket. In his grief, Jason didn't notice that Bob had stolen it while he was gone. I don't know why. After that, Jason didn't care about the treasure any more. He was an orphan, fearing arrest, so he fled to Australia. He fell in with a bad crowd and turned to crime again, as we know."

Stephanie sniffed and wiped her eyes with her sleeve. Emma had been waiting all this time to tell her story, and it was such a tragic tale.

"Years later Jason somehow found out that the treasure was a priceless diamond, and with his son, Paul, they devised a plan. Jason became bitter and greedy over the years. He sees it as his inheritance. He's been threatening Bob since he found out he stole the locket. He's been blackmailing him into helping them and passing on what you told him. Emma wants you to know Bob's in danger too, Jeff. She doesn't blame him for anything."

It was likely that with Bob's gift of psychometry he hoped that the locket might tell him where the treasure was. But he was wrong.

She turned to Jeff. "We have to stop Jason!"

She looked back at Emma who bowed her head in thanks, smiling. Her story was told, she was free.

Jeff took out his phone and called Mike, telling him where Emma's body was and asking them if they had Bob safe in custody.

"They haven't been to get him yet. We have to go!" said Jeff, standing up. "I told Mike where to find the body and I'll explain everything later. I probably broke a few laws here already, but it had to be done. She needed to be found."

Stephanie nodded. "It will take some explaining, how we knew where to look and why we decided to dig up her body!" she said with a smile.

As Jeff went to take Stephanie's hand to leave, suddenly he saw what she saw: Emma walking towards the bridge with her arms outstretched. There, coming from the other side of the bridge was Robert, walking towards her. He saw her and they ran to each other, then he held her tightly in a long overdue embrace. As the clouds shifted and a beam of sunlight hit the bridge, they vanished in each other's arms. Tears filled Stephanie's eyes again. It reminded her of Isabel and Tom. This was the side of her gift that she had come to love: helping spirits to find peace, telling their stories when they were no longer able to, and reuniting them with their loved ones. This, she felt, was her true purpose. Sadly, it was everything else that came with it which caused the problems.

As they turned to walk back to the car, Stephanie noticed something.

Behind the rock near the grave lay a bunch of wild flowers, dried and brittle now, but evidence that someone had been visiting this spot recently. The flowers were obviously placed in memory of Emma. There could be no other reason that anyone would lay flowers in such an obscure place. One thing was certain, Judd could never have managed such a task in his wheelchair. The location would have been inaccessible to him. That left only one person.

"Bob!" she said, explaining to Jeff what she had seen. "Maybe he kept the locket for sentimental reasons because he obviously thought highly of Emma," she added.

Bob's tears when he had talked with her about Emma the other day must have been genuine. It gave Jeff some measure of comfort to know that Bob had been paying his respects to Emma all these years. That he was not as evil a man as he had been painted in the last twenty-four hours. His faith in him had been restored, just a little, and that meant so much to him.

"You're very special, do you know that?" said Jeff as he took the shotgun off her.

Stephanie just smiled and picked up the shovel, and they walked away hand in hand. She realised that bringing comfort to the relatives of the spirits who spoke to her was also part of her role, a part which she liked very much.

"As for ghoulish apparitions and murderous gangsters, well those I can live without!" she thought.

***

"So, everyone has been lying to us!" Stephanie said, as they drove.

"Well Judd did say he didn't kill her, but he suspected she was killed in the woods. Jason never suspected him at all because he never saw him there, but of course Judd thought he did and he must have lived in fear all these years. We all know what happens to people Jason doesn't like!"

"But Bob knew we were going to see Judd. Maybe he told Jason about it. Did the police check on him?"

"Yes, he is apparently in protective custody; they're moving him to a safe house until Jason is caught. Mike told me earlier. Sorry I forgot to say. The only loose end now is Bob."

At that moment, they arrived at Curlew Cottage. The blinds were drawn.

"Bob never draws the blinds, even at night!" he said. "He likes to look out at the sea!"

He jumped out of the car, reached into the back seat for the shotgun, ran to the house and opened the door with a spare key. Stephanie followed him inside.

The house was dark and very quiet. She found Jeff in the sitting room, staring at the body of his great-uncle Bob, slumped in his armchair by the embers of a dying fire. Jeff felt his neck, he had no pulse but his body was still warm; death had only recently claimed him.

His walking stick stood by his side next to the hearth and on the coffee table was an empty vodka bottle, a glass, an equally empty bottle of sleeping pills and a note in elegant but shaky handwriting. It was addressed to Jeff, who stood there with clenched fists. He picked it up and underneath the note he found Bob's will. He sat down and read the note. Minutes later he broke down and sobbed as he handed the note to her. She hugged him then went into the kitchen and gave him privacy as she read the letter.

Bob wrote that he was sorry and told the story of what happened to Emma, his part in hiding the body. His version of events was identical to how Emma had just shown to her, apart from the fact that Bob had seen Judd running through the woods while Jason had been blinded with tears. He explained that he had been frightened of what Jason would do, so he had never told him, or anyone.

Judd feared what Jason had become and wanted to protect himself. Suspecting that Jason saw him in the woods, he told the police that Jason had killed her. Even though it was a lie, Judd suspected it to be true. But of course, they couldn't prove it because Judd didn't know where the body was buried. Bob had stolen the locket as a keepsake at first, then later he tried to use it to find the treasure. But guilt took over and he kept it in the hope that one day someone would find the body and his nightmare would be over. But Jason had figured it out. Bob hadn't told Jeff that Jason had been blackmailing him for information about Stephanie because he knew that she had the gift and might be able to find the treasure for him; once Jason had it Bob thought that she would be safe.

It seemed that Paul had targeted her from the beginning, just when she thought he couldn't stoop any lower. Jason knew about the legacy and Bob had seen her in a vision. Stephanie remembered how Bob had said he had been waiting for her; that he had known for a long time who she was. It had been years before she found out herself. He had told Jason, and Jason had sent Paul to target her. Stealing her credit cards was just a cover. What Paul really wanted was her fingerprints and DNA to connect her to the Trevelyan family.

Stephanie gasped when she read the next part, and her blood ran cold. Bob said that Jason had told Paul to marry her, to get access to her fortune then divorce her and get half, or maybe kill her and get it all. She felt sick when she remembered how easily she had been deceived. It was the ultimate betrayal of her trust and her love. She took a deep breath and carried on reading.

Bob was ashamed and he couldn't take the lies any more. His tears for Jason had been real; he missed the friend he had once had, a man who had changed so much. He could have told them where Emma was, but he was scared of Jason, of what he might do to him. In not speaking up he had put them in danger as well, for which he begged their forgiveness. But at least he could rest in peace knowing that Emma would finally be found.

Bob also hadn't told Jeff that he had terminal cancer and wanted to leave this world while he still had his dignity. He told Jeff to be happy and that he had made him his sole heir. He also said that Stephanie had been sent to Marlin for many reasons and she would need his help; that they were destined to be together, and he was never to let her go. He begged her to forgive him for his part in her misery.

Stephanie began to cry. She went back to join Jeff, who sat with his head in his hands and wept silently too, his shoulders shaking. All Stephanie could do was to hold him. When he composed himself he rang the police.

By this time, Stephanie had called to update Jan about Emma and Bob. Jan told her that the diamond was in safe hands with the solicitor, and the police knew where to find it. She also said that Judd had just been found at the safe house by the detectives protecting him. He had passed away in his sleep sometime in the past hour, around the time that they had found Emma's body. Stephanie told her about the note and Jan said that she was on her way back to Marlin and would meet them at The Lodge in a few hours.

Stephanie gently told Jeff about what Jan had said.

"Judd kept his word to Emma, as best he could, staying alive until she was found. Even after all these years he had still been too scared to tell the truth. Now, with Jason back in the country, he was terrified. They suspect a heart attack. I expect he simply couldn't take the strain any more."

Stephanie felt sympathy for Judd, a young man who had mistaken Emma's maternal affection for something else, and even when she rejected him he still tried to save her. He had only told the police what he believed to be true: that Jason had killed her. Yet somehow, she still found it hard to shed a tear for him. She felt like she had no more tears left.

"If I'd only come to see Bob when I thought about it, maybe he would still be alive," said Jeff, with bitterness in his voice.

"I think he did what he thought was for the best. Bob lied too, Jeff. He helped to bury Emma and didn't tell anyone," she said. "Even if it wasn't Bob or Jason that killed her. And he knew about Paul. It must have been so hard for him to bear the weight of all that. But you couldn't have known he would do this, no-one could. He was a proud old man, Jeff. He kept his cancer from you. This was his plan all along, I'm sure of it. If he had been arrested for helping Jason, he would have ended up in prison."

"I know. That would have finished him," agreed Jeff, the words sticking in his throat.

Suddenly, he looked lost, betrayed and abandoned by someone he thought would never let him down. Stephanie understood the feeling only too well. Jeff sensed what she was thinking. The thought that Bob had added in any way to the distress caused to Stephanie by Paul and Jason was almost too much to bear.

"I'm so sorry," he said. "Maybe it would have been better if you had never come here. All it's done is cause you more pain. I haven't protected from any of it, have I?"

"None of this is your fault, Jeff," she told him. "I came here because I was meant to. If anything, meeting you has been the one good thing in all this mess, and I will never regret that. I thought you felt the same?"

"I do," he said.

He took put his arms around her and they waited for the police to arrive, sitting in silence in Bob's living room looking out to sea.

***

The next couple of hours were a blur. An unmarked police car and an ambulance to arrive at Curlew Cottage. Mike and Phil arrived soon after and offered Mike their condolences. Stephanie explained that they had a tip from an anonymous informant which led them to find Emma's body in the woods; they couldn't very well tell them that the informant was Emma herself. The detectives took statements about that, and about finding Bob.

Phil and Mike were used to working with P.I. and they didn't seem surprised that she and Jeff had been present at both crime scenes. Phil received a call while they were there and reported that Jason Richards had been arrested at nearby Padstow, having rented a boat to bring him back from France. They had reason to believe he had killed the Trevelyans himself on the assumption that maybe the diamond had come to light somewhere in Sarah's possessions after her death. When he had failed to find it, or extract any answers from them because they knew nothing, he had simply tied up any loose ends by killing them. The beautiful blond child that Stephanie had seen playing with his toy car had grown up to be a vicious old man, and a cold-blooded killer.

"It wasn't the hex after all!" thought Stephanie, as she heaved a sigh of relief.

But it was small comfort. The couple were still dead, although not by supernatural means: they had been victims of another family's greed. The police had learned that Jason had associates waiting for him at the harbour. It seemed that he had built up quite a crime syndicate over the years. The men had been apprehended and didn't take much persuading to tell the police that he was on his way back to confront Stephanie at The Lodge. That was one encounter that both she and Jeff were happy to have missed out on. The police had rounded up all his other contacts too, including the men who had trashed Stephanie's home, and those sent recently by Jason to threaten Bob. Their network was crumbling, and without a leader it might soon fall apart, or at least that's what they all hoped.

Jeff looked at Stephanie and took her hand when they heard that the attending pathologist in the woods believed that Emma had died of a head injury and broken neck, consistent with a fall, exactly as Emma had shown her. Stephanie shuddered, not for the first time in the past few days.

It was four o'clock that afternoon when they arrived back at The Lodge. Grief, relief and exhaustion overtook them. It struck Stephanie that the house was still quite a mess, as Jan had described the day before. Although tidy, there was visible evidence of the damage caused by the cats a couple of days ago, with the ripped carpet and other breakages wrought by Jason's men, plus the hole in the office wall, unemptied litter trays, takeaway cartons, unwashed dishes and more. Stephanie didn't know where to start, or how she could pay to replace all those things. Her insurance would cover some of it, minus the obligatory excess payment for which she would have to obtain a police crime number. But the advance from her book and the money left over from the sale of her London flat wouldn't cover it. In fact, it was almost gone. She sank into an armchair and stared out at the sea.

'DON'T WORRY STEFFI. ALL WILL BE WELL!" said a familiar voice.

She sighed. Platitudes weren't going to help her this time. The stark reality hit her like a ton of bricks. From now on she needed to focus on writing her book. If she didn't earn some money soon, she wouldn't be able to pay her mortgage. Then she would lose the cottage. After all she had been through already, it seemed so unfair.

As if reading her mind, Jeff came in with a mug of tea, saw the look on her face and gave her and a hug. Just what she needed. Maybe life wasn't so bad after all. Then, Jan arrived; naturally Jeff had a coffee waiting for her.

***

"Jan, I don't understand!" she was saying, over and over. It seemed too ridiculous to even consider.

She had read and re-read the letter three times. It wasn't sinking in.

"It's all yours Steph! The cottage, the land the village stands on, the estate. Even the tin mine and the farms. Everything!" said Jan.

"How?" Stephanie asked.

"OK I'll explain it again as simply as I can. Focus on my voice! Andrew and Judy Trevelyan were murdered today. They died leaving you the sole heir to the Trevelyan fortune. This letter was left in the hands of their solicitor, just in case this day ever came. They didn't expect to die together, or so soon, but just in case, Andrew made provision for you to take over the estate immediately in the event of their deaths. When I went to their solicitor, Mr Markham, to take him the diamond, he had already been informed of their deaths and he handed me the letter. He's happy to handle things with the estate management team till you are ready to take over, but he sent you this cheque to tide you over for living expenses and so on in the meantime."

Stephanie stared at the cheque Jan gave her for £300,000.

"That's a lot of living!" said Jeff, with a tired smile.

"It's too much!" said Stephanie. "Too much money, too much to take in!"

"Well the Trevelyans were used to a comfortable lifestyle," said Jan. "Steph, the estate is worth millions! Squillions even!"

"That's not even a word!" she replied, the hint of a smile appearing on her lips. "This means I can keep the cottage?" The realisation dawned on her.

"Yes Steph, you can keep the cottage! You can pay off the mortgage on this place and buy as many cottages as you like!" said Jan. "Mind you, you own the estate and the village too, so why would you need to!"

"Really?" Stephanie asked, again, with a beaming smile spreading across her face. Stephanie finally understood. The cottage, her beloved home, was safe. That was all that mattered.

From within the cottage echoed shrieks of joy that could be heard far up the lane and even down on the beach where they vied with the cries of gulls that swooped and squawked, echoing the sounds of their celebration.

***

After the initial realisation and brief bout of excitement, none of them had felt much like celebrating. They were all exhausted and with Jeff also in mourning, they decided on an early night. Jeff excused himself after dinner and went back to Willow Cottage. Stephanie missed him as soon as he left. She chatted to Jan for a while over a glass of wine and took the opportunity to ask about his late wife, Melissa.

She had been blonde, blue-eyed and beautiful, and they had been teenage sweethearts. She was a teacher who had been the victim of what they suspected as a mugging on her way home one dark winter evening, resulting in her being fatally stabbed. It took two years before Jeff could go back to work and it soon became obvious that his heart was no longer in it.

Although he had spent the past three years searching unofficially for her killer, he had never been found. He had lost faith in the police force, and in himself. He had met Jan during a missing persons case that she had worked on in London. She had felt his gift and looked into his background. On sensing that he was looking for a change in direction, she asked if he wanted to join "P.I."

At first, he refused, so she told him to think it over. Then she rang him out of the blue just a month later and he agreed. That was a year ago, and he had been an excellent member of her team ever since, a leading light in fact. He had thrown himself into his work. With his intuition and strong deduction skills, he was invaluable to both aspects of the business, and he had told her that he felt like he was finally doing something worthwhile. She also realised a long time ago that he was perfect for Stephanie, so when the opportunity presented itself, and knowing he was the best man to protect her, she had engineered it so that they would find each other.

"And, that as they say, is history!" said Jan.

"I think we did OK, didn't we?" said Stephanie? "Emma is at rest with Robert, Jason is in prison, Judd and Bob have both already found peace in their own way. I get to keep my cottage and Jeff…" She paused. Something awful had just occurred to her.

"He's leaving now the case is over, isn't he?" she said, horror-struck.

"Not necessarily," said Jan. "There's something I want to discuss with you…"

***

It was a chilly when Jeff turned up at about nine o'clock the next day. Dawn had brought with it a red streaked sky, heralding bad weather. The wind blasted the last of the tinted leaves from their branches and it felt a lot more like autumn. Stephanie's heart lurched at the sight of him. She had had only just got up and Jan was still asleep. He had apparently been up early, planning the arrangements for his great uncle's funeral; he was just waiting now for the coroner to release the body. A suicide was the probable cause of death, but there had to be a post mortem. It was suspected that Judd had suffered a heart attack, but he had no relatives, no-one to plan a funeral for him. Stephanie decided to pay for it herself.

"I feel responsible," she said. "He was estate manager once and lived in my house. I feel I owe him that much. Does that sound silly?"

"Not at all," Jeff smiled.

Suddenly Stephanie remembered that there was somewhere she had to be.

"Lucy needs to meet her familiar!" she said.

Jeff said he would go with her and they left a Jan in her pyjamas making some urgent business calls, barely awake and bleary-eyed.

***

They decided to drive to The Forge, partly so that they would be in time to catch Lucy before she went to school and to avoid the sleet that was forecast for later. As usual, her mother Lisa had brought her over after breakfast for her to walk to school with her friend who lived a few doors away from Michael and Lisa.

When Stephanie walked in accompanied by Jeff, Michael smiled to himself. He too was pleased at the obvious happiness that Jeff had brought to his niece in such a short space of time. Jeff was carrying a well-pierced cardboard box tied up in a red ribbon. He put the box on the floor.

"Happy Birthday!" said Stephanie and Jeff in unison.

Lucy opened the box and her face lit up when she found the kitten. His toy puppy was in the food bowl again. The kitten woke up when Lucy stroked him.

"Meeoo!" he said and started purring.

"Hello, Shadow!" said Lucy.

She picked him up and cuddled him as his purring grew louder.

"How did you know his name?" asked Michael in surprise.

"Oh, Nanny Mary told me ages ago!" she said. "I've been waiting for him!"

The adults all looked at each other in shock.

"Nanny Mary?" thought Stephanie. *"The spirit of Mary Hall has been speaking to Lucy?"*

Bob had been right about Lucy. She had the gift, but what sort of gift did she have? Michael took out his spotted handkerchief and mopped his brow. Jessie sat down very firmly on a nearby chair. Stephanie looked at Jeff and they both stared at each other in surprise and dismay.

"That's who you've been talking to recently?" asked Jessie.

"Yes, and my other friends!" said Lucy, in a matter-of-fact way, her full attention on the kitten.

"We're going to have fun with this one!" said Jeff as they said goodbye.

"That's what I'm afraid of," said Stephanie looking grim. "Especially if she takes after Mary!"

***

When they got back, Jan was fully dressed, made-up and ready to leave, in a midnight blue trousers suit with a white satin blouse and killer heels. Her blond, bobbed hair was straightened and gleaming. She had made a pot of coffee, so they all sat around the kitchen table watching the waves break on the sand. Stephanie told her about Lucy. She too, was not pleased at the news.

"Watch her!" she warned and Stephanie nodded.

Today the sea was a bright shade of blue. There were no clouds yet, but it was getting colder as the morning went on. They sat for a while in silent contemplation, Stephanie thought about Lucy, and about Jeff, and the fact that it would soon be time for him to move on.

"Well, are you going to tell him, Steph, or shall I?" said Jan, the first to break the silence.

"Yes, I will! Sorry, seeing Lucy knocked it clean out of my head!" she said laughing. "Jeff, I'm buying into P.I. and opening a new field office here in Marlin, and I want you to run it with me. Please say yes!"

Jeff looked at Stephanie's wide-eyed enthusiasm and Jan who looked like she was going to burst with excitement.

"That sounds like an offer I can't refuse!" he said, surprised, but pleased not to be leaving either Marlin or Stephanie. "But what about your book?"

"I'm going to finish that first. I can write part-time while we set up the office. The paperwork on the estate should be finalised by then. Sorting out the premises should take a couple of months, by which time the book will be finished and I can work with you full-time. I already know the perfect location."

"Where?" asked Jeff, wondering why it would take so long to organise.

"Quarry House, of course, the scene of my first solo house clearance. What better place could there be!"

They others laughed. Jan was glad to hear Jeff laugh again. But there was a hint of sadness in his eyes. It would no doubt be there for some time to come, although she knew that Stephanie would be the one to banish it forever, if anyone could.

"I want to renovate all the houses in the courtyard too. Bring them back to life and rent them out as low-cost housing for young local families Michael told me that the village is crying out for them," Stephanie added.

"That's a brilliant idea!" said Jeff, beaming.

"Well, now that's settled, I'll be going!" said Jan. She stood up.

"Jeff, I want you to stay on here then and work out the details of the new office with Stephanie over the next couple of weeks, help manage the renovations and so on. I'm happy to fund it till the rest of Steph's money comes through. I'll hand your workload over to Dana and promote her to senior investigator. She deserves it. Steph, you and Jeff can feel free to employ any additional staff you need. I'll pop down from London now and then while you finish your book and we can open in the New Year. Does that sound OK?"

"Perfect!" said Jeff and Stephanie together, as he took her hand.

"OK then, time I was going!" said Jan and stood up to leave. Stephanie and Jeff followed her out.

As Jan opened the front door, she turned back and called out.

"Steph, I think you'd better see this!" She looked dumbfounded.

The ground at the front of the house, all over the doorstep and spilling onto the drive, was covered in baskets of fruit beside bread in the shape of wheat-sheaves and bottles of home-made cider. Corn dollies, baskets of home-made cakes, biscuits, pies and other foods were strewn everywhere.

"What the hell?" said Stephanie.

Jeff realised what was going on and smiled. "I know what this is! There's an ancient tradition on the estate to give the landowner gifts at Harvest time," he said. "Your secret is out! Is there a card?"

There was a gift card tucked in the biggest basket of all, and it said:

"For Lady Stephanie, Mother of Marlin."

"Steph and Jeff, have you got something to tell me?" Jan pretended to look shocked.

"NO!" they both yelled together, then they all laughed.

"Oh!" she said disappointed. "Haha, Steph and Jeff, I like the sound of that!"

"Stop!" said Jeff, laughing too, and attempting to ignore Jan as she winked at him.

"But what does it mean?" asked Stephanie, looking very puzzled.

"During my research, I came across an old parchment in the archives, telling of a local legend. It said that one day a woman would return to Marlin, a powerful woman who would unite two warring families and bring peace and prosperity to the area. They called her the Mother of Marlin. Mother is an old term used to represent a nurturer or protector. Everyone expected that the prophecy would be fulfilled by Isabel, but when she died, they lost hope. But it's you Stephanie! Because you are descended from the Trevelyan and Hall families who hated each other, you have united them in one person, yourself. The Trevelyans accepted you, in a way, even if they didn't want you to have their money they didn't really have a choice, and the Halls have welcomed you as part of their family. And, well, you can see from these gifts what the villagers and estate people think, and there is no denying what you can do. You've already brought the courtyard back to life by getting rid of Peter, and because of you they will be homes that people will feel happy to live in!"

"He's right!" said Jan, giving her a hug. "You're just what Marlin has been waiting for, Steph, you must see that."

Stephanie felt embarrassed, but proud at the same time. She did feel protective of the estate already. It was her home, her birth-right. She bore no ill will to the Hall family for the actions of their ancestor, and as of yesterday, she was the last of the Trevelyans. But her greatest inheritance was her paranormal ability, which she had yet to master, or even understand. She vowed then that she would use it for good, not for evil as Mary had done. She hoped that Lucy would do the same.

"Get some rest, the pair of you!" Jan called back through her open window as she drove off. "This part of the country is riddled with spirits just waiting to be moved on!" Then, with a wave and a smile, she was gone.

"She's not wrong there," Jeff said as Jan sped away. "Our work here has just begun."

They began to pick up all the gifts before the rain came in and ruined them.

"That's what I'm afraid of!" thought Stephanie, picking up the last basket.

Just then, a cloud passed over the sun, shutting out the last of the day's warmth as the sleet began to fall and a shiver ran down her spine. As she turned to go back inside, she remembered what Lucy had said earlier, and it worried her.

"Is Mary still hanging around, putting ideas into Lucy's head, corrupting the

child? If so, she will have a hell of a battle on her hands!" she thought.

Someone smiled as they watched her close the front door of her cottage.

"So, it begins!" they said.

PART FOUR: NEW BEGINNINGS

STEPHANIE WAS STRUGGLING with an onslaught of emotion. Happiness, love, excitement, nervousness, doubt and sadness, to name but a few. But the main thing she felt was overwhelmingly tired. It was mid-December, the week before Christmas and winter was tightening its hold on Marlin. Days were short and dark, staying very cold with inclement weather. Red morning skies were the norm, both beautiful and ominous like Marlin itself. Life had been very busy, to say the least. She felt like she had been swept away up by a tidal wave, thrown about a bit and dropped back onto dry land, like a castaway on a strange island. All was calm for now, but she had a feeling that something might happen to change that at any moment. She had taken refuge in her cottage, to recover and throw herself into her writing again.

She was finally making good progress with her book, finally working on the final chapter. She never thought she would make it. The book, after a shaky start and many interruptions, had ended up imitating reality. In her first book, it was as if she had been describing the man of her dreams, the love she was waiting for. A love which she thought she would never find. Now that Jeff Dawson had found her (or rather they had found each other when neither of them was even looking) the romance unfolded effortlessly in her story too, because she was living it. The deep emotions that she felt, the passion and her new zest for life were abundantly obvious in her writing, and on her face.

She had never believed in soul-mates until now. It felt like she had known Jeff forever, and she couldn't believe how lucky she was. They understood each other, often without words. They finished each other's sentences and had the same thoughts at the same time, something which she thought only happened in films or fairytales. Their love felt ancient and binding, yet it was new and delicate at the same time, and it its intensity excited and scared them both in equal measure.

From an early age whenever anything went well for her she waited for the "bad thing" that inevitably came with it; the downside, the Yin to its Yang. She feared that it wasn't meant to last, or that something negative would happen to counterbalance this great happiness that she had found. Her suspicion was usually right: anything good in her life, any achievements, had always been tainted.

She remembered how she had passed an entrance exam at 11 to a good local grammar school, but Jan had failed, so Stephanie chose not to go there. She had excelled at school, but Jan was not so successful academically. Her family had a comfortable life and Jan's family always struggled to make ends meet. When she graduated, Jan was already working at a modest clerical job, so the same thing happened. How could she celebrate her achievements and enjoy her good fortune when her best friend was heartbroken and had little money to spare? Stephanie didn't realise it at the time, but her caring nature and her empathy were what caused her these problems. It was also a part of her awakening gift and she could not ignore that either.

Stephanie had found love at 14. First love was precious, special, and she was happy, for a while, until her mother was tragically killed soon after. It seemed that every time she found happiness, something bad happened to someone she loved, and her joy was instantly overshadowed. Crushed.

"Maybe this time I'll be lucky," she thought, hopefully, then she remembered reading that in this world you make your own luck. Bu

what would be the cost of Jeff's love? Stephanie decided that there were some things that were worth taking a risk for. He was one of them, even though it was obvious from the start that she had no choice. It was a decision that had already been made: Stephanie Meares was hopelessly, helplessly in love.

***

Stephanie was also an heiress now, much to her surprise and sooner than she had expected. She had taken it in her stride, but not without a good measure of trepidation. Alan Markham was senior partner of the respected law firm Markham, Jolly and Ingles, solicitors to the recently murdered Trevelyans. He was now her solicitor by default. He had contacted her the day after Jan went back to London and sent her copious amounts of paperwork via courier, legal documents of the like she had ever encountered. Page after page to read and sign. She had to even take a trip to London herself a week later, to return them in person, give evidence of her identity; finalising the formalities. As of that day, she was formally the legal owner of the Trevelyan estate, including the village, ancient tin mine and farmland, houses and shops. Everything. It still hadn't properly sunk in, even two months later.

She had a meeting arranged for Friday with Simon Blake, a representative of management company currently managing the estate. He wanted to go through the accounts and bring her up to speed with all the business affairs relating to her inheritance. and to discuss its future direction. He was also making one of his regular inspections of the estate and had offered to give her a tour.

She had neither the time, the training nor the inclination to manage the estate herself, although she felt obliged to familiarise herself with everything, to make sure it was being managed properly. For some reason, she felt she had to see that everything was as Isabel would have wanted, and she fully intended to protect the interests of her residents and estate employees. Living up to her responsibilities as Mother of Marlin was something which she took very seriously. It would be a considerable challenge, but one that she was ready for, even though the whole situation still felt unreal.

In addition to finishing her book and getting to grips with the estate, she also had to oversee the renovations at Quarry House with Jeff. The sympathetic remodelling was slowly taking shape as per her vision. She had experienced a glimpse of the house in its original glory on the day that she banished Peter Trevelyan, so she had a definite idea of what she was working towards.

The renovation of the grand house was the first thing she spoke to Alan about after signing the papers. He had recommended a local architect. Blueprints were drawn up and submitted to the local council for planning permission which had been approved some weeks later. Funding had been released, local builders sought and contracted, and work had commenced in earnest.

Stephanie had no plans to live at Quarry House; it would just be a base of operations for "P.I. South West", as the branch had been aptly named by agreement between herself Jan and, of course, Jeff. As a new managing director of the main company, even though Jan still held the majority share, it was a huge undertaking. But her responsibility lay with this branch, in her beloved Marlin.

She would be its operational manager, Jeff would be the lead investigator, and they would work out the rest as they went along.

Additional plans had been approved for the rest of the courtyard to be repaired and modernised, so that the nine small cottages would be fit to rent out to local families. Her plan had been met with great approval in the village. She wanted to return the courtyard to the people of Marlin, now that Peter's dark presence had been evicted. She also felt that Isabel would approve.

***

Stephanie had also been doing some investigating. Well, in truth she had simply just interrogated Jan whenever she came down from London, which had been almost weekly. The subject was Jeff and, as usual, Jan had a wealth of information to offer.

According to Jan, Jeff was 36, a few years older than them. She said he was quite "comfortably off" in his own right so she could put her mind at rest that he "wasn't after her money." He had joined the police force at 18 and taken voluntary redundancy after 15 years, receiving, in her words "a not-too-shabby payment. Having moved to London eight years ago to take up a detective post, he also met and married Melissa there, and they had lived in a leafy London suburb.

After she died, he could no longer bear to live in the house, so he put all their furniture in storage and retired from the force. He had lived ever since like a nomad, staying in hotels and rented houses on P.I. expenses, never wanting to settle anywhere. He still had the best part of the proceeds of the sale of the marital home put away. His lifestyle as a lead investigator with P.I. already had taken him all over the UK in the past year and it meant he had saved a lot of his earnings too. Then there was the house and money that his great uncle Bob had left him, which Stephanie already knew about. It turned out that the will they found at his home had been properly witnessed and it remained uncontested by his remaining relatives. S

She learned that Bob had been a widower for many years and he had no children or other living family apart from Jeff's mother, Jenny, the daughter of Bob's late sister. Jenny was an attractive woman in her late fifties who lived in Wadebridge, a widow after Jeff's father had died suddenly of a heart attack in 2010. He had left her well provided for financially, and she also had an income from renting out Willow Cottage, their holiday home, usually to tourists.

Jenny knew that Jeff had been closer to Bob than anyone, always visiting him whenever he was in the area, so she was happy that he had been Bob's beneficiary. She was hoping that he would settle down and maybe put down roots again, especially with the new office and Stephanie in his life. The women had taken to each other straight away, and although they had only met briefly at Bob's funeral, Jenny could see that Stephanie and her only son were a perfect match.

Jan told her that the family "gift" had provided a bond between Bob and Jeff. It passed down through the men in their family, and Jenny had no brothers. Bob had none either, and with none of the distant cousins showing any sign of it, Jeff appeared to be the only remaining male member of the Bishop family who had any such ability. Bob had been his mentor, his confidante, and it was plain to all that he missed him terribly for many reasons.

Stephanie wished that she could have asked him about all of this herself, but she was afraid to intrude on his grief. She also wondered why her mother hadn't paid a spiritual visit lately. Jan had reassured her that she would pop in from time to time. In truth Jan suspected that it was because she felt that Stephanie was coping better on her own now that Jeff was around. It seemed that Grace had always been watching, since her death, trying to get through but she couldn't reach her till Stephanie had come to Marlin and stopped hiding from it. Grace had only ever wanted for her daughter to be happy, and helping her find love, giving her a nudge in the right direction (towards Jeff) had been part of that. She would be back, should she ever need her, of that Jan was certain.

Stephanie had also been wondering why a host of spirits hadn't converged on the village for Halloween, which she would have suspected. Jan had laughed as she told her that was all superstitious nonsense and the spirits who wanted to be there were already there, all the time. Somehow Stephanie hadn't found that thought to be comforting.

***

Jeff was still coming to terms with what had happened with Bob, both his death and his alliance with Jason, enforced as it had been. More than anything he was upset that Bob felt that he couldn't confide in him. But after a while be came to understand why Bob had felt that suicide was he better choice, considering his prognosis.

t was November by the time the three autopsies and inquests were completed, then the bodies were released. Bob's funeral had been an understated affair but well attended by the villagers, as had the one Stephanie arranged for Phil Judd. There had been a simple service for he interring of Emma's remains too, which Stephanie had also insisted on paying for. Jason had not objected, or requested to attend, much to everyone's relief.

The press had returned. Rumours were rife, and reporters were uninvited guests wherever they went. The news of the inheritance, and the various deaths that followed in their wake, had shrouded Stephanie and Jeff in mystery. It all naturally made for a good story, and the couple caused a stir wherever they went.

Of course, not everyone was happy about Stephanie being Lady Trevelyan (as she was now officially entitled to be addressed). But that was a matter for the locals, not a source of gossip to be shared with the wider world. The villagers had presented a united front.

"Marlin looks after its own." Michael had told them, and they had been touched by his words and the support of those around them.

The people of the Trevelyan estate had tried their best to support them both, shielding them with a wall of silence against outsiders, allowing them to retain as much as possible of their privacy and their dignity. But they had still viewed the continued attention interest of the press as appalling.

Sarah Trevelyan had been laid to rest in France. Her parents Andrew and Judy Trevelyan had left instructions with Alan that in the event of their deaths, they both wanted the same. Their final wish was not to be brought back to England, especially not to Marlin. So, Stephanie had respected that request, and they were buried in France alongside their daughter.

She fully understood their need to leave Marlin because of the curse and hailing from Devon, they weren't born in Marlin. It did however secretly anger her that they had been willing to accept the Trevelyan land, title and money, yet their last act as they left this world was to turn their back on Marlin. Not even wanting to be buried there felt somehow disloyal. She realised then that this village, the estate and everyone in it, already meant so much to her that she would defend it to the last, if necessary. Little did she realise what dangers lay ahead and how often her resolve would be put to the test in the weeks and months to come.

***

Recent events had brought Jeff's feelings closer to the surface around the loss of his wife too, as if any reminder was needed. At times Stephanie felt that Melissa's memory was always there between them, almost casting an invisible shadow over their relationship. He never mentioned Melissa and didn't seem to compare them. But occasionally Stephanie couldn't help but feel felt a little cheated, like she was second best. How could she hope to compete with his first true love and the memory of a murdered wife? She was like a saint, an angel that would never grow old, or fat, or have her looks fade. She wasn't jealous as much as saddened by that prospect. Her self-confidence had never been very strong to start with, and after Paul it was in the gutter. But little by little she was clawing it back.

She also had to deal with the recent intrusion of Paul again, into her thoughts and her life. The realisation that he had been even more devious that she had first imagined had left her feeling stupid, gullible and fearful. Yet the events since she moved into the cottage had shown her that she was stronger than she thought. She could see now that her instincts were good and her self-belief was growing. She was determined not to go back to being the scared, pathetic victim that Paul had created and preyed on, and Jeff was secretly determined that he wouldn't let her.

*****

Jeff and his mother had come to an arrangement following the funeral. Stephanie had met him at Curlew Cottage the following day to sort through Bob's belongings. Suddenly he turned to her and spoke, his words catching in his throat.

"I can't live here, Steph," Jeff said. "There are too many memories."

"I understand," she replied and just held him for a while.

He rang Jenny that evening, and they agreed that he would transfer Curlew Cottage over to her so she could rent it out. She would transfer Willow Cottage to him, but for Jeff it would become his home. It was an ideal solution, and he and Stephanie had continued living as next-door neighbours. That decided, they carried on with the awful task of stripping Bob's home of his identity and his memories, making it neutral and ready to receive guests. A lick of off-white paint here, a pale pastel cushion there, and all trace of him was gone; it was as if Bob had never existed. Although not to Jeff, or to Stephanie who mourned him too in her own way. Despite the circumstances, she had liked him very much.

*****

A week ago, she and Jeff had sat down over a mug of tea at her sunny kitchen table overlooking the beach, and had a long discussion about the issues that had been left unmentioned since the day of Bob's death: their relationship. The sea was grey, overcast by heavy clouds waiting to drop their payload of cold, winter rain. Night was falling. Strong winds howled around the cottage and buffeted the windows as she told Jeff that she knew all about his wife, and how sorry she was. He was glad that Jan had told her.

He said that Melissa was his past, and she was his future. Stephanie and Jeff both knew how deeply they felt about each other. They belonged together: that much was obvious, both to them and to everyone else. They both had ghosts to deal with, both living and dead. Nevertheless, they agreed to take things slowly, although they both knew that neither of them was going anywhere and they both knew that whether life kept them together or ripped them apart, they would never love anyone else. They sensed that they had been invisibly bound in love from the second that they met until their last breath, and beyond.

As he left that night to return to Willow Cottage, he stopped and turned to face her in the doorway. It was there, where they had met for the first time, that they shared their first kiss. There was no straggly, wet kitten, no spirits, no interruptions; in that moment, it was just the two of them; the only two people in the world.

"I think I love you, Stephanie Meares," he said, with one of his amazing smiles.

"I think I love you too!" she replied, with tears in her eyes. He hugged her, wiped away her tears and stepped out into the night.

As she watched him go, Stephanie knew that together, over time, they would help each other to heal. It was time for new beginnings, in ways that neither of them could even imagine.

***

Friday 18th December 2015 arrived. Jeff found her on the beach taking an early morning stroll at first light. It was so peaceful that they were able to forget her worries for a while. They had breakfast together, much to the delight of Maisy. She made quite a fuss of him and despite never having had a cat (or maybe because of it) he was quite taken with her too. Maisy had still not forgiven Stephanie for letting that fur-ball known as Shadow to invade her territory; she had been distant and as difficult as only a cat could be. The fact that Jeff had brought him there had been totally wiped from her memory and Maisy adored him. Slowly Stephanie came back into favour, helped enormously by the arrival of a straggly cat toy as a compensatory gift, which they named Baby. Baby had a habit of making an unwanted appearance in strange places, such as snuggled in Stephanie's slippers, or deposited on her office chair. She couldn't decide whether it was a compliment or an instrument of feline torture to punish her for daring to let another cat into the house. Jeff naturally found the tales of "the gift of baby" extremely amusing.

***

Stephanie answered a knock at the door at exactly ten o'clock that morning: the new estate manager was on time. Standing there was Simon Blake, tall and fair, with green eyes. A striking combination, and naturally, she noticed the fact.

"Come in Mr Blake, it's freezing out there!" she said, regaining her composure.

"Thank you, Miss Meares, or do you prefer lady Stephanie? Please, call me Simon!" he said, accompanied by a strong handshake.

"Oh no! Please call me Stephanie and this is Jeff Dawson, he will be managing the new offices at Quarry House."

Stephanie had asked Jeff to attend the meeting with her. Jeff instantly took a dislike to Simon on noticing his effect on Stephanie, but he was nevertheless relieved to see as they shook hands that his potential competition was wearing a wedding ring.

"Pleased to meet you!" said Jeff, smiling widely, feeling triumphant at winning a battle that had never quite begun.

Stephanie smiled to herself, immediately seeing through Jeff's enthusiastic welcome.

"Please come through. Tea or coffee?" she asked.

"A coffee would be most welcome, thank you!" he said. "It's freezing out there."

Maisy looked at him from the kitchen, closed one eyelid and hissed. The she went back to sleep, greatly unimpressed by their visitor. Maisy wasn't easily impressed by anyone.

The three of them settled down in the living room; Simon took an armchair and Stephanie and Jeff settled on the sofa. The sea lashed the rocks. The beach was empty apart from the gulls as Simon glanced out through the French windows while he sipped his coffee.

"What a wonderful location," he said.

"Yes, it's a lovely view," Stephanie replied. "Now where shall we start?"

Seeing Stephanie's keenness to get down to business, Simon

immediately switched to work mode. He asked where he could plug in his laptop, then he accessed the relevant documents and began his update on the current workings of the estate.

Apparently, the accounts were looking healthy. A good number of summer visitors had meant that business was booming in the village, and that meant that the shop-keepers' rent was always paid on time. Stephanie had a thought, which she aired.

"Surely if I own the estate and all the land and so on, why do I need to even think about making more money?"

Simon smiled, in the same sympathetic way which you would use with a child. His manner told her that he thought she was an idiot and a novice at this business, which she instantly resented.

"It's like this," he explained. "The wealth you have is on paper, like virtual wealth. Yes, you are wealthy and titled and you own property and land, but you still need to maintain the estate, repair the shops and houses and so on. To do that, the estate must pay its own way. The money you need to fund that, and drawings from the estate to live on, plus the cash to refurbish Quarry House and so on, that all comes from rent and various other forms of income."

Suddenly Stephanie understood. If her income ceased, it would all fall into disrepair. She was like those people she had seen on the television living in a crumbling mansion with the only way to stop it falling around their ears being to turn it into a hotel or a safari park. She had to make her land and property self-funding if it was to survive.

"Sorry, I'm rather new to all this," she said with obvious embarrassment.

228

"No apology needed. That's what I'm here for," he said with a warm smile. "It's my job to take care of the details on your behalf."

Stephanie smiled back, feeling a little more at ease. Jeff smiled encouragingly.

Simon continued, saying that the tin mine was now a tourist attraction it and housed a small museum and gift shop, which all added to her income. He said that there had also been an application to the management company to turn one of the outbuildings near the tin mine into a café and a bistro with thirty covers. This request by the landlord of the local pub, The Miner's Arms, needed her approval as the owner of the buildings. Stephanie instantly agreed; she felt like was getting the hang of this now. Decisiveness was the order of the day.

"Just what we need!" she said. "Approved!"

She signed the appropriate document, duly retrieved from Simon's briefcase, and he continued. Jeff nodded in approval.

Simon told her that the three farms on the property had been kept fallow, in line with the current EU agreement (which meant that they were paid money not to grow crops there). So, they were allowed to grow wild. Andrew Trevelyan had not cared much for business and despite suggestions to the contrary and warnings about wasted resources, he had been happy for them to remain like that. This was an issue close to Jeff's heart, as Bob had managed one of those farms when he was younger and he had hated seeing what had become of it. Stephanie agreed that the land should be brought back into use.

"What about renting it out to tourists?" she suggested. "For touring caravans and campers? Surely tidying the fields up, building toilets and shower blocks and adding a play area and clubhouse wouldn't cost too much, would it, with the current state of the accounts? And the farmhouses could be renovated to rent out to large groups of people?"

Simon nodded and Jeff smiled.

"That is a great idea," said Simon, "along the lines of one which I have broached with your predecessor in the past, but it sadly fell on deaf ears."

"Perhaps we could build some yurts or cabins later on too, depending on trade," she added. "And if we create more jobs, then less of the younger people will have to leave the area to find work!"

She wasn't totally sure that the locals would relish having more tourists in the area and neither did she. But as tourism was the village's main source of summer income, she didn't see how they could object when maximising their income potential was to everyone's benefit, at least financially. Tourism was, after all, the mainstay of many rural areas in modern times.

"I'll look into the cost and draw up a plan," said Simon with a smile. "Marlin is a popular tourist area so I'm sure it would be a lucrative project. I'll get back to you with the figures as soon as I can."

They mulled over a few other ideas such as llama farming, ostriches and such like, but agreed that tourism was their best bet, for the time being at least.

Jeff looked at her. "I think Bob would love the idea," he said. Then he leaned over to her and whispered, "In fact I know he would because he just told me!"

Stephanie looked a little startled. But then, she thought, *"Why should I be surprised, contact from the dead is becoming a regular occurrence at The Lodge!"*

Luckily Simon didn't appear to have heard him. He continued with his report. The quarry was another site which might need development in the future, but it was not viable for further granite extraction without becoming structurally unsound. Stephanie said that she would give it some thought.

"So, moving on, do you have any suggestions as to how we might increase winter trade, which is always a slow period here?" he asked, hopefully.

They all thought for a moment while finishing their drinks.

"What about writing or craft weekends?" Stephanie suggested. "People could do those indoors, whatever the weather. We could build an arts centre on one of the farms, perhaps by renovating one of the old stone barns. I know a few people who would make excellent tutors and I wouldn't mind teaching an occasional class myself," she suggested enthusiastically.

Simon nodded, agreeing that with her literary success, her expertise would be well received.

"You're good at this!" said Jeff, encouragingly. Simon smiled and made some notes on his laptop. He was obviously pleased.

"Excellent idea, it's so good to see you taking such an active and enthusiastic interest!" he said.

Then they discussed the status of the courtyard renovations. Simon told her that work was on target and asked when she hoped to launch the business.

"January 4th looks like the best date for the launch," Stephanie reported. "If the project is on target as regards budget and the building works keep to schedule, it should be ideal. Bearing in mind we have Christmas next week, of course."

She was proud of the fact that they had been able to use local craftsmen for the whole project as part of her plan for revitalising the area.

Simon agreed that her suggested date fitted well with his estimate.

"Then I will be able to get in and sort out ordering the furniture and furnishings straight after the New Year," she added.

"Jan is happy with that time-scale," Jeff agreed. "We have had a few enquiries to the main office about potential cases in this area which we will be able to manage more easily from here."

He glanced at Stephanie and raised his eyebrows.

"The paranormal kind, I expect!" she thought.

"Excellent!" she said.

"Very good! Now, moving on, have you thought about what you want to do with The Manor?" asked Simon.

It was then that Stephanie realised that she still hadn't been to The Manor. She felt uncomfortable at the thought of it. Simon explained that it was pretty much as it had been after the fire. It had been made safe, locked up behind a metal fence with padlocked gates, and abandoned. It was reputedly haunted.

Stephanie sighed. *"What on this estate isn't haunted?"* she thought. Jeff gave her a knowing smile.

"I think I need to see it first!" she said.

She told him that she had been busy with her book and other matters and hadn't had the time. In fact, she had been putting it off.

"Well, there's no time like the present!" said Simon. "I have nothing else to report so I would be happy to give you a tour of the estate, if you like?"

Stephanie reluctantly agreed. They finished their drinks, put on coats and scarves and went to Simon's car; a Land Rover Discovery. A vehicle befitting an estate manager.

'Time to bite the bullet, as Jan would say!' she thought.

***

Simon pointed out locations of interest as they drove. He told them that his family were originally from Marlin. His grandfather had been another of the tenant farmers on the estate, and his father after him, but then he had moved away for work when the farms became disused. Simon said he hadn't been to the village himself until he was assigned the Trevelyan estate contract in 2013. That was when the Blackmores left and the management company took over. He told them that Marlin had always held a special place in his father's heart, and now he understood why. He had a vested interest in seeing the farms being of use again and couldn't wait to tell his father about the plans.

Stephanie was pleased to know that also that the estate manager had such a close connection to Marlin. It seemed fitting somehow. Then Simon offered condolences to Jeff, on behalf of his father, and told him that he still remembered Bob fondly. It meant a lot to Jeff that someone still remembered him as the man that Jeff had known and loved. Not all the locals had been so kind, having read what was printed in the papers about his involvement with Jason, a known criminal. He thanked Simon sincerely. The man was pleasant enough, but there was still something about him that he didn't like.

"Shall we start with The Manor and work our way round to the tin mine?" he suggested.

Stephanie was agreeable to the plan.

***

They soon reached The Manor. The tall metal gates that were supposed to guard the premises were hanging off. The once proud house had collapsed, now a charred heap of bricks and mortar. Bramble bushes and ivy covered the sprawling expanse of decimated rubble and the grounds surrounding it. A cracked and rusted weather vane lay toppled next to a broken bird bath, amid tiles and bricks both charred and broken. The manor house was dead, yet at the same time alive with moss and grass grown wild. Nature had reclaimed the land, and it was once more a haven for wildlife.

It was a forlorn and dismal place, just as she had imagined it; a place that, in the grip of William Trevelyan, had brought only misery and death to her ancestors, on both sides. Isabel ran from there the night she was killed. He had himself ridden from there on the horse that threw him to his death, and his wife and son had been burned to death within its walls, now blackened and crumbled. She was filled with dread as she got out of the car and walked towards it.

"There is a possibility it could be rebuilt," Simon told her. "Andrew had quotes made and it would be very costly, but if that's what you want…?"

"Knock it down!" she said. "I want it removed, all evidence of its existence erased. Forever."

Jeff put his arm around her. She was shaking, tears poured down her cheeks. She felt a little dizzy, so she rested her hand on one of the gates to steady herself.

The wind whistled around them, crows called, robins fought for their territory. But all she could hear were the pitiful screams of the dead. Not one or two, but twenty or more. She felt sick, empty, as if her legs wouldn't hold her. She felt pain; searing pain all over her body. She was choking. Her eyes were dry and burning. She smelled smoke, acrid and deadly, taking her breath away as it filled her lungs. They howled in agony; there were so many voices. Then they faded and one voice remained. Stephanie closed her eyes and put her hands over her ears, not realising that the screams she was hearing were her own. Everything went black as she passed out in Jeff's arms.

***

When she became aware of her surroundings again, she was lying on her sofa with a damp cloth on her forehead, a blanket over her legs and her feet propped up on cushions. Jeff was sitting on a kitchen chair next to her, holding her hand. Simon was nowhere to be seen.

"What happened?" she asked.

"You fainted, but you're OK now!" said a woman's voice. Jenny, Jeff's mother.

"It's OK, Mum used to be a nurse," Jeff told her. "I knew she would be at Curlew Cottage, adding the final touches ready for a family who are renting it for Christmas. So, I called and asked her to come. I hope you don't mind."

"No, of course not. Thank you!" she said sitting up.

"I'll get you some tea!" said Jenny.

"How?" she asked. "How did I faint?"

"We were at The Manor. Don't you remember?"

It all came back to her. She buried her head in his chest and sobbed.

"It was horrible. So many people died there! I thought it was just Peter and his mother but…"

Jenny came in with a glass of water and a mug of sweet tea. "Here drink this," she said gently.

"I remember now, I saw it all. They had been celebrating Peter's birthday. Many of the guests had gone home, except a few that were staying the night. But the servants who lived in the house and others from the village who were clearing up afterwards were still there too. The fire started so quickly, none of them had a chance! I felt it, I felt the heat, their pain, and the smoke choking the life out of them. It was horrible!"

She stopped, took a deep breath and a sip of water. Jenny looked at Jeff.

"She has a strong gift, doesn't she?" she said putting her hand on his arm. He nodded.

"I'm sorry you went through that Stephanie," she said, facing her. "I've seem Jeff like this so many times when he was younger. It never gets easier."

"Are you OK?" he asked, looking extremely worried.

"Yes, I'm a bit shaken, but I'll be fine," she said draining her glass of water, the now familiar thirst taking over. She gulped down her tea. When she smiled at him, he looked relieved.

"What happened to Simon?" she asked.

"He looked confused to say the least! I made up some excuse about stress and he drove us back, said he had to get back to the office and left. He also said he would set things in motion for the demolition of The Manor. He said to tell you he hoped you feel better soon, and he'll email you in a few days."

"Good riddance to it!" said Jenny. "That place is hideous. Well then, if you're sure you're OK, I'd best be going too!" she said. Stephanie thanked her again and Jeff walked with her to the door.

"Thanks Mum!" he said, kissing her on the cheek.

"No problem!" she said. "Look after her!"

"I will!" he reassured her. "What worries me is that she went through all that and I saw and felt nothing."

"Well, it might be because it was related to her family," Jenny said.

"Maybe," he said, waving her goodbye.

He checked on Stephanie and she had fallen asleep.

"I need to call Jan," he thought, stepping into the kitchen in case he woke her.

Jan answered at the first ring.

"Hi Jeff! Everything OK?" she said.

They had only spoken that morning, so she was concerned.

"Yes, now it is!" He told her what Stephanie had experienced at The Manor.

"Did she touch anything?" she asked.

"Yes, she felt dizzy and leaned on the gate," he replied.

"That would be it then! It sounds to me like it might be linked to her psychometry. She picked up on the energy of past events, like she did with the locket before, but with so many images, so many people and so much negativity, it's no wonder she freaked out!"

"Why didn't I feel anything?" Jeff asked.

"Because that isn't part of your gift, Jeff. Occasionally you get premonitions and feel spirit energies approaching, and you have seen spirits. But you can't do psychometry. Hell, even I can't do that!" she said laughing. "But there is another possibility. Either there were no spirits there, and she was just replaying a past event, well as powerful and horrible as it was, it can't hurt her. Or, as I suspect, there were many spirits still trapped there, and the vision came to her because only she can move them on, as Mother of Marlin. You couldn't see Emma either, could you?"

"No, and I didn't see Peter, just what she did to him and the sound of his screams as he went straight to hell." he said. "But I did see Emma once she held my hand."

"That will come in useful," Jan said. "For now, just make sure she rests and eats something and drinks a lot of fluids. And doesn't do anything stupid!"

"You're right. She's fast asleep now. Don't worry, I'll keep a close eye on her, but that last part will take some work, she's very... pro-active, isn't she?" said Jeff.

"Tell me about it!" said Jan.

"Thanks Jan, I knew you'd be able to help," said Jeff.

"That's what friends are for," she said. "Give Steph my love and tell her I'll call her in the morning. Oh, before I forget, how was the meeting?"

Jeff told her about Simon's visit and discussed some P.I. business, then he said he would see her later.

He went into the living room and stood for a while just watching Stephanie sleep. He hoped that was the end of it. But he had a strong suspicion, like Jan, that this was not over and that thought made him very uneasy. She was new to all this and capable as he knew she was, he didn't want her burning out. He settled in the armchair nearest the sofa and tried to watch TV with the volume low as she slept. Maisy jumped onto his lap purring and kneading with her claws, so he picked her up and put a cushion under her feet.

"Those needles hurt, madam," he whispered.

Very soon, thanks to the rhythmic sound of the wind, night falling and the soothing purrs of a very happy cat, he fell asleep and so did Maisy.

***

When Stephanie woke up she was surprised to see that it was six o'clock, and already dark. She looked over and saw Jeff fast asleep on the chair with Maisy curled up on his lap. She smiled to herself and stood up. Her legs felt a little shaky as she went over to turn the TV off. She felt much better, although not having eaten since breakfast, she was very hungry. She went into the kitchen and started preparing an omelette.

Her thoughts turned to what happened at The Manor. It was as if she had been reliving the pain of every person that died in the fire. It had been unbearable; little wonder that she had passed out.

"How was that even possible?" she thought. *"What is the point of putting me through that?"*

Then she understood. The spirits were desperate to escape that place and only she could help them.

Soon Jeff was woken up by the sound of Stephanie clattering about in a cupboard, looking for a frying-pan. He went into the kitchen with Maisy close behind. Stephanie smiled when she saw him and gave him a hug.

"Thanks for catching me earlier," she said.

"You've put on a few pounds you know…" he said as she swatted him with a tea towel.

They ate in the kitchen. He told her he'd spoken to Jan and told her what she said.   "That all makes sense," said Stephanie. "It was so awful, Jeff! You're lucky you didn't experience it. I never even considered that anyone else might have been there in the fire, I thought it was only Peter and Julia," she said. "What Mary did…"

"I know," he said. "Grief can make people crazy."

He looked away, out to sea, into the darkness. He was lost for a moment somewhere in the past, in a time before she knew him, and Stephanie felt suddenly alone. After a few minutes of quiet contemplation, she spoke.

"I felt them, Jeff, all of them, pleading with me to end their torment. It wasn't just a vision, they're still there and they want me to set them free. I saw Julia, servants, guests, everyone but Peter, but of course we know he's already gone. If it had been just a replay of a memory, Peter would have been there too. They're earthbound spirits, Jeff, every one of them. I need to release them and I have to do it tonight. They've waited too long already."

"I was afraid you were going to say that," he said with a sigh. "I suppose there's nothing I can do to persuade you to leave it till tomorrow, at least?"

"Not a chance!" she said defiantly.

***

By seven o'clock they were in Stephanie's car. Jeff was driving because she still felt a bit disoriented. She was drinking from a bottle of water, silent and determined. Jeff was still trying to persuade her to wait till morning, and she was having none of it.

"If you had seen them…!" she started.

"OK, I give in!" said Jeff.

They arrived at the ruins of The Hall. They each had large torches that P.I. used for such nocturnal jaunts. which Jeff kept in the boot of his car along with a few other essential items. Burning sage would be useless on a night such as this, with high winds and now the slightest whisper of snow being swept about by the gale.

"Dancing and swirling like tiny, white moths!" she thought, reminding her suddenly of Isabel, and that thought gave her strength.

For protection, Jeff called in their guides. Stephanie realised that she didn't yet know who her guide was. Jan had told her that it was an ageless spirit, who had never lived in human form, but whose only purpose was to protect and guide her through this life. An ally who would be revealed to her when she was ready, or when she needed them most.

"If there ever was a time," she thought *"this is it! Are you there?"* she thought.

"I AM ALWAYS WITH YOU, YOU ONLY NEED TO ASK!" said a gentle

male voice beside her and she felt a hand on her right shoulder.

She turned and saw him, a tall distinguished-looking man of indeterminate age, in a smart black suit. He had pale blue eyes and a calming manner, and she felt like she knew him. His voice was somehow familiar even though she couldn't remember where she had heard it before. She wondered what his name was, and instantly he told her.

"LUCAS!" he said, and she silently thanked him.

"I'M HERE TOO, STEFFI!" came the voice of her mother.

Standing just behind her and to the left, Grace put a hand on her other shoulder. Stephanie was overcome with emotion she saw her and felt the love in her gentle touch. She tried to steel herself, taking comfort from her presence; she had work to do.

"OK then now we're all here, it's time to begin!" said Jeff.

He had heard both Lucas and Grace, but wasn't able to see them.

Stephanie, still fighting back the tears, just nodded. Jeff made the affirmation that they were safe and protected in a circle of love and light. He explained that it would help to reduce the effects of the emotions she had experienced before, protecting them both from their full effect so that she could do what was needed.

Suddenly The Manor appeared before her, whole but ablaze. Voices started screaming and the smell of smoke reached her nostrils. But this time it was as if she was an onlooker, not a participant in the tragedy. She felt no fear, or pain; there were no choking or burning sensations.

Instinct took over.

"STOP!" she cried, and the image froze before her eyes.

"COME!" she called, and one by one, more than twenty people rose up and stepped out of the flames.

"They're here, I can feel them this time!" said Jeff. But he still saw nothing but ruins.

They rose on broken limbs, in flaming, tattered, remnants of clothes. Their skin was sooty and blistered from weeping burns, and gashes caused by masonry when the ceilings fell and the house collapsed on itself. It was a nightmarish vision. Stephanie swallowed hard and blinked.

"Their spirits have been released from the flames!" she said in a faraway voice.

Their combined energy was making her nauseous, she could feel it getting stronger as they approached. Somehow the hands on her shoulders gave her strength. It was as if without words they were guiding her towards what had to be done, awakening knowledge that she already had. She took Jeff's hand and immediately he could see what she saw.

"My God!" he gasped. Unbidden tears clouded his vision. "Those poor souls!"

With his other hand, he wiped his eyes and glanced back at the house; it stood there intact and majestic, as it had been before the fire. Like a resplendent phoenix, it had risen once more from this place of the dead.

All the lights were on and there was music playing as the people walked away from it; a 1930s jazz band echoed through the stillness, a ghastly reminder of a happy evening that had ended in carnage.

The manor house that revealed itself to them now had certainly been beautiful. With four floors, it boasted Gothic-style arches, towers and turrets. It had ornate gables and brightly coloured stained glass windows adorned by thick, red velvet curtains. The impressive stone building bore all the hallmarks of Victorian charm, and stood in immaculately kept gardens.

Stephanie reached out her other hand and beckoned the people to her. As they walked, they began to glow. Their screams stopped, their injuries began to fade; disfigured faces healed and became whole once again, like the house they were walking away from. They looked as they had done in life before the fire; their torment was over. One by one the crowd came towards her, and as they did so, they all began to smile. They formed a group in front of her and Jeff, bowing to her in thanks.

They stood for a few seconds, looking at her in awe, the one that they had been waiting for. Servants in uniform, musicians, villagers and even a couple of guests who had died whilst waiting for their cars to collect them. Among them stood overnight guests in their nightclothes, struck down either getting ready for bed or having died in their sleep. No-one spoke.

Then silently, they moved aside to allow a woman to come to the front; she looked very much like Isabel. She was very attractive, and she wore a tasteful, black, beaded 1930s party dress. Her brunette bob of hair was set in waves, as was fashionable in that era, and a band of black, sequinned material adorned her head. Her eyes were bright with tears.

Before them stood Julia Trevelyan.

"Thank you, Lady Stephanie!" said the woman. "We have waited so long for you, but we knew that you would come. Mary, she wouldn't let us leave. Be careful! She…"

"Mother!" Suddenly a voice called from behind them. Stephanie turned around and there was Isabel, reaching out her hand to Julia. As she did, the hands that had rested on Stephanie's shoulders fell away as Grace and Lucas stepped back and vanished.

Julia stopped speaking and ran to her child, together once more after so long apart. As she and Jeff moved aside to let her pass, the others formed a line behind her and walked slowly, one by one in procession towards Isabel.

Each one whispered *"Thank you!"* as they passed Stephanie, their voices hushed as if in prayer. Isabel took her mother's hand. A wall of white light appeared, surrounded by a border of shimmering silver. The entrance to forever. As they watched in awe, Isabel led her mother through it, stopping only to wave in gratitude to Stephanie before she left. The others soon followed, vanishing into the light, free at last. Then the light shrank to nothingness and was gone. It was dark and still apart from the sound of the wind. Jeff looked back at The Manor and it lay once more in ruins.

"How the hell did I do that?" Stephanie asked herself.

She was reeling from what had happened. She had just met Isabel's mother, another innocent in all this, and freed her to join her daughter in a far better place than either of them had known in life, along with many other trapped spirits. She had also seen her own mother again.

after fifteen long years apart. Her shoulders shook and Jeff realised she was sobbing. She fell to the ground in the snow, unable to move or speak. No words could have been enough to describe what she was feeling.

Jeff put their torches in his pockets and helped her to her feet. The snow was coming down heavily by now and he wanted to get her back home. He had to carry her to the car: she was drained of energy. He opened the passenger door, made sure she was comfortable and did up her seatbelt. He marvelled at her achievement and felt desperately sad for the people that they had seen. He felt anger at the immeasurable pain that Mary had caused, not only to those that she felt responsible for her son's death, but also to Isabel and the other innocent victims of the fire. He understood loss and a thirst for vengeance, but what he had just witnessed went far beyond that.

He drove to The Lodge as fast as the weather and the snow-covered roads would allow. Stephanie appeared dazed, and she felt severely weakened. She began to fall asleep, but then she stirred, and Jeff handed her the bottle of water which she soon finished.

They had been out less than an hour, but the snow was already falling thick and fast; it had become a blizzard. He settled her on the sofa with an extra blanket and made some hot chocolate. They drank it in silence as the snow fell. Soon the ground became white, the snowflakes whirling and glistening like millions of stars, purifying the place where the souls of the lost had finally found their way home.

***

Stephanie woke up. She was surprised to realise that she had spent the night on the sofa. Her neck felt very stiff, but she also felt somehow refreshed. Then she remembered.

"The Manor!" she thought.

She felt sad, but pleased at the same time. She had done what she set out to do, however she had managed it. Maisy was lying by her side on the sofa, wedged behind her knees. She stretched, pushed her gently onto the floor and stood up. Jeff was again fast asleep in the armchair, he had insisted that he didn't want to leave her. She smiled. They hadn't spoken much after getting back; she had been exhausted. But she remembered how attentive he had been, how worried. She looked out at the bay and it was white with a snow; the sight struck her as odd. Unnatural. The beach just didn't look right with snow on it.

Her head ached like she had been drinking the night before.

"It must be dehydration!" she thought, as she made her way to the kitchen to make tea. Then she had even more of a surprise when she looked at the clock, it was almost noon. Just then her mobile phone rang, but she couldn't find it. She realised it was still in her jacket where it had remained since they got home the night before. It was Jan. She told her what had happened at The Manor.

"I told him not to let you do anything stupid!" Jan said. "Where is he?"

"When have you known anyone dissuade me from anything once my mind was made up?" she replied. "And he's still asleep!"

"What, you mean… he stayed over?" Jan said excitedly.

"In an armchair, Jan!" she said smiling. Jan sounded disappointed. "I fell asleep on the sofa when we got back and he must have been afraid to leave me."

"Oh, I see. Aaw, he's so sweet! I told you he was right for you! How are you feeling after last night?" she asked

"Exhausted! But a little pleased with myself!" she admitted.

"You should be! Steph that was an amazing thing you did," said Jan. "Talk about a baptism of fire! No pun intended," she said with a stifled giggle. "You will be a fine addition to P.I.!"

"Thanks!" Stephanie replied, smiling to herself. "Jeff helped, and I met my guide, his name is Lucas. Mum was there and..."

"Slow down! Who, what?" said Jan.

Stephanie explained.

"About time you met him!" she said. "The poor fella's been waiting a long time!"

Jan was pleased to hear that Jeff could see what Stephanie was seeing when she held his hand.

"I was right!" Jan thought.

Then Stephanie told her about what Julia had said about Mary.

"Powerful witches, even as spirits, can prevent weaker spirits from moving on. They're not satisfied with just causing their death, they want to control them even after death, extending the hex into the afterlife. It sounds like Mary is one of them. They can be very dangerous. That must be why Peter was still here too. They can even exert the same power on those affected by the hex after they die themselves, and Mary died not long after the fire. Serve her right!"

"Yes, but, you don't think…?" she asked.

"That Mary is still around? After that, hell, yes!" said Jan. "When spirits warn you you'd better listen. Wake Jeff, stay in and lock the doors, I'm coming down there!"

"What use would it be to lock the doors?" she asked. "Jan?" But Jan had gone.

"I didn't have time to tell her about the snow!" she thought.

***

Jeff woke up; he heard someone talking. At first, he was a bit confused to find himself in a chair at The Lodge, again. Then he remembered. Stephanie, where was she?

He found her in the kitchen making toast.

"Good morning!" she said, giving him a hug "or rather, afternoon!"

"Hi, how are you feeling?" he replied, giving her a kiss on the top of her head as she made him tea.

"Tired, headache, thirsty," she said, "but otherwise OK!"

He leaned his neck to one side, it hurt and gave a distinct click.

"Who were you talking to?" he asked.

"Jan. She's on her way!" she replied.

"Why?" he asked, looking concerned.

She told him Jan's reaction to the warning about Mary Hall.

"Good! We need all the help we can get! This snow is quite deep." he said, glancing out at the garden. "Did you tell her about it?" He said, picking up the mug of tea.

"No, she rang off before I had a chance," she said with a grin. "You know what she's like!"

"I know someone else like that!" he said, smiling. "Text her. If she can get to Wadebridge, maybe Simon could bring her over in his Discovery. I'll ring him first and arrange it," he suggested.

Jeff found that Simon was happy to help, so Stephanie left Jan a text message.

"Have some toast," she said.

They enjoyed a quiet breakfast watching the snow fall silently on the beach, creating a surreal landscape and obliterating the sand. They almost forgot about the night before and the dangers that the new day might bring.

After breakfast, Jeff said he had to go to Willow Cottage, to clear the snow from the drive and sort out a few things, but he promised to be back in an hour. After she'd reassured him for the third time that she was alright, he kissed her gently on the forehead and went out into the snow, relieved that he didn't have far to walk.

***

While he was gone, Stephanie had a shower and dressed. After feeding Maisy she washed the dishes and mugs from breakfast and dinner last night, which were piled up in the sink. As she did so, deep in thought, she stared absent-mindedly out through the kitchen window overlooking the beach.

Most of the snow was gone now, washed away by the morning tide. There was hardly a cloud in the sky as was often the case after a snowstorm. The sunlight was bright, and the glare bouncing off the snow that remained clinging to the rocks was dazzling. Stephanie shielded her eyes, then she spotted something else shimmering, to the left of the beach on the horizon. Something she had never noticed before.

When Jeff arrived back, she called him into the kitchen, pointed it out and asked him about it.

"Oh, that's Lapwing Rock," he said. "You probably haven't noticed it before because it blends into the horizon. But today the snow has made it stand out against the sea. It's a small uninhabited island and, yes, you own that as well!"

"We will have to take a look one day," she said.

"Good idea," he said. "It's about half a mile offshore, just past Fern Leap on the way to the tin mine. You might have seen it if we'd made it that far yesterday. You can walk to it when the tide is out."

Stephanie shuddered at the mention of the place where Isabel died.

"But for now, we need to concentrate on finding Mary," replied Jeff.

"I know just the person to ask," said Stephanie, getting up. "I just have to find my wellies."

Despite protestations about Jan's orders not to leave the house, he followed her outside. "Where are we even going?" he asked.

"To see Lucy! It's the Christmas holidays and Lisa is looking after her every day while Jessie and Matthew are at work. And The Forge is where Mary used to live. We'll be back before Jan gets here!" Stephanie said, excitedly. "AND it's a lovely day for a walk!"

Jeff had learned already that there was no arguing with her in this mood, or any mood really.

***

Stephanie was right. It was a sunny day, yet there was a biting breeze. She was pleased to see he had also cleared her driveway of snow. The lane was covered with about three inches, which was already beginning to turn to grey slush. The local children would most likely be making the most of the downfall, building snowmen and having snowball fights. Wrapped up in scarves and gloves, the walk to the village was bracing, but beautiful. Everything glistened as if covered in fairy-dust. Or so it seemed to Stephanie.

"We need to get some Christmas decorations," said Stephanie. "And a tree!"

"I know someone locally who sells real Christmas trees, leave it with me," said Jeff, walking with one arm round her.

"It will be my first Christmas in Marlin," she said, "and our first

Christmas together."

"A double celebration," said Jeff, turning towards her and kissing her softly. Just then, a voice shouted.

"Ahem! This is a respectable neighbourhood!"

"Morning Michael!" called Jeff with a grin, as they approached his house.

"Hi, I thought you'd be at work?" said Stephanie, smiling too.

"Nobody wants to buy antiques on a day like this," said Michael, catching his breath as he leaned on a shovel. "I opened up at ten, waited a couple of hours and gave up," he added.

"Let me help you," said Jeff. Michael nodded in silent thanks and gave him the shovel.

"I suspect you have something on your mind?" he asked Stephanie. Her face grew serious.

"Yes," she said, "and you're not going to like it."

They went inside and found Lisa in the kitchen making lunch. Stephanie declined a sandwich, but accepted a cup of tea.

Jeff soon joined them as they all sat around the kitchen table, enjoying the heat from the wood burner and chatting about nothing in particular.

"Now then, what is it you came about, my dear?" said Michael, after a polite interval, his curiosity getting the better of him.

Stephanie told him about The Manor and everything that had happened the day before, sparing as many of the gory details as she could. But Jessie was still shocked. Michael took out his handkerchief and mopped his brow. He instantly understood the purpose of their visit.

"Could Mary really have stopped them moving on?" she asked.

"Yes, no doubt," he replied. "She was an expert in some of the darkest magic ever known. Curses, hexes, binding spells. Going up against her is foolish, Stephanie. Let her be!"

"I can't!" Stephanie answered. "Not after what she's done. God knows how many other poor souls are trapped here because of her evil, her blind hatred. I need to find her. Is Lucy here? I thought she would be with you?"

"She's... she's not been herself recently," said Lisa. "Spends all her time locked away in the spare bedroom with that cat. Talking to Lord-knows-who! I know it sounds odd, speaking about a child like this, but she frightens me!"

"I know full well who she's talking to," said Stephanie, grim-faced. "She's talking to her great grandmother, Mary Hall! There is a link there that has to be broken."

"She's of the age now," said Michael, "the age when the gift begins to awaken. But in the case of witches, her power will also start to develop, if it hasn't already. With the right sort of guidance that power can be used for great good. But if it is twisted and turned by the forces of evil..."

"She will end up like Mary," Stephanie said, closing her eyes at the thought. "I won't let it happen, you can be sure about that."

"I know how strong the gift is in you, my girl, but I fear you may not be able to do it alone. You will need help of another kind," said Michael. "Someone with the gift, but also magical knowledge. I know of one such man. The gift was passed from father to son in his family and you will need his help if you have any chance to cast Mary out. His name is Simon Blake, and he is a warlock."

"Simon, my estate manager?" asked Stephanie, and Michael nodded.

"I think we need to get back to The Lodge," said Jeff, his face serious.

"Agreed!" said Stephanie. "But first I need to speak to Lucy."

"Upstairs, first on the left," said Michael. "But don't say we didn't warn you!"

***

Stephanie insisted on going alone, with the creaking stairs of the old cottage heralding her arrival. She came to the guest bedroom and knocked the door.

"Go away!" said a young voice.

She ignored it and opened the bedroom door. There in front of her were five coloured stones spinning in a circle about three feet above the bed where Lucy sat, staring at them. When she turned to look at Stephanie, they fell onto the bed with a dull thud.

Shadow was on her lap, purring. He had grown into a fine young cat, sleek and healthy. His eyes shone. Stephanie thought she saw them gleam unnaturally as he closed them and went back to sleep. She took a step into the room. Lucy looked away, her attention on her precious cat.

As she stroked him his deep, throaty purr became louder, hypnotic.

"Hello Lucy," said Stephanie. "I've come to talk to you about..."

"I know why you're here!" said Lucy casually, stroking Shadow without even looking at her. "She won't talk to you. But she told me to tell you she will see you soon, very soon."

With that, an unseen force propelled Stephanie backwards out of the room and into the wall on the landing. She took a breath, stepped towards the doorway and the bedroom door slammed shut.

Jeff was on the landing beside her three seconds later.

"What happened?" he asked.

"I'm fine, let's go!" she said.

Michael was right. If the child already had such power, the magic of Mary Hall was going to be a hundred times greater. They had no time to waste.

"Tell her I'll be waiting!" she called back as she went downstairs.

"Meeoo!" said Shadow innocently, blinking at them from where he now stood, on the landing windowsill. No-one had seen him come out of the bedroom and the door was still shut. As they fled, he simply licked his front paw languidly, purring loudly.

***

After chatting briefly to Michael and Lisa and trying to reassure them, they walked back up the hill. Stephanie explained what had happened; Jeff was astounded. When they reached the cottage, it was almost three o'clock. Stephanie made a pot of coffee while Jeff rang his mother; he had some questions about the Blake family. He wasn't prepared to trust Stephanie's safety to someone he hardly knew without at least getting a second opinion. His mother confirmed that she went to school with Simon's father, Jack Blake. His grandfather had, as Simon told them, been a farmer on the estate. She knew very little about Simon himself, but she knew his father well. They were good people, one of the oldest and well respected families in the area.

"What about the gift?" Jeff asked. "Did Jack have it?"

"Oh yes, everyone knew that," she said, "there was talk of magic in the family too, but I don't know much about that side of it. Actually…"

They chatted for a while longer, then Jeff thanked her and rang off. He went into the office to make a couple of other calls, then told Stephanie what Jenny said.

"Will this never end?" she thought aloud. "My family on both sides did such terrible things. I can never possibly hope to make up for it all."

"It isn't your responsibility to do that," he told her, putting both arms round her and holding her close. She pulled away from him.

"Yes, it is, Jeff! No-one else can undo the things they did. You saw last night. Those spirits had been waiting all that time in agony for me. ME!" He hugged her again.

"Well, you're not alone," he said. "I'm with you every step of the way and so is Jan!"

She looked up into his eyes. "I know," she said. "But I still don't thin

I'm strong enough to face her. Spirits are one thing. They don't bother me, even bad ones. But she's a with and pure evil, Jeff. Look what Lucy can do already, and she's only a child. I'm still trying to get to grips with my gift, whatever it is. I'm happy to admit that I need help and if Simon can help me, I'm all for it!"

*****

They spent the next two hours discussing Jenny's information and the events of the past few days, just trying to get their heads around the situation. She could see that Jeff was afraid that this was all too much for her. But she knew that just seeing Jan would make her feel better. Jan was strong, and that made Stephanie feel strong too; she took further comfort from the fact that Jeff was with her. She knew she could count on him, a fact which she was getting used to. Yet relying on his strength made her feel somehow weaker. She had accepted that she also needed help from Simon, and accepting help from anyone, especially virtual strangers, was something that didn't sit well. But she had a feeling that whoever else was there, she was the only one who could end this. The others just had to make it possible.

Jeff prepared a late lunch while Stephanie tidied up. Then Jeff helped her prepare the spare room for Jan to stay over. They also found blankets and a pillow for the sofa-bed in the office in case Simon needed to stay too, all depending on the weather. They watched the news while they waited, sitting on the sofa with Maisy curled up next to Jeff. At about ten past five, a car pulled into the drive; Jan and Simon had arrived. Maisy ran to hide.

"So, when exactly WERE you going to tell us you're a warlock?" Jeff asked sternly, then breaking into a smile and he shook his hand warmly,

"Not exactly a topic you raise on first meeting someone!" said Simon, smiling too, a little embarrassed.

"He told me, in the car just now," Jan said, giving Stephanie a hug and throwing an overnight bag on the floor at the bottom of the stairs, "or rather I told him. I sensed his energy. I've come to recognise people who are gifted in the magical arts, we see them a lot in our line of work!" she looked at Jeff, who agreed. "I brought him up to speed about last night. We need him Steph, if what you've told me is anywhere near as serious as I suspect, Mary is going to be a bitch to deal with!"

"I know," Stephanie said frowning, explaining what Michael had said.

"I think I have a few tricks up my sleeve which might help!" said Simon. "From what I hear, Stephanie is already a force to be reckoned with and Jan has told me great things about you too, Jeff," he said with a nod in his direction.

Jeff nodded back. "We will have a battle on our hands, that's for sure. Between the four of us, we may have a chance. But first, we need to make a plan!" added Simon.

"And we need coffee, plenty of coffee!" said Jan, collapsing onto the sofa.

"Definitely," said Simon, smiling at her.

Jan returned his smile in a way that Stephanie hadn't seen in a long time. She was pleased to see it.

Stephanie realised as she made the coffee, listening to the lively chat and laughter that filled the cottage, that she drank a lot of coffee when

Jan visited. Then, unbidden as they always were, a memory popped into her head.

As teenagers, they would meet up in Bristol every Saturday, to browse the shops, then visit their favourite coffee house, eat pastries and plan their lives. She wanted to be a writer, and Jan wanted to be a businesswoman. She yearned to meet a tall dark handsome man; Jan favoured a blond, blue-eyed Adonis. She was the quiet, cautious one, always unsure of herself and her choices, and Jan had always been the one to grab life with both hands with confidence and enthusiasm.

Stephanie had always made logical decisions based on meticulous research; Jan tended to act on instinct, going where the wind blew. They hadn't always seen eye to eye on everything, but that had made life all the more interesting. The only girl with two brothers, in a family with very little money and limited affection, Jan had always had to fight for everything. That experience had stood her in good stead, but had also led her to choose unwise romantic partners.

Stephanie had come from a middle-class family, never wanting for anything, but she had been almost starved of love after her mother died. They had clung together for support for as long as she could remember, and they had a lot of fun. But soon enough, those happy carefree days were gone forever. Paul had been her one big mistake, and she wished she had listened to Jan, who had hated him from the start. He hadn't been that tall, or dark and was only vaguely handsome. She had been drawn to him simply because opposites attract. He had been opposite to her in every way, and she had lived to regret every moment that she had wasted with him.

Jeff was nothing like him and she realised that she had never been happier. She took the coffee through to the living-room and found Simon sitting next to Jan on the sofa, obviously besotted and hanging on her every word. She hoped that Simon might be the one to bring Jan that sort of happiness too. Jan had a "type" and Simon definitely seemed to fit the profile.

She sipped her coffee. Little had they known back then where their lives would lead them: to this, to Marlin, fighting against evil that they never knew existed. Stephanie was certain that despite their differences in background and experiences, they would always be friends; it was a true friendship forged in pain and mutual understanding which transcended all boundaries and obstacles. Another thing was also obvious to her now: since she was learning to trust her instincts, developing her abilities and living in a place where logic did not apply, they were growing more alike by the day.

***

Jeff broached the subject first. "OK so where do we start?"

"Well," Stephanie said, "let's begin with what we know. Mary told Lucy she would see me very soon. Which to my mind means that either she somehow knows where we will be at any given time, or she intends coming here. What do you think, Simon?"

"I think she will attack where and when she thinks she has most advantage," Simon said, confidently.

"I agree," said Jan. "Steph, she will be mad as hell that you released all those souls. We have to make sure we fix the odds in our favour."

"Yes," said Jeff. "We need to bring her to us, pick a place we know, or one that we can defend easily, and set up plenty of magical protection. How do we get her there though?"

"A summoning spell," said Simon. "I can take care of that if you can both put the protection in place." He pointed at Jeff and Jan, who nodded. "Then Stephanie can work her, um, magic, for want of a better word, and get rid of her for good!" he said with a confident smile.

"It would be my pleasure," Stephanie said, with more confidence than she felt. "But where?"

For a few moments, nobody spoke. They all drank their coffee, deep in thought.

Then Simon spoke. "What about the old family chapel on the Trevelyan estate? It still stands on holy ground. What better place to fight evil!"

"Good plan!" said Jan, giving him a wink. "Now we just have to decide when?

"Let me think." Simon began. He looked at his watch, muttering to himself. "It's already dark now, it's almost six. By the time we eat something and make our preparations, and I need to do some research..." he fell into thought for a minute or two. Everyone looked at him, brimming with suspense.

Then to everyone, he said, "We will need to use some powerful magic to combat anything she may throw at us. I have a few defence and reversal spells I could use. But we need to plan this well and make sure we have covered all eventualities. If we leave here in about four hours, then go and make the place secure, we should be ready in time. All things considered, I suggest that we summon her at the chapel at midnight."

"How cliché is that," said Jan, smiling broadly. "I'm in!"

"My God, she's almost purring!" thought Stephanie, as she watched her friend flirting with Simon.

***

Simon got out his laptop and did some research. He had brought most of the essential items, but needed a couple of extra things which he went to collect from a friend in the nearby village of Sealby. While he was out, Jeff and Jan sat in the living-room and discussed protection techniques. Stephanie made dinner and fed Maisy while listening to the radio. By about half past seven they were all gathered round the kitchen table eating hearty portions of home-made lasagne and garlic bread. Stephanie was a good cook, having had to provide for herself for many years.

"That was great, Steph," said Jan. "Almost as good as mine!" Stephanie laughed, being the only person there who knew that Jan was incredibly bad at cooking. She always avoided it, even if no ready-meals were available, she was miles away from a restaurant and she was starving. She often teased her that she could burn water. In fact, Jan had once boiled a pan dry without thinking to check it, and her far-more-than hard-boiled eggs had exploded all over the kitchen ceiling, necessitating full re-decoration. She had never cooked again. Luckily, her income allowed for her expensive eating habits. She wondered how she maintained her figure with so many takeaways. But Stephanie decided not to share Jan's secret in present company.

After dinner, they discussed their plans. Jeff told them that the chapel was along a path behind the ruins of The Manor, standing near the cliff path and overlooking the bay. It had been built by the first Lord Trevelyan in 1745, shortly after The Manor itself.

The house had been altered and extended over the years, but the chapel had remained the same. Simon confirmed that it was still in use as a local place of worship for the villagers, shopkeepers and the few estate employees who escorted visitors on tours to the tin mine and worked in the gift shop. It was popular with visitors, due to its quaint and quirky appearance. It had a tiny steeple, beautiful stained-glass windows and fresh flowers, provided every few days by a few devoted women from the village and bought in from the next town. The vicar provided a service one Sunday a month, sharing his time with three other coastal parishes. Stephanie decided she had to visit it properly when this was all over, to take flowers for Isabel and Julia. They weren't just faceless ancestors to her any more, and she felt that she owed them that much.

The time passed quickly. Everyone knew what they had to do, and at half past eleven they gathered what they needed, and piled into Simon's car. It was time to face Mary Hall., and Stephanie was terrified.

***

The snow showers had returned during the evening, but the flurries had ceased, for now. Simon led them to the chosen location: Mary Hall's grave. Jan and Jeff set up a perimeter of protection around that area of the graveyard, so that only spirits they wanted there could appear. They all summoned their guides to act as gatekeepers and protectors.

"HERE, STEFFI!" said Grace, confirming her arrival to Stephanie, allowing Jeff and Jan to hear her too.

"*PRESENT!*" said Lucas, doing the same.

It was a cold night, quite clear and Stephanie saw stars shimmering in the distance. Although there was a full moon, heavy clouds passed across it now and then, blocking its illumination, so Jeff set up the extra lights he had brought. With no wind or snow, Jan could burn white sage around the area and offer up a short prayer of protection, asking that love and light should shine on their efforts to rid this place of evil. While she waited, Stephanie gazed at the tiny chapel, its stone and ornate stained glass had stood the passage of time well, despite being in such a bleak location. The graveyard was bigger than expected, with gravestones, angels and other monuments in memory of the dear departed. By day it might have been beautiful, but at night she found it extremely creepy.

It was time. The ancient chapel clock struck midnight. They all joined hands around the grave. Jeff and Jan stood either side of Stephanie and then they each joined hands with Simon. Jeff gave her hand a gentle squeeze. With Lucas and Grace beside her, the fear had abated and her face was a mixture of determination and resolve. She stood defiantly with her friends, with just one purpose: to rid this world of the vile Mary Hall.

Simon placed two artefacts on the grave: a symbolic silver dagger and a copper goblet filled with a dark elixir. Stephanie didn't even want to know what was in it. Then he began a summoning incantation. His voice became deep and resonating. There was a momentary break in the clouds and moonlight reflected eerily from the liquid in the goblet. As it did so, the contents started frothing and bubbling, overflowing onto the grave. Simon raised his arms into the air, mumbling the words of an ancient summoning spell. Stephanie's stomach turned over at the sound. This felt wrong. The hairs on her arms stood on end and an awful feeling swept over her.

"Mary Hall, I summon you!" said Simon, masterfully.

Dark clouds covered the moon and lightning crashed from the sky and struck a nearby headstone, splitting it in two. Everyone jumped. All of a sudden, the air became extremely cold, and the wind rose and howled through the graveyard. Two of the lights blew over and smashed, leaving the area around them in partial darkness. When the clouds dispersed, the moon cast a single shaft of light pointing in one direction.

"Look!" said Jan.

They all turned inland to look along a pathway suddenly lit up by moonlight. The flowers on the graves at the other side of the graveyard were gradually withering in turn on each side of the path, and the grass between the graves was turning black. Some invisible malevolence was making its way slowly but surely towards them, poisoning every living thing in its wake.

As the dark shape drew slowly closer, a hazy figure appeared that developed gradually into the body of a woman dressed in mourning clothes. She looked like a middle-aged version of Stephanie, but her eyes were lifeless pits of blackness. The resemblance was startling; it was Mary.

She wasn't ugly or crone-like as Stephanie expected of a witch with her reputation; she simply emanated eternal sadness. Stephanie could feel it coming off her in waves, deep sorrow and immeasurable clouds of grief. As she drew closer, it became obvious that she walked slowly because she was dragging her right leg, which was freakishly twisted. Her right arm lay useless at her side. The emotions she gave off soon gave way to desolation and despair and as she reached them, her eyes took on a crazed appearance; her expression was purely malicious.

Stephanie could see as she stood before her that half her face was disfigured and the right part of her skull was missing. Her hair that side was hanging in lank, bloody strings, giving her an even more ghoulish appearance. Stephanie realised she had never even wondered how she died. She whispered to Jeff who confirmed what she now suspected: Mary had thrown herself off nearby Fern Leap onto the rocks below, unable to life with her grief. Stephanie felt her stomach lurch with nausea, and she began to shake.

"Can you see her?" she asked.

"Yes!" Jeff answered his voice sombre.

He gripped her hand more tightly to comfort her, and Jan did the same on the other side. She was ready.

"Welcome, Mother of Darkness!" said Simon, with a sudden smile. "I have waited so long to meet you!"

They all turned to look at him.

"Thank you, dear boy," said Mary. "You make me proud!"

"What?" said Stephanie in disbelief.

She looked at Jeff and Jan. Their faces were resolute, and they did not seem at all surprised.

"Yes," said Simon, looking at her, "I orchestrated this so I could meet her, but more importantly, so that she could meet YOU!"

Jeff tried to let go of her hand so he could grab Simon, but found that his hands and feet wouldn't move. None of them could move; they had been bound to the spot.

"That's the beauty of magic!" he laughed, his face contorting and his true allegiance apparent to all.

"So," said Mary, to Stephanie. "You think you can summon ME? You have no idea who you're dealing with, do you?"

In an instant, she was standing beside her and Stephanie felt an icy hand on her left arm. It was as if a dagger had been driven into it. She felt grief and loss like she had never experienced, yet Simon's dagger remained on the grave. This was magic. She felt as if all warmth, light and joy had been sucked out of her body. She just stood there, helpless, as Mary draw all the good, positive feelings out of her, replacing them with fear and self-doubt. The terror returned along with all her feelings of inadequacy.

But then as suddenly as it began, it stopped, as unseen hands dragged Mary away by the shoulders and threw her to the floor.

"GET AWAY FROM MY CHILD!" said the voice of Grace Meares.

She materialised in front of them, her face ablaze with anger. Stephanie's eyes filled with tears. Grace, the man who Stephanie now knew as Lucas her guide, and two other unknown spirits had wrestled Mary to the floor and were pinning her there by her shoulders. Stephanie assumed that the others were guardian spirits belonging to Ian and Jeff. She could feel that Mary's dark energy was strong and her energy was growing, and she knew that even four protective spirits, strong as they were, wouldn't be able to hold her for long.

Simon's eyes were half closed, and he reminded Stephanie of a snake. He started to chant. He had let go of their hands, but they were still unable to move. He moved away from them and stood closer to Mary.

Jan took her chance and whispered something to Jeff and he nodded.

"Jacob, Adam, Rachel!" she called.

Two men in dark clothes appeared from behind nearby gravestones and a woman in similar attire ran out from the tiny chapel porch. They instinctively linked hands around the fallen spirit of Mary Hall, joining forces with the four guides, chanting around her where she lay on the ground.

Jan began speaking some words in a language that Stephanie had never heard. Their hands suddenly became free and they could move again. Jan ran to join the circle of strangers as the wind howled, thunder crashed and lightning ripped the air apart. Stephanie fell to her knees as Jeff punched Simon hard in the face and he fell to the ground. He deftly rolled him over on his face in the gravel, secured his wrists and ankles with plastic cable ties from his pocket, and put his scarf round his mouth to gag him. He left him there, groaning and struggling on the path, and ran to Stephanie, putting a protective arm around her. Magic was not one of his talents.

They others walked in a slow circle around Mary as their chanting became louder and more rhythmical. Mary struggled to get free. She began an incantation of her own, then with a massive burst of dark energy, she threw off her captors and vanished. Jan, Jeff and the three newcomers lay on the floor, and all the spirits were gone.

"Stephanie, now!" called Jan, and Stephanie moved closer.

Her arm still felt a bit numb from Mary's touch, but she was able to move it. She suddenly became very calm. Her fear was gone. Seeing her mother rush to defend her like that had awakened strength that she never knew she possessed. As she stood up and took a step towards Jan and the others, Mary appeared in front of her. Her injuries had vanished, her hair was whipped up by the wind, and her dark eyes glowed with hellish flame. She raised her hands to the sky and a lightning bolt struck the earth next to Stephanie.

Stephanie ignored it. With the hint of a smile on her lips, she raised up her hands and directed them towards the sky, as if she was bathing in the energy of the moon. The others rushed to form a circle around them. A glow of light suddenly appeared around her. Stephanie's aura became visible and started to grow, and she felt a surge of energy. She heard her heartbeat drumming in her ears, and she became acutely aware of the blood coursing through her veins. She instinctively knew what to do; what to say.

"I am safe, you cannot hurt me. I am protected by the love of my friends, my family and my loved ones, both in life and in spirit."

As she spoke Mary's hands dropped.

"I have what you cannot take from me. I am alive, Mary and you are just a memory!"

Mary took a step back, the brilliance coming from Stephanie was so dazzling that the circle of people around her had to close their eyes. She could see that Mary was growing weaker, as if the light was draining her darkness away, and her strength

"Impossible!" said Mary. "You are no witch, so how…?"

As she started to walk towards Mary, Stephanie spoke again.

"We might be related by blood, but I am NOTHING like you!"

Stephanie directed her hands towards her ancestor and a pure white light shot from them, the light of goodness and love. Mary stumbled backwards as the blast hit her full in the chest, filling her heart. She shrieked in pain.

"No, please, I did it for Tom!" she whimpered. "My son! They killed my boy!"

"NO excuses! Tom was a good man and he would be ashamed of you!" said Stephanie. "I'm sorry for your loss," she said, "but you had no right to do what you did, to Julia, or to the others. They did NOTHING to you."

She sent another blast of love and light at Mary.

Mary started to whine, a high-pitched shrill sort of keening sound, like a soul in utter torment. The pain of the love that she was experiencing was too much; it was the pain of loss, the pain that she had been unable to live with, and died trying to escape.

"It hurts, doesn't it, the light of love and goodness? Has it been so long since you felt those things that you forgot what they feel like? Maybe they are feelings that you never knew, or do they simply remind you what you have lost?"

Mary fell to her knees, screaming "NO! STOP!"

But Stephanie carried on, moving closer to her. As Stephanie reached her, she bent down and raised Mary's head. Then she looked into her pleading, defeated eyes and put her arms around her in a firm hug, flooding the spirit with light.

"It's over!" she whispered.

As she said those words she held her close, and Mary's spirit burst apart, dissipating like a cloud of dark ash, falling from her hands as it disappeared into the ground. Mary Hall was gone. The remaining lights blew, a cloud covered the moon, and the graveyard was thrown once more into darkness.

"Ashes to ashes!" Stephanie muttered softly in a monotone, as she fell to the ground and passed out.

***

She woke in her bed thinking she had been in the throes of a ghastly nightmare. Then she saw Jeff asleep in her rocking chair next to the bed and Maisy snoozing in her favourite place by her side. Daylight streamed through the bedroom windows and the sound of happy voices carried from downstairs. She sat up and Jeff woke.

"Morning!" he said. "Sleep well?"

"Yes, thanks! I feel fine! Why are you there and who's downstairs?" she asked.

Then she remembered: Mary; the graveyard; the three strangers.

At that moment, Jan came in with a mug of tea.

"I thought I heard your voice," she said. "Drink this!"

First Stephanie drank the full glass of water that she found her bedside table, then she started on the tea.

"Thanks! I'll see you both downstairs in a minute," she said. "I just want a quick shower and some clean clothes!"

"OK!" Jeff said. He gave her a peck on the cheek before he and Jan left the room

Her memory of the night before was clear now. She couldn't believe what she had done, the power that had been channelled through her was not her own, that was certain. It felt like what she had experienced when Isabel passed through her that night with the doll. Pure love. How was she able to do what she did? Whatever the reason, it felt good to destroy Mary. Too good. Unease crept into her mind about her feelings. She thought about the way she had taunted and tortured Mary at the end.

"That can't be good, surely?" she thought.

As she sat and started at herself in her bedroom mirror, she examined her face, feeling a darkness surround her; her unease was growing. She wondered if what she sensed was coming from within her, if her own dark nature because of her evil lineage was becoming visible, maybe drawn out by contact with Mary. But then something happened that she was not expecting, the face in her mirror began to change. Her reflection slowly faded before her eyes, blurring and shifting. She wanted to look away, but she was riveted. Slowly but surely, the face in the mirror had altered into the face of a man with dark hair and darker eyes. She knew who it was, she felt it. The face glared at her a level of hatred she had never seen before. The darkness she felt was not her own, but was coming from him. She gasped and ran to the bathroom.

***

Fifteen minutes later, she had showered, dressed and was sitting in the living room, with no make-up and wet hair. She couldn't bear to look in a mirror again, and for now, she kept her vision to herself.

"Steph, I'd like to introduce you to three more members of P.I. Meet Jacob, Adam and Rachel Hollow! I told you we have regular dealings with some magic experts, and these three are the best I know!" They nodded and smiled.

"Seriously? Their name is *Hollow*?" Stephanie whispered. They all smiled. "No offence!" she added.

"Yes!" Jan said. "I was surprised when I met them too, but it's an old Cornish name!"

She explained that Jacob and Adam were brothers and Rachel was their sister. They were all tall, in their late twenties or early thirties, it was hard to tell. They were all extremely attractive, with long, jet black hair, dark brown eyes and black clothes to complete their image. As a modern-day witch and two warlocks, they certainly looked the part. Jan explained that they had driven over from working on a case in Exeter last night as soon as she called them.

"I'm sure you'll be seeing a lot more of them. I will be assigning them to your office!" said Jan. "You need more people who know this area well and they're originally from Sealby, but like the rest of us, they move around a lot."

Jeff obviously knew then and was already aware that they would be working with them. He seemed happy with the addition to the team.

"Pleased to meet you, welcome to the team and thank you so much for your help last night!" said Stephanie with a broad smile, as she shook their hands.

"No problem, you didn't really look like you need anybody's help!" said Jacob, the eldest. "Really, you were kick-ass!"

Stephanie found herself blushing. On shaking their hands, she realised just how powerful their energy was, and feeling suddenly dizzy, she sat down in the armchair by the window. Jeff rushed over, looking concerned, and passed her a glass of water.

"You need to take things slow until you get your strength back," he said.

"OK!" she said, squeezing his hand.

The Hollows all smiled, they knew true love when they saw it, and they were happy for them both.

Stephanie turned to Jan. "OK, I'm lost, when did you have time to call anybody, and what else went on that I don't know about? And where exactly did you know work out that Simon was working for the dark side?"

Everyone laughed. Jeff explained first.

"When I spoke to my Mum about Simon, she told me more than I let on. She said she'd heard rumours that he belonged to a magic coven in Wadebridge, where she and Simon both live. She gave me the name of someone she knows locally and while you were in the kitchen, I called them. Then, when my suspicions were confirmed, I rang Jan to warn her."

Jeff and Jan had wanted it to appear as if they had been taken in by him.

"Well you convinced me!" said Stephanie.

"We decided not to let you in on the plan because we knew that whatever you feel always shows on your face, and we couldn't let Simon become suspicious," added Jan.

Jeff also said what a terrible liar she was; a fact which he quickly emphasised as a good thing.

"Fair enough," she said, a bit peeved at being left out, but at least now she understood why.

"So, when Simon went off to get potion ingredients, and you were making dinner, Jeff and I concocted a plan. That's when I called the others!" Jan told her.

"And Bob whispered in my ear that I shouldn't trust him," said Jeff, smiling but with a hint of sadness.

Stephanie was pleased that Bob had been in contact with Jeff again; she knew how comforted Jeff would be by his presence.

"Where's the lovely Simon now?" Stephanie asked.

Jeff grinned as he answered her.

"He is at a P.I. safe house. He hasn't actually committed any crime that we know of, but we will be suggesting *most strongly* that he never shows his face in Cornwall again!"

"Well you can tell him from me that his arse is fired!" she said.

Everyone found that comment extremely amusing.

"He told us everything, anxious to save his own skin, the little worm!" said Jan. "He used magic to make sure he got the estate manager's job, so he could find out about you and get close enough to put his plan into effect. He blames your family for his father losing the farm and Mary used that to persuade him to use his magic to bring her here to kill you. And he was the one that brought the kitten here, Steph. It was a gift to Lucy from Mary. He said that he's been watching the cottage for some time. He left the kitten outside and hid behind a hedge until someone picked him up, which just happened to be Jeff. I don't think he'll risk showing his face here again. He's petrified of you!"

"So he should be," Stephanie muttered.

"Don't worry, the power of three will take care of him, I'm sure," said Adam.

"What's that?" asked Stephanie.

Rachel explained that if magic was used with the intent of harming anyone, no good would come to the witch or warlock that cast it. It was believed that the damage that they intended to be done to others would come back on them threefold.

"That sounds terrifying, considering how he wished my death!" said Stephanie. She sat in silence for a moment.

"And Mary finally got HER just reward!" she thought.

"Has anyone checked on Lucy?" she asked, looking concerned.

"It seems she's back to normal," said Jeff, "now that Mary won't be bothering her any more. I called in earlier today and told Michael and Lisa what happened. They were extremely happy. They said to thank you for saving her from Mary's influence. She still has her gift, of course, but without Mary's interference, I'm sure that between us we can guide her to use it in the right way. And she's keeping the cat. He seems somehow different too, a little less, well, weird!"

"Well, that's a relief," Stephanie said. "I'm sorry things didn't work out for you and Simon," she said to Jan with a wink. Jeff laughed.

"I knew the slimy, lying bastard was bad news the minute I laid eyes on him!" Jan said.

"Nothing to do with my phone call then?" said Jeff.

"Well, I suppose it helped, but he had a bad vibe! You didn't really think I liked him did you Steph? Evil warlocks are NOT my type! I was just playing along. Mind you my acting was always amazing. Remember in school when we did the Wizard of Oz?"

"You played Second Munchkin in the first crowd scene," said Stephanie, laughing.

"Yes, well that's true, but Mrs Jones told me I was the best Second Munchkin they ever had!" Jan replied proudly.

"You were six, and she lied!" said Stephanie as everyone laughed.

Jan looked deflated at first, then she smiled too. It felt good to Stephanie that her cottage was finally filled with so much laughter, with so many good people, new friends and old.

"Anyway," said Jan, "since it's been crazy busy lately, I thought we'd close P.I. for a week, and that means I can stay for Christmas, if you'll have me?"

"I wouldn't have it any other way," said Stephanie warmly.

"By Christmas you're going to need to decide on a colour scheme for Quarry House. Then you'll need furniture and furnishings. That's one serious shopping trip, Steph! And I can help you to organise the launch," she said, her eyes wide and gleaming.

Stephanie just smiled and nodded, she knew how much Jan loved shopping.

Jeff proposed a toast. As they all clinked their mugs he said, "To P.I. South West, and to Stephanie!"

"Yes," said Jan. "Thank God it's over with, and we can all relax!"

***

As the toasting, laughter and merriment went on around her, Stephanie looked out of the window at the dark waters of Lapwing Cove and shivered. Jan was wrong; it wasn't over. There was someone that Jan, that everyone, had forgotten about; someone else who was being kept here by Mary's hex. Stephanie knew without a doubt that she still had one more invisible enemy to face.

Evil was rising in Marlin. An entity even more terrible than Mary. There was one more vengeful soul to send on their way before she could lay all her family ghosts to rest, and that this would be the hardest battle of them all. She had felt the darkness as soon as she woke up that morning, then she had seen him, taunting her in the mirror. She already had a feeling that she knew where to start looking for him.

"A penny for your thoughts?" said Jeff, putting his arms around her. She jumped involuntarily, then turned around to hug him.

"That won't be nearly enough," she said wistfully.

Ian called him into the kitchen to help her distribute fresh coffee, and he left her to her solitude. She couldn't tell him or anyone what she'd seen. She wasn't ready to drag them all into more danger. She just stood there staring at the sky clothed in its many shades of grey, at the darkness that was looming over the bay in the direction of Lapwing Rock. She had only one thought. One purpose.

'William… I'm coming for you!"

PART FIVE: THE DARKNESS

IT WAS MONDAY January 4th 2016. At eight o'clock Stephanie woke up and stretched; she went to look out of her bedroom window at the waves lashing the rocks. The tide was in.

"Wake up," she said, "we have a business to launch!"

Jeff opened his eyes. Maisy was lying across his chest and her bedraggled Baby toy was draped over his face.

"This bed wasn't built for three plus a cat toy," he said, smiling, throwing Baby to the floor. Maisy woke and pounced on it, purring.

"You love her really," she called as she walked across the landing to the spare room, to wake up Jan.

He sat up and threw Baby at her head as she walked out.

"Jan, get up, it's Launch Day!" she called.

To her surprise, after taking a quick shower and putting on a smart new suit, she found Jan in the kitchen, already dressed, made-up and ready for the day. She was already halfway through a pot of coffee.

"Morning, Steph," she said. "It's a beautiful day, and the sun is shining!"

Christmas had come and gone, the first Marlin White Christmas in thirty years and the best one that Stephanie could remember, surrounded by family and friends, old and new. The snow had melted, re-frozen and finally disappeared without trace. Jan had been to tie up loose ends in London for a few days and was now back for the opening day of P.I. South West.

Stephanie's book was finally finished and with the editor, so she expected last-minute comments very soon. Quarry House was ready to open its doors to clients and things were going incredibly well with Jeff, so much so that they were now living together. Everything was perfect, for a change, which made her feel oddly unsettled; it was like she was waiting 'for the other shoe to drop'.

"Is that man of yours still asleep?" asked Jan with a grin, bringing her back to earth with a jolt.

"Not yet, he will be down shortly," Stephanie said.

Jan was glad to see Stephanie and Jeff so happy. That night at the graveyard, Jeff had been frightened for her. They had both realised that life was too short; even spending another minute apart would be too long. He had moved in on New Year's Day, rented out Willow Cottage again, and they had been inseparable ever since.

"New year, new start!" Stephanie had said.

It had been a very sudden development. Some might have called it madness, but as Jan herself had told her, "When it's right it's right." Everyone who knew them could see they were meant to be together, and they both agreed.

Stephanie made tea for herself and Jeff, trying to shrug off the feeling of dread that had swept over her. He came into the kitchen and started cooking bacon and scrambled eggs for them all.

"Isn't he lovely," said Jan, batting her eyelashes and smiling at him.

"Shut up, Boss!" he said, with one of his grins that could melt permafrost.

"Well actually, as of today, Steph's your boss," Jan reminded him. "And I'm HER boss, so that still makes me your boss, too, really…"

"STOP!" he said, serving breakfast. "My head hurts."

The women laughed while they all sat down around the kitchen table to eat.

"I'm glad Amy was able to start today," said Jan, putting ketchup on her eggs and almost spattering her expensive, white silk blouse.

Amy Porter was their newly appointed receptionist. She had been recommended by Michael and Lisa, and was a lifelong friend of Jessie, their daughter-in-law. She was 23, tall, attractive and blonde with big, blue eyes. A perfect choice in fact; she oozed confidence, had plenty of previous experience in administration, was good with people and didn't care about the paranormal aspects of the job. She was an empath, someone who felt what others were feeling, and that would come in useful when dealing with potentially distressed clients. They were lucky to find her. Jan mentioned that Adam Hollow, one of their new team members, was already smitten with her after their first meeting, and it seemed that the feeling was mutual.

"Not sure I really approve of office romance," muttered Stephanie, spearing bacon with her fork.

"Hypocrite!" said Jan and Jeff together.

Stephanie laughed and quickly finished her breakfast. She went to put her plate and mug in the sink, then she fed the not-so-patient Maisy who had been savouring the aroma of bacon with relish. Much to her disappointment, there were no leftovers to share with her, so she made do with gourmet cat food.

"Come on, or we'll be late on our first day!" Stephanie said, walking towards the front door.

Jan drove her sports car, and Jeff and Stephanie jumped into his car. Stephanie took one last look at the folder of documents which she had brought with her as they made their way through the village. Jeff beeped the horn as they passed Michael and Lisa, who were seeing Lucy off to school on her first day back after the Christmas break.

"See you later!" he called through the partially open window.

They all waved back and shouted that they would be there for the launch.

The offices were opening for business at nine o'clock, but there was to be an official launch party that evening at six o'clock, with family, friends and the press. Jan intended to drive back to London after the party.

"Good morning!" said Amy with a welcoming smile, as they walked in through the door at Quarry House. Like the others, she was smartly presented in office wear, even if she was wearing maybe a touch too much lipstick.

They all greeted her. Stephanie was already satisfied that she made the right choice in employing her. Amy sat behind an imposing curved reception desk, in the building's equally splendid hallway with its marble floor and antique oak panelling, yet she looked in total command of her surroundings. She told them there had been no visitors and that none of them had any messages. Stephanie thanked her and told her where they would all be for the foreseeable future, absent-mindedly tweaking the flower arrangement on the desk as she walked past.

She was pleased to see the office finally ready for business, and it was indeed a beautiful office. Behind Amy, a wide staircase swept upwards, opening each side onto a large landing. Downstairs, to the left of her, was a comfortable waiting room leading into Jeff's office, where he went now to catch up on email and phone calls. To the right, the same arrangement existed for Stephanie. Her office was the same room where she had met and despatched the spirit of Peter Trevelyan. Somehow it felt right.

To the rear of the staircases, accessed by both sides, was a large kitchen with a staircase to the basement, used for added storage. Next to the kitchen was a staff lounge, and opposite them was a large conference room with video-conferencing facilities for inter-office meetings.

On the next floor was an office used by Jan when she was in Marlin, and a larger one for the Hollows (currently finishing up a case in Exeter). There were more offices to be shared by permanent branch employees who would soon appointed, and for any visiting operatives who may need to call in from time to time. There was a library containing an abundance of information on the supernatural, with rare and ancient books on all aspects of witchcraft and wizardry, local lore and legend, and so on. It also held copies of books on Cornish history and ancestry, and old maps of the local area. In fact, it was a much more comprehensive specialist collection than any public library could offer. It was just what they needed to help with the type of unusual cases often undertaken by P.I.

Alongside the library, they also had rooms where they stored equipment for their various business needs, which could be anything from state of the art surveillance equipment to potions, police radios, cameras or EMF readers and other devices to locate, record and remove unwanted spirits. There was also an impressive computer room and technology suite, and a huge wardrobe room, with clothing, make-up, prosthetics and disguises of all types. On the top floor, there were five, twin-bedded, en suite bedrooms, for any staff member from other offices who needed to remain overnight in the area, and anyone who lived locally, worked late and needed to stay over. Much of their surveillance and activity was nocturnal by the very nature of the business.

In addition to their supernatural endeavours, P.I. catered for a wide array of clients, and its operatives' needs in the pursuance of their work were many and varied. This branch would be no different. With thoroughness, discretion and professionalism, Jan had built an excellent national reputation; Stephanie was determined that this office would be a credit to her good name, and a worthy addition to the business.

No expense had been spared. Stephanie had ensured that the décor and furnishings complemented the elegance of the house, restoring as much as possible of its original features whilst tastefully combining them with modern-day style and convenience. Polished hardwood floors and leather seating, double-glazed sash windows, solid oak desks and plain curtains and cushions made from rich fabrics, all added to the charm and functionality of what were, after all, business premises.

The staff lounge was her favourite room, designed with floor to ceiling windows. The walls of the room were painted in pale lemon, light and bright to contrast with the dark wood floors, with the comfortable, black leather furniture that was the theme throughout. But here it was accented with plush, yellow, satin brocade cushions, giving the room a hint of sunshine even on a cloudy day. It opened out onto a small stone courtyard garden. There she had installed a relaxing water feature, and there were oak benches from which to enjoy views to open fields beyond.

The staff lounge was where the launch party would be held, and where she and Jan went now, to put the finishing touches to the decorations and other arrangements. There were tables laid with crystal glasses ready for champagne or orange juice, and silver ice buckets, glass jugs and crisp white tablecloths gleamed in the sunlight. Silver bowls for snacks sat beside folded piles of yellow napkins, all ready for the waitresses who were coming in from the village café to pour drinks and serve attendees. The decorations simply consisted of a tasteful banner. Everything was ready, simple yet elegant.

"You've done a great job, Steph," said Jan giving her a hug.

"Thank you," said Stephanie, "although I'm actually looking forward to getting this launch out of the way and getting my teeth into some real work," she added.

"Like going after William?" Jan asked, blunt as usual.

"How did you...?" asked Stephanie.

"I've known you since you were a toddler, Steph. Do you think I can't tell when there's something on your mind? Your book is almost in print, the business is up and running. You have the man of your dreams, more money than is probably decent, and yet you still look like someone just peed in your cornflakes!"

Stephanie smiled. "You're right," she said. "It has been playing on my mind since we dealt with Mary. I need to put it all to rest."

"I know," Jan said, "you need closure so you can get on with your life."

"Finally," came Jeff's voice from the doorway. "I wondered how long it would take you to mention it. OK, so how do we do this?"

Stephanie turned and smiled. It seemed that his well-honed intuition was still working, yet he didn't tend to use it much any more. Not since his great-uncle Bob died, in fact. It had failed him with Bob and he had lost faith in his ability. But it seemed that his instincts when it came to Stephanie were always extremely accurate.

***

They all prepared a hot drink in the kitchen and went back to Stephanie's office. As they passed Amy she said, "Miss Meares, there's a package for you."

"Thank you, Amy," said Stephanie, "By the way it's OK to call me Stephanie, unless we have clients present."

She picked up a small padded envelope from the reception desk. Only her name was written on it, and it had no postmark so it had been delivered by hand.

"Who left this for me, Amy?" she enquired.

"Oh, one of the painters popped in with it just now. He said he found it in the basement when he was storing the last of the leftover paint. It was in a box along with some other things and he thought you might want to look at it in case it was important, so he put your name on it. He said there were antiques down there too. Just let me know if you want anything taken away, and I can arrange it for you."

"Thanks!" said Stephanie with a smile. "We'll be in my office if anyone needs us."

Jan and Jeff sat on the sofa and Stephanie settled in an armchair opposite. She put down her tea on the coffee table between them and opened the package, tipping its contents onto the table. There were two brass keys, one which was large and plain, the other small and ornate. She picked up the large one first. As it touched her skin, she saw a flashback.

It was as if she was looking through someone else's eyes. The person stood outside an old stone shed-like building in howling wind and rain. She heard waves slashing on rocks and gulls calling. Bending down a little the person used the key which unlocked a low door, then they ducked to step inside; she suspected that this person was a man. The interior was dark and musty, with cobwebs around the beamed ceiling. There were small mullion windows and dried leaves lay scattered around the flagstone floor. It looked like an old fisherman's cottage. It was all on one level with a single makeshift bed in one corner, a small fireplace at the far end and an empty table with two chairs under the window. On the floor by the back wall were old fishing nets.

She told the others what she had seen.

"It sounds like the tiny cottage on the island," Jeff told her, "the one you were asking about the other day, you know, Lapwing Rock."

"How do you know that?" asked Jan in surprise.

"I used to play there as a child during the summer holidays, all the kids did," Jeff replied. "What does the other key tell you?"

Stephanie picked up the smaller key. She was back in the same room, but this time the table had a large, carved, oak box on it, covered in metal studs and bars. It looked strangely familiar. It was like a large, oak jewellery box in the shape of a chest, and inside the lid was a mirror, As the person opened it, she saw that she had been correct; the reflection of a man with thick, curly black hair and dark eyes stared back at her. It was a face she recognised. Stephanie immediately dropped the key, ending the vision.

"What is it?" Jeff asked. Stephanie explained.

"What was in the box?" Jan asked.

"I don't know, I didn't see. But I know one thing, the face... the man in the mirror was William!"

She picked up the key again, hoping to replay the scene and this time see what was in the box, but nothing happened.

"We need to go there," she said.

"When?" Jeff asked.

"As soon as we can. There's no time today with the launch and we need to do it in daylight, when the tide is out. So, it will have to be tomorrow," she said.

"We could check out the basement now though?" Jeff suggested. "There might be other clues there."

"Good idea," Stephanie agreed, and they drank their drinks quickly and made their way to the staircase. Jeff told Amy where they were going as they passed her desk, in case anyone wanted them for anything.

They went through the kitchen and found the stairs to the basement behind a door next to the gleaming catering cooker. Jeff went first, putting the light on. The wooden stairs were steep, leading to a small room with whitewashed stone walls containing tins of paint, tools and old dust sheets. This room opened onto a larger room full of items from the house: the remaining antiques which had not been stolen or damaged over the years. There was a pile of paintings stacked together in the floor facing one wall. Stephanie pulled a sheet off them and set them aside one at a time. There was one of a woman she recognised as Isabel in a fine ball gown, then one of Peter in a smart suit. There was also a portrait of the former Lady Trevelyan. Julia had been as beautiful in life as Stephanie saw her in spirit, only in the portrait, her eyes looked sad and a little frightened. Beside her, was a tall, imposing man. Staring back at her was the face she had seen before, but only in mirrors, William Trevelyan himself.

"I was right!" Stephanie said. "Look, that's him. William."

"What could he have been hiding in a wooden box on Lapwing Island?" Jan asked.

"No idea, let's carry on looking round," Stephanie replied.

She had a look at a few more portraits of people that she had never seen before, either living or dead. Jan found a tray of old silver cutlery, Jeff investigated a tea chest filled with china crockery. Then they came to an old oak dresser against a wall in the second room.

"This is lovely!" Stephanie said. "It would look good in my kitchen."

"We'll ask Amy to have it sent over for you," Jeff said, smiling.

"Sadly, I don't think there's room!" Stephanie said.

She realised that she had referred to it as *her* kitchen, even though it was Jeff's home now too. She was relieved that he didn't seem to notice, or maybe he simply didn't mind. He didn't seem to be intimidated by the fact that she owned the whole village when a lot of men might have been. Jeff was not bothered about worldly possessions, and it was just one of the things which she loved about him.

Stephanie opened one of the cupboards in the base of the dresser, and in it was the large, carved, wooden box with metal bars and studs.

"How odd!" she said, "Look, it's the box I saw."

The box was locked. Stephanie tried to open it with the smaller of the keys, but it wouldn't budge.

"Either it's rusted with age or it's the wrong key," Jeff said.

"No, it isn't that." said Jan. "I think it's been sealed with magic, dark magic. Call Jacob, he'll know what to do."

Jeff rang him; he reported that they were done with their case and were on their way back, which was expected to be in about ten minutes' time.

Stephanie suggested that the group should wait for them in her office so they went up there.

While they waited, Amy rang Stephanie to say that Michael was on the line for her. He didn't have Jeff's number, and he wanted her to tell him that a police detective had been in the village looking for him. He had called into the antique shop and Michael had given him directions to Quarry House. He said his name was Detective Sergeant Ray Thomas and he would be there within the hour. Jeff looked worried when he heard the name, and so did Jan. Stephanie was about to ask him about it when Jacob arrived.

"I have to take care of something," said Jeff. "Will you two be OK to deal with this?" he asked. They reassured him and he left. His face looked dark.

"OK. If you need me, I'll be in my office," Stephanie replied. But he had already left.

On the way, he told Amy to show the man straight in when he arrived which she did soon after.

***

"Well you were right Jan, this is going to need some work," said Jacob "I'll need to get my kit from the car. I'll be right back."

While they waited, they examined the rest of the cellar. There they found three large locked doors at the far end, but they had no time to find keys because very soon Jacob returned with a large black leather case. He placed the box on a nearby table opened his case and took out some of the tools of his trade. He began to recite quietly and confidently while he waved a wand of the purest Brazilian quartz over and around the box.

"Try now," he said.

Stephanie took the smaller key and tried the lock. There was a clicking sound, and the lock popped open.

Someone had obviously taken a lot of trouble to conceal what was inside. Stephanie leaned over and gingerly lifted the lid. Suddenly all the lights in the basement went out, the temperature plummeted and a chill breeze filled the room, swirling round their heads. They heard a crack. Jacob continued chanting, and the lights came back on. Stephanie watched in amazement as an icy fog-like emanation streamed from the box, flew around their heads and up the stairs. As it vanished, the temperature in the room became instantly warmer.

"What the hell did we just let out?" asked Jan.

"Not a clue," said Jacob. "But it can't be good."

Stephanie and Jan peered into the wooden box; it was empty. Neither of them dared to touch it. Jacob looked forlornly down at his crystal wand which had turned a cloudy, grey colour and lay in two parts on the table. The damage was obviously the origin of the cracking sound and it looked like all the energy and goodness had been sucked out of it. He put it in his pocket without a word, planning to bury it in the garden later; giving it back to the earth where it belonged. Its work was done, and he believed that it should be laid to rest with dignity, like every other living thing.

"I'll start cleansing this area," Jacob said, frowning and drawing invisible symbols with his hands on the walls, floor and ceiling. "This place has been filled with negative energy."

"Good idea!" sad Jan.

Stephanie looked at Jan quizzically. "Magic?" she asked.

"No Reiki, he's a Reiki Master!" Jan explained. "As well as a therapy, Reiki is a powerful way of cleansing anything. Rooms, crystals even people. He's drawing the symbols to cleanse and protect the room."

Stephanie nodded. She still had so much to learn. She felt compelled to pick up the box. Instantly she saw an image of the fisherman's cottage again.

This time the man, who they now know to be William, was gazing inside the box. Inside he placed a smaller box made of silver, engraved with a filigree pattern and a letter T etched in the centre of the lid. He locked the small box with a tiny, silver key and placed it in his pocket. Then he began mumbling words which she couldn't understand and waving his hands over it. He did the same to the larger box, then with a self-satisfied smile he placed both keys in his pocket.

Then Stephanie found herself back in the present. She began telling the others what she had seen.

"We know the large key opens the door to the cottage on the island," said Jan, "but we still have a few questions to answer. First, how did the keys come to be in this basement? Second, where is the silver key and the silver box, and third, and most important, since when did William Trevelyan know dark magic?"

They turned as they heard Jeff come down the stairs into the basement.

"I have to go," he said. "Jan, Ray has a lead. Stephanie, I'll be as quick as I can." He kissed her and left.

Stephanie stood in stunned silence for a moment then she asked Jan "I have a question too, who exactly is Ray and what the hell is going on?"

***

Jacob said he would continue cleansing the rest of the premises because they had no idea what they had let out of the box, or where it would end up. Jan and Stephanie went up to Stephanie's office, collecting a coffee on the way.

"What's going on with Jeff?" asked Stephanie.

"Ray is Jeff's old partner," Jan explained. "He has presumably found a lead to locate the man that killed Melissa."

Stephanie instantly understood: Jeff had to do this. After all this time, he had a chance of finding the man who killed his wife. What she didn't understand is why he felt that he couldn't talk to her about it. But she let it go, for now.

"I don't think we need to take the others away from their work just yet, but after what we saw earlier, we need someone with magic skills in on this. I propose that we keep it between us and just work with Jacob," Jan said.

Stephanie agreed.

"William did his best to protect the contents of the silver box, so it must be important. We really need to get to that island. We also need more information on William, so we know what we're dealing with," Stephanie said.

"Well it was pretty strong, dark magic, so my guess is he was in the same league as Mary Hall," Jan said, instantly resigned to the situation. "This is not going to be easy."

"Just what we need," Stephanie said, frowning.

"You don't think that William's spirit was locked in that box do you, and we just let him out?" Stephanie asked, looking horrified.

"Maybe," Jan replied, "but whatever it was, it was pretty nasty. Steph, you focus on making sure the launch goes smoothly and Jacob and I will do some research. Don't worry, you're not alone and we *will* get him," she said giving her friend a hug.

"We have to go to the island tomorrow without fail, Jan." Stephanie was adamant. "I have a feeling we'll get some answers there."

"Absolutely! Now drink your coffee and relax, see you later!" Jan said, and left the office.

Then Stephanie's mobile rang. She heard a familiar voice.

"Hello love, everything under control?"

She recognised the greeting instantly.

"Hello, Dad?" she said. "What a surprise!"

***

It was only lunchtime, and she already had a headache. The day she had long awaited wasn't exactly going to plan. She sat on a bench in the courtyard, enjoying the solitude of the garden, eating a sandwich and trying to take in what her father just said to her. He hadn't been in contact since she'd left London, but after reading about where she was living and finding out about her inheritance and her new business, he had done some research on P.I. When he found out about the supernatural side of the business, he felt it was time that she knew a few things which he had kept from her since her mother died. There were events which he knew had been set in motion a long time before that, and they were relevant to her present situation.

What he had told her had come as a shock in one way, but made perfect sense in another. He told her that her mother, Grace, had a gift. A second sight she used to call it. It was something that had brought her much pain over the years, in not being able to understand it or control it. Stephanie understood that feeling only too well.

It seemed that Grace's mother known to Stephanie as Nana Jean (and daughter of Isabel) had also been blessed in the same way, but had refused to entertain the idea. Nana Jean had once told her son-in-law a story of one night seeing a woman in white floating above her bed accompanied by a tiny white moth, and she had been so terrified that she never spoke of it again. Stephanie realised with sadness that it had been Isabel, trying to contact a lost daughter who had never known she was adopted. Jean, in her fear, knew that something wasn't right, saw the ability to see such things as a curse not a blessing (like many people before her). She had denied her gift and refused to discuss it beyond admitting its existence. Stephanie said nothing to her father about her own gift, and he didn't ask, although she had the impression that he already assumed that she had it.

He continued to say that Grace had experienced premonitions since she was a small child which often came true, sometimes not as she imagined them. Often fragmented as her own prophetic dreams tended to be, they usually made no sense. Like her daughter, Grace had wondered why she had them at all, if they weren't clear enough for her to be able to warn anyone. She also had what Stephanie understood from her father's vague description, as some ability in psychometry, just like she had. He went on to say that in the last year of her life, Grace had been plagued by dreams of a place near the sea, of a woman falling from the cliffs. She became obsessed with finding answers. She only worked part-time as a doctor's receptionist, so she spent all her spare time on research. He said that she had openly shared all of this with him, and he had tried to help her as best he could, but he had felt powerless because he didn't really understand it himself. He had watched the woman he loved fall apart before his eyes.

Stephanie had been chilled to the bone when she heard that on the night she died, her mother was driving to Cornwall. In fact, she was on her way to Marlin. She had never known, never even asked where her mother was when she died. All she was told was that she was killed in a terrible car accident. Her grief took over; her mother was gone, and the details didn't matter. Apparently, for some unknown reason Grace had lost control of the car and crashed onto the central reservation of the M motorway, near Exeter. A driver had pulled over to see if he could help He had stayed there holding her hand until an ambulance arrived, sadl too late to save her. The man later told the police officers attending th scene that she was hallucinating, rambling about a white angel reaching out to her. Stephanie had no doubt that it was Isabel. Might it have bee the hex that killed her? She strongly suspected that it was. Stephanie's family life had been torn apart at an early age by Mary Hall, and she hadn't even known about it.

Her father then told her that he had been keeping something for her, some items that her mother had with her at the time of her death. Grace had felt them to be very important, and he wondered if they might have been connected to what drew her to Marlin. He was afraid that what drove Grace to her death might do the same to Stephanie. He asked if he could drive down and give them to her in person and she had agreed and reassured him that she was fine. He was on his way and would be there in time for the launch.

Her mind was racing. Her thoughts drifted back to other memories that had surfaced in recent weeks. The time that she knew she wouldn't see her father's cousin alive again. The days she had sat alone in the spare room of her childhood home and sensed other people in there, talking to her. The spirit children she had played with. The many times she had felt someone standing beside her, giving her silent messages and consolation. She now knew that it had been Lucas. Her uncanny knowledge of where to find lost possessions, and her many dreams of events that later came true. Her childhood had been full of these inexplicable moments, some reassuring and some frightening to a child, although she had unwittingly become used to them. Memories which she couldn't face; events which she had buried.

There were so many things that she hadn't wanted to remember, so she had put them all in a room in her mind and locked them away in a box of her invention. Or so she had thought. She now realised that it was an identical box to the wooden chest with the studded metal bars that had become so important to her now. That's why the box had looked so familiar to her; it had been another premonition. Like the box that she opened that morning, the box in her mind had been unlocked now too, and all the memories she had sought to deny had all spilled out, just like whatever had soared away up the stairs from the basement that morning. It was time to face the truth, and finally she was ready.

But she also knew that the box she was looking for now held more than her blocked psychic memories; it held the secret to destroying William, and other secrets of a very different kind.

***

Jan made her jump as she joined her on the bench. Stephanie told her about the phone call and what her Dad had said.

"It makes sense," Jan said. "Do you remember that day you fell off the climbing frame in the school playground when you were eight? When your mother unexpectedly arrived before the Head had a chance to call her? We were kids. We thought it was just a coincidence. How wrong we were."

Stephanie cast her thoughts back to her childhood.

"Yes. I know what you mean. I also remember that morning before I left for school, the last time I spoke to Mum. She said 'Goodbye Steffi, have a good day!' She said goodbye Jan! She never usually said goodbye. I wondered about that for years: whether she… knew."

They looked each other. They both knew the answer.

Stephanie felt a new memory creep into her mind, a memory so awful that she had buried it. She was 14. She woke up in the night screaming. Her father rushed to her bedside, and she explained that she had a dream about her mother: that she was in a car crash and that she was dead. She heard the impact, felt a searing pain in her head, just as her mother would have. She gasped in her sleep as her mother took her last breath, the link between them had been that strong. Her father told her it was just a nightmare. But in the morning, she had woken to find police in her house and her father in shock.

She had never even told Jan about it, but she told her now and Jan hugged her. Then Stephanie told her about all the other memories that had been surfacing. She listened silently; she understood as Stephanie knew she would. Jan had been through some similar experiences, but nowhere near as terrifying, yet she had embraced them from an early age. No wonder Stephanie had avoided all Jan's attempts to get her to develop her gift; that is until she came to Marlin. She no longer had a choice. Jan held her friend tightly, wishing she could spare her more pain. Stephanie had been through a lot in her life already, and no doubt that there was worse to come.

They sat in silence for a few minutes then Jan got up.

"Come with me, I have something to show you," she said.

Jan was dreading what she had to do next. Taking a deep breath, she gently took Stephanie's hand and led her upstairs to her office. What she was about to say would not be easy for her friend to hear, but it still had to be said.

***

Jan had found a useful book during her research. She showed Stephanie an old leather-bound book: "A History of The Trevelyan Family." It was an old biography of her family and the estate, including a long section on the ongoing feud with the Halls. She had typed out a summary of the important facts.

"I'm sorry, Steph, but it isn't all good news," Jan said. "The feud between the Trevelyans and Halls goes back a long time, further even than William and Mary. I'll give you the short version," Jan said, then read from her notes.

"It says here that The Manor was built in 1745 by the first lord of the manor, as we knew. His name was Sir Adrian Trevelyan, owner of the tin mine. The mines themselves date back to the Bronze age, to over two thousand years BC. Tin, as you may know, when mixed with copper, forms bronze, making it much sought-after, and in the 18th century, mining here reached its pinnacle, with Cornwall as the world's major producer of tin. Adrian, owning a lot of the surrounding land, and wanting to flaunt his money. decided to build a grand house with a chapel, rows of homes for his workers and a pub. That's when the village of Marlin sprung up and the land was developed into three farms to provide for his family and the workers."

"OK," said Stephanie, "so where does the magic come in?"

"I was getting to that!" Jan said. "Well, it says that all went well for the family until the early 1800s when his great grandson, Harold Trevelyan, met a local woman named Josie Weekes. Josie was a white witch, and she also had an eye for his older brother Luke, but he wasn't interested. She used a harmless love potion to make him fall in love with her. Harold, who in his jealousy wanted to break the spell, teamed up with some local coven in Wadebridge. It was the Blake family, Steph, and we all know what they're like, having recently met dear Simon. Harold learned to use dark magic to break the spell, but something went wrong because in his envy, he wished ill on his brother because of it and Luke died."

Stephanie was shocked. More death associated with her family. Their history was steeped in blood.

"Josie was heartbroken. She hated Harold and would have nothing to do with him. He tried to make her love him using magic, but she used powerful protection magic and it failed. As you know, the power of three takes care of those that use magic to harm others, and he died horribly, although no details are given, thankfully. Josie, it seems, only used magic to protect herself from Harold, not to harm him or anyone else. She fell in love again and went on to marry a villager called Samuel Hall, one of the farm hands on the estate, and she lived a long and happy life. They had three children, one of whom was her daughter Alice, a white witch like her. Alice's line was the one that gave rise to the lovely Mary."

"That's how magic came to be in the Hall family," Stephanie said.

"Looks like it. The Hall magic was used for good for a long time. It seems that they were all white witches till William killed Tom Hall and set Mary off." Jan said. "Josie was a good person and so were her descendants. She was a healer, using herbs, magic and potions only to help people, using magic only in their best interests. And Alice continued her work when she died. That must be where you inherited your ability to heal spirits, Steph," said Jan. "Now, back to the Trevelyans!"

Stephanie nodded, it all made sense.

Jan told Stephanie that the Trevelyans blamed Josie for what happened to both Luke and Harold. After Harold died, it seemed that the use of magic in the Trevelyan family died with him. But the family hatred of Josie Hall didn't, and hatred for all the Halls became a family feud.

"Then a few generations later, William was born and took over the estate and married Julia. But he started dabbling himself in the dark arts. It says that his business dealings extended far beyond the tir mines, Steph. He used magic to make sure he kept increasing his fortune, getting the best deals and destroying competitors, making people do exactly what he wanted them to, even killing them. He remained rich, even through the Depression of the 1930s, and carried or expanding his empire. When other people were starving and thei businesses failed, he was thriving on their misery."

Stephanie was speechless; this was worse than she expected. He inheritance was gained by dark magic, greed and blood money.

"There's more." Jan said. "His wife Julia was gifted, not in magic as fa we know, but in the gift which we now know to have been passed dow to you. It's no wonder you are so powerful, Steph, you've got it on bot sides of your family, and that's quite rare, believe me!"

There it was, confirmation that what her Dad had said was true. Grac probably did have the gift from the Trevelyan line, and so did Jean, a did she. It didn't only come from the Halls.

"Jan, there were witches on both sides of my family. Was what Mar said wrong all along? Could I be a witch? Or do I just have this powe because I inherited the gift on both sides? Could I also have some sort c magical inheritance too, like Lucy? But I don't cast spells. I wouldn't know where to start!"

"There are such things as natural witches," Jan said. "I think we'll have to research into that side of things a bit more before it all makes sense."

Stephanie was horrified. As well as having an incredible gift, she might also be a witch and she was heiress to a tainted fortune. She was filled with panic.

"I don't want the inheritance, Jan. Not any of it, I don't want his money. I want to give it all away!" Stephanie said, with tears in her eyes. "I knew he was wicked, but this…! I can't take it all in. My inheritance is corrupt and stained with the deaths of so many innocent people. And even though Josie started off good, it was because of Mary that magic was used for dark purposes in that line too!"

"It's a shock I know," Jan said, getting up and putting an arm round her. "But be sensible. Think of all the good you can do with it, the good you've already done in so short a time. Even if you are a natural witch, you're nothing like him Steph, and nothing like Mary, don't ever think that. Think of Julia, Isabel, Jean and Grace. And Josie and Alice! You come from a long line of strong women with extraordinary talents, good people who chose only to use them to help others, despite the darkness all around them. This is your chance to make it right, to make Marlin a good place again. You can make the Trevelyan name synonymous with benevolence and happiness. Set up trust funds, build schools and hospitals. Do anything you want with the money. But don't forget, you have a responsibility to this estate. You're Lady Trevelyan now, like it or not!"

Stephanie was silent. Then she spoke, almost in a whisper.

"You don't understand, Jan. I enjoyed it."

"Enjoyed what, being rich?" Jan said, smiling. "Who wouldn't!"

"No, destroying Mary. Near the end, I could feel her pain. She begged me to stop, but I carried on tormenting her. I enjoyed it! What kind of monster am I becoming? This power... it's dangerous! It lures you in and..."

Stephanie was in tears now.

"That doesn't make you a monster, it just makes you human!" said Jeff.

He was standing in the doorway, and she was happy that he was back, even though she was embarrassed that he heard what she just said.

"To destroy someone that caused your family so much pain, who hurt so many people, just to make sure they never hurt anyone again? That's a good thing, in my book. And if you really were a monster, you wouldn't be worrying about it!"

He walked over and put his arms around her, and she instantly felt certain of everything.

"No-one should ever be ashamed of who they are, Steph. You were given your gifts and your money to use for good, so don't be afraid to use them," said Jan with a smile as she left the room. "See you later!"

"What did I miss?" asked Jeff as Jan breezed out. She brought him up to date on everything that had happened since he left.

"No wonder you're in bits, that's a lot to take in," he said. She nodded and wiped her eyes.

"What happened with Ray?" she asked, sniffing.

"The tip he received was a dead end, but this new contact might eventually lead to something, if we're lucky," he said, his eyes looking sad and distant. "I'm sorry, Steph," he added. "I should have told you I was still looking into her death. It's just that so much has happened, and I didn't want to burden you with anything else...."

"I understand," she said. "But please, don't keep things from me. You don't have to protect me from everything!"

He nodded and held her close. Suddenly he pulled away, looked at Stephanie and brightened up.

"Come on, let's get ready, we have a party to go to, Milady!"

***

Stephanie showed the waiting staff from the village café how she wanted everything set up, then she told Amy where they would be in case of an emergency. Jan was staying at the office, elbow-deep in dusty old books; she had her outfit with her in the car. Jeff drove Stephanie to The Lodge to get changed for the launch. She was silent all the way home. All the information she had learned from her Dad then from Jan was roaring round in her brain. Jeff fed Maisy then phoned Ray to check in while she was having a shower.

Her head felt like it would burst. As she was straightening her hair, she heard voices downstairs. She dressed quickly and applied her make-up, looking in the mirror as briefly as possible, relieved to see only her own face reflected back at her. Soon she was ready. She looked perfect for the occasion in a sapphire blue satin dress with matching satin shoes. She usually lived in jeans and felt completely out of place in such clothes, but Lady Trevelyan had to put on a show; her public expected it. Her jewellery was a pair of plain, silver stud earrings and a simple silver and sapphire pendant which had once belonged to her mother.

She rushed downstairs to see who was there. It was her father. He looked older, thinner, had many more lines around his eyes and his hair was a little greyer at the temples. The years had not been good to him, he was only 58, and something about him made her feel uneasy. He looked both well and ill at the same time. Jeff was making them all some tea.

"Hi, Dad, I see you've met Jeff!" she said, with genuine affection.

Her father explained that he had arrived at the office early and Amy had given him her address.

"Wow," said Jeff. "You look amazing! That reminds, me I'd better get ready too. If you'll both excuse me…"

Her father nodded and Jeff kissed her on the cheek as he went upstairs to change. A string of expletives could be heard coming from the stairs, followed by "Sorry!" They were all directed at Maisy, who had left her toy known as Baby on the stairs to trip him up, yet again. Stephanie explained what had happened and her father smiled. Maisy appeared on cue and hissed at her father, in true Maisy fashion, and Stephanie told her off for being rude towards their guest.

"Jeff seems like a good man," her father said. "He has very sad eyes though. He's suffered a great loss, hasn't he?"

She nodded and said nothing; she didn't need to. Her father was observant and a good judge of character, probably why he was such a good solicitor. He had such good instincts that she often wondered whether he had the gift too. He was certainly empathic.

'Good to see you Dad, let's sit down," she said as she led him into the kitchen and passed her father his tea. They sat at the kitchen table overlooking the sea, the horizon lay in the distance, resplendent in the setting sun.

"You have a beautiful home," he said. "I love the view!"

She thanked him, then came straight to the point.

He looked at her and spoke. "I have something to say. I'm sorry we've grown so far apart, Steph. I never wanted things to end up like this. After your mother died, I was lost. I retreated into myself and left you to fend for yourself. I'm so sorry."

Any bitterness she had felt for him melted away. But she struggled not to become emotional; now was not the time.

No need to apologise, Dad. It was a long time ago. We'll have plenty of time to make up for the past."

She took his hand with a smile.

As she did, she saw a picture of herself attending a funeral. She realised that they wouldn't have long at all. Her father was grievously ill, and he knew it. He had come to make amends before it was too late.

"..." she began, but the words wouldn't come.

"You know, don't you?" he said, and she nodded.

She looked at him closely and she realised then that he had a glow around him. She had heard of such things before, but had never experienced it, or maybe she had and hadn't realised what it was. This was the sign that she had picked up on in others without ever seeing it, but now that her gift was getting stronger, it was clear as day. This was what made her uneasy when she first saw him just now; she could see that his spirit was starting to escape from its earthly home, his body. It happened when people were terminally ill, or about to face some life-threatening event which they were unlikely to survive. Maybe it was linked to her psychometry, but for some reason she was able to see it. She gasped, and he noticed her looking at him.

"Your mother used to get that look too, whenever she picked up or something unpleasant. It's stage four cancer, Steph. Three months, six at most they said. I want to put things right between us while there's still time. Please forgive me."

She put her arms round his neck and held him, clung to him like she did when she was little. He was back: the Dad she adored. She remembered how he had taken her for walks in the country on Sunday mornings and the stories that he made up just for her. He had encouraged her in her writing, in her poetry, in everything. He had often stood outside the door as she sang and played guitar in her bedroom, then popped his head in to say how much he loved it. He had made her believe that she was invincible, and that nothing was impossible.

She felt the closeness return, that bond that they always had before he had changed, before her mother's death had changed him; before the time when he no longer noticed she existed, or at least that was how had felt. It was like she had lost him a bit at a time over the years. Without her even noticing, he had started to slip away.

He had always been there for her when she was little; she and her mother were his life. Even though he often had to work long hours, he had always made time for her. Then when her mother died, the light went out of his eyes and he had just slipped away, out of her life and she hadn't understood why. She knew now that he couldn't help it; he had been protecting himself from his pain as best he could and trying to protect her from it too. Also, it hurt him that she had reminded him so much of her mother. She wished now that she had made more effort.

"If only we could have helped each other," she thought. Maybe she could help him now.

"There's nothing to forgive," she told him. "I was as much to blame. Now, is there anything I can do? There must be some treatment, anything, money is no object now."

She let go of him and he shook his head.

"Nothing, Steph. I've had surgery, and further treatment will only delay the inevitable for a short time. No more can be done, so there's no point in prolonging things. I have made my choice, to enjoy the time I have left, not bedridden in hospital. Not until I have to be there, at least. It's OK, really. We must make the most of the time we have left. I'm so proud of you, Steph! Your mother would be too, your book was wonderful, you know how she loved to read. She would have loved it."

He wiped his eyes with his handkerchief.

"YES, I AM PROUD, STEFFI!" said her mother. She thanked Grace silently.

"If only he knew, she's right here with us!" she thought, yet she didn't know how to tell him. She sensed that the knowledge might bring him more pain than comfort.

"I'm surprised you read it. You know you only like cowboy books and war stories!" she joked.

"I read it because you wrote it," he said, smiling, and she knew that he would have.

She was crying now and laughing at the same time.

"OK, so what did you bring me?" she asked, suddenly overcome with curiosity.

She wiped the tears away as he handed her a parcel. It was wrapped in brown paper and inside that were two objects wrapped in tissue paper. She unwrapped the smaller of the two. It was a tiny silver key on a silver chain.

"I don't know what it's for," he said.

Stephanie knew instantly what it was, the key to the small, engraved. silver box from her vision. William's silver box.

"But where is the box?" Stephanie wondered *"On that island?"*

She didn't touch it; now was not the right time. She simply wrapped it up again in the tissue paper.

"Thank you!" she said. "I know exactly what this is for!"

The other object turned out to be a small leather-bound book. She opened it, and it was her mother's diary. As she flicked through it, she could see that it contained her thoughts, visions and dreams, which she knew would be invaluable to her, like a piece of her mother for her to treasure

"I don't understand it. I don't know what's going on, but I hope you get a chance to explain it to me one day," he said with a weak smile.

"Yes Dad, I hope so too," she replied, hugging him again.

Jeff came into the kitchen looking at the clock.

"Sorry to interrupt, but we need to go," he said.

She placed the items carefully in her handbag then went upstairs to reapply her ruined make-up and brush her hair. She could hear the men chatting happily downstairs. It meant a lot to her that they were getting along. She pulled herself together and moments later she appeared in the hallway

"Ready!" she said, as she picked up a warm coat from the hall stand.

***

Soon they were driving back to Quarry House. Her father had insisted on following in his own car so he could leave for Bristol straight after the party, refusing her offer to stay over at The Lodge. Stephanie took the opportunity to tell Jeff what she had just found out. The concern in his eyes made her want to cry again, but she couldn't let herself give in to it. Not now. She had to make sure that she made the party a happy memory for her Dad; for them both.

What she hadn't told her father, what she didn't even want to think about, was that she doubted she would see him alive after tonight. The thought of losing him again, when she'd only just got him back, was breaking her heart.

***

It was almost six o'clock. Guests were starting to arrive and Jan had already rung her while they were in the car, panicking that they wouldn't get there in time. She explained about her father. Jan was saddened to hear about his illness, she had always been very fond of him when she was growing up. She had always thought of James Meares as her father too, and she welcomed him as such when they arrived. He was obviously just as pleased to see her.

Music played, the press was in attendance. Michael and Lisa were there with Matthew, Jessie and Lucy. Jenny had driven over to celebrate with them too. The Hollows and some other P.I. operatives from London and elsewhere, known to Jeff but new to Stephanie, mingled happily with the crowd. Local shopkeepers, estate workers, tin mine staff and even her solicitor had been invited, and everyone had been happy to attend. Champagne flowed, and it was soon time for her speech. Stephanie stood in front of them all nervously. As Jan introduced her, cameras clicked and flashes blinded her.

"I give you Lady Stephanie!"

Everyone clapped as she stepped forward. Then the lights went out.

The French windows at the rear of the room flew open and a wild wind howled around them. Glasses smashed, people screamed and started running outside into the courtyard. Amy was at the front. She had instinctively grabbed Stephanie's father by the hand and was leading everyone through the back gate to safety before anyone could cut hurt by flying glass. Stephanie was proud of her, and grateful. This was not the weather; this was an angry spirit.

Jacob, Adam and Rachel joined hands with Jan, aiming to cast magic and ward off what was attacking them. But an unseen force separated them and flung them into the corners of the room. The rest of the P.I. operatives found torches, and some joined the trio, forming a wider circle. They all started chanting ancient rites while others ran to the Hollows' office at Jacob's request to fetch the bags containing their equipment. Glass shards, chairs, tables, in fact everything in the room, was being hurled around as if it weighed no more than matchsticks. Everyone was cut and battered, bleeding and bruised. They were knocked down time and time again, but they still kept standing back up. The air stank with decay, terrifying howls filled the air and torches flickered and died as their batteries were drained, all the energy being used to fuel the rage of one entity.

Jeff, Jan and Stephanie knew who it was and what he was after. It was William, and he wanted the silver key, hidden for now in her office. He was willing to kill everyone in that room to prevent them finding what he'd hidden. He had no form; what lay before them was a shapeless ball of thick, dark, swirling evil, and he was winning. Her team were exhausted.

Stephanie stood in the middle of the room, pulling Jeff to her side. Jan in to the other and soon, as they all called in their guides, Stephanie beckoned all the remaining P.I. operatives to hold hands and form a line. Her people were being hurt, and she wouldn't stand for it. She was their protector, he had made her angry, and anger made her strong.

"YOU are not welcome here, spirit!" she called. "LEAVE NOW!" Her voice was chilling as it echoed through the room. With the aid of magic and spiritual intervention, led instinctively by Stephanie, they all joined forces.

Using all their strength of purpose, and with every ounce of energy that they had left, they started to push his energy backwards. Witches chanted, psychics channelled their guardians and everyone else just stood their ground defiantly. Stephanie began glowing, and her energy spread from one to another down the line until they were all glowing too. Gradually, inch by inch they walked forward towards the door together, forming a barrier of impenetrable light, banishing the darkness and forcing William's energy out of the room. As the doors slammed shut, the lights went on. Stephanie slumped to the floor, her energy spent.

The music started playing again. As they looked around, they were all shocked to see that the room had somehow been reset as it was before the party. Glasses were unused, bottles were full, and the buffet lay untouched as it had been at the start of the evening. Also, everyone was unscathed, without even one cut or bruise; Stephanie's light had healed them. The team stepped back in admiration and relief, looking at their surroundings. Then one by one they just stood and stared at Stephanie. Jeff rushed to her side, joined by Jan.

They had all seen some incredible sights, fought some deadly spirits during their time with P.I. but nothing had come close to that. It had been astounding. Not only had she used her inner light to stand against their unseen attacker, to fight him, but she had given them the power do so too. She was a natural leader, inspiring and unselfish, the rightful protector of Marlin.

Then, with help, she stood shakily to her feet and said a few simple words that filled them all with dread.

"Thank you, everyone, but I think that was just the beginning. He will be back, and we need to be ready."

***

The guests were waiting outside the gate, anxious for news. The group inside quickly composed themselves. Jeff went out and ushered the guests back in, reassuring them that it was just a freak wind that caused a power surge and that peace had been restored. Everyone trooped back in, not seeming to notice that the food and drink were untouched; or maybe they simply assumed that they had restocked. All that is except Stephanie's father, who didn't believe a word of Jeff's explanation. But he didn't pry, he was just glad to see that they were alright.

Stephanie regained her composure in the privacy of her office with the help of some water, and then Jeff helped her back to the party. She fought back her exhaustion, walked into the room with her head held high, and everyone broke into spontaneous applause.

Stephanie gave a short but genuine speech, thanking everyone that she needed to thank, both for welcoming her into their village and into their hearts. She told them that P.I. was there for everyone, however they needed it. In that comment, there was an unspoken promise to rid the village of the evil that had hung over it like a pall for generations; waiting for her. Many people there understood, and her team firmly believe that she could do it, if tonight's display was anything to go by.

The party went on to be a huge success: the launch had been a truly memorable event.

As her father left that night, he told her that he would always be there for her if she ever needed him. She smiled and told him "Likewise," as she fought back the tears. He hugged her and looked at her, then smiled and said, "Goodbye Steph."

She caught her breath when she looked into his eyes. In that moment, she knew that this was the last time they would meet, and he knew it too. Just like when she saw her mother for the last time, this *was* goodbye.

***

Jan held an emergency meeting after the party in the conference room. As owner and overall manager of P.I. she told everyone that she wanted all those present to remain in Marlin and support the P.I. South West team until William was dealt with. She said that tonight had shown that it would be a very dangerous mission; that he was possibly the deadliest spirit that they had ever come across. She said that any one of them could decide to pass on this case, if they chose to, and she told them that their jobs were safe whatever they chose. Everyone agreed to remain, without even a second thought, and Jan gave them her thanks.

Stephanie thanked them too, for their support and for their prompt actions earlier. She told them that she had some idea of how to progress, which she would share with them in the morning, but for now, they all needed rest.

The team members sorted themselves out as far as overnight accommodation was concerned, making full use of the suite of company bedrooms. Jan would be staying indefinitely at The Lodge, which Stephanie had already arranged with her. Amy lived in the village so she went home by taxi, and Adam saw her to the door.

Back at home, Stephanie told Jeff that she needed to speak to Jan before she went to bed, and he gave them privacy. She was beyond exhausted, but she had burning questions and she hoped that Jan could answer them.

"Jan, I don't understand what happened tonight, how did I do all that? I gave everyone light, shared with them the power to push William away then I healed them. I don't know how I did it!" she said, in obvious distress.

"I know, isn't it awesome!" her friend replied, beaming at her.

"No Jan, it's terrifying," she said, in tears. "I feel like some sort of freak of nature. The energy, the light, it's too much!"

"Steph, what you did tonight was incredible, and it was for the sake of good. You protected and healed everyone around you. That can't be a bad thing! Does it really matter if you don't understand it? This gift, the most wonderful thing I have ever witnessed, was given to you for a reason. Just accept it!"

Reluctantly, Stephanie agreed to do just that.

"I suppose I'm stuck with it, aren't I?" she asked, this time not expecting an answer. Jan laughed and hugged her before saying goodnight.

Stephanie went to bed. But as she tried to sleep, wrapped in Jeff's arms with Maisy at her feet, she realised that it didn't matter how she did what she did; the important thing was that she just kept doing it.

***

The next morning, at nine o'clock, a tired but determined makeshift team of people sat around the large conference table at Quarry House, armed with copious amounts of coffee. There was Amy, Jan, Jeff, Stephanie, the other P.I. members from the night before, plus another local employee who had been called in by Jan that morning.

The building smelled of smudge sticks. As promised, Jacob had been cleansing any residual negative energy from the building by burning them in every room throughout the premises. He had added Reiki and sound for additional cleansing, and he had been rigorous. In some rooms, such as the reception area and conference room, he had used the more palatable Palo Santo. As he had explained to Stephanie in detail as she drank her coffee, it was the wood of a mystical tree that grew on the coast of South America and was particularly suitable to the purpose. It gave off a pleasant, citrus smell due to the oils in the wood itself and was less likely to induce coughing (a common side effect of burning white sage). That particular inconvenience would not be welcoming to visitors, or beneficial to the smooth running of their meeting.

Stephanie's mind wandered as she waited for the meeting to start. Sleep had not come easily the night before. She had tried counting sheep and drinking hot milk, then when they failed her, she stayed awake till the early hours reading her mother's diary cover to cover. It had made her realise that there had been so much more to Grace than she had ever imagined; so much that she didn't know. Its contents had come as a great shock. It was like reading the innermost thoughts of a stranger, yet she could have written it herself. The torment that Grace had endured:

the visions, the unanswered questions that Stephanie had a team of colleagues and friends to help her with. All of that, Grace had faced alone. Even though her father had obviously understood and supported Grace in his own way, her mother went through all that without anyone to guide her. It was unbearably sad. She must have thought she was going out of her mind, which she had heard that some psychics and mediums often experience. Without Jan's guidance, Stephanie knew that she would have felt the same, and at times she still did. Especially when she first came to Marlin and was stalked by the doll from hell.

However, the diary had held no further clues to help Stephanie with her current task or her own personal journey. It had just given her a deeper understanding of her mother. Although reading it had upset her, she also treasured the opportunity to get to know her mother better. They had been robbed of so much time. She had always known that they were alike, and it had never been more apparent than now. At least she still had Grace's spirit around her, for the time being at least. Grace hadn't spoken to her while she was reading the diary, or afterwards. No words were necessary; it was just another one of those unspoken bonds that they now shared.

Her thoughts were drawn back to the meeting as Jan began. There had been no time for formal introductions the night before, so Jan invited everyone to give their name, usual work location and area of expertise, and Amy made a list. Stephanie had no need to introduce herself or explain what she did; they had all seen it, and it defied description.

Stephanie took the list from Amy. Then she, Jan and Jeff stepped out for a while, relocating to her office. They needed to discuss how to best use the team for the challenges that they might face in the dark days to come, and decide on the tasks of immediate importance for that day. Soon they had a firm plan, at least for now. Their plans had a habit of changing, like the Marlin weather, as if they too were at the mercy of the tides.

Jan updated the team. The first thing that needed to be put in place were circles of magical protection; one around Quarry House and one at The Lodge. Jacob and Rachel were allocated that task.

They agreed that the fisherman's cottage on the small island of Lapwing Rock was the likely location of the silver box, or that it might at least provide Stephanie with clues via psychometry. On hearing that Laura from the Exeter branch also shared that gift, it was decided that she would go with Stephanie and Jeff to the island to maximise their potential for finding leads.

Then Jan addressed Suzy and Faith from Bristol.

"We would like you to combine your summoning skills, please, to find ways to draw out William, at a time and place of our choosing. Adam will work with you, advising on spells and rituals to help you to do so, Jan said. Suzy, Faith and Adam nodded their agreement.

"Jacob and Rachel, could you please join them when you back from The Lodge? We need you to work on protection magic and keep the team as safe as possible from any of William's future attacks. Also, we need to devise ways to reverse and remove any spells preventing us from opening the silver box when we find it."

The pair agreed.

Jan asked Hunter to start preparing any appropriate equipment th they might need, such as communication devices. He was one of the London team, their new technology expert who was due to start at the Marlin branch the following week,

Dawn and Abbey from Swindon agreed to use their clairvoyant and precognition skills. Martin, a local historian and cartographer (originally from Marlin but now living in Wadebridge), would assist by working through the ancient books and maps in the research library. His task was to try to pinpoint locations of importance to William that might be alternative hiding places for the silver box (should it not be on Lapwing Rock) and suggest other places that he might manifest next. It was expected that Martin would also join the team at Quarry House, making best use of his local knowledge.

A former London vicar, Robert, now fighting for the souls of the world in a less orthodox but more direct way, was asked to investigate appropriate passages from scripture to give them support in the tasks to come. Although demonic possession was not likely, there were other aspects of his training and knowledge that might come in useful. Stephanie, not being religious in any way, looked sceptical.

"Psalm 37, for example, is often used to break hexes and other religious passages are uses for blessing and cleansing," Adam informed her, allaying her doubt to a certain extent.

Stephanie nodded in embarrassment, vaguely remembering that someone was reciting scripture at the lunch the night before when William attacked. She freely admitted to everyone present that they needed all the help they could get and thanked Robert for anything he could add. Robert smiled warmly, obviously used to scepticism around his beliefs. She could see that he appreciated her openness.

"Amy and I will stay here," said Jan, "Amy could you please deal with any press and public enquiries after the launch, and make appointments for new clients?"

Amy agreed willingly, frantically scribbling notes as Jan went along.

"I'll be busy contacting existing P.I. clients, soothing ruffled feathers for those cases where operatives have been called away, and reallocating the cases of the operatives that have been seconded to Marlin," Jan added.

Everyone now had a role, and it was obvious that they were determined to fulfil their duties as best they could. Stephanie had only known most of them a very short time, but she hoped that a couple of them would be staying with her in Marlin and intended to discuss it with Jan in due course. She already had no doubt about the calibre of the people that sat before her, and she was impressed with the range of their skills. She knew, absolutely, that they would stand beside her in a heartbeat; wherever she led, without hesitation. Their aim was the same as her own, to rid this world of evil in the form of William Trevelyan and anyone else that came along to cause trouble. For the first time since this sorry mess began, she felt like they might just stand a chance.

***

With two hours left before the tide came in, Stephanie, Jeff and Laura set off. They decided to call in at The Lodge first, so that Stephanie and Jeff could change into more suitable clothing than suits for tramping round the island in rain and biting winds. Laura had was already appropriately dressed in jeans and a thick jumper with a warm coat, gloves and a scarf. She waited in the living room, gazing out over the choppy sea and stroking a delighted Maisy.

Jeff picked up his backpack and put in some torches, energy bars and bottles of water; then they drove to the tin mine and left Jeff's car in the car park. Stephanie had never visited the tin mine, but this was not the time to play tourist. As they walked, she stared sadly at Fern Leap where Isabel met her death at the hands of William and Mary took her own life. It carried an energy of despair and tragedy. They took the steep steps down from there to the beach, being careful not to slip. The steps were narrow and worn. There had been a shower of rain which had ended just when they left the office, leaving the steps particularly precarious to the unwary. They were in a hurry, but safety came first.

That area of beach was rocky and full of pebbles, and the wind blowing in off the sea was as cold as they had anticipated. The tide was out, and the sea was a long way off. They skirted the base of the cliff, and started walking past the high tide line marked by seaweed and driftwood, the occasional piece of plastic, crisp packets and an old beer can. Stephanie frowned, making a mental note to have more bins installed on the beach and along the coastal path. They walked out towards the sea, following a rough path between two rows of sea-worn, wooden posts sticking up from the ground.

"There used to be a bridge here when I was a boy," Jeff said, pointing to the posts and breaking the silence that had fallen on them since leaving the car. "When it fell into disrepair after a particularly bad storm, parents decided not to rebuild it to discourage children playing out there. The island had the reputation of being haunted."

"Understandable," Stephanie said.

"It didn't stop us though," Jeff laughed. "We simply waited and walked over at low tide!"

He made conversation with Laura, knowing her well from past cases. She seemed friendly, if a little serious, but obviously very committed to her work. Stephanie was lost in thought. The January wind blowing off the sea stabbed like needles though their coats, gloves and scarves.

They reached the island, and climbed another more dangerous set of steps, the first few being covered in barnacles and slimy pieces of draped seaweed. The route was treacherous; covered with recent seawater from the morning tide. There was also a strong smell of rotting fish. At the top, they reached a level area surrounded by grass, heather and old stone blocks from other former dwelling places. There were iron hoops set into a low stone wall next to the top handrail, presumably a place to secure the ropes from small rowing boats used to reach the island when the tide was in. Gulls heralded their approach, the sky was brilliant blue and cloudless, which accounted for the low temperature that they were experiencing. The wind was blustery. Grateful for the metal handrail, they made their way carefully up a steep path which had deliberately been covered in broken shells to add purchase for anyone visiting the island.

The view from the top was breathtaking. Stephanie could see the whole of Tern Bay, with the beach at Lapwing Cove stretching all the way from Curlew Cottage on the far left to the tower of the tin mine on the right. She worked out that The Manor would have been somewhere on the cliff beyond that, and clearly visible before the fire from where they now stood. Further on into the distance, she could see what she recognised as the roofs of the village; she could just make out the houses and shops, and the pub.

Then as they turned away from the cliff, sheltered a little way down the other side of the hill, they came upon the small cottage. There were two stone steps leading down to it and it looked exactly as it had in Stephanie's vision. She took the large key from her coat pocket with her gloved hand and unlocked the door.

Jeff went in first in case anyone was there, but it was empty, so the others followed him inside with their torches lit. It was quite dark inside, with tattered, moth-eaten curtains covering the windows, and it smelled of mould, dust, and the now familiar aroma of fish. It had no inhabitants apart from the spiders and wood lice that had set up home in there, and an occasional beetle that wandered in.

A gust of wind caught dried leaves that lay on the floor, spinning them round with clouds of dust motes which lit up like fairy dust in the beams cast by the torches. It was just as Stephanie had seen in her vision. As Laura shut the door the leaves fell, lifeless once more, to lie dormant in new places on the cold, dirty flagstones until they rotted away, or someone else came to disturb their slumber.

Jeff shone his torch on a table in the centre of the room, familiar only to Stephanie. On the table was a large, carved, wooden box with metal studded bars, identical to the one that she had found back at Quarry House.

She tried the smaller key from her pocket and the box clicked open. She jumped as she caught sight of her own windswept reflection in its mirrored lid. This box was empty.

"So, there are two boxes which both open with the same key," she said.

She took off her gloves and touched the box; nothing happened.

"In that case, why was there no protection magic on this box?" Jeff asked.

"Maybe the other box was William's, and this one belonged to someone else?" suggested Laura.

"Who, Peter? Would he trust his criminal son with something as important as what was in the silver box?" asked Stephanie.

"Maybe he stole it?" Jeff wondered.

Laura touched the box and also saw nothing. None of this made sense. Jeff looked at his watch.

"We'd better go, the tide is due in," said Jeff.

He picked up the box and put it in his backpack. Stephanie took the larger key from her pocket to lock the door while the others waited by the steps. As she touched the door key with her bare hand, her consciousness was transported elsewhere. Another vision.

She was in the cottage. There was a raging wooden fire spitting and crackling. An oil lamp was lit, the curtains were drawn and the small room was warm and welcoming. William was there, and he wasn't alone. Peter was with him and they were arguing.

"Where is it? I know it was in there and it's gone!" said William, enraged.

"How would I know? I'm not the only person who comes here, you know!" said Peter, flippantly.

"You're the only one with a key! Do you know what this means for me if anyone gets hold of it?" William bellowed.

"With all the spells you used to secure it, I wouldn't worry," said Peter, not particularly bothered by his father's bluster and posturing, and obviously used to it.

"It isn't your immortal soul that's at stake, is it?" shouted William, pacing back and fore. "Don't you care?"

"Well if anything happens to you, dear father, I will be filthy rich. So, no!" said Peter in defiance. With that, William turned to face his son, towering over him, and slapped him so hard across the face that he fell backwards into the table.

"I wish you were dead!" said Peter, storming out of the cottage, slamming the door behind him hard enough to rattle the windows.

William turned to the fire, seething in anger.

"Steph, are you OK?" she heard Jeff calling from far away.

As abruptly as she had left it, she was back by the door of the cottage, weak and shaken, with her knees about to give way under her.

***

Jeff and Laura helped her up the steps into the bracing sea breeze. Stephanie still felt light-headed and nauseous, and they had to hold her up. They led her to a flat rock outside where she sat, shaking, and Jeff gave her a bottle of water. Laura refused the offer of one. The causeway to the beach was covered; they were already too late. They were trapped by the tide. Stephanie told them both what she had just seen.

"That box really is important to him, isn't it?" Laura said.

"Yes, and we don't have a clue why, where it is, or what's in it!" said Jeff. "We can't do anything stuck on this damned island!"

Stephanie tried to stand up, but she was still dizzy. Every time she connected with one of William's memories she felt worse.

Jeff tried to call the office, but there was no phone signal.

"Well, it looks like we'll be waiting here a few hours until the tide goes out again," he said. "Unless you want to swim for it? Personally, I don't fancy catching my death of cold."

"I can't swim," admitted Stephanie, dismally, drinking her water.

"Well that idea is definitely out then," laughed Jeff. "Have a rest here, unless you're OK to explore the island?"

Stephanie said she was feeling better after a drink. She stood up. Laura had already walked off, drawn to something at the back of the cottage, so they both followed her.

***

Following the path behind the cottage they spotted a large rusted metal age-like object, about eight feet high, which looked like it had been used as a brazier to house a beacon at one time. As they drew nearer, they saw Laura standing there, staring up at it. A thought occurred to Stephanie.

"Jeff, was this place used as a lighthouse?" Stephanie asked. "From here it would have been easy to signal to The Manor and the village beyond." she said.

"Not as a light house as such. Smuggling, as you know, was commonplace in this area. But the wreckers were the worst.

"What are wreckers? Stephanie asked.

"The story goes that in the 18th and 19th century people would light beacons like this one, to lure ships onto the rocks out there in the bay. When the ships ran aground, they would steal the goods that came ashore," Jeff answered. "Some people like Peter Trevelyan made a decent profit from it, and they didn't care about the people that were killed. Some of them even murdered the survivors so that there would be no witnesses. But others did it because they had no money and no choice. They were very hard times. In places like Chesil Beach in Dorset, many ships were wrecked, often by accident too and they capitalised on it. Hundreds of people died."

"That's horrible!" said Stephanie, shivering

"Later on, the authorities stepped in and built a proper lighthouse to the north of the cove, at Angove Head. Then, in the 1930s, the island was used by Peter Trevelyan to signal to boats bringing in contraband. He would signal the pub in the village where his men would be waiting to come down and collect their shipments."

"You're a mine of local knowledge," Stephanie said with a smile.

"I like to read, what can I say!" Jeff replied, with a wink

They reached Laura and told her what they had been discussing.

"Maybe Peter's energy is on this, if he used to light it," she said.

She stepped forward, and touched the old, rusted, iron brazier with her bare fingers. Instantly, an image flashed before her eyes.

"Tunnels!" she said. "There are tunnels from the island, one leading to the cellar of The Manor and one that comes out underneath Quarry House. If we can find them, we can follow them to get off the island!"

She quickly found her gloves; the wind was rising and getting colder. Encouraged by her vision, they walked a little further, following a path downwards which led them over to a small sandy beach on the other side of Lapwing Rock. The wind pulled at their hair and sand flew straight at their eyes as if to blind them. They came across a small wooden platform to the right of the beach, and there they found what looked like an old well with a lid covering it. On closer inspection, the wooden cover had started to rot after years of battering by the damp salty breeze, and there were rusted metal hinges covering half of it. It was more like a trapdoor. Jeff knelt down and tried to lift it, and with some effort and grinding of the hinges, he gave it a heave and it flapped open, landing with a thud, causing some of the crumbling planks to shatter as it landed. The smell of mould rose from the tunnel. Inside was an old metal ladder, riveted to one wall.

"Is this an old well?" Jeff asked. "And if so, why would it have a ladder?"

He picked up a pebble and dropped it down the shaft, but there was no splash, just a clink as it hit the bottom. Laura shone her torch down and there, at the bottom, a solid floor.

"This isn't a well, it's an entrance to the tunnels!" she said, confirming what everyone was thinking. She bent down and touched the trapdoor.

'Peter's energy is strong here, he used it a lot."

'Probably to avoid detection by the authorities," Jeff said. "Let's see where is comes out, we have no choice, unless we want to stay here for 1ours, and we might find something useful down there."

eff went first. He turned around and lowered himself in, trying the adder first to make sure it would hold his weight. The opening was quite narrow, so he had to slide his backpack off his shoulders and hang t on one arm. Edging his way slowly down the ladder, holding on with •oth hands while holding his torch in his teeth, he made his way to the ottom.

Be careful!" he called. "The rungs are very smooth with wear."

tephanie waited for him to step off before she stood on the ladder, caring it might not be able to withstand more than one person's weight t a time. She shone her torch down the shaft to help light his way.

ss soon as he set foot on firm ground she went next, with her torch in er pocket. While she descended, Jeff shone his torch for her, then he id the same for Laura. When they were all safely down, the women lit neir torches again and they began to investigate the tunnel.

***

oon they came to a place where the tunnel spilt into two.

Vhich way shall we go?" asked Stephanie.

1ura felt the wall on each side. "This way," she said, pointing to the ft. "His energy is strongest here, so it's more likely that this is the one hich took him home to Quarry House."

Jeff suggested that they split up, so he could investigate the other tunnel, but Stephanie reminded him that if it led to The Manor, it was likely that the exit was buried under tons of burnt wood and rubble. She shivered at the thought of going there again.

"Fair point," he admitted.

At first the tunnel smelled dank and stale. Suddenly Laura started screaming.

"My neck, something cold touched the back of my neck!" Jeff rushed over to her and shone to torch on the back of at her neck and saw water droplets. He looked up and saw a narrow shaft leading upwards, a long way through the rock. Presumably it led out to the top of the cliff letting fresh air into the tunnel.

"It's OK, probably just water dripping from a ventilation shaft," he said "It's easy to imagine all sorts of things down here in the dark."

Laura didn't quite seem convinced, but they carried on.

As they went further on, occasionally they felt a breeze on their faces and decided that there was some sort of built-in ventilation system in place to keep the air fresh. It made sense when they remembered the first part of the tunnel which would have been under the beach and therefore under water at high tide. It had smelled stale from lack of access to fresh air.

"Whoever built these tunnels knew what they were doing," Stephan said.

"Yes!" agreed Jeff "The smugglers were probably tin miners out make some extra cash. They had to know how to dig shafts and tunnels safely, their lives depended on it."

He added that the tunnels had been roughly hewn out of the rock by hand, judging by the pick axe markings. Stephanie admired their skill and Laura seemed more at ease on hearing this. So long as there were no icy, ghostly fingers clawing at her, or spiders dropping from the ceiling for that matter, she was happy to continue.

They reached a fork where the tunnel opened out on one side to form a cavern. The air was rancid. As Jeff stepped in to have a look around, he shone his torch on the ceiling and a colony of tiny Pipistrelle bats woke up. They took flight, swooping and diving around their heads, escaping mainly through the tunnel to the island and some flying up through the air vents. The smell was obviously from the amount of their droppings caked on the cavern floor. Jeff was glad he hadn't walked too far into the cavern for the sake of his shoes.

Laura started screaming again. This was all becoming too much for her.

"William wasn't a vampire, was he?" Jeff asked, grinning.

"I bloody hope not," said Stephanie. "I hate garlic!"

They comforted Laura, reassuring her that the bats were harmless, and carried on walking. After some time, they noticed that the path was leading gently upwards. On the floor at the sides of the tunnel they passed further open areas probably used for storage. One contained some broken crates, then further along they came to one with empty barrels and a couple of broken wine and brandy bottles. It was all evidence of the illegal imports of the former tunnel users. Stephanie was afraid to touch anything in case she had a vision of the wreckers' activities at close quarters.

The walls of the tunnel were dotted with little ledges periodically set high up. They were hand-crafted crevices where remnants of candles still stood, presumably to light the way for early smugglers and the latter day criminal element.

After about twenty minutes they came to an area of the tunnel where the rock changed to brick. It looked like they had reached the foundations of a building. Ancient tree roots had pierced the floor in places, sending snakelike tendrils which crisscrossed over the path that lay before them. They had to step carefully to get past them. Finally, they came to some wooden steps leading up to a door. Jeff tried the handle, but it was locked.

"I wonder..." thought Stephanie, taking off her gloves and retrieving the larger of the two keys from her pocket. The lock was a bit stiff from lack of use, but the key unlocked it. As she went to push it with her bare hands she had another vision, one of Peter's memories, and this time it was very brief.

"I know where to find the third box!" she said, triumphantly.

***

As she opened the solid, old, oak door, she emerged at the bottom end of the basement at Quarry House. It was the middle door of the three which she had noticed the last time she was down there with Jan. Without a word, she put on the lights using a nearby switch on the wall, turned to the door on the left and opened it with the same key. Inside was a collection of shelves, containing an ancient wine collection. Jeff's eyes lit up. There, amongst the bottles, on the lowest shelf, was also an object wrapped in purple velvet.

Stephanie put her gloves back on. She bent down, took out the object and placed it in her left palm, gently unwrapping it with her right. As the heavy cloth fell away from the object nestling in her hand, it revealed a gleaming, engraved silver box bearing a large letter T. It was smaller than she had envisioned, just bigger than a pack of cards, and very light. It had been protected by the cloth and the cupboard where it had lain, so it was untarnished. But it was also bristling with negative energy.

"Laura, please could you go and see if Jacob is back and bring him here?" she asked. Then to Jeff she said "Could you get Jan down here, please, and fetch the silver key from my top, right-hand desk drawer?"

They both agreed. She promised Jeff she wouldn't touch it directly till it had been checked. After they left, she sat on a nearby chair, examining the box with her gloves on. The engraving covered all the sides except the base. The letter T, presumably for Trevelyan, was only on the lid, in a slightly raised oval section set above the centre of its surface. She shook the small box; it made no sound. She had always done the same with her Christmas presents, which had amused Jeff greatly. She smiled at the memory; their first, wonderful Christmas together already seemed such a long time ago. She wondered what might be so important yet light enough that it didn't even make a noise; she could hardly bear the suspense after all the waiting and searching. Most of all, she really hoped it wasn't empty.

Then there was a sound of voices and footsteps on the stairs. Jeff appeared first, followed by Jan, Jacob and Lauren. Adam and Rachel trailed behind them. Jeff gave her the tiny key on its chain, which she placed in her pocket.

"I asked Adam and Rachel to come too. Depending what's in the box, we will need their help," Jan said.

"Yes, it might contain an object used in dark magic to help restore the spirit of a dead person seeking immortality. I've read about objects like that," said Adam.

"That doesn't sound good," said Stephanie, remembering the cold mist that had "Could William's spirit have been what was in the first box we found in the basement?" she asked. "You know, the icy mist?"

"No, I suspect that box was a decoy, put there by William and covered with protection magic." said Jacob.

"I agree. What he wanted to protect is in this box. It's protected by far more intricate magic," said Adam, whose expertise was binding spells and using puppets as effigies of dark spirits to control them. "But I think it's likely that what came out of that box alerted him to the fact that we'd opened it and drew him here."

"Well let's hope this box doesn't have the same effect!" said Jan. "I need at least one more coffee before we face him again!"

Jacob and Rachel spent some time using the spells they had developed that morning, working hard to undo the dark magic currently preventing anyone from opening the small box. Adam began to cast a spell to bind any associated spirits to the box, should the contents be as they suspected.

"This could take a while," said Jacob. "Why don't you grab that coffee and I'll text you when we're ready?"

They all agreed; it was mid-afternoon by this time and the three explorers were cold, tired and hungry. They gladly went upstairs to the staff room for a mug of something hot and a welcome snack. Jeff updated Jan on their trip to the island, and she told the three of them all about the team's progress in their absence.

Jan was pleased that Laura had been of so much help, and she thanked her. Then she reported that she had rearranged all the P.I. cases. She had also fended off calls from concerned clients, a task with which Amy had provided sterling support. The Lodge and Quarry House were protected as best as could be managed and preparations were all in place for manifesting and (hopefully) trapping and defeating William. Just then, Jan's phone rang. Martin had found some interesting information, so Jan asked him to join them in the staff room.

Martin arrived in due course, carrying an old yellow map with edges that look like they had been chewed, and a small, dusty blue book. Abby came with him while Dawn stayed in the library to continue her research.

Jeff updated Martin quickly about what happened on the island. With his thick glasses on he had an air of an academic about him. He informed them that he had also come across evidence of the tunnels and he unrolled the ancient hand-drawn map, bearing the Trevelyan crest of a plain white shield with a black gull in the middle holding a fish in its jaws. The Latin phrase "Semper Dives" sat in black letters on a white scroll above the bird. Martin translated it as "Wealth Forever" which he said referred to someone who was always surrounded by riches, as befitted the greed of its owner. It was the first time that Stephanie had seen it and the motto made her feel sick, knowing its connotations and the lengths William had gone to in order to preserve and increase his fortune.

The map also showed the exit of the second tunnel and it ended at The Manor as suspected. But before reaching it, it also forked again along the way, so there was a third tunnel. This tunnel, led to the tin mine.

"It was another route for the smugglers, later used by Peter and his men to escape from the authorities."

Abby spoke, in a small, very quiet voice.

"Dawn and I both think we will find him at the tin mine. It represent the main source of his wealth, you see."

Stephanie thanked her, saying that it was a plausible option.

"Now, to the matter in hand," said Martin. "The final box!"

He asked about the size of the box and looked overjoyed when they told him.

"It sounds like a keepsake box, as I thought, where people of the Victorian era, usually, ladies, would keep items of personal significance."

He showed her photographs of boxes in the book he was holding, which did look similar.

Then Jan's phone rang; they were ready in the basement. They all trooped back down there, Martin and Abby included.

"Finally, some answers," thought Stephanie.

***

The small box was beautiful. It was now free from any sort of magic and it had been quite a task to free it from the spells which had been had cast upon it. Also, surprisingly they had not been dark in origin, so the negativity must have been coming from its contents. Adam had been right about the complexity of the spells.

Stephanie picked up the box, and as her skin made contact with its energy, she was surprised to see Julia. She was placing something in the box. She appeared frightened and kept looking over her shoulder. Stephanie could see clearly what was in her hand and what she was doing. Then the image faded.

Without saying a word to anyone, she took the small, silver key from her pocket. It made a small click as the lock disengaged and she opened the lid; it was empty. She ignored the cries of disappointment and expletives from Jan. She closed the lid, picked up the box and began twisting the small oval panel on the lid in a clockwise direction. As she did this, the base box slid open, revealing a hidden drawer. In the drawer lay a curl of jet black hair tied with a fine, dark blue ribbon.

The others looked at her in astonishment. "How did you...?" Jan asked.

"I saw Julia do it in my vision," Stephanie answered with a grin.

"Julia? said Jan.

Jacob stopped Stephanie as she was about to pick up the hair.

"Wait, let me check it out first!" he said.

He examined it and declared it clear of dark magic. In fact, there was no magic at all, which surprised everyone.

She took the lock of hair out of its drawer and as she held it she was transported back to the early 1900s. Julia and William were young, and they seemed very much in love as they stood together in a beautiful drawing room, presumably at The Manor. They were giving each other a gift on their first anniversary. This was a time before William discovered the dark arts and became consumed by greed. Julia had given him a silver pocket watch containing her photograph. He was handing her a box containing a large, gold locket in the shape of a heart, and inside it was a lock of his dark, curly hair as a keepsake, as was the custom of the era.

Then the vision faded, and she was taken to a time many years later when William was lost to magic and money. By this time, Julia feared him, Tom was in prison and she just found out that he intended to make Isabel get rid of her child. She had hidden her away in Bristol. But William had found her, and when the child was born he had her adopted. Julia was as distressed as Isabel. But he was too powerful, and they had no ally in her weak, selfish son. The women couldn't fight William alone and she feared for Isabel. But she also knew magic, and after Isabel died, she realised the importance of the lock of his hair. She concealed it in the drawer and cast magic herself to protect the box. Then Stephanie saw Peter's involvement with the box, and the events that came after.

Stephanie found herself back in the present day, in the basement, holding William's lock of hair. The energy coming off it was strong and evil. She dropped it onto the table in disgust.

"I think I understand now," she said, motioning as if to brush something from her palms, then she explained what she had seen.

"You see, it was Julia's keepsake box. She is the one who sealed it with magic. It looks like she was quite skilled too because no-one has been able to break through her spells in all these years, until today. It seems that William began to get nervous after Mary hexed the family, fearing he wasn't long for this world. The hair was somehow important to him and she knew that. He found out where Julia hid it, but he couldn't open it. So, he locked the silver box in the bigger box and made a copy of that to throw people off the trail."

Stephanie stopped and paused for a moment. "I dread to think how Julia suffered for hiding it," she added.

"How did Peter get hold of it?" asked Jan.

"Peter found the original box and thought the magic was William's. I didn't see where he hid it then, maybe in the tunnels or somewhere on the island. I don't suppose it matters," Stephanie said. "He kept it as insurance in case his father ever turned against him, like he did with Isabel."

"How did they both get here?" asked Jan.

"The one on the island was the original and somehow he opened that and removed the silver box. He left the outer box there because he had no use for it, but after William died he brought it here, to his home. He hid it, unopened, in the basement. He never knew what the silver box contained. Then when he found the copy, he hid that here too, thinking there might be some treasure in that. He died not long after his father, so they remained hidden and unopened all this time. It looks like when we opened the copy yesterday it sent some sort of warning to William.

But I wasn't shown the significance of the hair." Stephanie added.

"Yes, why would the hair be important?" asked Jeff.

"Because it gives us a way to control and destroy him," said Jacob, and the others all nodded in agreement. "It's just what we need!"

"What do you mean?" asked Stephanie looked as confused as Jeff.

"The hair is a physical link to the man himself, to which his spirit is also linked in some way which we don't properly understand," Adam explained. "But while this lock of hair, the last remnant of his physical body, remains on this earthly plane, he has a link to it. Evil men often fear where will end up after death, Hell, damnation and all that, and he wanted his spirit to remain earthbound. He didn't want the hair falling into the wrong hands, the hands of people like us or Mary, witches and warlocks who could use it against him. William had plenty of enemies, as we know!"

"And that's just what Julia was hoping for. With this hair, she left us a weapon to get rid of him, once and for all," said Stephanie. "If Peter had found it, I expect he would have destroyed him. How awful to be afraid of your own wife and son. He didn't live long after Isabel though, did he? I suppose he's been in Marlin all this time, just waiting for revenge. For me."

The idea was a sobering one and Stephanie wondered just what they would be facing.

"He deserved it," said Jan, seeing that Stephanie was getting a little nervous. "Now it's time to send him on his way!"

"If you give the hair to Adam," Rachel explained, "he can use it to create an effigy of William. Then we can bind him to it, secure and constrain his power within it, and burn the effigy, sending him away forever," she said.

"Just like we did with the evil entity in the doll Mary made," Jan added, "Mary used a strand of his hair then to bind the hex against his family to the doll. We can do the same with him."

"Take it," said Stephanie, pushing it across the table to Adam. "It feels nasty!"

"And be quick," said Jan. "He will be back again tonight, and twice as angry, and it will be dark in just two hours."

"It won't take me that long!" said Adam.

Then Jeff's phone rang. "It's Ray," he said. "I have to go!

***

Darkness fell and Quarry House was a hive of activity. All the preparations had been completed, and the team trooped out to the company cars. Their destination was the tin mine.

Jacob and Rachel had already been out to the site and put in place an area of containment with spells of protection. Adam carried an effigy, a small doll which he had carefully prepared in the likeness of William Trevelyan with the help of the portrait from the cellar. He had sewn the lock of hair to it, to bind William to it using powerful magic. He had set his intention of preventing harm to the team and the wider world, so that William's spirit should be released from this plane and sent to wherever it needed to go.

Adam was skilled, and Stephanie found the doll terrifying, especially given her experiences with the doll made by Mary. She asked Adam about something that she had wondered about: why Mary's doll had appeared old if it had been an effigy of Tom Hall as a young man. He explained that the doll had aged in appearance over time due to the dark magic and evil energy attached to it, which had shrivelled and shrunk it. She wished she hadn't asked, but now she was even happier that it was gone.

Faith and Suzy had prepared spells to summon William's spirit to the tin mine and bind him there. But this could only be done for an indeterminate limited period and they had to be cast once they were all in place. Laura, who also had the gift of precognition, had used it to help predict the best time to summon him, to guarantee their preferred outcome. She would be on-site with Dawn and Abby who had helped locate the best place to lure him. They would help in any way they could, as they did the night of the party. The whole team had an energy and goodness which their gifts provided, and there was safety in numbers, especially with such a formidable enemy.

Tonight, there would be a full moon, but it was cloudy, and they needed the full light of the moon to optimise the spells, so that left them only narrow window of opportunity. Their well-crafted plan depended on the weather. To save time, Hunter had already set up all the equipment which they would need at the chosen site and he would monitor them remotely from the office. There were infrared and night vision cameras and motion sensors. Everyone had an earpiece for him to communicate to them and indicate William's position, especially useful to those within the team unable to see spirits: not all of them were clairvoyant. The technology would also prove invaluable in assisting them to gauge the team's effectiveness and help them to defeat him It was common too for recordings to be made on such occasions, providing unique research data to help improve P.I. team tactics in future cases.

Martin would remain with Hunter back at Quarry House to give what support he could, advising them on the layout of the mine and its myriad of tunnels, should William evade them and venture deep into the mine itself to hide. But Stephanie had a feeling that their adversary was more than ready for a confrontation and had no intention to hide if the launch night was any indication of his plans.

Robert was armed with all the support that religion could provide. He rode in the car with Stephanie, and as Jan drove them, he prayed silently. Jan was also silent, for a change; her full attention was focused on traversing the coast road in the dark without any street lights. Stephanie soon became lost in her own thoughts.

She realised she was trembling; she was awash with emotion. Anxiety about what awaited them, nervousness about her own power and what it could do. Fear that she might lose herself again in her apparent subconscious quest for vengeance, even though her conscious intentions were purely to protect. She also had doubts whether she would really be able to defeat William. But mostly she was worried about Jeff, hoping he would find who was looking for and scared about what might happen if he did. Losing him terrified her more than the spirit she was about to face. She was lucky; she had a team with her. Jeff probably just had Ray, or at least she hoped he did. He might even be facing a murderer alone.

"What if…?" she thought. Her heart was thumping in her chest.

"We're here," said Jan.

No more time for thought: it was time to act.

***

Hunter had seen their cars approaching and had switched on an array of industrial sized halogen lights which he had positioned at the mine. He had been given permission by Stephanie, as owner or the property, to access the lighting and security cameras already in place around the site. All the equipment was fully functional by the time they reached their destination.

Stephanie gazed at the imposing, ruined mine buildings. Before her stood the skeleton of a four-storey, granite structure and a tall, round stone tower. While the others made last minute preparations, she asked Martin back at the office to tell her what their functions had been. He told her they were the engine house and chimney stack, which was often all that remained now at most old tin mine locations. He also gave her a short version of the mining process. She promised herself that she would come back another time and visit the small museum; if she lived to see another day.

Jacob and Rachel were reinforcing the protection magic while Adam put the doll in place and cast the final binding spell. Abby checked on the equipment to make sure that the lights, EMF meters, sound recording equipment and speakers all had battery packs as backup in case the electricity blew, or the arrival of William drained the energy (which was more likely). She also sound-checked the video cameras that Hunter had already installed around the scene.

They were a well-oiled team, and Stephanie was impressed by their skill and professionalism. It felt to her as if she was on the set of a ghost-hunting television show and she half-expected a large woman in flowing robes to waft into view holding a crystal ball. The thought made her smile; but this was unfortunately real life. Far too real, in fact, and everyone around her was practically dressed in jeans, jumpers, coats and other suitably warm clothing.

Robert was pacing back and forth uneasily, blessing everyone with holy water, doing what he could while the others prepared. They were all relaxed and at home in such situations, but like Stephanie, he was relatively new to this. Out of respect for his beliefs she had worn a small, ornate, gold cross which her religious aunt, her father's sister, had given to her after her mother died. He smiled when he saw it and seemed a little less on edge, but it brought her no more comfort now than it had done then.

The clouds had slowly been blown out to sea on the tide. The moon appeared in her glory in the clear night sky, shining down on them at precisely the time that Lauren had foretold.

Faith and Suzy began to cast the summoning spells. Stephanie saw that a circle of stones had been prepared in the area nearest to the mine entrance. In the middle of the circle lay the doll, surrounded by a ring of clear quartz crystals, sparkling in the moonlight and interspersed by Rachel with herbs and flowers. The location was prepared; the bait was set.

"Ready!" called Jacob.

The air sizzled with magic. It was time.

They team moved as one. They took their places, forming a ring around the circle of stones. Jan was to her right, but this time it was Jacob who stood to her left. She thought again of Jeff and immediately put him out of her mind. She had a team to lead and a job to do. They all called on their guides and she felt her mother standing close to her left shoulder and sensed Lucas putting his hand on the right. Then they waited. But they didn't have to wait long.

Suddenly Hunter called out, "There's a cloud of cold air heading right at you."

"HE'S HERE!" whispered Grace.

PART SIX: CLOSURE

The car park was in confusion.

"I see him!" Stephanie said, but she was the only who could.

"Where is he?" called Jan.

"Join hands," Stephanie shouted, as the wind whipped up around them.

Because they were linked to her, they all saw him too. All that was visible was a face attached to a plume of thick, black, impenetrable darkness, like sentient fog. But it was his face, and he was smiling.

Thick clouds covered the moon, then all hell broke loose. Lights and cameras came crashing to the ground, leaving them in pitch blackness. Stones and pieces of equipment came flying at them from all directions.

Soon the backup batteries burst into life and the area was ablaze with light once more, albeit at ground level. Abby was struck on the head by flying debris and fell to the floor, breaking the circle. She was alive, but dazed. She pushed the others off as they tried to help her up. She told them to leave her, to carry on without her. They joined hands once more. Next thing, she was hurled sideways into the side of a parked car. Laura started screaming so Jan told Laura to go and help Abby and stay with her. Suzy cast spells of protection on the pair of them and helped Laura to take Abby into the car where she lay on the back seat, pale and ill.

William, or the entity that he had become, was raging, spouting vile spells and curses as the black fog span around them all. But as they joined hands again and held firm, the stone circle remained untouched;

353

protected.

"Now!" yelled Jan.

Robert started reciting a psalm, Adam started chanting and all the others joined in. It was a spell to lure him in, seal his power and bind him forever to the doll. Suzy ran back from the car and joined the circle repeating the spell in unison as they stood with the others once more.

Then a huge gust of wind blew them so hard they fell to their knees breaking the circle once more. As the circle broke, once again only Stephanie could see him because the others were no longer linked to her. A whirlwind of blackness hovered before them, inside the circle of stones. It was working; the cloud of evil had been drawn into the circle.

Little by little, a wispy shape appeared. It was a tall, dark-haired man in a long, black cloak. The spirit of William Trevelyan had fully manifested now and stood proudly before her. His head didn't loll about in death as Emma's had, although he had died of a similar injury; his dark energy and his pride were too strong for him to appear like that. He stood upright, bold and arrogant. His cloak flapped open like the wings of death itself, fluttering in the gusts of wind. At his beckoning individual, smaller shadows crawled out from underneath it and spread out on the ground around them, the spawn of his magic. Each dark patch of fog grew upwards, transforming into a host of grotesque human-like spectres before her.

The team stood up, unaware of what was going on. William had successfully been trapped inside the circle of stones, but something was wrong: he still had his power. He also wasn't alone, and they hadn't prepared for that. When the wind had scattered the team, their spell was incomplete, and he had taken advantage of it.

"The thermal cameras are showing cold spots everywhere!" Hunter called through their ear-pieces.

"Watch out!" Stephanie cried, helpless to protect them. "His power hasn't been bound!"

She told them what she saw. Their plan was failing.

"He must be drawing on spirits to do his bidding," said Martin. "It's an ancient, heinous form of magic, a spell which he's using to control them. They'll do exactly as he says."

"I can't see them!" called Jacob, and the others agreed, all searching blindly for what Stephanie was describing to them.

The team could see neither the host of entities, nor William, only sense their presence and see the damage they caused. Only Stephanie was privy to the horror that surrounded them, and she could only stare helplessly as the spectacle unfolded. She struggled to link hands with her team, but the wind forced her away. She was quickly becoming drained of energy.

She alone witnessed the arrival of at least twenty spirit people. Smugglers, wreckers and other criminals appeared, people that once lived and died in Marlin. Captive spirits who were helpless, unable to do anything but that which William ordered. They were totally under his control, deformed by his dark magic. They all attacked at once, dissolving into many thick clouds of choking fog, heavy with the stench of death; each of them launching itself at one of the team. William just stood there and roared with laughter, enjoying the spectacle while the spirits shrieked in agony, unwillingly doing as he wanted while trying unsuccessfully to get free from him.

The team were swept apart from each other, blown around the car park like leaves in the wind. But it wasn't being caused by the wind. Only Stephanie saw them: entities of dark fog with ghoulish faces and the strength of many men. The team were being attacked by what they perceived as invisible forces. But what she saw was an unwilling army of spirit puppets acting out his will, according to his script. She was scared rigid, appalled and sickened by the sight, full of sympathy for the poor lost souls being manipulated so cruelly, and at the same time worried and fearful for her friends. She suspected that his magic was binding her too. She was powerless to help them.

"I can't move and he's using other captive spirits to attack us. You have to stop him!" cried Stephanie, the only one who knew what was going on.

"Martin, find… a counter-spell," called Jan breathlessly. "Stop them. Bind him!"

Then there was silence as the team fell to the ground like lifeless dolls themselves, gasping for breath, and the foul host flew to William, drawn to him as I they were marionettes and he was pulling the strings. They gathered around him as they took on their dark human shapes again, unable to resist. Tortured souls, begging, pleading to be released. While her team lay scattered and helpless, struggling to even stand, he strengthened his grip on the puppets of fog. They no longer struggled against his will. They were lost.

They formed a line facing Stephanie, between her and their shadowy master, growling menacingly now like animals. The creatures of darkness were getting ready to pounce on their prey: Stephanie. William floated above them, chanting his abominable magic, within the inner circle, but still very much in control.

Stephanie stood alone in front of William, trying to summon her energy, struggling to fight back, but she was unable to think, as if the darkness was draining her and dragging her thoughts away into nothingness. He floated to the ground, glaring at her, his eyes like tar pits of blackness. His menace and his beasts were meant for her eyes alone, to intimidate her, to scare her. His aim all along had been to isolate her from her friends, and he had succeeded.

His unintelligible words resonated in her head and she found she was unable to move her legs. She was unable to do anything, he had seen to that; she was at his mercy. Was she to be his next puppet? Was he going to use her to harm her team? She would rather die than do that.

Then she heard a noise behind her; she turned her head and couldn't believe what she saw. Villagers were walking into the car park, led by Michael. Beside him stood his three sons: John, David and Matthew. Behind them came his wife Lisa and his daughter-in-law Jessie, with Miss Broom the librarian, then the lanky girl from the café. Two young women she recognised from the supermarket and the pub landlord and his son followed behind. Even Amy was there. Twenty or more, she lost count. They kept coming, even people she didn't know, many she didn't even recognise. Her eyes filled with tears. She tried to tell them to run, but she couldn't speak. They couldn't even see what they were facing, and they probably thought he was alone. Their actions were noble, but they were walking into a trap.

"No, you have to RUN!" she thought, but she couldn't say the words. She felt as if she was floating away from her body, from her friends.

"Did you think we would let you face him without us?" Michael called above the chanting. "Last time he came, we turned and ran, but not any more. This is our village too!"

William gave an order and the spirits turned and attacked the crowd once more. The villagers all ran forwards. Some had the gift so they *could* see William and the fog creatures, others were casting magic, some stood praying. Others fought unseen foes with their bare hands, dragging the team away to safety. They all did what they could. While the villagers kept the darkness at bay, the team got to their feet. Jacob told them what to say. They all joined hands around Stephanie and William and recited the spell together, breaking his hold on the weaker spirits, setting them free at last and forcing the black fog to dissipate.

Suddenly, Stephanie could move. She could feel her energy surging and the villagers' presence gave her renewed hope. But it was short-lived.

William's puppets were gone, and he was furious. He raised a gale around them again and blasted everyone to the ground. They all scrambled to their feet, exhausted, weakened.

"We're not strong enough," said Jacob, gasping. "We can't take much more of this!"

Stephanie became angry, angrier than she had ever felt in her life. One of her own had been hurt, the rest were deteriorating. The villagers, even her own family, had come to help, risking their lives, and it was not going to be in vain.

"I can't let him win, but it's taking everything we have to just hold him off. How can we defeat him like this?

***

The battle continued. Winds howled, magic crackled in the air. Stephanie called on her mother and Lucas who instantly appeared at her side. Somehow, she began to feel stronger, she had no idea why. Then her energy surged, and from nowhere, she began to glow. Something had broken William's hold on her.

Then she saw them. They were floating a few inches above the ground, approaching slowly across the cliff path from the graveyard in single file. Jerking in and out of view as they jumped in space and time, coming a few feet closer each second. Then they were there, beside them. The villagers and those members of her team who could see them looked on in wonder and made way for them to pass.

Isabel was at the front, behind her came Julia. Grace went to join them and Isabel motioned to two other women, ones that Stephanie hadn't seen before. Somehow Stephanie knew without doubt that they were Josie, the white witch who had brought magic into the Hall family, and her daughter Alice. Then her own grandmother, Jean, appeared from the midst of the crowd, nodding and smiling at her as she came closer. Stephanie's eyes welled up with tears at the sight. Dressed in white with eyes that glinted like crystals, they were all there because of her.

Isabel and Julia stood either side of her and beside them stood Jean and Grace, then Josie and Alice. Mothers and daughters of three generation, both Trevelyans and Halls alike. Along with Stephanie they formed a group of seven women, a powerful magical number. Hand in hand they stood, all victims in one way or another of betrayal, hatred and greed. These were all strong women, some that she had known and loved, and others who were just strangers, but they were all family. Her family. In their own way, each of them had played a part in bringing her here. The mothers of Marlin had come home, one last time, and this is where the legend would end. They joined hands with Stephanie and formed a circle around William, encasing him in light, instantly binding his power.

Something moved at the edge of the Stephanie's vision. She turned and saw that the procession wasn't finished. Now other spirits came. Before her eyes appeared the horde that she had saved from the eternal suffering of the fiery blaze at The Manor. All of them were perfect beings of light, and even though she had sent them to a better place where they could be free, they had chosen to come back to help her to rid Marlin of William Trevelyan forever.

She didn't even know their names, but she had been there for them all without hesitation, releasing their souls from torment. She had been willing to fight for them and to tell their story when no-one else could. Now they were here to fight for her, standing beside her, their final wish to help her destroy the most evil threat that ever existed to the village and to protect their descendants, her friends and her family. The time had come; the final battle had begun.

They formed an outer circle, working as if by some unknown plan. Standing with the team and their guides who had reappeared beside their charges; each lending her their strength as she had, in the past, lent them hers. William, in seeing the horde, on sensing their energy so radiant with goodness, began to screech like a soul in torment, which by this time, he was.

On and on they chanted until his magic was sealed away. He had lost control; the man who was used to controlling everyone, everything around him. He could sense defeat, and he was petrified, rooted to the spot by fear and white magic.

The inner circle began to glow as Stephanie's brilliance amplified theirs. The glow went round and round the circle at dizzying speed, pulsing and growing in intensity as it went faster and faster, trapping William in the centre of the circle with the dreaded doll. He howled like a caged beast, confined within his prison of light, desperately trying to get away, to no avail.

The team were stunned. Some shook, some wept, all were drained and could barely stand, but still they did so. Strong, defiant and proud. The villagers moved forward, joining the living and the dead. They couldn't quite believe what they were seeing, but they were strangely unafraid; they just wanted to do what they could, to be part of it. To help Stephanie.

"Begin the ritual!" called Jan, and Adam dashed forwards with Jacob and Rachel. They advanced as one, stepping easily through the spirits who allowed them to pass through them as if they were mist, although they had felt solid when they held their hands. Their energy invigorated the Hollows, who formed a small inner circle. The trio of powerful white witches began casting the final spell to draw William into his effigy. Now it was time for Stephanie to play her part.

She began to shine with an unprecedented level of luminescence, and beams of light shot from her eyes, piercing holes in the blackness before her, the last refuge of the soul of William Trevelyan. The light passed harmlessly through the Hollows as they worked; those that were good could never be harmed by it.

Stephanie spoke to William, in a voice that was steady and clear.

"You are FINISHED!"

He screamed. The people in the outer circle covered their ears at the sound of his screeches: they were like the baying of the hounds of hell themselves. Each beam of light tore into another section of his loathsome darkness, causing him excruciating pain with its purity. Stephanie stared unblinkingly at him, her eyes like lasers, boring channels of light through the deepest shadows of his spirit. Like a knife through butter, she was methodically carving his soul, piercing it with goodness and tearing him apart.

Each shaft of light that seared through him carried a piece of his shadowy form with it, propelling bits of his essence downwards, again and again, into the doll. His wife, his daughter and his descendants stood firm before him, fuelling her power, fighting not out of revenge, but with a weapon which he knew he was pitifully unprepared to overcome. He had been defeated by the one thing that he had thrown away so many years ago. Love.

Stephanie didn't hesitate. She was resolute and ruthless. She channelled the love of the souls beside her, the will of every man and woman there, from the past and the present. They all had one thought: to erase him from existence. The circle closed in until they were almost touching him. Then the spirits beside her let go of her hands, and she stepped closer to what was left of William. The Hollows stepped aside to let her through, and they joined the inner circle. The final spell was cast. All that remained of him was his shadowy face, a writhing mass of vileness, burned full of holes.

"Now, child!" said Isabel. It was time for the final blow.

Stephanie gently put her right hand on William's ravaged face and quietly whispered the last word that he would ever hear, one word full of meaning, for him alone.

"Goodbye."

As soon as she touched the ruined semblance of the face of William Trevelyan, it hardened like a mask. He let out an ungodly scream as if her hand had burned him, and the final vestige of his spirit fragmented like a piece of black, volcanic glass. As the last shard fell, he was sucked into the doll. Trapped forever.

She turned to the women beside her as the glow faded from her body. She blinked away tears as she looked at each of them. One by one, they nodded and said goodbye to her. Isabel, Julia, Josie, Jean, Alice. She thanked them all, and she suspected that she would never see them again. All, that is, apart from her mother. Stephanie was certain that Grace wasn't ready to go yet; she still had one more task to complete.

She was right. Grace was waiting to meet her husband when his time came; to walk hand in hand with him once more on their final journey, just like Robert had waited for Emma. For now, she had faded quietly away, as had the other spirit guides and supporting spirits. All of them were waiting in the shadows until they were needed.

The clouds parted and a bright beam of moonlight shone onto the ground. As it did so, Isabel waved and turned away to lead the others into its glow. She walked into the shaft of light without even looking back, then she started running. Stephanie soon saw why.

A man was waiting; she knew instantly that it was Tom Hall. Isabel's work here was done and they could be together at last. They shared a love which not even death could destroy. He had waited for such a long time while she remained to avenge them both, and now they would be together for all time. Suddenly Tom turned back and reached out his hands. Jean, the daughter that he had never known, ran into his arms and Isabel cradled them both; a family reunited.

One by one the others followed Isabel and vanished into the light, as if absorbed by it. First the women from the inner circle disappeared, then the people from the fire. Stephanie no longer fought back the tears of joy that flowed down her cheeks as she said goodbye to every one of them, just as she had done once before. But this time, she was the one saying thank you.

As the last of them departed to their rightful place, she felt something touch her cheek. It was a tiny white moth, a gift from Isabel. A final kiss goodbye. She watched as it flew back to Isabel and followed its owner into eternity. Stephanie blinked away a tear, and when she refocused her eyes, the moth and the light were gone. The car park was in darkness once more, save for the light of the faithful moon.

***

Seconds later, all the lights flickered on again. Stephanie turned to face everyone. There they stood, exhausted and battle-worn, and most of them had tears in their eyes, still unable to believe the remarkable scenes that they had just witnessed. She dried her own tears with her sleeve and walked over to thank them all in turn and they expressed heir gratitude to her.

Then she turned away and walked over to the car where Abby was still ying, in great pain, with a wound on her forehead and her right wrist ed, swollen and obviously broken. Laura sat beside her, obviously haken at what she had just seen. Stephanie opened the car door and vithout a word she placed one hand on the top of Abby's head and the ther on her wrist. Instantly, the wound and swelling vanished, along vith her pain and any other unseen injuries. Abby looked at her ncredulously and thanked her, and she smiled warmly in return. Iowever, this development did nothing to help Laura's nerves, so she ently touched her forehead too and she stopped shaking. Then the ree of them walked back together to join the rest of the team.

he villagers were all standing or sitting on the ground now, itermingled with her team, drinking bottles of water that Jan had rought. As Abby and Laura joined them, they welcomed them in lence. Jan put her arm around Stephanie as she spoke to each of them, aking sure that they were all unharmed. Nobody replied, they just odded. They had no energy left with which to form a response.

e spoke for them all as she said "It's time to end this."

ney gathered to follow Adam, as he picked up the doll from the circle nd took it to an old, galvanised steel dustbin in the corner of the car rk, which they had brought with them and protected with magic. He rew it in and covered it in petrol, then handed Stephanie a box of atches. The procession of onlookers formed a circle around them and od well back.

"Déjà vu!" said Jan, as Stephanie lit a match and threw it in, igniting the petrol and setting the doll alight. A journey that had started with the destruction of an evil doll had come full circle and was ending with the burning of another one.

"It seems fitting," she thought.

Unlike Mary's effigy, it said nothing. There was no unearthly screeching, or wailing, and Stephanie was secretly grateful for that. William was sealed away, already silenced by magic and love. They al watched as the flames danced and the doll burned away to nothing in seconds, taking him with it to oblivion.

"Dust to dust," whispered Stephanie, and the merest hint of a smil played on her lips. This time, she knew it was finally over.

***

They all remained there, watching until the last of the flames died ou Then Jan turned to Stephanie and wrapped her arms around her necl She held her for a moment, then pulled away and just looked at her, fu of love and admiration, echoing the feelings of her team, her family an the villagers.

Jan was so proud of her. There she stood, an unassuming woman wi mousey hair, a dear friend that she had known all her life, who ha moved to this sleepy village a few months ago, just looking for a fres start and peace and quiet to write her books. Instead she had dealt wi tragedy and unspeakable horror and found a soul-mate. Defeated ev again and again, and grown into the most incredible healer that she, anyone else, had ever seen. She wiped a small tear that had someho escaped.

"Come on, Steph," she said. "Let's get you home!"

Stephanie just nodded, realising that this time, despite what had just happened, she hadn't passed out. The energy that the spirits had given her still flowed through her veins, bursting out of every cell of her body. She had never felt more alive.

Jan turned to speak to the team.

"Thank you everyone, great work! Pack up and take the equipment back to the office then get some sleep, we'll have a meeting at ten in the morning."

They all just nodded. They were still dumbfounded; awestruck. This was a night which they, and the villagers, would never forget.

Stephanie realised that because if her, the prophecy had reached its conclusion; Mary and William were gone and the darkness of the feud that had overshadowed Marlin was lifted.

Suddenly Stephanie remembered.

"Jeff!"

Without him, none of this mattered. One thing could wipe her happiness away in an instant. Losing Jeff. Yin and Yang. Darkness to put out the Light. She took her phone from her pocket. No calls, no messages. She had to get home. She had the horrible feeling that for Jeff, facing a darkness of a different kind, time was running out.

***

As Jan drove Stephanie back to The Lodge, they both silently prayed that Jeff would be there. But the cottage was dark and silent, and the only one to greet them was a very hungry Maisy. Jan said she was sure that Jeff would be back soon, but they both knew it was a platitude.

Jan was worried too; it wasn't like him to not keep in touch. He would receive a piece of her mind when they found him, for worrying them both. She asked if Stephanie wanted her to stay, but she said she was fine and she would be going straight to bed. Jan simply hugged her and reluctantly left to drive back to Quarry House. She wanted to help the team put away the equipment, and sort out a few things ready for the morning, and she expected it might take a while. She told Stephanie not to wait up; she had the spare key and she would let herself in quietly so as not to wake her.

Stephanie hugged her and watched her drive away. As she closed the door against the cold night air and went back inside, the cottage felt too quiet. Empty. She fed Maisy and slowly sipped a mug of hot chocolate in her living-room overlooking the bay. But it brought her no comfort. Watching the moonlit tips of the dark waves wash over the sand usually calmed her, but tonight that too brought her no solace. She knew she should feel triumphant, but somehow all she felt was panic about what might be happening to Jeff, and dread at whatever news the morning might bring.

She went to bed and Maisy settled by her side. As she tried to sleep, horrifying images flashed before her eyes.

An ornate-handled hunting knife with its blade dripping with blood. Jeff lying on the ground. A graveyard.

She sat up, with beads of perspiration on her brow, shaking. She knew it hadn't been a dream. This was one time when she wished that her intuition might be wrong, but she knew it wasn't. It was real, she could feel it. Her insides churned with despair, her heart ached with worry. Jeff was in danger and she had no idea where he was.

**

The following morning, after a restless, but thankfully dreamless night with no more terrible visions, Stephanie woke up early and found herself alone. Jan had come back around midnight and she had still been awake. She had insisted on taking Abby to hospital last night, but when they got there, they found nothing wrong with her so they had sent her home. Pleased that Abby had made a full recovery, Stephanie had told Jan about what she had seen and Jan had done her best to reassure her. At around two, Jan had gone to bed and insisted that she do the same, but she had only dozed, waking often. Wired with energy from the spirits at the tin mine and worry about Jeff, eventually her body had sucked her into slumber from sheer exhaustion.

She was beside herself with worry. Jeff still hadn't come home; she hadn't heard from him all night and the whole situation was really starting to frighten her.

"I can't lose him now!" she thought, over and over, willing him to be safe. *"Is this where life comes and takes my happiness away again?"*

She knew that the man Jeff was searching for was a dangerous criminal, the man who had killed Melissa. He could easily kill Jeff without a second thought.

But there was nothing to be gained by worrying, and now that it was day, he was more likely to turn up at the office than come home. Much as she hated to, she had to put all thoughts of Jeff aside and get ready for work. She had a business to run and a team depending on her. She knocked on the spare room door and receiving no answer, went in to wake Jan. But Jan had already left; a note on the pillow said that she had some things to sort out and would meet her at work.

***

After a short shower and a mug of tea, Stephanie fed Maisy and set off in her car for the office. It was a cold morning, so she had wrapped up warmly. She arrived at half past eight, to be met by a smiling Amy.

"Good morning, Stephanie!" said Amy.

"Hi Amy! Any calls or messages?" she asked.

"Nothing so far. Too early for the post too," she said. "Jan said to tell you she's in her office if you need her."

She thanked Amy, and went straight to see Jan, who smiled widely at her.

"How is the heroine of the hour?" she joked, then the smile faded as she saw the expression on Stephanie's face. "What's wrong, Steph? Is Jeff back"

"No! He didn't come home, Jan. I don't know what to do!" Tears welled up in her eyes.

Jan smiled reassuringly.

"He'll be fine. He's ex-CID and hard as nails. Don't worry! He's been in worse situations than this," said Jan, with conviction.

"If you say so, although I'd rather not hear about them right now. I suppose I'd better try to focus on work and keep busy. Anything happening I should know about?" She spoke in a measured voice, which took some effort, but her stomach was churning.

"After last night, I thought we'd better discuss your team situation," Jan began. She was just as worried as Stephanie, but trying not to show it.

"OK," said Stephanie. "As it stands, this office currently has myself and Jeff," his name giving her another pang of worry as she said it. "Also, we have the three Hollows, Hunter and Martin and, of course Amy. That makes seven," she added.

"Yes," said Jan. "And you never know what type of cases you're going to get. Jeff can handle the everyday investigation cases with the help of his intuition. You will have support from the others in a non-psychic capacity too, namely Hunter on surveillance and Martin on research. I can make Dana available too whenever you have need of her particular skill-set. I was going to suggest giving you Laura because she worked well with you yesterday. But she is still very new to all this and a bit nervous, so I think she'll need more training and experience, if she decides to stay. Abby was pretty shaken up too. I think I'd better keep her with me for now," Jan said. She gave a sigh then continued.

"I know this type of work isn't for everyone, no matter how gifted they are, and the events in Marlin haven't exactly been our usual type of case. Anyway, you already have admirable psychometry skills yourself. I thought of giving you Dawn with her precognition and past-lives skills, and Faith with her summoning expertise and psychic drawing ability. They are more experienced operatives too. Then the Hollows can take care of all protection spells, effigies and binding, curses and hexes, and so on, to make it a fully balanced team." asked Jan. "How do you feel about that?"

"Sounds great!" said Stephanie, genuinely pleased.

"I thought you'd be happy. Everyone is in the office already. We will have a debriefing session at ten o'clock, and then, on your behalf I will give them the rest of the day off. They need time to get themselves sorted, go home and collect their stuff and so on."

Just then Stephanie's phone rang. She gave Jan the thumbs-up sign and left the room. It was her editor, not Jeff, as she was expecting. She had emailed Stephanie the proposed editorial changes to her book, saying that if she could go through them this morning and give her approval the book could be at the printers within days. Stephanie agreed and went back to her office to work on them straight away, welcoming the useful distraction. She was happy with the changes and emailed her editor back. The book was finished at last, but at that moment, she didn't even care.

She went into the kitchen in search of a hot mug of sweet tea and cake. If ever there was time for cake, a missing boyfriend stalking a crazed killer fitted perfectly. Luckily Jan had bought doughnuts. She sat alone in the staffroom, eating, drinking and worrying.

By ten o'clock the team, apart from Jeff, were all waiting for her in the conference room. First of all, Jan thanked everyone for their remarkable efforts at the tin mine, and Stephanie thanked them too. Jacob asked after Jeff and she said that he had been called away on personal business and would return soon, which she secretly hoped would be the case. She informed them all about Jan's proposed additions to her team those mentioned were delighted, but those who were not chosen looked disappointed.

Jan assured them that it was nothing to do with their ability, it was just that they were more needed elsewhere, which seemed to put their minds at rest.

As the team stood up to leave, Abby thanked Stephanie again for healing her the night before. She told her that she was amazing, and on behalf of everyone that had been present last night, she said that they would all be proud to work for her whenever she needed them. It put Jan's mind at rest about anyone leaving the company, and Stephanie flushed with embarrassment. The ones who were leaving Marlin said their goodbyes. Then the new team members left for the day, to collect their belongings and return the next morning, ready for work.

As she reached her office, her phone rang. This time it was Jeff.

"I'm in Exeter but I can't get hold of Ray. He had to go off to another case. I found him, Steph! Damn it, my battery is almost dead. Can you get in touch with him and get him to meet me at this new location? Keep ringing him, please!"

Jeff managed to tell her the address before his phone went dead. She was so relieved to hear from him, but at the same time worried that he would go ahead and confront the man by himself and get hurt. The images from the night before flashed through her head; she had to find him and warn him.

She went to her laptop, searched online for the number of the Exeter police station and spoke to one of the officers who had come to The Lodge a few months ago, when she had the break-in and knew Jeff; DS

Philip Dennis. He said that Ray wasn't there, but he gladly gave her Ray's mobile number and his own, and promised to pass on a message if he saw him. She rang Ray's phone, but it went to voicemail. She left a message asking him to meet Jeff at the address he gave her. Then she grabbed her coat and scarf and ran to her car, telling Amy to let Jan know where she would be, and driving off before Jan could have a chance to stop her.

***

The location was a scruffy café in a rundown area of Exeter. As she went in she saw Jeff, gripping a large mug of what looked like sludge, but which turned out to be just very strong tea. There was just one other customer, a dishevelled old woman seated in the far corner, as unkempt in appearance as the establishment itself. Jeff's face was a mixture of pleasure and concern when he saw her. She sat down warily next to him, unwilling to even touch the table, let alone order anything.

"Why did you come, it isn't safe," he said softly, taking hold of her hand.

She told him about not being able to reach Ray and leaving messages.

"I couldn't bear to think of you here all alone!" she said.

"Thanks," he said and smiled. "It is really good to see you."

He was exhausted and looked terrible, like he hadn't slept in days. It came as no surprise when he told her that he had been up all night speaking to Ray's contacts and chasing any potential sightings of the man he was looking for. She sensed that her presence would only add to his worries, but it was too late to change that now. She didn't have the heart to yell at him for worrying her. He explained why he was there.

"He's using the name Jake Albert. We know it's an alias, although we don't know his real name," he said. "He's a former drug dealer turned addict, who served time for several violent attacks on women. He is very dangerous, suspected in another recent death as well as Melissa, but he keeps evading the police. He isn't getting away this time. Steph, he's here in Exeter!"

His weary eyes shone with hope, for the first time since she met him. She didn't know what to think.

"Where is he now?" Stephanie asked.

"Over there by the newsagent's," Jeff said pointing at a scrawny, wiry-looking man with wild hair and eyes, smoking on the street corner opposite the café.

"What are you going to do?" she asked, dreading his answer.

"Follow him!" he said, getting up as the man stubbed out his cigarette on the wall and walked off around the corner. "Stay here and wait for Ray," he ordered.

"Jeff, wait, I...!" she called after him, but he was already halfway through the door.

"I haven't had a chance to warn him!" she thought.

Stephanie had to do something. He had looked so determined and she knew she wouldn't be able to stop him. She stood up and watched him walk away, with panic stirring inside her. But then, as soon as he crossed the road and turned the corner, she did the only thing that she could do. She left the café and followed him. She couldn't let him face a murderer alone, not knowing what her premonition had shown her.

As she turned the corner, the man known as Jake Albert was facing Jeff. He stood about two feet away, waving a knife at his face. It was the same distinctive weapon that she had seen in her vision. Jeff had followed him into an alleyway, he could see that there was no way out and he was pacing; his energy was as taut as a catapult ready to launch.

"Put the knife down!" commanded Jeff. "The police are on their way and you're not going anywhere!"

Then he heard footsteps behind him. He turned and saw Stephanie.

"Run!" he said. "Call Phil, get help!"

It all happened so fast. Stephanie just stood there frozen as the scene unfolded before her eyes. She could easily believe that he had killed; a cloud of negativity covered him like a shroud. His aura seemed to be jangly, something she had perceived before when she came across someone who was on drugs.

The man lunged at Jeff with the knife while his back was turned. Jeff fought him off, landing a punch near his eye that sent him reeling. The man shrugged it off, twitching with obvious drug-fuelled energy. He ran straight at Jeff, waving the knife wildly at him, slashing his right arm as he tried to defend himself. Jeff let out a yelp of pain. Then the man knocked him into some crates and kicked him viciously in the ribs. Jeff's head hit the floor with a sickening crack, and he just lay there. Motionless.

It was exactly as she had foreseen. Blood was soaking his jacket from the wound on his arm, but at least she could see his chest rising and falling. He was alive. She sighed with relief. Then the man saw her and smiled in a way that made her heart lurch in her chest with fear. He started pacing again; his eyes were wide open, stating with tiny pupils. He looked irrational and jittery, acting on instinct and ready to pounce.

With Jeff lying there, Stephanie felt vulnerable. Jake stood between them, preventing her from helping him. She was torn between wanting to run to Jeff and running away out of fear. But she was aware that that she was also standing in Jake's way, blocking his route to freedom and there was nowhere else he could go. The alleyway was a dead end. He was trapped, and he was as dangerous as any wild animal that was backed into a corner.

Jake continued to grin and stepped closer, inching his way towards her, while pointing the knife at her, twirling the point. The knife with Jeff's blood still dripping off it as he approached. He looked like he was going to run at any moment and she was in his way; just another expendable victim. He would not hesitate to lash out again, to hurt or kill her. But at that moment her own safety didn't matter to her; all she could think of as that Jeff was hurt and needed her help.

Stephanie felt sick. She had no chance of fighting an armed man. So, she did the only thing she knew how to do, she closed her eyes and silently called upon her guides for help.

Lucas instantly appeared behind her and put his hand on one shoulder, indicating his presence. Grace appeared and put her hand on her other shoulder, giving her the reassurance that she needed.

"BELIEVE!" said Grace.

Her fear subsided, her mind became calm. The world became silent apart from the sound of her heartbeat. Her ears started ringing and then she felt it: the energy, building up within her. The man carried on moving slowly towards her, weaving from side to side with a grin of sadistic satisfaction on his face at the sight of her apparent helplessness. His intention was obvious; to kill her. He had almost reached her when she started to glow.

"What the..." he muttered and stopped.

The air crackled and her aura became visible and bright. He took a step back, realising that behind him was a dead end and she was blocking his exit. He wanted to just to barge past her and flee, but the incredible sight that lay before him chilled his blood and his feet felt like lead. He was rooted to the spot.

She couldn't let him get away, not after all this time; not after everything Jeff had been through. He had hurt the man she loved, and he was going to regret it. Her anger rose like bile in her chest, and vengeance filled her thoughts. A familiar sensation was coursing through her veins, and she was enjoying every second of it. Her hands were tingling as her voice rang out, strong and calm, unlike how she had felt only a moment ago.

"You think you can run, from ME?"

The man looked terrified. Then, without even thinking, she walked towards him, and he backed away. She lifted her right hand and a ball of pure, white light blasted from her palm, propelling him backward. As the blow landed, his head snapped back and the force of the blast sent him flying into a brick wall at the end of the alley. The energy from the night before was still there, magnifying her power, vibrating through every nerve, cell and fibre of her body. Never again would she be weak; Stephanie Meares was no longer a victim. The legacy of light remained. It was hers now.

She saw that the man had been instantly knocked out, maybe even killed. In that instant, she didn't much care either way. That sorry excuse for a human being would never hurt anyone else again; she would make sure of it. She raised her hand again, ready to send another blast his way.

"ENOUGH!" commanded Lucas, his familiar voice resounding in her head, startling her out of her anger.

The realisation of what she had been about to do suddenly hit her. She lowered her hand. As Jake slid to the floor, she sank to her knees.

"If he hadn't stopped me, would I...?" she wondered.

She raised her head to see Jeff sitting up, rubbing his forehead and gazing at her in amazement. He stood up and struggled over to her; she was leaning against the wall in shock, not at her actions but at what she might have done.

"Jan was right, you are an asset to P.I." he said, with a broad smile.

He helped her to stand up, then she hugged him tightly, relieved that he was safe. That they both were. As she did so, he winced from pain in his ribs. She released her grip, and he walked over to where the man lay, checked his pulse and was relieved to find he was still alive. As much as he would have preferred that he was no longer breathing, he knew

Stephanie could never live with herself if she had taken a life. Little did he know that she was already reeling from facing the possibility that she was capable of such a thing. What if Jeff was wrong? She could have killed an innocent man.

Jeff put him in the recovery position, telling Stephanie to keep an eye on him in case he was pretending to be unconscious and tried to run off. Jeff checked the security cameras in the alley, and to his relief they weren't real, just dummy cameras set up as a deterrent. Any recording of what had just happened would have been very hard to explain to the police. He went back to Stephanie.

"I'm so sorry! I distracted you. If I hadn't interfered…" she began.

"It's OK," he said kissing her cheek. "You saved me, Steph. We got him!"

He hugged her and helped her to a nearby crate where she sat while he made a phone call to Phil. Phil told Jeff that Ray was back in the office and they would both be there shortly. Stephanie took off her scarf and stemmed the bleeding from his arm. He sat on a crate and waited for the police, in a lot of pain from the blows to his ribs. She wanted to heal him, but already she could hear sirens, coming quickly closer.

Within minutes, two cars turned up; one was unmarked and driven by Ray, with Phil beside him and the other a patrol car with flashing lights. The Scenes of Crime unit would soon be there. There was no doubt in Jeff's mind that the knife that slashed him was also the one used to kill Melissa, and probably others too. He prayed that their tests would show that, and his nightmare would soon be over.

Soon after, an ambulance arrived. One of the uniformed officers accompanied Jake, who it turned out was really called John Evans, as he was checked over in the ambulance. He had come round, but he was still very stunned. One of the paramedics also took a look at Jeff, bandaged the slash to his arm and bound his ribs, already developing bruises and possibly broken. He suggested x-rays and advised him to go to the hospital, but he refused. They gave him some advice on symptoms of concussion. But he insisted on signing a form saying that he was refusing their advice, and they reluctantly had to let him go.

Stephanie was dazed and shaken, but still full of energy. Jeff assumed that she was weakened as usual, but she could feel that she was shaking from struggling to contain the new level of power within her. As she waited for Jeff it slowly subsided.

Two burly police officers led the man to their car. "She threw a ball of light at me!" he said, pointing at Stephanie, who tried her best to look innocent and shocked.

Jeff laughed. "Must be the drugs," he said.

Ray looked amused too. "Yea, he's really out of it," he said, laughing, obviously assuming that Jeff was the one who had laid him out.

"Thanks Jeff," he said. "I'm glad you finally got him. It must be such a relief."

"You have no idea," said Jeff. "And thanks for not giving up on this case. It means a lot."

Ray shook his hand firmly and drove off with Phil. The other officers followed in the police car with their extremely confused prisoner, leaving them alone in the alley. They would both have to attend the police station the day after to make a full statement, and there would of course be a trial. But for all intents and purposes, Jeff could finally relax.

As they walked back to their car, he stopped and turned to her.

"Now that's over, there's someone I want you to meet," he said.

"Of course, but first let's deal with your injuries," she said.

As much to his amazement as her own, she healed them there and then in the alley.

***

Adrenalin was beginning to kick in, making Jeff a little shaky, so Stephanie drove. They took her car because he had taken the train there. To her surprise, he directed her to a nearby cemetery, and they arrived just as dusk was falling. Then she remembered her vision of a graveyard and smiled. He took her hand and led her along the rows of graves until he reached a fairly modern one. Stephanie understood; she had guessed who was buried there: Melissa. As she approached the plot, Jeff let go of her hand.

"I've never been back here," he said. "Not even once since the funeral. I couldn't, it didn't feel right. I promised Melissa I would visit on the day I caught him. Today I did, and I couldn't have done it without you Steph. I hope Melissa understands why I couldn't come here before."

"She does," said Stephanie, as Melissa appeared before them. "She's here, looking at you now."

"Why can't I see her, why have I never been able to see her?" he said, with tears in his eyes. "I tried so many times, ask Jan. She tried, we both did."

"You weren't ready," Melissa said gently. "You felt guilty because you weren't there, because you couldn't save me, because you couldn't find him. But I understand that, all of it. It's OK!"

Stephanie told him what she said. He seemed relieved by her words.

"Thank you!" said Melissa to Stephanie. "I died so that you could meet, and you met so that he could get over losing me. Life is funny like that," she said and smiled. Stephanie looked confused.

We were so young when we met. I was his first love," she went on and that's a very powerful love. But it isn't always lasting, not like what you have. We would have grown apart; I had already felt it happening. Yours is a true, binding love, eternal and magical, and I'm happy for you. Tell him, please."

By this time, Stephanie was crying too, but through her tears she told off what Melissa had said.

"She's right," he said. "I want to see her, I'm ready," he said. "Will you help me?"

Without a word, Stephanie took his hand. As she did so, and he saw Melissa, his face lit up. She smiled at him. She looked beautiful and happy as he always tried to remember her. Until now all he had been able to visualise was the way she looked when he saw in the mortuary to identify her body. All at once, his heart was filled with joy and grief, sadness and regret. But most of all, he was aware of his love for Stephanie. To know that they had Melissa's blessing had set him free. Now he could finally move on.

"Goodbye, Melissa!" he said. "I will never forget you."

He held up Stephanie's hand, raised it to his lips and kissed it, then let it go, just as was ready to let his wife go. In that moment, he found that now, he could still see Melissa, even without Stephanie's help.

"Goodbye!" said Melissa. "Be happy, both of you!"

As they watched, she turned and walked away, and as she did so, she dissolved into tiny particles of light and was gone.

Jeff took a deep breath and said the words that Stephanie had been longing to hear.

"She was my past and you are my future," he said. "Let's go home."

"Not till I've taken you to a hospital!" she insisted through her tears. This time, he didn't argue.

***

After they arrived back at The Lodge that night, they just sat chatting and relaxing in the living-room with Maisy. Stephanie sat in the sofa and he lay down with his head on a cushion on her legs.

They felt they should celebrate, but they didn't much feel like it. Jeff had been advised to avoid alcohol in case of delayed concussion. Needless to say, his ribs weren't even hurting, thanks to Stephanie, and any trace of a headache was already gone. He didn't bother mentioning the slash his arm: it had already vanished.

Melissa was of course the main topic of conversation. They were both glad to have seen her find peace at last. Jeff seemed lighter too, like huge load had been taken away. For so long he had carried the burden of guilt, and the weight of his buried anger and need for vengeance. She could sense a change in him; she was glad that he could get on with his life at last, with her. The ghost between them had been laid to rest.

Stephanie was feeling anxious about her part in the capture of John Evans. She felt that she needed to tell Jeff about how she had felt when she attacked him.

"Jeff, I welcomed the energy. I felt superior, and I enjoyed the fact that I had such devastating energy. I felt invincible. I wanted... I think I would have killed him if Lucas hadn't stopped me."

"No, you wouldn't!" he said, with certainty. "A gift like yours will take a lot of getting used to," he said. "But you will master it. Think of it this way. There's an old Cherokee tale that Bob once told me. A young boy was walking with his grandfather, who told him that inside of each of us there are two wolves. One is all the good things in that person and the other is all the bad. They are locked in a permanent state of conflict. The boy asked which one will win, and his grandfather told him it's the one that you feed. There is good and evil in all of us, Steph, but it's our choice which path we take. I know deep down that your good wolf will win."

She understood, but even knowing that she acted in self-defence and to help Jeff, and that she had no choice, she still felt ashamed of what she could have done. What she had wanted to do.

"How did you get to be so wise?" she asked.

"I told you, I read a lot," he said.

She smiled. She told him she was still shocked that she had been able to use a gift that was meant for good to hurt a living person, and that she feared what might happen if she ever used it again.

Jeff was sitting next to her now, he turned to face her and looked her straight at her. "I have no doubt that if you hadn't, we would both be dead right now," he said firmly, and she knew he was right.

Suddenly, he stood up and knelt down on the floor beside her.

"What are you doing? Get up you'll hurt yourself," she said.

Jeff ignored her, gently took her hands, looked into her eyes and spoke.

"I'm fine, thanks to you. More than fine, in fact! Steph, I've spent too much time living in the past. But thanks to you, I don't need to do that any more. I want to spend the rest of my life right here, with you, trying to make you as happy as you've made me. Stephanie Meares, will you marry me?"

"Yes!" she said without even a thought. "Yes, of course I will!"

"FINALLY!" said a familiar voice.

"Goodnight, mother!" said Stephanie firmly, but she was smiling.

She could barely see him through her tears, but she had never felt happier or more complete than in that moment. Jeff made hot chocolate, and they drank it while they sat in comfortable silence, just looking out to sea by candlelight. All of a sudden, Jeff remembered something.

"By the way, you never told me what happened with William," Jeff asked.

"I forgot all about that!" she said. "You're not going to believe this..."

"If it involves you, I can assure you I will," said Jeff, with admiration in his eyes and more than a touch of pride in his heart.

***

The next day Stephanie drove them both to the police station in Exeter. Ray was still there, he told them that had already spoken to John Evans, who had been so terrified by his experience the day before that he had made a full and frank confession. They smiled at each other, knowingly. Jeff had caught the man who killed Melissa and the other women, and he would finally pay for his crimes. In fact, Ray thought it was likely that he'd die in prison.

After he took their statements, Jeff said that he would like to tell Melissa's parents in person that the man who killed their daughter had final been brought to justice. He felt he owed them that much, and Ray had honoured his request. Stephanie understood, and after she saw him off on the train to London, she went back to Marlin and arrived at about noon.

After checking in with Amy, she persuaded Jan to join her for lunch at the village café. The waitress nodded to them both in acknowledgement of recent events and they smiled in return. Stephanie noticed for the first time that she wore a name badge. Her name was Rosie.

After they had ordered and were sitting alone at a quiet table at the back of the room, she told Jan what had happened the day before and that he was in London. Jan was amazed by what Stephanie had done.

"You really need to be more careful, you know. He had a *knife* Steph.

But wow, that was amazing! And what you did with Melissa... Jeff must be so relieved to be able to put it all behind him."

Stephanie agreed. She had to laugh at Jan's face; it was an odd mixture of shock and awe. Then she told her about her self-doubt; what she might have done.

"I don't think you have anything to worry about there," Jan said. "Just listen to Lucas. His job is to protect you and advise you, even if that means saving you from yourself." Stephanie nodded. She really needed to get to know her guide better.

She changed to a happier topic by telling Jan about their engagement. Jan couldn't have been more excited if she was getting married herself.

"You're engaged? CONGRATULATIONS!" Jan shrieked, as she stood up, ran around the table and hugged her, to the amusement of the other café customers.

She asked coyly if she had chosen a maid of honour and Stephanie assured her that, of course, as she already knew, it had to be her: nobody else would do. Jan squealed in glee like a small child, much to the further amusement of everyone else in the café. As they sat, chatting happily about the future, Stephanie's expression became serious.

"I have a few questions about things that have been bothering me. Why do spirits stay earthbound? And Why is Marlin so full of spirits who can't seem to find rest?"

Jan smiled. "Well, these are things I suppose I should have told you before now, but we have been a little busy. And you have had a rather hands-on introduction to it all, haven't you?"

Stephanie nodded and gave a wry smile.

'Basically, as in other places, some spirits remain because they don't know they're dead, others simply refuse to move on because they have an attachment to a place or person. And there are those who remain here or come back to help loved ones through difficult times like Grace, or because they have unfinished business, like Isabel and the others. Recently we have dealt with a lot of unfinished business, simply because there has been a lot of tragedy here. Most spirits can be helped to move on quite easily once they decide to go."

Stephanie nodded to confirm that she understood.

'People don't change their personality much when they die. There are types like Mary and William, strong-willed and powerful in life and death. They can be very difficult to get rid of," Jan added.

'I definitely don't want to meet any more of them! Are there any particular conditions in Marlin that make it easy for spirits to come back and contact people? Or is it just the fact that so many people are attuned to them?" Stephanie continued. There was so much that she still needed to know.

'Well, I asked Martin the very same thing, and he told me there's a rare set of circumstances at work here. Firstly, Marlin is by the sea and has a river flowing through it, and water attracts spirits like moths to a flame."

This reminded Stephanie of Isabel's moth and she smiled to herself.

'Secondly, it's a place where ley lines cross, ancient electro-magnetic energy lines, which is another factor which draws them in. Thirdly, when you add the amount of witchcraft that has taken place here, plus the amount of people with the gift, well, we have an energy which lures them in, like a beacon. Imagine if you were lost in a strange land. You would be drawn to the people that understood you, wouldn't you, who speak your language? Well, that's what spirits do. They latch on to the people that can hear and see them."

"Ah, I see!" said Stephanie. "Marlin must have an invisible supernatura sign above it that says come on in."

Jan laughed. "That's about right!" she said. "Also, most of the spirit you have dealt with came to you because of who you are. They were linked to you in some way. Family is a strong bond, even in death. And you are the Mother of Marlin! Only you could have done it, Steph. I was your destiny to come here and help them. You have an amazin amount of spiritual energy; your aura is like nothing I've ever seen an your power is immeasurable. Just look at what you did for Jeff, and the wasn't even in Marlin!"

Stephanie felt a bit embarrassed.

"Look on the bright side," Jan said. "There should be enough spook events alone to keep you in business here, even without adding ar cases from the run of the mill investigative side!"

The waitress brought their lunch and Stephanie thanked her by nam this time. The girl looked as if she had had been blessed by the god She smiled, blushed, and left them in peace to eat.

"You've got a friend for life there," said Jan, grinning.

Stephanie smiled. Seeing Rosie reminded her to ask Jan one final thir that had been bothering her.

"Last night," she said, "the villagers that turned up to help us, some of them had the gift, didn't they?"

"Yes, some of them did," Jan agreed

"How many of them are there, do you think?" she asked.

"I have no idea Steph, there isn't a list or anything! People tend to keep that sort of thing to themselves. Michael might know, you could try asking him?" she suggested.

"Yes, I might just do that," Stephanie said. "It would be useful to know who we could call on, if we ever got into a situation like that again," she added.

"God forbid!" said Jan.

They both burst out laughing, then they finished a welcome lunch, interspersed with normal, casual conversation. As they left the café, Stephanie turned to Jan.

"If there's nothing important for us to do in the office this afternoon, there's something I'd like to take care of. Will you come with me, Jan?"

"Yes of course," said Jan. "What is it Steph?" Jan looked worried

"Something I've been meaning to do for a while," said Stephanie, with a smile.

***

An hour later, after a trip to the nearest town, they were walking through the graveyard of the chapel just beyond the ruins of The Manor, both with their arms full of flowers. It was a crisp, clear January afternoon without a cloud in the bright, blue sky. Waves crashed onto the rocks below and sea birds squawked to each other in the distance. Their breath formed clouds as they crunched their way along the gravel path. It was so cold that the early morning frost hadn't even melted.

Stephanie soon located the first of the graves that she was looking for in the ancient graveyard.

"Thank you!" she said, as she placed the first bouquet for Isabel. Then she did the same for Julia, Mark and Tom Hall and their father John. Also for Josie and Alice. After that she placed flowers on the more recent graves of Emma Jones, Bill Judd, and Bob Bishop.

The next bouquet she placed gently on the Trevelyan family monument just outside the church; in memory of Sarah, and her parents Andrew and Judy Trevelyan who were still her family, even if they had abandoned Marlin. She also laid a bouquet there for her mother Grace and her grandmother Jean. They were also Trevelyan descendants, even if they hadn't known about it in life. She wanted to honour the fact that their spirits, at least, belonged there.

Stephanie stood in silent contemplation for a few moments with tears in her eyes. So much tragedy had been caused just from two people falling in love. She thought of the ill-fated romance of Josie and Luke, then of Isabel and Tom. History repeating itself. But it wasn't love that had caused it all; it was purely due to the evil and hatred of the Trevelyan family, and later the Halls. In that moment, the realisation finally hit her. The feud was over, ended by her actions. She thought about what it meant to be the last Trevelyan; the fact that, as foretold, she had beaten the hex and laid all the troubled souls to rest.

"It's really over," she muttered, to no-one in particular, as she fell to her knees and sobbed.

The weight of that responsibility had been heavier than she realised, and now that it had been lifted she felt like she could breathe again. At last she could build a future with Jeff instead of worrying about simply fulfilling an ancient prophesy, and without the feeling that she was competing against his dead wife.

Jan rushed to her side and knelt there just holding her. She had watched in silence as her friend said a final goodbye to people to whom she owed so much, even those who she had no reason to even like; nevertheless, all of them had shaped her destiny in one way or another. She knew the enormous burden that she had endured with such courage and dignity, admiring her strength, leadership and formidable commitment. She had been so proud of the way that she had held it all together for everyone else, but she had secretly been worried for her. She welcomed this moment, relieved that Stephanie could finally release it all after holding it in for so long. Jan smiled as a single tear rolled down her own cheek; because now she knew that her friend would be alright.

***

Later that afternoon, Stephanie stood on the beach below her home, watching the grey cloud-tinged waves ebb and flow. She was idly passing the time while waiting for Jeff who had texted her to say he was on the way home from Exeter. Her thoughts drifted back to what had brought her to this place, on this day.

The past few months had been a roller-coaster ride of ups and downs; from exhilarating excitement to the deepest sadness. Days and nights filled with laughter and tears, terror and finally, triumph. She still had so much to learn about her family and her gift. But the most important thing that she had learned since coming to Marlin was that love was eternal; love was more powerful than anything, even death.

She had no idea what the future held for her. But she knew she didn't need to hide any more. She wasn't alone any more and there was much to look forward to; so much for which she was truly grateful. She had the business and her inheritance. She had Jan, as ever, her trusted, reliable, quirky, crazy best friend, and a team of wonderful, talented, dedicated people to support her. She was part of a family, the Halls. She had her faithful cat Maisy, and she had reconciled, at last, with her Dad. Her second book was finished, and she was taking a long break before starting the last in the trilogy. The feud was over, a host of spirits had been laid to rest and Marlin was at peace again.

Best of all, she had found Jeff, the love of her life and they had a wedding to plan. When they met, they were both broken people, trying to piece themselves and their lives back together again after heartache and pain. Each had different causes, but they were just as damaging. Stephanie had dealt with the ghosts of her past, and so had he, and in doing so they had both finally found closure. She had felt it that first moment when they met on her doorstep in the rain: he was her soul-mate, and she was his. They knew that they would always be together, in this life and the next, like Isabel and Tom.

She stood on the beach now, her beach, looking out to sea in a cocoon of contentment. She was Lady Stephanie, the new Mother of Marlin, and she would always do what was needed. With no regret; without hesitation.

A wave of excitement rose within her as a chill wind blew off the sea, raising the sand around her feet.

"The best is yet to come!" she thought.

"AND THE WORST!" said a voice that she knew so well.

THE END

ACKNOWLEDGEMENTS

The idea for this book began with a chance visit to a small antique shop in a quaint little Cornish seaside village. There I saw an old doll, a little old man sitting in a child-sized wicker chair, and it gave me the shivers I quickly left the shop, but the seed was sown. Many years later I wrote a story for my daughter about the doll, a short creepy story that lay forgotten for many years.

One day, I created the character Stephanie Meares to bring the story to life again. More time passed, and I resurrected and rewrote the story then I decided to extend it into a novel when I realised that Stephanie'. story was far from over. "Mother of Marlin" was born, the first of . series of books that became "The Marlin Chronicles."

Many of the paranormal events in the book are based on my ow experiences. "Truth is stranger than fiction," as Mark Twain so rightl said. But with the addition of fiction, the truth can become somethin even more mysterious and magical; the edges become blurred and the you have a unique creation. The characters all have a thread of truth to they are fabrications made from my observations.

Stephanie is part of me. I feel her pain, and that is because what sh experiences is often based on moments from my life. Unless you kno me well, you will never know which ones they are, and like mine, h story is far from over. I have laughed and cried with her as I wrote th book. I hope "Mother of Marlin" brings you the joy, tears and shive that it gave me when writing it, although in truth, it wrote itself wi very little help from me, as if it was just waiting for me to release it.

I have so many people to thank for their encouragement and suppo

Above all, I would like to thank my family who have given me the confidence to be who I am; without you, this book would not have been written.

I have learned that no dream is impossible if you want it enough; if you believe in yourself and trust your instincts. My instincts have led me to some incredible places!

Just remember: we are never truly alone while we have our memories - and that love is eternal.

[Names, characters, businesses, places, events and incidents are either the products of my imagination or used in a fictitious manner. Any resemblance to actual persons, living or dead, or actual events is purely coincidental.]

FEEDBACK AND CONTACTS

Thank you for reading this book. Your comments and feedback are so important to me. Please contact me on Facebook or visit my website where my blog will be updated periodically with release dates for the rest of the books in this series. I welcome your reviews on Amazon and Goodreads too, but no spoilers please!

I would love to add you to my new e-mail list. Just go to my website and use the form provided. All I need is your name and email address. You will receive information on release dates before they appear there or on my Facebook page, plus first access to any offers and exclusive giveaways ONLY available to mailing list members. These might be book previews, book cover releases, sequel descriptions, even free early access to a novella which will take place between the books in the series, but it is a stand-alone story (details below).

Rest assured, I will not pass your email on to any third party, or send you any other information apart from that which relates to The Marlin Chronicles series.

https://www.facebook.com/alysonmountjoyauthor/

https://www.alysonmountjoyauthor.yolasite.com

COMING SOON

SEQUELS: The other books currently awaiting publication in "The Marlin Chronicles" series will be available on Amazon worldwide, and there are more to come. I hope you will join me again in Marlin very soon, to see what other trials and triumphs are waiting for Stephanie and her friends there.

Book 2: "Children of Marlin"

Book 3: "Whispers of Marlin"

Book 4: "Nightmares of Marlin"

NOVELLA: A novella "Out of Marlin" will also be released soon. It takes place between Book 1 and Book 2 of the series, but it is a stand-alone story. It has no impact on the series and contains no great plot spoilers, so you can pick it up at any time. Join Stephanie as she decides to take a weekend break from Marlin with Jan, with surprising results. (Members of my email list will receive this novella free of charge in digital format prior to its release on Amazon).

Alyson Mountjoy – March 2017.

MOTHER OF MARLIN

Printed in Great Britain
by Amazon